For Jana Iverson ~
how disappointing to
realize that my book
is going to Hawaii,
but I'm not ~

bon voyage!

Dolly Kyle
2008
Psalm 91

PRISONERS OF THE HEART

the second novel of a trilogy by

DOLLY KYLE

Arkansas Inspired, LLC
Little Rock, Arkansas

 Published in the United States by

Arkansas Inspired, L.L.C.
1818 North Taylor St. #336
Little Rock, AR 72207

Phone 501-664-KYLE
Dolly@DollyKyle.com
www.DollyKyle.com

Be sure to read the first novel of Dolly's "Heart Trilogy"
PURPOSES OF THE HEART
ISBN 978-0-9802159-1-5
The 1st & 2nd novels may be enjoyed in either sequence.

For information about a book-signing event,
for notification about the 3rd novel of the trilogy,
for making comments/suggestions, contact above.

In the interest of saving paper and preserving the environment, there is no dust jacket with this book; the usual dust jacket "Bio" information is on page v.

Elvis Presley's song "Wooden Heart" was recorded on the RCA label; the words were written and copyrighted by Berthold Kaempfert, Ben Weisman, Kay Twomey & Fred Wise.

PRISONERS OF THE HEART

ISBN 978-0-9802159-2-2

Manufactured in the United States of America

FAMILY AND FRIENDS FIRST EDITION

With gratitude and love, I dedicate this book
to my excellent teachers -- especially

my late parents (in memoriam)

Rita Marie Pozzi Kyle and Slater George Kyle
who started my life on the right path
and taught me to think critically

Sister Mary Joanna
who taught me to read and cipher
and introduced me to our Almighty God,
to His Holy Spirit who inspires me daily, and to
His son Jesus, who saved me from myself

"Mrs. Belk" (Evelyn Simpson Belk)
who made the Garland County Library feel like a home to me

Sister Mary Amata
whose very name means love

Kenneth David Stuart and Leona Iattoni Diedrich
who built on the piano lessons started by my mom

"Miss Ann" Gidcomb
who tried for ten years to make a ballerina of me

Hazel Ricker and Elizabeth Buck
who brought a dead language to life

Lou Wood and Bedford K. Hadley
who gleefully made me work hard for those A's

Lennart V. Larsen
who welcomed my three little daughters in property law class

Bill Streng
who made tax law understandable as well as interesting

Mary Ellen Carroll
who taught me by example to be a caring and helpful cousin

Huey and Sally Crisp
who made going back to school so much fun

Betty Carlson Crain
who still saves me from math muddles and is a great friend

Allyn Florini
who enthusiastically encourages me
to live the lessons I have learned

ACKNOWLEDGEMENTS and THANKS

In my first book, I didn't plan enough space to thank everyone who helped me along the way, so I promised to do it later. Now it's later, and there are even more people to thank. My immediate family members have been truly wonderful. They prefer to remain anonymous, which is fortunate because it would take a whole page to list them. Several other people prefer to stay off "lists" -- for good cause.

I greatly appreciate every moment of emotional, physical, intellectual, financial, and spiritual support from the following (in alphabetical order):

Dallas Alinder
Nancy Baker
Barbara Bannon
John Bertrand
Ron Boyle
Julie Brenner-Walker
John Bronaugh
Diane Brown
Kathey Burks
Ben Clark
Ellie Clark
Mary Helen Cuellar
Mary Fou
Elaine French
Rebecca Garza Greenan
John Greenan
Arthur Hailey
Roger Hailey
Sheila Hailey
Jerry Hamlin
Richard Harwood
Sam Hilburn
Gloria Hocking
Sam Hocking
Robert Kelley
Sandy Connell Kelley
Phil Kemp
Durwood Knight
Jean Kyle-Jury
Louise Lueken
Charlotte McDaniel
Peggy Orchard
Lynn Riddle
Robin Riddle
Anamarija Sloan
Jack Swain
Mark Wells
Julia Woodward

In addition, I owe a special thanks to three professionals in various fields who read Prisoners of the Heart from their unique perspectives, and made valuable suggestions:

Beverley Best, transcriptions and editing; BestWord@cox.net
Bobby Harwell, actor and producer; more info at IMDb.com
Steve Stephens, media and public relations guru, Little Rock

Dolly Kyle was raised in Arkansas where she received a diploma from Hot Springs High School in 1964 and, three children later, a BA from the University of Arkansas at Little Rock (1972). She spent her early life in the family real estate business, and moved to Dallas in 1974 to attend SMU School of Law, accompanied by her three daughters who were then entering kindergarten, first and third grades.

Dolly passed the Texas State Bar Exam prior to graduating in the top 5% of her SMU Law School class (J.D., 1977). She is a Fellow of the Texas Bar Foundation, an honor which is limited to 1/3 of 1% of Texas attorneys.

She founded the non-profit Lawyers for Affordable Housing (LAH) to assist low-income homeowners with real estate issues. Dolly recruited 350 volunteer lawyers whose *pro bono* work affected multi-thousands of Texas housing units. LAH was featured in an ABA monograph, and was nominated for the State Bar of Texas *Pro Bono* Organization Award.

Dolly co-chaired the first Dallas Bar Association Home Project which still builds a Habitat for Humanity home annually. She served as an author and speaker for the State Bar of Texas Professional Development Programs.

Dolly is very proud to be a songwriter member of ASCAP (American Society of Composers Authors and Publishers) and of the CMA (Country Music Association). She has worked as a choir director, a math and music teacher, and as an Adjunct Professor in the Writing Department at UALR.

Though trained as a classical pianist, Dolly prefers to write country/western and Christian music. In over twenty years of playing a cheap guitar, she has deliberately limited herself to learning only six chords, so it's all fun and no work.

Dolly is now focusing on writing both novels and music. Her children are grown and healthy; her pets have all been buried; and most of her house plants are silk. Life is good.

PRISONERS OF THE HEART

INDEX

This is not the sort of book that needs an Index. If, however, a reader wants to compare scenes in this second novel to those in the first one, PURPOSES OF THE HEART, the reference to dates will make it easier. It certainly helped me while I was writing it. As always, I'll appreciate reader feedback. ~ Dolly

PART IV - LONG AFTER THE PROM

PROLOGUE

July 24, 1994

The Sunday edition of the *Vicksburg Daily Chronicle* sprawled across the kitchen counter, its headline proclaiming "PRESIDENT HOME FOR REUNION." Christi stared at the huge, front-page, color photo of Cameron surrounded by some of their childhood friends. She smiled to note that Kelly was not among them. As far as Christi was concerned, her friend Kelly should have gotten Cameron Coulter out of her life a lot sooner than she did.

Christi squinted to decipher the newsprint, but vowed that she would not give in to the need for reading glasses. Forty-seven was too young.

The telephone rang twice before Christi noticed it.

"Christina Boudreaux?" asked an unfamiliar voice.

"Yes," Christi answered tentatively.

"Please hold for President Coulter."

Christi frowned, wondering why Cameron would be calling her now, after everything that had happened. Maybe he was finally going to apologize.

Moments later, Cameron's early-morning, raspy voice greeted her cheerfully, as if there had never been a problem.

"Hi, Christi! How are you?" the President asked.

"Fine," she answered flatly. "You sound sick."

"Been up most of the night," he confessed with a light chuckle, "and my allergies are bothering me, but it's nothing serious."

"That's good," Christi responded automatically, then paused to let a silence grow between them.

"We all missed you last night," he offered lamely.

Again the silence.

She finally asked, emphatically, "Did you really?"

"Of course we did. Would I lie to you?"

Christi let that one ring in his ears until the silence was deafening.

Cameron cleared his throat nervously. Christi closed her eyes and pictured him tightening his jaw. Still, she didn't speak.

"Well, anyway," he began again, more hesitantly, "we did miss you last night. It was a great party."

Christi smiled to herself, listening to the publicly-smooth-talking Leader of the Free World groping for conversation as he used to do in high school whenever Kelly was around. It made her suspect that his call had something to do with her old friend. She waited, determined to make him work for it.

"Kelly was there," he said with forced brightness.

Here it comes, Christi thought, but didn't respond.

"She told me she finished her book."

Again, the silence.

"I'll bet it's good. She's a great writer," Cameron continued, trying to ignore Christi's lack of response. "Have you seen it?"

"No."

"Well, I was wondering," Cameron cleared his throat again, "if maybe she would let you read the manuscript before she sends it off to a publisher. I mean, you've always been such close friends."

"You've been more intimate with Kelly than anyone else has," Christi noted sarcastically.

Cameron glossed over her comment. "I'll bet she'd be happy for you to read it. I'm sure you're in it too."

Christi was beginning to get exasperated. "Let's get to the point," she suggested firmly. "If you're calling to ask me to read Kelly's manuscript and then advise her not to publish it, you're barking up the wrong tree. She's been working on that book for nearly ten years and she's not trying to hurt you with it. If Kelly had wanted to hurt you, she could have sold out during the election, and she's not the only one who had that opportunity. Ask her to let you read the book, and if you don't want it published, you tell her. From my perspective, it looks like she always does whatever you want."

"Whew!" Cameron exclaimed. He took a breath before continuing. "Listen, Christi, things are different between Kelly and me right now. I was just thinking that maybe you could get her to back off it for a while. She's been working on it for nearly ten years, so what difference could another couple of years make to her? In the meantime, you might like to do something like be our ambassador to the Bahamas. Invite Kelly to spend time with you down there. She loves the beach and y'all could have a great time. Then we could help her get the book published later on. I'm sure it's a good book, but it might make me look bad, and I don't need that in the next two years. It's just that I could never come right out and ask her not to publish it. That book means too much to her."

"But you want me to ask her not to publish it."

The silence returned.

"No," Cameron finally replied, "I'm not asking you to do that. Forget we talked about the book, Christi. I just called to say we missed you last night. You can tell Kelly that. You can tell her I called to say we missed you last night."

"I will tell her that you said to say that," Christi replied. "I suppose I'll leave out the part about the ambassadorship. And, by the way, I'm not interested in being an ambassador - to the Bahamas, or anywhere else. You know what I want, and I hope that someday it will become politically expedient for you to deal with it. Otherwise, it's just a matter of doing the right thing, or following through on your promises, and I've learned never to expect either of those from you."

Christi heard Cameron catch his breath, but didn't give him a chance to respond. With finality in her voice, she added, "Have a nice trip back to Washington. Good-bye."

"Uh, Christi, uh, I, uh, didn't..."

"Good-bye," Christi repeated, more firmly than before. She hung up the phone, not hearing nor caring if the President had echoed her "Good-bye."

She returned her attention to the newspaper in front of her. The camaraderie of the photo looked forced now. Staged. Empty. She squinted and blinked again, trying to read the article that dominated the front page. *Maybe glasses wouldn't be such a bad idea.*

Christi remembered that Cameron had reading glasses now, although he wouldn't wear them in a picture. She recalled seeing a news clip of Cameron exiting the voting booth on election day, wearing glasses that he quickly removed when he realized he was on camera. Christi counted back, calculating that Cameron had been forty-six the day he was elected President and was caught wearing glasses.

"At least I'm not the only vain survivor of Vicksburg's Class of 1964," she mumbled half-aloud.

Survivor. The word began to play in her mind like a bad melody that wouldn't go away.

She didn't pay any attention to the tears forming in her eyes, and continued to squint at the words that were now swimming together across the page. Christi blinked a few more times, trying to focus, and then gave up.

Maybe I should call for an eye doctor appointment tomorrow, she thought. Christi glanced at her calendar and started to make an entry, but the date itself grabbed her, and the memories came crashing back.

PART I

THE SUMMER OF '59

Chapter 1
July 25, 1959

"Christi! Christi, wake up! You're a celebrity!"

The young girl's muffled moan under the covers didn't stop her excited friend from rushing to the window and pulling open the heavy drapes. Christi slowly sat up in bed, blinking and rubbing her eyes, resigned to the unwelcome intrusion of summer sunshine and Kelly's loud exuberance.

"Look at this!" Kelly waved a newspaper. "Just look!"

Through her early-morning haze, Christi recognized the *Vicksburg Daily Chronicle* opened to the society section. Kelly held her finger on the *"Comings and Goings"* column.

"Here. Read it out loud. I want to hear how it sounds."

Christi read the first few lines to herself, then, smiling, sat up straighter in bed, and started over in a pretentious voice, *"Clem Boudreaux (civic leader and owner/president of Boudreaux Cadillac) will miss his beautiful wife and daughter this week as the popular pair of stunning brunettes travels to Savannah.*

"Helêne Boudreaux will give the bridesmaid's luncheon for the daughter of her college roommate Christina Demarest. (Yes, that is Mrs. Claude R. Demarest III of Willow Creek Plantation, for you history and society buffs.) If you've been reading Southern Society *(and we trust you have), you will know that young Delores Deeana Demarest ("Dee-Dee" to her many friends) is marrying none other than William Lee Culpepper IV of the Georgia Culpepper's. Need we say more?*

"Vivacious and oh-so-popular Miss Christina Boudreaux is the namesake and godchild of Christina Demarest, so it's all practically family. The stylish-beyond-her-years-pre-teen Miss Boudreaux has been seen shopping in all the best stores with her French-born mother, who still favors Coco Chanel. You will recall that Helêne has headed Vicksburg's "Best Dressed" list since her marriage to Clem brought her to our fair burg a discreet many years ago.

"Christina Boudreaux, with her own unerring good taste, reportedly chose several one-of-a-kind specialty items that have recently arrived from fashion capitol New York City. This is not to imply that Miss Boudreaux is any less of a Southern belle, but she does have that international flair that is so refreshing for our quaint river city.

"We can hardly wait to see the wonderful pictures of the Demarest wedding, and of our own special envoys, that will surely grace the next issue of Southern Society. *Until then, Helêne and Christina, 'Bon Voyage!'"*

Christi and Kelly observed several moments of awed silence at the end of the article. The celebrity was the first to speak.

"Wow!" Christi exclaimed.

"'Wow' is right," Kelly echoed, still standing in deference to her now-famous friend.

Christi looked up at Kelly and, for the first time since they met, realized the one-year difference in their ages. Twelve was definitely more sophisticated than eleven. The young blonde girl suddenly appeared awkward and tom-boyish to the *"stunning brunette"* with *"that international flair."*

"Sit down," Christi invited, condescendingly patting a spot on the bed, feeling magnanimous to her social inferior. Kelly obliged. The two girls leaned back against the wooden headboard and re-read the article together. By the time they had each taken a half-dozen turns reading it aloud, they not only had memorized it, but they also had returned to the social equality that they had enjoyed since Kelly "skipped" into Christi's third-grade class. If the upcoming article in *Southern Society* didn't do any damage, they would enter the seventh grade as perennial best friends.

The dainty white Princess phone beside Christi's bed rang quietly.

"That will be your daddy," Christi said, picking up the receiver and handing it to Kelly. "No one else ever calls this early on a Saturday."

"Boudreaux residence," Kelly answered politely. It was her father.

"May I speak with the *'vivacious and oh-so-popular Miss Christina Boudreaux?'*"

"Oh, Daddy, you'll embarrass her," Kelly admonished.

"I certainly hope so," Clayton McCain responded with a laugh, "and then I'll pick you up for breakfast."

Kelly handed the receiver to the celebrity.

"It's one of your fans," she smiled. "You better figure on sitting by the phone all day."

Christi put the receiver to her ear. She giggled and blushed at the words, "Is this *'the vivacious and oh-so-popular Miss Christina Boudreaux?'*"

"The same," she replied with the pretentious voice that she and Kelly had adopted for reading the article.

Christi motioned for Kelly to scootch over closer so she could hear too. The brunette head and the blonde cradled together, basking in the fame of the moment.

When Kelly left for breakfast with her father and his friends, Christi dressed casually, but carefully, in a cotton knit shorts outfit that she had bought for the trip to Savannah. *Might as well wear it in Vicksburg first,* she thought. *After all, I have a reputation to uphold.*

Christi bounded downstairs with a decidedly local flair. Her mother was in the kitchen, sipping coffee and reading the rest of the newspaper.

"Did you see this?" Christi grinned at her beautiful mother.

Helêne nodded and smiled, "Kelly showed it to me first. She tried hard not to wake you up, but apparently she couldn't help herself."

"And I'm glad!" Christi beamed. "Where's Daddy? Did he see it?"

Helêne shook her head. "He left very early, without coffee or the paper. It's the last Saturday of the month, you know."

Christi nodded, knowing the car business well enough. It seemed there was always some big promotion or contest from the factory and her daddy always wanted to win. His dealership was the largest in Mississippi, so he won more than he lost. He never admitted losing, though, because win or lose, he was still selling cars. Even when the new-car business might slow down, there was the used-car section. Clem

Boudreaux also silently owned several out of town car lots that would never merit the Boudreaux name and upstanding reputation.

"May I ride my bike downtown to show him this?" Christi asked enthusiastically.

"Mais oui, ma chère," Helêne replied gently, *"aprés le petite dejeuner."*

Obediently, Christi fixed herself a small bowl of cereal and ate a few bites. She was too excited to sit still. She gulped down a glass of orange juice, kissed her mother on each cheek in the continental style, and headed for the garage to get her bicycle.

Though it was still early, the air was hot and motionless. Christi pedaled briskly, reveling in the self-created breeze. Then, eagerly anticipating her daddy's reaction to her first big newspaper story, she pedaled faster and faster, foregoing her usual detour along the ridge overlooking the river where you could see the Mississippi lying broad and flat and brown, happy in the sun, or green and angry when the thunderclouds rolled in on it. She sped past the colored peoples' shoebox shacks and the white peoples' houses built long after The War, with their porches and railings, turrets and gingerbread trim, past the houses with names like Twin Oaks that had been built, or at least started, before The War, where the same families had lived for a hundred years, passing down the houses and furnishings, clothes and letters and diaries, silver and china, useful relics of their past lives and daily reminders of The War ~ The War that had taken almost everything there was to give, the fathers, sons, brothers, cousins, and husbands of the women of the South, leaving them shaken but stronger, alone but not lonely, cautious but unafraid, and proud of their men, of their own new strengths and of the land that was still theirs, if only a garden plot behind the house where they used to own hundreds of acres rolling down and along the Mississippi lying broad and flat and brown, happy in the sun, or green and angry when the thunderclouds rolled in on it.

Christi cruised into the huge asphalt lot of Boudreaux Cadillac and as usual swelled with pride at seeing her family name in big fancy letters on the neon sign out front, above her daddy's parking space. Eager as she was to see him, she succumbed to her habit of touring around to the back, past the service bays and the car wash, just to see what was going on. Nothing. It was still early and the service department was only open from ten until four on Saturdays. The salesmen would come in at eight.

Completing the circuit, Christi rode once again past her daddy's "loaded" white Cadillac with custom gold trim that he parked out front as part of his advertising. Clem ordered the same car for himself every year. It was his trademark and the only one of its kind in Vicksburg. He would have the gold trim removed before selling the "demo" to one of his friends at a bargain price. The deal included their promise not to re-apply custom gold trim. It was a small vanity, but Clem was known for it. Christi didn't give it a thought as she parked her bicycle, took the precious newspaper out of the basket, and headed toward the short sidewalk that led between the main office and the service department, around to the unseen private entrance she could enter with her key.

A chameleon darted across her path, and Christi stopped to watch it. The tiny reptile paused beside a huge green leaf, then decided to scale the office's brick wall. Matted green vines leading up to the window gave plenty of cover. Christi waited for the miniature creature to change colors, but was disappointed that he seemed to be on a mission, unaware that he was not blending into his surroundings very well.

Christi thought that he deserved to be caught for his carelessness. She could take him home as a pet. She had rubbed chameleons before and there was something sweet about them. She took a stealthy step toward her new friend.

The chameleon stopped abruptly when he reached the sill. Suddenly aware of Christi's interest, he turned to face her bravely. Christi admired his audacity and decided that he would, indeed, make a nice pet. She bent closer, staring straight into his beady little eyes. The chameleon, crouched on the edge of the sill, stared back at her, unflinching.

In the stillness, Christi noticed some movement in the background behind the chameleon. Although the slats of the horizontal blinds were shut against the morning light, there was a small slit at the bottom where the blinds didn't reach to the sill. In that small space, Christi could see clearly into her father's office. She let her eyes refocus from the chameleon into the spacious wood-paneled office beyond.

The movement she had first noticed had been her daddy's new secretary, Mrs. Jander, going in and closing the door behind her. Christi's father was sitting at his desk in his huge leather chair, talking on the telephone. Mrs. Jander started walking slowly toward him, touching the front of her red blouse. As Christi watched, transfixed, Mrs. Jander started unbuttoning it. Christi looked over at her father to see what he would do, but he didn't do anything. He just sat there and watched his new secretary coming closer, closer, closer, unbuttoning her red blouse.

Christi wanted to run away, but she couldn't move. Right under her nose, the chameleon started changing his color to match the red brick, but Christi didn't notice. She only noticed the color of that awful woman's orangey-red hair and the red bra that she was wearing under her red blouse. The woman took the red blouse and red bra off completely, and Clem Boudreaux just kept watching her and talking on the telephone.

Mrs. Jander had breasts the size of a woman nursing twins. Christi had only seen breasts like that one other time and they were full of milk. She wondered if Mrs. Jander was full of milk too. As if to answer Christi's unspoken question, Mrs. Jander reached up and grabbed her own breasts in her two hands and began squeezing and pulling on her very pink nipples, but Christi couldn't see if milk was coming out or not. Her father was watching closely and still talking on the telephone. He put down his pen. His right hand disappeared into his lap.

Rubbing and pulling on her own breasts, Mrs. Jander stood in front of the desk, rubbing and pulling, pulling and rubbing until Christi thought she was going to scream. Then Mrs. Jander walked around behind the desk and went up very close to Christi's father. He rolled his chair back. Mrs. Jander somehow slipped out of her skirt and she wasn't wearing any panties at all. Christi could only see the back of her bottom and then it disappeared below the desk as Mrs. Jander sat astride her father's lap, facing him and putting one of her huge breasts into his mouth.

He stopped talking, but he kept the telephone to his ear. Christi wondered who could be on the phone with him. Mrs. Jander started rocking back and forth on him, back and forth, back and forth, with her breast in his mouth. Finally, he hung up the phone and grabbed her other breast with his hand and he started rubbing and pulling on her nipple and he began to rock back and forth too, back and forth, back and forth, faster and faster until Christi thought she was going to scream. Back and forth, back and forth, back and forth, faster and faster, faster and faster, back and forth, back and forth, back and forth, and then they made a strange, muffled noise, and then they stopped.

After a few minutes of not moving at all, Mrs. Jander stood up and grabbed a handful of tissues from the desk. She wiped herself as if she had just urinated. Then she leaned over to get her clothes. Her great huge breasts hung down in front of her as she pulled on her skirt. Still leaning over, she stuffed her great huge breasts into the skimpy red bra. Then she stood up straight and tucked her breasts in some more. Then she put on her tacky red blouse and tucked it into her skirt. Then she straightened her ugly red hair that had not moved at all the whole time she had been rocking back and forth.

Mrs. Jander stood very close to the desk and they were saying things that Christi couldn't hear, and finally Mrs. Jander walked out of the room. Suddenly Christi was afraid she might be seen. She wanted to disappear like a chameleon. Then she noticed that the chameleon was still resting immobilized on the sill. He had tried to blend in with brick. Instead, he had turned into the color of Mrs. Jander's hair.

In a flash, Christi grabbed her rolled-up newspaper and smashed the chameleon against the edge of the brick sill. She abandoned his flailing, dying body and the society pages of the *Vicksburg Daily Chronicle* in the dirt outside her father's office window.

Chapter 2
July 29, 1959

Christi bought a half-dozen postcards as soon as she and her mother got to Savannah. She forced herself to write one to her father. She didn't really know what to say and wondered if she would ever be able to look at him again. Finally settling on sending everyone the same message, she wrote:

"Hi! Having fun! Miss you already! Love, Christi."

Duty done, Christi sat staring out the upstairs guest room window. Her heart was heavy and she would have given anything to talk to Kelly. She opened the fancy leather box on the dresser and rubbed her fingers across a soft white envelope with its beautifully engraved script pronouncing the return address of *Dr. and Mrs. Claude R. Demarest III, Willow Creek Plantation, Old Willow Creek Road, Savannah, Georgia.*

The heavy matching letterhead had a fancy crest at the top and repeated the engraved return address. Christi realized that she was in really high cotton. If only her spirits could be. She picked up a pen and began to write:

Dear Kelly,

I wish we had more time to talk before I left. Something really terrible happened and I didn't know how to tell you. Don't worry. I don't mean something really terrible like somebody dying, but in a way it's that bad. And, it's not about you and me. I know this sounds really stupid.

Anyway, it's about my father. He is doing something bad and I don't know if I should tell my mother or if she would even believe me if I told her. It's not something terrible like he could get arrested or anything, but it is terrible, I think. Actually, I don't know what to think and I don't know what to do, but most of the time you and I can figure things out if we work on it together and I'm sorry I didn't tell you when I was at home. I can't wait to see you.

Love,
Christi

She put down her pen and re-read the letter. She was correct in what she had written in the first paragraph. It did sound really stupid. She tore the letter into tiny pieces and carried them into the bathroom. As she flushed the fluttering scraps of paper down the commode, she began to cry quietly. Then she went back to the bedroom, chose another piece of the elegant stationery and began again:

Dear Kelly,

I wish you could have come with us. Savannah is beautiful — big trees like Vicksburg and a blue-water river. Mama's friend lives out in the country in a house bigger than ours (plus they have two guest houses and quarters) and we're staying in an upstairs bedroom in the main house. (You can see from the stationery, they call it Willow Creek and there's a giant willow tree outside my window that's creepy at night.) There's a ton of people and lots of parties because this is a big deal! The best news is about the reason for the wedding, but it's so juicy I'm going to save it until I get back, cause you probably wouldn't even believe it unless I was there to cross my heart and swear to die. Can you guess?

I'm riding horses and swimming every day. There's lots of people here to fix the horses and everything. I wish you could be here. I'd like to stay forever, but we'll be back next Wednesday night, so see if you can come over. I miss you.

Love,
Christi

Christi re-read the second attempt and decided that it would do. She also decided then and there that it would be best to forget what she had seen in her father's office and never, ever, mention it to anyone. Probably no one would believe her anyway and she would just get in trouble. She convinced herself that the incident between her father and Mrs. Jander was a once-in-a-lifetime terrible event that occurred on the 25th of July in the year 1959, and would never, ever, happen again. Feeling guilty and not knowing why, she addressed an envelope to Kelly, stuffed the revised letter in it, and quickly sealed it shut before she could change her mind.

By the evening of her arrival back home in Vicksburg, Christi had managed to relegate *the July 25th incident* to a distant place in the back of her brain. It surprised her by jumping out clearly in front of her eyes as they pulled into the driveway. She was even more surprised to be embarrassed when she saw Kelly sitting on her front porch, playing jacks, waiting excitedly to see her as if nothing had ever happened.

Kelly came running out to the car. "Christi! It's about time! Hi, Miz Boudreaux. Mama sent a casserole. She says I may stay if that's all right with you, or Christi may come spend the night with me."

"Why, thank you, Kelly. Of course, you're welcome to stay. I'll call your mother. You girls give me about an hour to get settled and reheat the casserole. Then we'll eat. Now don't go off and get lost."

On cue, the girls ran to their hideout above the garage. From there, they could keep an eye on most of the neighborhood, and in the winter, when the trees were bare, they had a good view all the way to the river. Now, all Christi could think about was *the July 25th incident,* so she immediately sought another topic to distract herself.

"It was a shotgun wedding!" she proclaimed boldly.

"I don't get it," Kelly frowned. "What's a shotgun wedding?"

"I didn't know either," Christi confessed, "but I found out." Her blue, blue eyes opened wider. "It's when you have to get married because you're pregnant!"

"But, I thought only married women could get pregnant and have babies."

"Don't feel stupid. So did I, but Michelle Demarest, she's the bride's cousin, told me all about it," Christi nodded, dark curls bobbing. "She's thirteen and she knows."

"So what happens?" Kelly wanted to know too.

For a second, Christi thought about her father and Mrs. Jander, and wondered if Mrs. Jander could be pregnant now. She blushed, and started into the story she had heard.

"Well, when a boy and girl are going steady, they do a lot of kissing and stuff."

"I know that," Kelly remarked impatiently. Christi was very flushed now, but Kelly didn't seem to notice.

The older girl took a deep breath and continued authoritatively, "Eventually, they go to the drive-in and they get in the back seat of the car under a blanket and then — you might not believe this, but Michelle swears it's true and I believe her — then the boy puts his wiener up inside the girl and she gets pregnant."

"He puts his wiener where?"

"Up inside the girl."

"I know, but where? Exactly where?"

"In the hole you pee out of."

"You're kidding. "

"No. I swear."

"Yuk."

"I know."

Silence followed. Christi blushed again, thankful that Kelly seemed to be lost in her own thoughts. She pulled a splinter of wood from the floor and cleaned under her clean fingernails with it as Kelly stared out toward the unseen river.

Finally Kelly asked, "What do they call it?"

"Call what?"

"'It.' What do they call it when a boy does that to a girl?"

"There's lots of words for it."

"Name some."

"Making love. Doing it. Screwing."

"Are they all the same thing?"

"I think so."

"Name some more."

"I can't think of any. There's a big one, though. It's the technical name for it. Actually it's two words, but I can't remember. "

"Is it sexual intercourse?"

"Yeah! That's it. How did you know?"

"Lucky guess."

"Come on. How'd you know that?" Christi really wanted to know. She felt scared.

"Ran across it in the dictionary."

That was enough to satisfy Christi, although she never would understand her friend's habit of reading the dictionary just for fun. She wondered if there were any way that Kelly could know about *the July 25th incident,* and so she asked, "Then you know all about it, huh?"

"No more than you do," Kelly confessed. "Just what I read in the dictionary. And another word."

"What?"

"Fuck!"

"Yeah. I heard Billy DeVito say that one. I wondered what it was. He got in trouble for it," Christi recalled.

"It's a trouble word, that's for sure," Kelly agreed, and Christi wondered again.

Christi watched a squirrel dangling upside down from the tip of a limb, carelessly clinging with his back toes to the pencil thin branch, his tail looped over the neighboring twigs. With his front paws, the squirrel was grabbing tiny berries and thrusting them into his mouth. Another squirrel approached, and the first one scrambled upright, chattering. They chased each other around and around the tree, up and down, leaping onto other trees and then back again. Around and around. Scared.

Christi cleaned her clean fingernails with the splinter, waiting and hoping that Kelly would change the subject, but Kelly obviously wasn't finished with it because in a few minutes she volunteered, "Mary Margaret McCafferty told me to go fuck myself."

"Mary Margaret McCafferty said that?"

"Yeah. Sunday."

"What did you do to her?"

"Nothing."

"I can't believe it. Mary Margaret McCafferty? She's so prissy. Wonder why she said that. You sure you didn't do something to her?" Christi insisted, knowing Kelly.

"Sure. She's just weird."

"Yeah, she's weird, all right."

Finally, Kelly changed the subject with her favorite line, "I'm hungry." Christi felt enormous relief as Kelly added, "Let's go help your mom set the table."

* * *

"This is a delicious dinner, Kelly. You be sure to thank your mother for it."

"Yes, sir, I will," Kelly mumbled at her plate.

Christi noticed that Kelly didn't look at her father when she replied, and then Christi noticed that she herself wasn't looking at him either.

"I'm afraid it would have been another night of sardines and crackers for me. I wouldn't expect Miz B to fix dinner after such a long, tiring trip. No, siree, I wouldn't."

Christi wondered why her father couldn't fix a better dinner for himself than sardines and crackers. *And why couldn't he have fixed a nice dinner for our homecoming? Kelly's father can cook, although he doesn't do it more than once or twice a year, except breakfast. Why doesn't my father? And how did Kelly's mother know that he didn't cook? How well does Kelly's mother know my father anyway?* For a second, she imagined Mrs. McCain in her father's office instead of Mrs. Jander.

Christi blushed and glanced around furtively to see if anyone noticed. They were all eating and talking about the trip. Everyone seemed normal. Or did they? Christi couldn't remember how it had felt before.

Nothing had changed, but everything was different. Were they all pretending? Did they all know about *the July 25th incident*, as she did?

Her beautiful mother was smiling. Christi heard herself tell a funny story about the trip and they all laughed, even her father. How could he laugh? How could they all laugh and act like nothing had happened? But of course, Kelly couldn't know and her mother couldn't know. Christi realized that she was the only one who could know, besides her father, and he was laughing. How could he keep laughing?

Christi heard herself laughing. *This is crazy*, her mind raced. *The world is upside down and everyone is laughing.* Kelly was laughing so hard that she started choking, but Christi just stared at her as through a fog. She wondered if Kelly would sit there and laugh and choke until she died and would never know about *the July 25th incident* because Christi was afraid to tell her. She wondered how she could be so afraid. After all, she was still laughing.

"Honey, are you okay?" Mr. Boudreaux patted Kelly on the back.

"Yes, sir, I am," Kelly mumbled at her plate. She still wasn't looking at Christi's father, and Christi wasn't looking at him either.

* * *

Christi was afraid to go to sleep too early. She was afraid that she would wake up again in the middle of the night and think about her father and Mrs. Jander, or even her father and Mrs. McCain. She was afraid that if she thought about it too much, she would accidentally say something to Kelly, so she changed the subject by talking on and on with endless details about Willow Creek Plantation, the parties, the magnificent church, the wedding itself with twelve bridesmaids and groomsmen, and the extravagant reception at Willow Creek with two bands and dancing until three in the morning.

"I don't get it," Kelly finally confessed. Christi panicked, afraid that her brilliant friend had seen through her subterfuge. Her stomach tightened. She was relieved when Kelly went on with her question.

"If they had to get married," Kelly frowned, "wouldn't they want to keep it a secret? It sounds like everybody in Georgia was invited to their wedding."

"I asked Michelle about that. She said that Mrs. Demarest always wanted a big wedding for her daughter because she didn't have one. And Dr. Demarest said, 'Why not? The bigger the lie, the more people believe it.'"

Chapter 3
August 6, 1959

"The bigger the lie, the more people believe it."

Helêne Lepeltier Boudreaux was contemplating that very truth as she rose early to fix breakfast for her husband. She gathered her long dark hair into a clasp at the nape of her neck and took a quick look in the mirror. Definitely French, not Cajun. That part of the story was true at least. Aristocratic? A possibility. Wealthy? A laugh.

Helêne Lepeltier grew up as a street urchin in Paris, never knowing her father, ashamed of her prostitute mother, and then found herself in the same occupation at the age of thirteen. But Helêne had resolved to be different. She avoided the drugs. She saved seventy-five percent of her ill-gotten earnings, and traded her favors for the things she would need to escape — tutoring in English, lessons in piano and voice, elegant, tasteful clothes, and finally, along with her legitimately earned *diplôme* from the local *lycée,* a glowing letter of recommendation from the disgusting old *professeur de français,* setting forth not only her outstanding intellectual capabilities, but also the illustrious heritage and social connections of the Lepeltier family. Sophie Newcomb College in New Orleans, Louisiana, United States of America, welcomed nineteen-year-old Helêne into its soft protective bosom.

The French girl felt surprisingly at home in the foreign country, surrounded by girls a year or two younger, and quickly adapted to the Southern manner. By the time of her senior year, as her money was rapidly eroding, she had no trouble securing a marriage proposal from Clement Boudreaux, assuring her future as a comfortable, if not wealthy, United States citizen. She thought she could love him and might have been relieved to know that her motives were not too different from the bevy of her classmates who flowered the South with their summer weddings.

Helêne told everyone that her entire family had been killed during the occupation of Paris, so that a large wedding would be inappropriate. The chaplain at Tulane University performed the Catholic ceremony in the presence of their friends Claude Demarest and his young wife Christina, who appeared quite pregnant for a recent bride. Christina and Claude Demarest stayed in New Orleans where he was in medical school. After a brief honeymoon in Biloxi, Helêne and Clement Boudreaux drove to Vicksburg.

The Boudreaux family, as would any Americans who made their money the hard way, welcomed Helêne as that most prized acquisition, an aristocratic Western European (probably related to royalty though it was too painful for her to speak of her sadly departed relatives), sophisticated, accomplished in the arts and fluent in four languages. Helêne took her place in Vicksburg society and set about the business of making a home and learning to love Clement ("you-can-call-me-Clem") Boudreaux.

After several annual trips to her trusted gynecologist in New Orleans, Helêne had been convinced that it was safe to conceive and soon thereafter a daughter, Christina Lepeltier Boudreaux, began and completed their family. At twelve, Christina was everything her mother had wanted — pretty, popular, smart and healthy. She would have all the advantages that Helêne had missed, from the love and attention of two parents to the material trappings necessary for moving in the right circles from which a suitable husband could be selected. It didn't matter to Helêne that her own marriage was not idyllic. She never looked at another man, and always proclaimed, verbally and physically, her love for Clement. They never argued, and, though there was a lack of passion, there was no lack of admiration from their friends who considered them to be the perfect family.

Occasionally, Clem Boudreaux, hearing more undiluted praise of his beautiful wife, felt a little uneasy, but could never find any fault with Helêne. He finally concluded that he must have some terrible character flaw that made him unappreciative of his good fortune.

Clem was feeling that way again as he sat down to breakfast across from the perfect French woman. Consciously, he compared Helêne to his new secretary Vayda. Mrs. Jander. There was no contest. Helêne clearly excelled in every category, from her thick, luxurious, wavy hair to her thin ankles and beautifully shaped feet.

Vayda had over-permed reddish hair with dark roots, a few extra pounds around her middle from drinking too much beer, and thick ankles above her square feet. Clem wasn't even sure what color her eyes were. She was smart enough, for a secretary, but lacked the refinement that everyone prized in Helêne. Even as he wondered what he saw in Vayda, his heart did a little skip and he knew he was too anxious to get to the office.

Christina and her friend Kelly McCain slipped into the kitchen and sat down at the table just as Clem was leaving for work. He looked with pride at his daughter — and his wife. Yes, he was doing damn well for himself. Best not to mess it up with fooling around.

He felt Kelly's cool presence in the room and turned to say "good morning." She had always been so friendly to him, but now this strange aloofness. He imagined that she knew his secret, but ridiculed himself for the thought. She was only a child. How could she even think of such a thing?

"Morning, girls! You're up early. Got big plans for the day?"

"Yes, Daddy."

Once again, Clem felt the strange aloofness from his own daughter. He responded in the only way he knew how.

"Need any money?" he asked hopefully.

"No, sir, thank you," Christi answered politely, but looking away. "I still have some from the trip."

"How 'bout you, Kelly? Need a coupla dollars for a special treat?"

"No, sir, but thank you anyway," Kelly mumbled at her plate.

It seemed to Clem that Kelly hadn't looked directly at him since Christi returned from Savannah last night. He felt rebuked, and the cloud of Kelly's unspoken disapproval followed him all day. *Must be my guilty conscience,* he thought. *I'd better do something about it. Maybe I'll just get another secretary. Hell, they're all the same.*

This resolution was no better than the previous ones he had made and not much different from the ones that would come later. The only thing to change would be his conscience. Eventually, it would wear down.

Christi and Kelly sped off on their bicycles immediately after breakfast. By eleven o'clock, they were hungry again and near enough to Kelly's house to drop in for lunch. However, both girls were specifically hungry for a Dairy Queen hamburger and a strawberry shake.

"Let's go," Christi started off.

"Can't."

"Why?"

"Don't have any money," Kelly confessed sheepishly.

"But you told Daddy you did."

"I lied."

"Why?" Christi asked, blushing. *Why would Kelly lie? Does she think I'm lying by not saying anything about the July 25th incident?*

"I don't know," Kelly lied again, blushing and hoping Christi wouldn't notice.

"Stop here," the older girl ordered. "Let's see if I have enough for both of us."

Christi counted. "Nope. Sorry. Why don't we go by your house to get some?"

"We might get stuck there, especially if Nellie Mae has something good started for lunch. And she'll want to hear all about your trip. Then my parents will want to hear it."

The girls sighed together. All they could think of now was a big juicy hamburger with lots of mustard and onion. And a cool thick strawberry shake. There had to be a way.

"Christi, I got it! Follow me."

Minutes later the two girls were talking to Kelly's neighbor Old Man Everett through his screen door. Christi remembered that the Everetts had been in Florida while she was in Savannah, but the Everett's news had rated only a small paragraph in the *"Comings and Goings"* section of the *Vicksburg Daily Chronicle.*

"Yes, sir," Christi heard her friend say, "I kept those kids from riding through your yard the whole time you were gone.

And, in case you didn't notice, I cleaned out your garbage can real good so it wouldn't draw rats and I watered your garden some, while I was at it."

"Martha, come here. Did you hear what all this nice child did while we were gone?"

"What? Oh, it's Kelly McCain. Good morning, Kelly, how are you?"

"Fine."

"And who's your little friend here?"

"You remember Christina Boudreaux, don't you?"

"Yes, of course. Good morning, Christina."

"Good morning, ma'am."

"Now what's all this you did? Won't you come in and have some barbecue? You know we've always got plenty of barbecue!"

"And it's great barbecue, too, but no, thank you, ma'am. We were just on our way over to the Dairy Queen for a hamburger and strawberry shake."

"Some other time then, but now, Kelly, you tell Mrs. Everett what all you did while we were gone."

"Oh, it wasn't really all that much."

"Wasn't much? Why, this child kept those other kids from riding all over our yard … "

"Do tell."

"… and she watered the garden …"

"No!"

"… and even scrubbed out that filthy garbage can just so's the rats wouldn't come."

"Well, glory be."

Kelly shrugged her shoulders. "It wasn't really all that much. I just wanted to stop by and see if you had a good trip and…"

"We sure did, honey, but it's awful nice to come home, especially when we have such nice neighbors. Herman, don't we have a little something from Florida for Kelly and her friend?"

Old Man Everett shuffled to the kitchen and returned with a box of salt-water taffy.

"We were going to bring this to you anyway, but seeing's how you kept an eye on things for us, here's a little something extra," he added, reaching into his pocket and coming up with a one-dollar bill and two fifty-cent pieces.

"Now don't eat all that candy before lunch. I don't want Nellie Mae getting on me."

"Yes, sir. Thank you. That's real generous of you. I didn't do much. Really."

Kelly and Christi sped off again on their bikes, this time for the Dairy Queen.

Christi waited until they were halfway through their feast before saying, "You've done some dumb things in your life, Kelly McCain, but cleaning out the Everett's garbage can has got to be the dumbest."

"Not so dumb," Kelly grinned, "we're eating hamburgers, aren't we?"

"Sure," Christi acknowledged, "but there must be more to the story than that."

Kelly nodded, "There is, but it's kind of a secret. You tell me a secret, and I'll tell you this one."

Christi glanced away, then lowered her eyes. "I can't think of any secrets right now."

"You're lying," Kelly challenged boldly.

Christi blushed, and stammered, "Whuh, whuh, why do you think I'm lying?"

"Because I know you. I know what you think," Kelly announced loudly. Then she leaned forward and lowered her voice to a whisper, "I never told you this before," she confided, her pale green eyes piercing Christi to the soul, "but I can read your mind."

Christi's face paled. She stared wide-eyed at her friend. She tried to think of something other than *the July 25th incident*. There was nothing else in the world. She felt her face and neck prickling with heat. She saw her father and Mrs. Jander rocking back and forth, back and forth, back and forth until she thought she would scream.

"NO!" she screamed at the top of her voice. "NO!"

Kelly stared in disbelief as Christi yelled right in her face. Everyone in the Dairy Queen turned around to stare at them.

Christi dropped her hamburger and jumped up from the table, knocking her purse to the floor.

"NO!" she screamed again and burst into tears as she ran to the girls' bathroom.

Kelly sat in stunned silence. She didn't even care that everyone was looking at her. She waited for a few minutes that seemed like an eternity, but Christi didn't reappear. Kelly had never heard Christi raise her voice. No one in the entire Boudreaux family, cousins and all, ever raised their voices.

She tried to remember exactly what she had said that made Christi so upset. The words "I can read your mind" echoed in the silence of her heart. She never should have told such a lie to her friend, but of course, Christi couldn't have believed it. Maybe that was it. Christi was upset because Kelly had lied to her about being able to read her mind.

Feeling guilty and suddenly concerned that people were still looking at her, Kelly bent down slowly to gather Christi's little purse and its contents. Everything was spilled out. Lipstick, mints, pens, stamps, change, junk.

Kelly stuffed it all back in the purse, straightened up, and walked blindly through the Dairy Queen to the girls' bathroom. She wanted to cry. *What's wrong with me? Am I crazy? What did I do?* Feelings she couldn't define welled up in her and she wanted to be sick. When she opened the bathroom door, she could smell that Christi already was sick.

"Christi? Christi, are you in there?"

"Yeah," came a weak voice from the last cubicle.

"I've got your purse."

"Thanks."

Kelly went to the sink, ran water on a paper towel, folded it and held it under the door.

"Here's a wet paper towel," she offered.

"Thanks," Christi replied feebly, reaching for it.

Kelly heard the commode flush. She waited, and waited.

"Are you going to come out?"

"Unless I can figure some way to flush myself down the sewer."

"Aw, Christi, come on. It's not that bad, is it?"

"Yes."

"Listen. I'm really sorry."

"You didn't do anything."

"I made you scream and cry and throw up a perfectly good hamburger," Kelly replied.

Christi couldn't help chuckling about the reference to the hamburger. That was so like Kelly.

"It's not anything you did, Kelly."

"Do you want to talk about it?"

"No. It's Nothing with a capital N."

"Okay, but come out of there and listen to me."

Christi slid the latch over and the door creaked open.

"Look at yourself in the mirror."

"I don't need to look."

"I said 'Look!"

Christi' s blood-shot eyes stared back at her.

"Now, you can either go around looking like that and making yourself miserable over 'Nothing with a capital N,' or you can tell me what's wrong and we can figure it out."

Christi managed a weak smile.

"So you really can't read my mind?"

Kelly shrugged, returned the weak smile, and found a way out of her predicament.

"Of course not, Dummy! And why would I want to? There's nothing like a Webster's Dictionary in there. Reading your mind would probably just bore me."

"Yeah," Christi agreed gratefully, nodding and beaming at her friend. "Yeah, it would probably just bore you."

Chapter 4
August 8, 1959

"It's not fair!" Christi complained to her mother as they stood at the sink drying the dinner dishes. "Kelly's a whole year younger than I am and she already has a boyfriend. She doesn't even want to be over here. I can't believe it's Saturday night and she's sitting at home by herself just in case Cameron might decide to call her. Where does that leave me? It's not fair. Kelly always gets everything."

Helêne looked around their large, beautiful kitchen and sighed, "Some people might think that you have everything, *ma chère*. Besides, she just met him today. She's excited, but it won't last forever. You're her best friend. That lasts forever. Try to be happy for Kelly and be patient. Someday you'll have a boyfriend, too, and you might need Kelly's patience."

"I'll never have a boyfriend," Christi whispered loudly. "Never."

"Of course you will," her mother assured her. "Of course you will."

"No," Christi insisted. "I won't. I don't want one. Boys are nasty."

"Look at me, *ma chère*," the elegant Frenchwoman cooed, cradling her daughter's face in her hands and looking straight into her eyes. "You don't mean that."

"I do mean it!" Christi glared at her mother, thinking about *the July 25th incident*. "You just don't know how nasty they can be."

For a moment, Helêne thought back to her life on the streets of Paris. *Boys can be nasty, indeed, but Christi is too young to know that.* Helêne felt her own shame, and looked away.

"Some boys are nasty, *ma chère*, but I'm sure that young Mister Cameron Coulter is not. You said that he's nice and smart and tall and funny and handsome. I'm sure that someday you'll have a boyfriend like that too."

"Like Daddy?" Christi asked defiantly.

Helêne glanced away momentarily before assuring her daughter, "Your Daddy is a very nice man. Everyone in Vicksburg likes him. We're fortunate that he takes such good care of us. Don't you forget that. You'll find a nice man who will take care of you, too, but there's no rush. Now, why don't you go call Kelly and be sweet to her?"

"She doesn't want me to call. She doesn't want the line to be busy in case Cameron calls her. It's just not fair. Kelly gets everything!"

Christi finished her part of the dish drying without another word, wondering why her father couldn't be like Kelly's. Mr. McCain would never do anything nasty with that nasty Mrs. Jander. Clayton McCain was the most nearly perfect man in Vicksburg, maybe in all of Mississippi. Why did he have to be Kelly's father and not hers?

Christi decided that if she ever got a boyfriend, he would have to be like Clayton McCain — tall and handsome and smart and nice to everybody and always interested in what she had to say. She smiled to herself, thinking about his call to *"the vivacious and oh-so-popular Miss Christina Boudreaux."* Clayton McCain would never, ever let her down as her own father had already done.

With that thought, Christi walked disconsolately through the den, past her disappointing father dozing in his big leather recliner. She slowly dragged her feet up the grand staircase to her exquisitely decorated bedroom. She didn't turn on the lamps, but got ready for bed in the dark, then lay there alone, staring at the ceiling, thinking about *the July 25th incident.*

It had been exactly two weeks, and the images of it still tormented her night and day. The nighttime was worse. She tried to stay awake to avoid dreaming about it, but a fitful sleep came, bringing the torment that she had come to fear and hate. When the phone beside her bed rang early the next morning, Christi felt as if she had just fallen asleep.

"Christi, wake up," Kelly whispered loudly into the phone. "I have to tell you something very serious and important. Are you awake?"

"Mmm-hmm, I'm awake," Christi mumbled. "Did Cameron call you?"

"This is not about Cameron," Kelly continued solemnly. "But no, he didn't call."

There was a long pause on the line.

"Then what is it?" Christi asked, sitting up straight in her bed, disturbed by the tone of Kelly's voice.

There was another long silence.

"When I got home from church this morning, my Daddy wasn't at home."

"No!" Christi exclaimed, thinking instantly of Mrs. Jander.

Kelly was silent again.

"Is he home yet?" Christi asked, hating Mrs. Jander and her red hair and her tacky clothes.

Kelly sighed, "No."

"Do you know where he is?" Christi questioned, with a sick knot forming in her stomach. "Do you want me to help you look for him?" she offered, recalling Mrs. Jander's address.

"I know where he is," Kelly whispered.

Christi felt guilty. On top of everything else, Kelly was a better friend than Christi could ever be. Kelly was going to tell her a secret about Clayton McCain and Mrs. Jander. Christi felt her hand getting sweaty on the phone. She didn't want to hear it, but she waited for the words she was dreading. The silence was deafening and interminable.

"My daddy," Kelly paused, and a chill went over Christi, "went to the hospital early this morning. Old Man Everett took him."

"Oh, no," Christi gasped, but there was some relief in her voice. "What happened?"

"He had a heart attack," Kelly said softly. "I don't know if a heart attack hurts or not. Do you think it hurts, Christi? I mean, we can't usually feel our hearts, you know."

"I don't know anything about heart attacks," Christi murmured, realizing that she was lying. She knew that you could die from a heart attack and that they did hurt, but she didn't want to worry her friend. She tried to sound cheerful as she said, "I'm sure he'll be okay, though."

There was another great long silence. Fear clutched Christi's throat. She tried to swallow and nearly choked.

"He will be okay, Kelly," she tried to assure her friend and herself at the same time. "He has to be okay."

"He's not going to be okay, Christi. He'll never be okay. He'll never come home again."

"What are you saying, Kelly? Tell me straight out how bad it is."

Again, the silence. A longer silence.

"He's dead," Kelly whispered, as though her heart would break.

"NO!" Christi shrieked into the phone. "NO! He can't be dead!"

"My daddy is dead, Christi," Kelly responded quietly. "Maybe you could come over before everyone else gets here."

"Oh, Kelly, I'm so sorry! Oh, my God! What are you going to do?"

"Maybe you could get your mother to come over and talk to my mother," Kelly asked plaintively. She paused a long time before adding, "I think there is something wrong with my mother. After the doctor called to tell her that Daddy was dead, she told me not to tell anybody."

"Then, maybe it isn't true," Christi said hopefully. "Maybe your mother was upset and she got confused about what the doctor told her."

"He's dead, Christi. I called the hospital. Then I called the funeral home. They're going to pick up..." Kelly paused a moment, "... his body."

"We'll be there in a few minutes," Christi promised. "We'll all be right there."

"Thanks," Kelly sighed. "I knew I could count on you."

Christi hung up the phone, slid back down in bed, and collapsed on her pillow. She felt hot tears forming, and was crying softly by the time her mother came into the room.

"I heard you scream again, *ma chère*. Are you all right?" Helêne asked gently.

"Nuh, nuh, no, I'm not," Christi sobbed as her mother sat beside her on the bed. "Kelly called. Her fah, fah, father had a heart attack. He's dead."

"Mon Dieu!"

Helêne embraced her daughter and felt her own tears coming.

"Mon Dieu!" she cried, rocking her child back and forth. *"Mon Dieu!"*

* * *

Christi sat on the sofa in the McCain's front parlor and listened to the awkward whisperings of the classmates and neighborhood kids who had come to call on Kelly. Kelly herself was spending more time with the adults because her mother wouldn't come out of the bedroom to talk to anyone.

Christi felt helpless, despondent, and alone. She didn't know what she should be doing, so she just sat and cried intermittently, while she listened to the subdued buzz of conversations and the droning of the air conditioner.

It was nearly one-thirty. The dining room table was crowded with platters of food that people had brought already. It looked as if half of Vicksburg had decided to bring their Sunday lunch instead of eating it at home. Someone handed Christi a brownie on a napkin.

She stared at it and remembered how much Mr. McCain had liked brownies. *I had always planned to make some brownies for him, but I never did. I never did. No, I never did, and now it's too late.* Hot tears came to her eyes and brimmed over, spilling down her cheeks. She let them fall onto the brownie.

The room became stifling hot. The air conditioner was running constantly, but it was over a hundred degrees outside and there were too many people in the house, or coming and going and letting the front door stand open. Christi wanted to get up and shut it again, but she didn't have the energy. She felt too empty inside.

She glanced into the dining room and saw her father standing beside Kelly, talking quietly with some of Mr. McCain's friends. She supposed that her mother was still in the kitchen with the women and Nellie Mae. She wondered if Mrs. McCain would ever come out of the bedroom. Maybe she should go knock on the bedroom door and talk to her, but what would she say? Regina McCain was always nice to Christi, but they had never actually talked about anything. Maybe this was not a good time to start.

The group standing in the open doorway stepped back for another visitor, and Christi saw the new priest up close for the first time. There was a momentary lull in the conversations as the houseful of Baptists and Methodists and Presbyterians paused to scrutinize the Catholic cleric.

He was young, mid-to-late twenties, tall and athletic, with dark wavy hair. He looked around the room for a moment and then walked toward Kelly, who apparently had sensed his arrival and disengaged herself from the group in the dining room.

"I'm Father O'Connell," Christi heard him say gently, with a soft Irish accent. He took Kelly's hand in both of his. "Sean O'Connell. I came as soon as I could."

Christi watched as Kelly led the priest through the crowd, upstairs toward the master bedroom. She felt compelled to follow them, though she didn't know why. She waited a few minutes, put down the brownie that she had made soggy with her tears, and started up the stairway, hoping that no one would notice. Feeling guilty, she stood outside the master bedroom door and tried to hear the conversation.

It seemed that only the priest was talking. Christi was mesmerized by the sound of his voice, soft and lilting, gentle and reassuring. She sensed, as much as heard, what he was saying — words about eternal life and rest in God. She tried to picture Clayton McCain in Heaven. She smiled, remembering his stories about picking cotton when he was a kid and wrestling alligators in Panama and fighting with bayonets in the Marine Corps. She could almost hear him singing the Marine Corps Hymn in his deep off-key voice:...

"If the Army or the Na-a-vy
ever gaze on Heaven's scenes,
They will find the streets are guarded by
The United States Marines."

* * *

Christi heard herself mournfully humming the Marine Corps Hymn like a dirge as she dressed for the funeral on Tuesday afternoon. It was the hottest day of the year, without a breath of air stirring or a cloud in the sky — not a good day to wear black. Christi stood in front of her mirror and wished it were cold and rainy outside, to match her mood. She had cried so much she was exhausted. Suddenly it occurred to her that she hadn't seen Kelly cry at all.

Kelly had asked her to sit with the family during the service. It was the highest honor a friend could bestow, but Christi was too sad to feel at all proud as she took her place in the small room off to the side where the family could see but not be seen.

Christi sat beside the family niggers Nellie Mae and her daughter Prudence in the row behind Mrs. McCain and Kelly and Kelly's younger sister Mandy. Funerals and weddings were the only times that white people and colored people ever sat together, and so it was the first time that Christi ever sat beside Prudence. She realized that they were the same age and that Prudence seemed to be as upset as she was that Mr. McCain was dead. She vowed to go out back and talk to Prudence the next time she was at Kelly's house.

* * *

The procession to the cemetery was interminable. A couple of older cars overheated along the way, and others stopped to pick up the stranded mourners. It was after three o'clock by the time everyone got situated at the graveside. The sun was unmerciful, even under the tents and the shade trees.

Christi felt sweat mingling with the tears running down her cheeks. She looked over at her best friend, sitting straight and silent in the white folding chair on the fake green grass carpet. Kelly didn't seem to be crying or sweating. She was just sitting there, staring at the open grave and the shiny casket suspended over it on belts.

The Baptist preacher prayed on and on. Then Father Sean O'Connell prayed on and on. The sun beat down, and Christi thought she was going to faint. She wondered how Father O'Connell could stand there in all those robes and not die from the heat. She thought about Clayton McCain being up in Heaven, watching all of them sweating around a box that held only his body while his soul was safe from the weather and from everything.

Then Christi began to wonder what would happen if her own father died. Would he go to Heaven? She panicked at the thought of her father and Mrs. Jander being together and dying and going straight to Hell.

She became aware of a lingering "Amen," followed by some uncomfortable shifting and coughing among the crowd. Then, in eerie silence, the casket was lowered slowly into the ground until it disappeared from her sight. She watched the funeral home attendant ceremonially scoop a shovel full of dirt and walk over to Mrs. McCain with it. He held the shovel out toward her and stood respectfully still. She looked up at him, with her big brown eyes so scared, and she shook her head from side to side. Other than that, she did not move.

There was another uncomfortable shifting of the crowd and a few more muffled coughs. Kelly stood up and took the weighty shovel from the man. Slowly, resolutely, steadily, she carried it across the carpet of fake green grass to the very edge of the open grave. She held the shovel over the gaping hole for the longest time. There was no shuffling of the crowd. No coughing. No breathing. There was nothing but the silence of stifling, still, summer air.

Finally, Kelly turned the shovel over. Dry dirt and rocks thundered onto the shiny new casket, and the rumbling echo of death was the only sound heard in Mississippi for the rest of that long, hot, August afternoon.

PART II

THE SOPHOMORE YEAR

(*sophos* - wise / *moros* - foolish)

Chapter 5
Thanksgiving 1962

"...for which let us give thanks as our families gather together and bless this food to the nourishment of our bodies, from Thy bounty, through Christ, Our Lord. Amen."

That blessing is just like me, Christi thought as she made the Sign of the Cross during the silence following the unanimous "Amen." *Part Boudreaux. Part Lepeltier. Part father. Part mother. Part old. Part new. What am I anyway? Fifteen years old and what am I? A sophomore. Sophos - wise. Moros - foolish. So what am I? Well, whatever I am, I'm better off than that turkey.*

All eyes were on the perfectly browned bird in front of Clem Boudreaux. He stood to carve, and conversations resumed.

"Now, hurry up, Clem. You know all those babies cain't be good for long," Billy Boudreaux interjected as Christi's father poured his second glass of wine.

"Help yourselves to the vegetables and start passing things around," suggested Helêne Boudreaux, the perennially gracious hostess.

Always the same admonitions. Every year more babies. Only now it would be Nellie Mae and Prudence trying to keep all the babies quiet during the Thanksgiving dinner. One o'clock. Nap time for most of them anyway. Christi was cousin to twelve girls now, all but the eldest living in Vicksburg.

Besides the teen-age Christi Boudreaux and her California cousin Maggie Stevenson, the other girls were under five years old, all offspring of Clem's younger brothers, of whom Billy was the most vocal at dinner conversation, as usual.

"Well, I don't care. I don't see why a nigger would want to go to Ole Miss anyway!"

Christi closed her eyes and let the voices blend together. It was almost impossible to tell one Boudreaux brother from the next without looking at them. Christi didn't want to look.

"I think it's those damn Yankees puttin' ideas in their heads, that's all. No self-respecting Mississippi nigger would want to go to a school where he's not wanted."

"I think you're right about that. They've done fine going to their own schools, and damn lucky to have schools if you ask me."

"That nigger Meredith won't live to graduate, you mark my words."

"Well, at least Governor Barnett did what he could, sending the state police to keep him out. Who would'a thought Kennedy would butt in with federal marshals?"

"Anybody with a brain might'a figured he'd do it. Lookit the damn laws he's pushed down everybody's throat."

"Yep. Lettin' niggers ride in any seat they want on interstate buses, lettin'm sit in airports and train stations right next to white folks."

"Cain't say I was too surprised to see the President back up them marshals with fifteen thousand armed troops."

"Well, I'm just surprised only two people got killed."

"That's the truth."

"Don't forget them two hundred wounded. I hate to think how many I'da taken out if they'da started throwing tear gas in my fraternity house."

"It's them damn Yankees. All they wanted to do for the last hunnert years is come down here and tell us how to take care of our niggers. It's enough to start another war."

Silence.

"Sure is good dressing, Helêne," Billy complimented, remembering his manners. "A body might think you were born and bred right here in Vicksburg, Mississippi, 'stead of Paris, France."

"Thank you, Billy. Have some more giblet gravy on it."

"B'lieve I will."

"The next thing you know, little Christi here'd be going to high school with niggers. Now, you just try to imagine that."

"I wouldn't mind if Prudence went to school with me," Christi interposed in the lull.

Everyone stopped for a few seconds to stare at her.

"Have you been running around with that nigger again?" her father asked. "I should've left those two at the McCain's instead of trying to help out bringing them over here. I've told you a hundred times that nice white girls don't run around with niggers – not even in their own back yard!"

Christi's face flushed at being called down in front of the whole family. She bit her tongue to keep from asking him who he was running around with. She didn't say anything. The Boudreaux brothers resumed their usual conversation, oblivious as always to the comings and goings of Nellie Mae as she refilled the serving bowls and tended to their unspoken needs.

"I swear, there's no telling what this place is coming to. My own niece running around talking to a nigger gal and willing to go to school with her. Clem, boy, you better take charge of your daughter."

"She doesn't understand that it wouldn't be just Prudence. Once you let one nigger in, you're gonna have'm all."

"Yep, you mark my words. If that nigger James Meredith lives to graduate from Ole Miss, God forbid, there won't be no end to it."

"That's the truth. Why, twenty years from now, you could have a nigger football team at Ole Miss, and Grambling out trying to recruit white boys."

Another silence fell as all considered the enormity of that prediction.

"Niggers in the dorms, a nigger roommate, for God's sake."

"White kids would have to go outa state to college."

"Imagine a nigger homecoming queen at Ole Miss!"

"I'm afraid that's the day I'd become a card-carrying member of the Klan!"

"We don't carry cards."

"I know that. It's just a figure of speech."

"Well, the Klan better git busy, 'cause things are goin' down hill fast."

"Next thing you know, niggers'll be wanting to eat inside at Tolbert's Ice Cream Parlor."

"Naw. Tolberts don't serve chitlins and skins."

"Yep. And they don't serve niggers."

"Not yet, but you just look what's goin' on all over. So-called 'civil rights workers' down here stirrin' up trouble, signing up niggers to vote. Hell, most of 'em cain't read."

"Cain't none of 'em think."

"So you know this ain't their doin'. It's damn Yankees tryin' to do their thinkin' for 'em. Gitt'n 'em all stirred up. Making promises they cain't keep."

"It's the same old thing it's always been. Hard 'nough for a white man with good sense to scratch out a decent living, and now they wanta give hand-outs to the niggers."

"Can you imagine how much of our hard-earned tax money it took to send them federal marshals and fifteen thousand troops to Oxford just so's one coon could register at Ole Miss? Now how many more are they gonna have to send down there to tutor that boy?"

"At that rate, this country can't afford too many more niggers in white colleges."

Christi interjected, "But that federal court ordered the University to register James Meredith."

"With all due respect to you, Miss Christina Boudreaux, I don't believe we need nigger-lovers or federal courts or any other kind of courts to run our schools."

Christi closed her eyes again and listened to them going on and on.

"So there, you see, even if, and I'm saying 'if,' even if it was just a question of rights, there's nobody in the South wantin' those rights started down here by a bunch of left-wing Commie Yankees coming from New York and Dee-troit City and Washington, DC, tryin' to tell us how to run our schools and our bus service and our lunch counters and our public facilities."

"How'd you like to go to a picture show and find out they let the niggers come down out of the balcony and sit beside you?"

"Yep. White folks have got rights too and we don't want to have to drink at a water fountain where any nigger can come up and spit in it, or go sit on any public john where some nigger just sat. For Christ's sake, I don't know what this country's coming to. Niggers are gonna be the ruin of it..."

* * *

"Gracious Heavenly Father, we thank you again, as we leave to go our separate ways, for the opportunity to gather here together as a family on this Thanksgiving Day, in peace and love, to enjoy the fruits of Thy Harvest, this food for the nourishment of our bodies, from Thy bounty, through Christ, Our Lord, Amen."

"Amen."

Clem Boudreaux opened another bottle of wine. Chairs scruffed across the hardwood floor, china and crystal clinked to the kitchen, and televised football droned through the house, occasionally punctuated by lazy conversation and a few snores. Christi surreptitiously picked up the black hall phone.

"Kelly, can I come over?"

"Sure. Y'all finished eating?"

"Ate at one. Everybody's still here, but I don't care."

"What's wrong?" Kelly asked.

"I don't know. Maybe nothing. Maybe it's just me. I'll be there in fifteen minutes."

"Okay," Kelly agreed, and immediately went to get her bike out of the garage. She wiped the cobwebs off and dusted the seat with a handful of fallen oak leaves, then rode slowly up and down the driveway waiting for Christi. She tried to see how slowly she could go and still maintain her balance. It helped that the wide tires were nearly flat.

Christi had found her tires flat too, so she got her father to air them up, figuring the gas station would be closed.

"Thanks, Daddy. See you later."

"Now don't be out on the bike after dark."

"I know. We won't."

"Call if you're gonna spend the night there."

"Daddy, I always do."

"I know. It's just my job to remind you."

"Okay."

"How about taking the pump? You haven't ridden that bike in a while. There may be a leak."

"I can make it to Kelly's. She has a pump if I need it. Please stop worrying about me. I'm fifteen years old!"

Under his breath, Clem Boudreaux admitted, "That's why I'm worrying."

"Bye."

"Now don't forget to call."

"Okay. Bye."

"And, honey, be careful."

At the corner, Christi turned left away from the direction of the McCain's, taking a detour to be able to report on the whereabouts of Cameron Coulter if she could ascertain as much from riding past his house. Their porch light was on, the garage appeared to be locked, and the big Buick was gone.

Christi headed to Kelly's at full speed.

"What took you so long?"

"I had to put air in the tires."

"Me, too."

"And then I rode by Cam's to see if he was at home…"

"Oh, Christi, no! Tell me you didn't! On your bike? I could die!" Kelly moaned.

"What? I thought you'd be happy."

"Happy? Are you kidding? If he saw you ride by he'll know you were spying on him for me. Oh, no! And on your bicycle, like a little kid! Jesus, God, I could die!"

"Kelly! How could you talk like that? Taking the Lord's name in vain! What's getting into you? And what's so bad about being on a bicycle?"

"Little kids ride bikes. I could die! He'll think I'm a little kid and he'll never call me again! Oh, how could you?"

"Calm down. It wasn't you riding by, it was me, and I'm not a little kid."

"But he knows you're my best friend. It's all the same thing. He'll know you were spying for me."

"Kelly… "

"What?"

"He wasn't home."

"Oh, no! Where could he be?"

"It looked like everyone was gone."

"How could you tell?"

"Porch light on in broad daylight, garage locked, car gone, no sign of life."

"Oh, my God! No sign of life? Maybe they've all been killed and the murderer stole their car!"

Silence.

"Jesus, God! What do you think?"

Silence.

"Christi! Maybe we should go over there! What do you think?"

Christi looked at her friend for a full ten seconds and then said quite seriously, "I think you're crazy."

"But Cameron and his whole family could be dead!"

"Or, they could have driven down to Bogalusa to have Thanksgiving dinner with his grandparents."

Kelly sighed with relief. "I'll bet you're right. They probably drove down to Bogalusa to have Thanksgiving dinner with his grandparents. I'm so glad you thought of that."

"Know what else I think?"

"What?"

"I think you're crazy."

"Thanks a lot. What a nice thing to say."

"Just listen to yourself. Worrying about Cameron seeing me on a bicycle, worrying about Cameron never calling you again, worrying that Cameron's been murdered just because the family is gone for awhile — this is not your usual way of thinking."

"Maybe it is. Maybe I just don't tell you everything I'm thinking. Maybe I think about some really weird things you couldn't even imagine," Kelly retorted.

"Well, if you get any weirder than thinking Cameron's been murdered, don't bother to tell me about it or I'll be visiting you in your padded cell."

Kelly shoved off down the driveway into the street. Christi followed.

"Has he called you lately?" Christi asked sarcastically from twenty feet back.

"Not exactly."

"What does that mean?"

"Well, you always know every time I talk to him, and you know I'd have told you if he called again, so you're just asking to be mean. I talked to him last week at the Dairy Queen."

"I know. But that was accidental."

"That was Fate."

"Don't be dramatic."

"I'm not. It was Fate. Just like when we met."

"That wasn't Fate either. Cameron was on the golf course with his brother and you were on the golf course with me and Mandy. We all played golf a lot. How can you call that Fate?"

"It was Fate that he moved to Vicksburg."

"And I suppose it was Fate that caused you to be here in Vicksburg waiting for him? That Fate got your parents together so you could be born here in Vicksburg and be waiting for him?" Christi taunted.

"Why not? You're just jealous because I wanted to talk to Cameron instead of you at the Dairy Queen."

"Here you go, talking crazy again. Where did I put that straight jacket?"

"You just don't understand," Kelly complained as she picked up speed.

Christi kept pace. "I think I do. You met a guy three years ago, fell madly in love, but he only calls you once in a blue moon, and so your little brain flipped out. Simple."

"That's really mean," Kelly replied over her shoulder, still pedaling fast.

Christi's voice softened, "You've gotta face it, Kelly. He's just not interested."

They pedaled along in silence for a few minutes, in and out of the dappled shade on Cherry Street.

"Maybe he's shy."

Christi laughed. "Cameron Coulter, shy? Ha! Now I know you're crazy."

"I think he is. He's too shy to call. He's afraid I'm not interested in him, so he doesn't call unless he can come up with a good excuse. Why don't you give him a hint?"

"Sure, like, 'Cam, why don't you call Kelly more often? She'd love to talk to you, but she's too shy to let you know.'"

"Yeah, something like that."

"You're serious?"

"I'm serious."

"Well, okay, I'll do it."

"No, don't! I'd just die of embarrassment. If he's going to call, Fate will take care of it."

"Then, I'll go back to my original statement. I think you're crazy."

"Just wait. Just you wait, Miss Christina Boudreaux, until you feel like this about somebody and he doesn't call you for a long time. You'll think about him, and you'll talk about him, and you'll wait forever if you really care about him."

"No, I won't. I'll figure he isn't interested, and I'll go look for somebody else."

"You <u>think</u> you will. You just wait."

Chapter 6
Monday after Thanksgiving, 1962

Miss Fennstemmacher walked briskly into the noisy classroom, carrying desolation and silence in her satchel.

"Good morning, Class. I apologize for keeping you waiting," she glanced at her watch, "but I was detained in the principal's office. I'm sure that you industrious students made valuable use of the past five minutes in order to prepare for a little pop test this morning."

Gasps. Groans. Grumblings.

"I trust you all had a pleasant Thanksgiving holiday. Now let's stand for the Pledge of Allegiance. Whose turn is it to read our Scripture passage? Thank you, Lucinda."

"I pledge allegiance to the flag of the United States of America and to the republic for which it stands… "

Christi's mind wandered as the familiar words came out of her mouth of their own volition and fell to the linoleum floor. The room was too hot. She glanced over at Johnny Chambers. He was wearing his ninth-grade letterman's football jacket, heavy wool with leather trim. Beads of perspiration formed on his forehead and his upper lip, clinging to the light brown hairs he was hoping to shave soon.

Johnny was big for his age, and a good-looking boy, but that was the problem with him. He was immature, a boy, nothing at all like Grover Jones. Christi smiled, thinking that the new guy in the high school might be just what she wanted.

Back in September, Grover had caused quite a stir in the halls as the head football coach and three assistants had shown him around the school. Rumor had it that Grover was an eighteen-year-old-junior who was transferring in from the county just to play football for Vicksburg High. He was six-four and huge and really cute, in a rugged sort of way. As a sophomore, Christi hadn't managed to get introduced to him yet, but occasionally she would see him in the hall and she would give him "a look." She smiled again, in practice for the next time she might see him.

Johnny Chambers sensed someone's eyes fixed intently on him and he looked around, surprised to find that it was Christi

Boudreaux. She always acted so snobby to him. Maybe she saw him make those great tackles against Natchez last week. Something had happened. She was smiling. Staring right at him and smiling. He smiled back. She blinked and stopped smiling. Girls. Always coy. He resolved to talk to her between classes. This was the most encouragement Christi had ever given him and he wouldn't waste the opportunity to make a move.

"Before our little test this morning, we have one item of homeroom business. It's time to decorate the classroom doors for Christmas and as usual there will be prizes awarded for the best designs in two categories—religious and novelty theme. It is a matter of great personal concern to me that my homeroom should win one of these prizes this year. Your assignment this week from my homeroom, in addition to your regular English homework and the outline for your term paper, will be to submit a design for our homeroom door.

"You may sketch your idea on regular notebook paper. Do not worry about the quality of your artwork. I'm sure we have plenty of competent artists in here who will be able to bring the design to life. What I want to see is the idea. The religious category is self-explanatory. The novelty category should relate Christmas to the fact that this is an English classroom. You may submit a design in each category if you wish. In fact, you may submit as many ideas as you have. As I said, it is a matter of great personal concern to me that my homeroom should win a prize this year. If you fail to submit an idea, you will receive a zero in English this week.

"If you have any questions about this, please see me after class. Now take out a sheet of paper and put your name in the upper right hand corner with the date … "

What a witch, Christi thought to herself. *'Matter of great personal concern to me.' Who in the world cares? Miss Fennstemmacher cares, that's for sure.* Christi wondered why. *Could she be in trouble? She was 'detained in the principal's office' this morning. How could the door prize help? Funny. 'Door prize.' Play on words. Hmmm.*

Johnny Chambers made a point of walking next to Christi as they left the classroom. "Did you see the Natchez game?"

"Yeah."

"Did you see me make those tackles in the last quarter?"

"Yeah."

"What did you think?"

Christi looked around and saw at least half a dozen girls eyeing her enviously just because she was walking with Johnny Chambers. She did another quick appraisal of him. Definitely handsome, in a young sophomore sort of way. Nothing like Grover Jones, though. Johnny was only the star of the sophomore team. Kelly probably wouldn't be impressed.

Still, Johnny was considered a real catch by everybody else. She could do worse for the time being. After all, she was the only cute tenth-grade girl who didn't have some kind of boyfriend to talk about at slumber parties or at the Dairy Queen or Tolbert's Ice Cream Parlor.

"Well, what did you think?" he repeated.

"About what?"

"The tackles. My tackles in the last quarter."

Christi took another look and saw more eyes on her and Johnny.

"To tell you the truth, Johnny, I thought they were extremely aggressive and excellently executed."

She smiled. Everyone was watching.

"No kidding? You mean it?"

"Certainly. In fact, it occurs to me that you might be the best football player to come out of Warren County since Glynn Griffing."

"No kidding? You mean it?"

"Of course, I mean it. By the time you're a senior, every college in the conference will be after you. That is, if you keep on trying as hard as you did against Natchez."

"Aw, I can do better than that. I know I can."

"You can if you think you can, Johnny. I'll be watching."

"Would you like to eat lunch with me in the cafeteria today?"

"I thought you always sat at the jock table."

"I can sit wherever I want."

"Like a six-hundred pound gorilla."

"Huh?"

"You know. The old joke about 'where does a six-hundred pound gorilla sit?'... Anywhere it wants to.'"

"Oh, yeah," Johnny chuckled, "well, how about it?"

"Sure. I'll meet you in there. Better go to class. See you later."

"See y'at noon."

Christi ran into Kelly on the way to the cafeteria.

"I heard you're meeting Johnny Chambers for lunch."

"Where'd you hear that?"

"It doesn't matter, I heard it so many times. When did all this happen?"

"Nothing happened. We just talked after English, and we're going to eat lunch together. It's no big deal."

"Maybe not to you."

By Thursday afternoon, Christi was wearing Johnny's jacket ("only as a token of our friendship, Johnny, 'cause I don't want to go steady") and cheering him on at the "B-team" game. His coach wondered about the spectacular improvement in an already outstanding player. Too bad the season was over. Johnny Chambers almost single-handedly shut down the entire Greenville offense. The celebration at Tolbert's Ice Cream Parlor was loud, but ended quickly. It was a school night.

Christi got home after ten o'clock wearing the hero's jacket, and was finishing her homework when she remembered the 'door prize' contest. She hadn't thought of anything and now her brain was tired from unscrambling 'sentence fragments' and 'run-on sentences,' differentiating subordinate from independent clauses. Suddenly, she brightened. *Thank you, Jesus!* She found a piece of red construction paper, some old Christmas cards, scissors and glue.

* * *

"You may work quietly on your term papers while I look through these designs," Miss Fennstemmacher announced through lips more tightly checked than usual. "If you find it necessary to speak to your neighbor, please be considerate of those who are working independently."

Johnny immediately turned to Christi to hear more about her impressions of the game. She frowned and shook her head. Disappointed, he talked to a fellow jock. Christi opened Huckleberry Finn and pretended to read. She was watching Miss Fennstemmacher.

There were only three designs turned in on construction paper, one blue, one green and Christi's red one. These had been shuffled to the bottom of the stack, Christi's last. Slowly, Miss Fennstemmacher made her way through the pieces of notebook paper, frowning. She sorted the efforts into two stacks, one receiving frowns, the other getting frowns plus pursed lips and an occasional glare over her glasses at the artist who had failed so miserably.

As the original pile diminished into two smaller ones, the glares increased in frequency and duration. Miss Fennstemmacher's acorn eyes got smaller and darker. At last she came to Christi's. She picked it up in her left hand and held it at arm's length. She stared at it. Her tight mouth quivered slightly at the corners. Her nostrils flared almost imperceptibly.

The shoulders of her brown dress began to move in jerky rhythm with the air coming from her nostrils in short, audible puffs. Her bullfrog throat swelled up with each puff, the puffs coming louder and faster like a locomotive leaving the depot.

Finally, a squeak came with each bit of air and her lips separated. Christi noticed her teeth for the first time. Miss Fennstemmacher opened her mouth wide and leaned back in her chair. The squeaks became guttural bellows and her whole body moved with them. Miss Fennstemmacher was laughing. Ugly, old Miss Fennstemmacher was actually laughing.

* * *

At the Christmas open house, Principal Bullock himself guided the distinguished guest around the school, stopping at the end of the tour in front of Miss Fennstemmacher's door where Christi's winning design was displayed: a large Santa Claus and his mate sitting in front of a glowing hearth, around them a half-dozen baby Santa's, and above it all the greeting

'Merry Christmas from Mr. and Mrs. Santa Claus and all the Subordinate Clauses.'

"We're quite proud of your daughter, Justice Fennstemmacher. She has provided us with a very creative class project. She's a real inspiration as a teacher."

"I had hoped that she might become a lawyer," the justice replied quietly, glancing back and forth from the principal to the daughter who had never quite measured up to his expectations. "I always thought she was bright enough."

"No doubt. No doubt, Your Honor, but there are other considerations. An inspirational teacher can provide the turning point in a young person's life. A lawyer is seldom able to match that kind of accomplishment. It's fortunate that your daughter has chosen this profession and fortunate, indeed, for Vicksburg that she accepted a position here. We're mighty proud. Mighty proud."

Justice Fennstemmacher gazed at the ceiling and remembered old Mrs. Jensen, Lord rest her soul, who had taught his tenth-grade English class and encouraged him to participate in the debate club that she sponsored. Her influence had, indeed, started him on the long satisfying road to the Mississippi Supreme Court. He looked directly at his daughter for the first time in years, and jovially asked, "Is there an ice cream parlor around here, Alexandra, my dear? I believe this calls for a celebration."

* * *

Miss Fennstemmacher walked briskly into the noisy classroom. Smiling.

She sat down at her desk and looked at her thirty-two students. Smiling.

"Wonder what got into her," Johnny whispered across the aisle to Christi. "Get it? 'What got <u>into</u> her?'"

Christi gave him her drop-dead stare and pretended not to understand his vulgar implication. She thought about *the July 25th incident,* and pictured Johnny Chambers with Mrs. Jander.

"Good morning, class. As you well know, we won the prize for the best Christmas door in the novelty division, thanks to

Christi's idea and the artistic contributions of most of the class. I think we owe ourselves a round of applause." Smiling.

Enthusiastic applause.

"For our prize, in addition to the blue ribbon that you see hanging on the bulletin board this morning, Mr. Bullock will give our class a little party in the teachers' lounge when we come back from Christmas vacation." Smiling.

Whoops, hollers, and more applause.

"In addition, I am very pleased to report that your parents scored perfect attendance for our homeroom at the open house last night. As their reward, I am going to give you an additional week for the completion of your term paper, so that you might recover fully from your vacations before you have to begin the final draft. This should give you plenty of time to do the work yourselves without asking for parental assistance." Still smiling.

More applause, whoops and whistles.

"And because it is the last day before Christmas vacation and I am so genuinely pleased with this class, we will have our own little celebration today."

On cue, one of the cafeteria workers rolled in a cart with two large bundt cakes and three dozen cartons of milk.

"I baked two cinnamon swirl cakes last night so that we could have a party today instead of the 'pop test' that the more cynical of you might have anticipated." Smiling.

Whoops and hollers and whistles and applause, during which Johnny leaned over toward Christi and warned, "She probably put arsenic in them!" and Christi curtly replied, "Shut up! Can't you see she's trying to be nice?"

"Now, if you will all please stand for the Pledge of Allegiance…" Smiling.

That afternoon Christi tried to avoid Johnny by ducking into the girls' bathroom instead of going straight to her locker. *That guy is getting to be a regular pain in the something-or-other. He is so juvenile with his dumb jokes. This whole thing was a totally stupid idea. If I want Grover Jones, I should go after Grover Jones. There must be some way to get to know him. I should give Johnny his jacket back. I could do it right now. The jerk is probably still hanging around my locker, waiting.*

Kelly came running into the bathroom. "Thank God I found you! You'll never guess who's been standing out by the side door for the past five minutes!"

"Grover Jones?"

"Yes! The one and only Grover Jones!"

"Oh, my God! How do I look?"

"You look great, but that won't matter if he's already gone!"

"Do you think he's waiting to see me?" Christi asked breathlessly.

"Of course. Who else? I saw the way he looked at you in the hall last week. Johnny Chambers is going to wet his britches when he has to sit on the bench behind Grover Jones next year. Come on! Hurry!"

The girls ran frantically down the hall, past Christi's locker, turned the corner and dashed for the side exit, inadvertently picking up Johnny Chambers on the way.

"Christi! Where are you going in such a rush? Wait! Christi!" Johnny called, running behind them.

At the end of the long hallway, Christi and Kelly slammed into the push bar on the big door together. It swung wide into the vestibule and crashed into the wall. Then they casually opened the outer door, and stepped slowly and demurely into the December afternoon sunshine.

Bigger than life, Grover Jones was walking toward them. He smiled in recognition. Christi's heart stopped. She tried to say his name, but the sound wouldn't come. Suddenly his face turned to stone, and he walked brusquely past them into the building.

"Christi, why were you running away from me?" Johnny whined.

Christi whirled around to face him.

"Because you make me sick!"

"What? But you're wearing my jacket."

"Not anymore!"

Christi dropped her books on the pavement and tore off the jacket.

"There!" she flung it at him. "Take your damn jacket! I hope it keeps you warm!"

She pulled open the huge outer door, paused a moment in the vestibule, then ran to the girls' bathroom, choking back the tears until she was safely locked in the last stall.

Kelly bent down slowly to pick up Christi's books and everything that had spilled out of her purse. Johnny stood by helplessly, watching her gather the lipstick, pens, change, junk.

"Why do you suppose she did that, Kelly?"

"I don't know. Maybe she's playing hard-to-get."

"Yeah, maybe," Johnny shrugged his shoulders and put on his jacket. "Girls are funny that way."

Grover Jones had run blindly down the hall to the opposite exit. He wanted to cry, but decided on anger instead. *Typical dumb girl, walking around in some jock's jacket that doesn't fit, smiling, all full of herself with her stupid boyfriend tagging along behind. I could smash his skull!* Grover looked around for a victim.

What's wrong with me? Am I crazy? I saw this girl a week ago and haven't had a three-minute conversation with her yet, so I want to smash some guy's skull because she's wearing his jacket. I should never have come here. I should have stayed out in the county with the rest of the hicks where I belong. I could never have a girl like Christi Boudreaux.

My daddy's right. I'll never amount to anything. No, I'll never amount to anything. I never should have come to Vicksburg. These coaches are just filling my head with crazy, uppity notions. Feelings he couldn't define welled up in him and he wanted to be sick.

* * *

"Christi? Christi, are you in there?"

"Yeah," came a weak voice from the last cubicle.

"I've got your books and your purse."

"Thanks."

Kelly went to the sink, ran water on a paper towel, folded it and held it under the door.

"Here's a wet paper towel," she offered.

"Thanks," Christi replied feebly, reaching for it.

Kelly heard the commode flush. She waited and waited.

"Are you going to come out?"

"Unless I can figure some way to flush myself down the sewer."

"Aw, Christi, come on. It's not that bad, is it?"

"Yes."

"Listen. I'm really sorry."

"You didn't do anything."

"Do you want to talk about it?"

"No."

"Okay," Kelly replied, with compassion in her voice.

"Okay," echoed Christi's voice behind the closed door. "It's just that I'll never get a chance to see Grover and talk to him and find out who he is and let him find out who I am and if we might like each other and I don't understand why I feel like this about him when the honest truth is that I haven't even had a three-minute conversation with him, but it seems like I've known him forever, yet I don't know what he's thinking of or if he likes me at all, but when he looks at me I could just die-and-go-to-heaven and something tells me that he feels the same way, but how will I ever know? I mean, why would he smile like that, you did see him smile, didn't you?, and then just walk past me without stopping to talk or even say hello?"

"Maybe it was because Johnny was there," Kelly suggested.

"Don't be ridiculous! I wasn't paying any attention to Johnny. I didn't even realize he was there until he started whining about my running away, and that was after Grover went inside."

"Well, you were wearing Johnny's jacket."

"Kelly! He wouldn't have even noticed that, he walked by so fast. Besides, I don't care anything about that dumb old jacket."

"Grover couldn't know that."

"Sure he could."

"How?"

"He could ask me."

"Okay, here we go into the Twilight Zone. Christi, come out of there and listen to me."

Christi slid the latch over and the door creaked open.

"Look at yourself in the mirror."

"I don't need to look!"

"I said 'Look!'"

Christi's blood-shot eyes gazed back at her.

"Now, you can either go around looking like that and making yourself miserable or you can put all this Grover Jones nonsense in perspective. You're a pretty girl when your face isn't all twisted up from crying. Let him see how pretty and nice and smart you are when you can, but don't go crazy trying to make it happen. Why don't you just relax and let our friend Fate take care of this?"

"You know I don't believe in Fate!" Christi whimpered, sounding as if she would start crying all over again.

Kelly shook her head, and patted Christi on the cheek. "Who else but Fate would have started a silly thing like this?"

* * *

Indefinable nightmares tormented the young minds and, restless in the morning, their fated souls instinctively sought solace in nature. Alone, Christi Boudreaux and Grover Jones walked their individual aimless paths to the ridge above the Mississippi, sometimes less than a block apart, blinded by the heavy December fog that obliterated the landscape.

Dense gray-brown mountains of clouds rushed into each other, then backed away slowly in apology, only to meld again like herds of amorphous elephants, drunk on loco weed, confused, twisting, turning in slow motion, sinking and rising with the fog that separated them from the roily renegade river. The sun appeared only occasionally, as a full moon will sometimes trespass feebly into the late morning, a timid child in the corner waiting futilely to be noticed.

PART III

THE CLASS OF '64

Chapter 7
October 7, 1963

Grover Jones found his precious Christi talking with Kelly McCain and senior class president Cameron Coulter on the Confederate Street side of the school. His heart skipped a beat as he noticed a tall, red-headed stranger with them. *The guy better not be making a move on Christi.* Grover approached the group in a rush.

"Christi, I've been waiting at your locker."

"Sorry, Grover. We got to talking."

"That's all right. Hey, did you see that Corvette parked in front of my truck?"

"Yeah. That's what we were talking about. It belongs to Larry Llewellyn here. Larry, this is my boyfriend Grover Jones."

Grover felt relieved to be called "boyfriend" by Christi. It was still hard for him to believe his good fortune. *It looks like Cameron Coulter might be in for some trouble, though. The red-head guy with the fancy car seems to be totally smitten with Kelly, and she's being a little too flirtatious. Probably doing it to make Cameron jealous. Not a good idea.*

"Related to the George Llewellyn who just bought out all the Dalton Department Stores in Mississippi?" Grover asked.

"Guilty," Larry confessed. "That's my dad. Anyway, I'm pleased to meet you, Grover," the newcomer said sincerely. Looking up at Grover's wide face, Larry asked, "Am I correct in assuming you're the largest high school football player in Mississippi?"

"Biggest white one," Grover shrugged. "Don't know about the niggers."

"Grover made All-State as a junior," Christi beamed. "He actually lives out in the county and is supposed to go to Jett, but he's such a great player, we got him to come to town."

"You play ball, Larry?" Grover asked.

"I did in New Orleans, at a small prep school. I'd be afraid to try it in Mississippi, though. You all take your football too seriously for me."

"It can get you off the farm, Larry. That's serious," Grover confessed. "Yep. That is serious."

"Hmmm," Larry acknowledged with a nod. "Well, I'd better get moving. I need to get a locker assignment before class. It was nice to meet all of you. I'll see you after school, Kelly."

The newest Vicksburg High School senior walked quickly through the double doors, followed more slowly by Grover and Christi. They left Cameron Coulter standing on the sidewalk, staring wordlessly at Kelly McCain.

"Christi, you ought to tell Kelly not to keep trying to make Cameron jealous," Grover suggested quietly. He glanced back over his shoulder as if he could still see the pair on the sidewalk. "It's not going to help the situation any," he added wisely.

Christi shrugged and shook her head. "Have you ever tried to tell Kelly anything?"

* * *

Grover Jones watched from a second floor window of the high school as the sleek, black Corvette eased into the parking space in front of his forty-nine Chevy pick-up. He was surprised to see Cameron Coulter get out of the passenger side, laughing and talking with the new red-head kid. Grover was not the only student to notice and to conclude that the transferee with the fancy car must be all right since he was a friend of Cameron.

Grover grinned and stepped aside to his easel when a kid yelled, "Hey, Big Guy! Move over! You're blocking the light!" At nearly six-feet-six, two hundred seventy-five pounds, Grover did block a lot of light, but he never intentionally threw his weight around, except on the football field. He nodded at the runt who hadn't even said 'please.'

Lunch period was not quite over and Grover already had his materials assembled for class. The fifty minutes in art seemed to go by so fast that he would arrive early, even though it cut into his time with Christi. His dark heavy brows knitted together above cow-brown eyes as his huge hands sorted the tiny brushes. Then his wide face relaxed into a gentle smile as he looked at the promising beginnings of a still life on the easel. If it turned out as well as his art teacher predicted, he would give it to Christi for Christmas, matted and framed if he could come up with the money. Even her parents might like it.

Clem and Helêne Boudreaux had not been enthusiastic about Christi's choice of boyfriends, and Grover didn't feel welcome at their house. After having dinner there twice, Grover had told Christi not to push it anymore. He wouldn't come in the house after that, but would always call to be sure Christi was ready to go, so that his visits with her father at the front door never lasted more than a minute.

Then on the third Saturday in September, two weeks ago, when he went to pick her up, thinking she was ready, he stood on the front porch waiting through four rings of the door chimes. His big heart was pounding with worry that Christi's father had decided she couldn't date him anymore. Mentally, he prepared for a verbal confrontation with Clem Boudreaux, but Christi herself opened the door, wearing a filmy yellow silk gown.

"Christi!" Grover had gasped. "You shouldn't go to the door in something like that! Where are your folks?" Grover's eyes darted everywhere but at Christi.

"They're in Jackson for a Chamber of Commerce dinner. With speeches!" Christi laughed as she took Grover's damp hands and led him into the house. "Til midnight!"

"Oh, God!"

"Don't you remember what day this is?"

"Well, sure. Nine months from the day we officially met. I even brought you a present."

Grover took the small box from his pocket and handed it to Christi. He lowered his eyes.

"It's not much, but I thought they might be pretty on you."

Christi opened the package and found two matching mother-of-pearl barrettes.

"Oh, Grover! They're lovely!"

"Do you really like them? Tell me the truth."

"Don't be silly! They're beautiful! I love them!" Christi swept part of her long dark hair up on one side and clasped it with a barrette. As she reached up to the other side, her arm brushed across her breast and a dark nipple stood erect against the pale yellow silk.

"There," she said, the barrettes in place, "how do you like them?"

"The bar-rettes? Or the bar-reasts?"

Christi giggled and crossed her arms over her chest.

"The barrettes," she teased. "I believe we discussed the breasts previously."

"The barrettes really do look pretty in your hair, Christi. Go look in the mirror."

"I have a big mirror in my room. Come on upstairs with me."

"Do you think we should?"

"Look in my mirror? Sure. No one's here and I have an anniversary gift for you."

"Where is it?"

"Come on upstairs. I'll show you."

Christi took his hand and led him up the spiral staircase and across the landing to her large, exquisitely decorated bedroom. Late afternoon sun filtering through white lace curtains cast a golden glow on her wallpaper's yellow roses. White lace and yellow roses were everywhere — at the windows, on the bed, at the dressing table.

"This is a beautiful room, Christi," Grover whispered. "Prettier than I ever dreamed."

"I'm glad you like it. Now stand here at the mirror with me and look at my new barrettes. Aren't they lovely?"

Grover stood beside Christi in front of the mirror and laughed, "When we live together, Christi, we'll have to hang the mirrors higher. My head's cut off!"

"I guess we'd better get wider ones too. No, on second thought, I might look better with half my rear cut off."

"I love your little rear! Don't change it a bit." He grabbed her ample bottom and turned her toward him. "Don't ever change anything!"

"Thank you for the barrettes. And for always making me feel so special."

"You are special, Christi. Everybody knows that. I'm just lucky you want to be with me."

"Well, then, we're both lucky. Now, give me a kiss and you'll get your present."

Grover lifted her off the floor as they kissed, then set her down gently.

"I can't take too much more of that without getting carried away. Better get the present now."

Christi twirled around lightly, the gown billowing in a yellow cloud around her.

"I'm it! Your present! If you still want me."

"You? Here? Now?"

"Why not? Remember, last week it almost happened in the truck. Wouldn't it be better here?" Christi walked over to the bed and pulled back the yellow, lace-trimmed coverlet. She twirled again and smiled at Grover, "Now? In a place we will always remember?"

Grover stared at the yellow roses forming on the easel, and remembered. He knew he would always remember.

Chapter 8
October 22, 1963

Hurricane Nora came to life as a small tropical depression sometime after dawn on Tuesday, the twenty-second of October. One of many storms that season to be spawned near the Tropic of Cancer, Nora was first charted at approximately twenty-four degrees north latitude, ninety degrees west longitude, halfway between Key West and the thinly-populated northern coast of Mexico, over three hundred miles due south of New Orleans.

For twenty-four hours, she churned an erratic path through the Gulf, picking up speed and velocity as she struggled to focus on a victim coast. Inhabitants of all the port cities from Ft. Myers, Florida, to Corpus Christi, Texas, went about their business as usual, paying casual attention to the United States Weather Service reports that were being broadcast with the hourly news.

On Wednesday, as Nora headed northerly at about twenty miles an hour, a heady mix of excitement and apprehension quickened the pace of the typically languorous coastal population. Housewives from New Orleans to Biloxi to Panama City added bottled water and extra batteries to their grocery lists, while their husbands made sure they had enough wide masking tape to cover their storefront windows and enough gas in the cars for an emergency evacuation.

At the Grand Cayman Yacht Club, the bartender plotted Nora's course with toothpicks stuck through his new gulf chart into the pockmarked corkboard wall. This method of tracking hurricanes and diverting them from his home island had worked for twenty-two years and Stringer wasn't about to change his ritual now.

"One more?" he asked the tall, weathered American who was pondering Stringer's wooden line advancing upon the southern United States.

"No, thanks, Stringer. Better get going."

"Pulling out, are you?"

"Not yet. Waiting to see what Miss Nora will do," he replied, putting an American ten-dollar bill down on the bar.

"I don't have to be in New Orleans until the first. Plenty of time to move after landfall."

"Right you are, Cap'n. Plenty of time."

Stringer nodded, picked up the money, and wiped the spotless bar with a clean cloth.

"I hear you got a new owner," the bartender added, as an apparent afterthought.

Rundy Pryor stopped and turned back to Stringer.

"New owner?"

"Yeh," Stringer replied absently, wiping the bar again.

"Where'd you hear that?"

"Around."

"Thanks," the captain acknowledged, putting an American hundred-dollar bill on the bar. "Maybe you'll hear something more by tomorrow."

"Maybe," Stringer winked. "Walls talk around here," he grinned, jerking his head toward the chart.

Pryor put on his sunglasses and pulled down the brim of his cap, shielding his light blue eyes from the late morning glare off aquamarine seas as he strolled to the end of Pier Three where *La Muestra* lay waiting.

The impressive, steel-hulled Chris Craft, the flagship of an anonymous fleet, had been in his sole care since Arnie had bought and registered her in the Caymans only two years ago, right after the hurricane season of nineteen-sixty-one.

Occasionally her owner had been aboard or had made her available to some of his clients, but usually Pryor was alone at sea with only his illicit cargo and a girl he might pick up along the way — preferably a black-skinned Bahamian or a nubile Jamaican — grateful to be freed from her island prison.

The captain's pace quickened as he remembered the young beauty who would be lazing in the master stateroom's wall-to-wall bed. He had met her in Cartagena last week on his usual Colombian layover. She had said her name was Tawanya, that she was a nineteen-year-old American model, and that her boyfriend had put her off his sailboat at Aruba after a fight.

The girl's story was plausible enough, which made the captain less likely to believe it. But what did it matter? She was probably at least fifteen, if not twenty-five, and she knew her way around a boat. He could almost imagine keeping this one. Arnie would never have to know.

But now Arnie might not be the owner. Pryor frowned and wondered what kind of trouble had precipitated the change, but in his fifty-one years, he had learned to take what comes and not ask too many questions. For his part, he had always done a good job, skimmed off a lot less than most men in his position would have done, and had been very discreet. None of the girls he had traveled with along the way were ever seen with him in port.

Pryor's eyes caressed the large yet sleek white ship as he automatically checked the blue water line running her length. *At least the homebound stash is lighter than all those damn guns going south, but no matter. The storm will have passed.*

He padded silently across the teak deck, dropping his cap and glasses on the pilot's seat as he went below, the sound of his movements muffled by the generator's quiet hum. The deep blues and greens of the salon and galley soothed his eyes as he fixed himself a gin and tonic.

A shadow emerged from the stateroom door.

"Rundy?"

Tawanya stood framed in the doorway, tall, supple, her hair, eyes and skin all the same shade of warm, soft, milk chocolate. She was wearing nothing but the white coral necklace he had left out on the dressing table. He smiled at her. She parted her lips to let her tongue trace their contour.

Pryor finished his drink and put the glass on the counter. This girl could arouse him with a look. There was something different about her. Maybe he would keep her awhile. He reached down and touched the front of his white cotton ducks. Tawanya placed her soft hand over his.

"Let me," she whispered, pressing with one hand as her gentle fingers found the drawstring. "You're a magnificent man, Rundy Pryor," she caressed with her eyes and fingers, moistening her lips as she slowly knelt before him.

He stood transfixed, lost in the rhythm of her movements, more soothing at first than the gentle rocking of a sailboat at anchor, then undulating as a great yacht crests the swells in a heavy sea, finally as powerful and insistent as the pounding of the ocean's surf against a rocky cliff, until at last he exploded, and the sea was calm once more.

Spent and limp, Pryor leaned back against the counter and stared at the white coral necklace.

* * *

In New Orleans, a seventeen-year-old mulatto boy slipped the *Charleston Lady's* bowline off its deck cleat and dropped to the dock below. The big Pacemaker glided from its mooring laterally, its twin screws counter-rotating to move the yacht crab-style away from the pilings before reversing to ease out into the marina.

Picky, picky, picky, Jody French thought, as the *Lady's* owner himself guided her toward the harbor and finally upriver. The Crescent City Yachting Club and Marina would be almost empty by Wednesday afternoon, most of its members opting to move their expensive boats farther inland under the threat of Hurricane Nora.

Jody's eyes followed the progress of the beautiful white Pacemaker until it disappeared around the bend, leaving barely a trace of wake in the turgid brown water. Then he looked around for something else to do. It was frustrating to the young mulatto that he always wanted more work, but no one would trust him with anything important.

The sky darkened and Jody's heart beat faster. *If the hurricane hits full force, I'll be a hero,* he thought to himself, trying to imagine what he might do. He caught a Styrofoam cup that was being kicked along by the wind and dropped it into the trash barrel beside the diesel pump as a dark blue sedan drove into the guest parking area. Jody trotted over to open the driver's door.

"Thanks, Boy," the man said flatly.

"May I help you? My name's Jody."

"Okay, who's in charge here?"

"Mr. Watson, sir, but he's ferrying a boat upriver right now. Is there something I can do?"

"Maybe you can. I'm thinking about moving my big fishing boat up here from Destin, Florida. Just wondering about security around your marina."

"This one's as secure as any in N'Orleans. We lock those gates at night and only members have a key."

"How about getting in by water?"

"Can't lock up the whole harbor, sir. That's the only way to get in at night. By boat. 'Course, we have a night watchman too. He'd hear a boat coming in."

"Well, good."

"What d'ya fish, sir?"

"Huh?"

"What d'ya fish?"

"What do you mean?"

"What kind of fish are you after? Marlin? Tuna?"

"Yeah. Tuna."

Jody decided to ask a stupid question to see if he could figure out what this guy was trying to do.

"Would you be wanting an open slip, sir, or a covered one, or a private boathouse?"

"Oh, a regular slip would be fine. One like that'd be nice," the older man said, pointing to the pier of low, covered slips where a few day cruisers bobbed. "Well, thanks, Boy, you've been very helpful. Tell Mr. Watson I may be back later because of you."

"Yes, sir. Thank you, sir. And may I tell him your name?"

"Burns. Bill Burns."

The wind picked up as he slammed the car door.

Jody watched Mr. "Bill Burns" drive away and then mused aloud. "'My big fishing boat,' the guy brags. In a day-cruiser berth?" He shook his head. *"Fishing for tuna without a tower? Does he think I'm an idiot?"* Jody chuckled to himself, wondering what the real story was, knowing that if he kept his eyes open, he would probably figure it out, eventually.

* * *

Hope I'm not making a big mistake here, Alexandra Fennstemmacher thought as she watched the ancient Chevy pick-up truck back into her driveway to within a few feet of the old quarters' front door. The huge boy she had met just yesterday got out from behind the wheel. Young Cameron Coulter stepped from the other side. In a few minutes they had unloaded a double-bed frame, mattress and box springs, a small dresser, a rickety desk and chair, and a dozen odd liquor boxes of stuff.

Better not be alcohol in there, she stiffened at the thought, peering harder at her overgrown new tenant, who supposedly would pay for his "keep" by doing odd jobs around the place and tending to some long-neglected maintenance. In all her years of teaching, not a single coach had ever even dared ask her to mark up a grade for one of the dumb jocks. Now, here, she had one, a big one at that, needing a roof over his head. Miss Fennstemmacher was still surprised she had agreed to the arrangement for one Grover Jones. *That Cameron Coulter is a persuasive young man.*

The old spinster sniffed the air through the musty screen and frowned. *Here it is Thursday already. Wish that hurricane would get on with it. Unstable air isn't good for anybody.* She closed the window with a thwack.

* * *

At Tolbert's Ice Cream Parlor, Kelly McCain fretted about the weather over her sundae. She had never been on a yacht before, and Larry Llewellyn's invitation to fly to New Orleans with his family and cruise up the Mississippi to Vicksburg on their new boat was almost more than she could stand. At first, Kelly was amazed that her mother agreed to let her go, since she had only been out with the tall, red-headed Larry a couple of times. She suspected that her mother was reacting more to the Llewellyn family money than to Larry himself. Kelly decided not to think about that. If nothing else, she could have a good time with Larry, and maybe even make Cameron jealous at the same time.

"But Larry, what if the weather's too bad and your boat doesn't get to New Orleans by the first?"

"You worry too much, Kelly. The boat's especially fast, and there's plenty of time left. I didn't realize you were looking forward to the trip that much."

Kelly glanced down at her ice cream. She realized she wasn't being very coy about this trip. She didn't want Larry to get the wrong impression.

"I guess I'm much more concerned about the Homecoming Queen election that day. I want to be here to vote for Christi," Kelly said.

"We'll be here for that," Larry assured her. "Now, finish up your sundae and let's get going. I promised Grover that we'd stop by to help him get settled. It's certainly nice of old Miss Fennstemmacher to let him move into her quarters."

"Wait till you see the place before you decide how nice she is. The house is a mansion, but run-down. You wouldn't put your dog in the quarters."

"Still, it's a place to live, so he doesn't have to drive that dilapidated truck so far every day. I think it's nice of her."

"Fine," Kelly agreed flatly, "but it's probably the only nice thing the witch ever did."

* * *

Hurricane Nora, at her best, spiraled winds of a hundred-eighty miles per hour around her calm eye, with torrential rains extending hundreds of miles beyond. Moving sporadically through the Gulf for three days, she efficiently completed her job of drawing excess heat from the water into the cool upper atmosphere, venting her fury without a direct assault on the coastal cities.

Nora sent her heavy, moisture-laden clouds up the Mississippi River valley past Memphis, drenching Vicksburg with a furious Friday-afternoon thunderstorm that continued through the night, turning the football field into a muddy battleground, wrenching the last leaves from red-oak trees and plastering them together in sodden puddles upon the gummy black soil, quenching the Indian Summer's thirst and more as the storm faded into a gray drizzle that spread across the South and lasted the dismal weekend, while four-day-old

Nora herself was spinning harmlessly toward an uncharted ocean grave.

* * *

Rundy Pryor was Stringer's only customer at ten-thirty on Sunday morning.

"You know we don't open till eleven, Cap'n."

"Then this'll have to be on the house. Gin and tonic."

"Bad night, Cap'n?"

"A good night. Bad morning."

"Pulling out today?"

"No rush. I'll be right here until sometime tomorrow."

"Storm's no problem now," Stringer volunteered, inclining his head toward the toothpick spiral that was Nora's path.

"We all hear the same weather reports."

Stringer shrugged his shoulders and continued polishing wine glasses, sliding them into the overhead wooden rack.

Pryor stared out the window at *La Muestra*. When he set his empty glass on the polished mahogany bar, Stringer replaced it with a fresh one.

"No more after this," Pryor mumbled, putting a ten on the bar. Stringer shrugged again and began filling the nut dishes.

"Hear anything new?"

Stringer nodded.

"Well?"

"You're in trouble, Cap'n, if you show up in New Orleans with a mulatto girl you picked up in Columbia."

Pryor stood and reached into his front pocket. He pulled out an American hundred-dollar bill and put it on the ten.

"Thanks," he nodded, turning to leave.

"Cap'n?"

"Yeah, Stringer?"

"Real trouble."

The rugged seaman looked straight through the bartender, fishing another hundred-dollar bill from the same pocket and putting it on the bar.

"Don't mention it, Stringer. And, don't worry about it," Pryor scoffed as he made his way to the door.

"Me? I don't worry 'bout nothin,' Cap'n Pryor," Stringer shrugged, popping a salted peanut into his mouth. "No, sir. I don't worry 'bout nothin.'"

Business at the Grand Cayman Yacht Club picked up by eleven-thirty and it was almost one o'clock before Stringer noticed that *La Muestra* had slipped quietly from her berth, headed for the open sea.

Chapter 9
October 29, 1963

George Llewellyn bore no resemblance to his son at the moment. Both of the Llewellyn men typically appeared relaxed and quietly in control, their brown eyes never giving a hint of emotion. This afternoon, the man known as "PapaLew" to family, friends, and foes, was clearly furious. He clenched his teeth, took shallow breaths, and clutched the telephone mouthpiece closer to his pale lips. Beads of perspiration glistened on his balding head. His slight frame hunched forward, as if he were ready to pounce on his prey.

"God damn it! I know she got on in Columbia! I want to know where she is now! Exactly where she is! Don't give me that patronizing 'now-now-PapaLew' shit! I'm sick to death of your fucking excuses! This won't happen again, you sonofabitch! God damn it, this won't happen again!"

* * *

"Why don't you take the afternoon off, Jody? Looks like we'll be busy this weekend when the boats start coming back in, so take a break now."

"Thanks, Mr. Watson, but I'm okay. Maybe I could help ferry some this afternoon."

"I said, beat it, Jody. Go take in a movie. Come back in the morning."

"But tomorrow's Wednesday, my regular day off."

"Then I'll see you Thursday," he added absently, glancing at the wall clock above the water cooler. "Get moving."

The brown-skinned teen-ager picked up his duffel bag of extra clothes and headed for his bike. He was a quarter mile from the yacht club when he remembered the tennis shoes he had left drying on the workshop radiator. Making a U-turn, he sped back toward the marina, gliding through its gates unnoticed, leaning his bike against the chain link fence while he ran in to get his only other pair of decent shoes.

A dark blue sedan drove into the guest parking area and Jody noticed that Mr. Watson waved the curious visitor — the purported "Bill Burns" — around to the space beside his own car on the far side of the clubhouse. Jody frowned and took a closer look before moving his bike. No one saw him leave that second time.

* * *

"You're the best, Tawanya. I don't know what it is about you, but you're the best."

The young girl lounging on a towel across the bow cushions stretched and rolled luxuriously onto her back, exposing the front of her rich full body to the afternoon sunlight. She smiled and her teeth glistened like the white coral necklace she wore.

"No. You're the best, Rundy Pryor," she purred. "This has been the best two weeks of my life."

"Hasn't been two weeks yet."

"What day is this?"

"Tuesday, on this side of the globe. Come here. You're too far away from me."

* * *

"God damn it! Get someone to chart a ship's course from the Caymans to N'Orleans. Send a plane out over the Gulf on that heading. Get a reading on that fucking boat! Call the Senator. Send a Coast Guard cutter to board her."

PapaLew wiped the perspiration from his brow as he listened intently.

"Fuck! I don't give a rat's ass if she's loaded!"

He sighed heavily into the phone.

"God damn it! That much? Shit! You've goddamn tied my fucking hands!"

With his left hand, PapaLew rubbed his eyes as he went on quietly, "All right, all right then, forget the plane. Fuck the Senator. Fuck the Coast Guard. But if anything happens to that girl,..."

* * *

Christi sat on Kelly's bed, watching her pull clothes from her closet.

"Maybe you're right," Kelly nodded. "I'm probably making this whole thing into too big a deal. It's just that I've never been on a yacht before. I don't want to look stupid."

"You could never look stupid, Kelly, but wear the navy blue pants suit," Christi insisted. "Navy blue is nautical and it won't show dirt."

"It's nice that you're always so sure about what to wear," Kelly sighed. "Thanks."

"Now you promise you're going to be there to vote for me in the run-off, right?"

"Of course. Don't you think I'd do just about anything to keep Carol Jean Tolbert from being Homecoming Queen? She's always trying to get her claws into Cameron. She makes me sick," Kelly spit out the words.

"I really want to win," Christi whispered. "Wouldn't it be perfect? Grover just got elected captain of the football team, so he'd be my escort even if we weren't going steady."

Hearing Christi recount the Homecoming protocol, Kelly realized with sudden clarity that the runner-up, the "loser," the Senior Maid, would have to be escorted by the Senior Class President. Cameron Coulter. She felt ill.

"You'll win, Christi," her young friend reassured her. "Now, relax. It will be all over by three o'clock on Friday. I only wish I could be there to hear the announcement."

Christi laughed, "Sure, you'd rather be at school than on a yacht. Don't start lying to me now!"

* * *

"Tawanya! Good, you're awake. Come watch the sunrise with me. It promises to be almost as lovely as you are.... Wait. Where's your coral necklace?... Sure, go get it, and take time to put on your robe....

"There now. That's much better. Come on up here with me.... Watch your step. Don't trip on the robe.... No, silly girl. Don't take it off. Wrap it around you. It's chilly up here.

The end of October, you know. You could catch your death...."

Tawanya shivered momentarily in the early morning sea breeze and leaned her back against the captain's chest for warmth. He encircled her from behind, his powerful arms pulling her body closer to him.

The yacht cruised effortlessly through the rolling swells as the couple swayed together gently on the bridge. They watched silently, mesmerized as the pinkness of a perfect dawn broke through the heavy cumulous clouds above the horizon, casting an iridescent glow on the ship's bow. Moments later, the quiet pearlized pink of the sky deepened to a more and more brilliant rose as the sun ascended above the clouds and recklessly flung its most brilliant color before them - an astonishing red that irradiated the dazzling sea with a billion sparkles of effervescent light.

"The promise of a new day," Tawanya whispered, letting her head fall back to rest on his shoulder.

Rundy Pryor felt himself becoming aroused. He let his hands drift down from Tawanya's stomach to the opening in her robe.

Now, touch me, he thought, and in that instant he realized that Tawanya's hand was already there. Her fingers explored him with curiosity and excitement, as if she had never felt a man before.

She seems so innocent, he frowned. *If I hadn't had her myself, I'd swear she was a virgin.*

As her other hand joined in the caress, it became stronger, more insistent. He thrust himself harder into her hands against the top of her buttocks and she responded with an equal force, pushing her shoulders back into his chest and arching her body upwards.

His left hand massaged her in rhythm with his own pleasure, and he let his right hand trace a moist path up her soft brown body, pressing and releasing, pressing and releasing, finally stopping only when he felt her flood with satisfaction. She sighed and rested her head easily against his shoulder while her hands behind her continued their insistent stroking of him.

"Bend over," he whispered, lifting the back of her robe.

Pryor entered her from behind, immediately came to a raging climax inside her, then jerked her upright and crushed her body back against him.

Encircling her so tightly with his left arm that she couldn't move, he reached over to the boat's console and grabbed his fish knife. With one, swift, practiced stroke, he sliced the girl's neck from left to right, severing artery and windpipe in a fraction of a second. There was no sound but a gush of air and a gurgle of blood as she slumped lifeless in front of him.

The terrycloth robe absorbed most of the mess. He bent down, unfastened the white coral necklace, and dropped it into last night's glass of gin to prevent the blood from drying on it. Then he tied the red-tinged robe tightly around Tawanya's limp body and picked her up. Being careful to support her bobbing head as he crossed the deck, Pryor dropped his ruined cargo off the stern.

The few splotches of blood on the deck wiped off easily with a damp cloth. Pryor straightened from his task and noticed the sunlight sparkling on the glass of gin and coral. He sighed, picked up the glass with the necklace in it, and carried it to the fantail. As the boat cruised indifferently on autopilot, Pryor stood staring at the rosy froth in its wake.

"It's a shame to treat you like all the rest of them, Tawanya," he said aloud, tossing the beautiful strand of white coral into her uncharted ocean grave.

"You really were the best."

Pryor descended through the salon to the galley sink and washed the smell of her juice from his left hand and the stain of her blood from his right. Then he poured himself a bowl of corn flakes and sat down to breakfast.

* * *

"God damn it! This is Thursday afternoon! It's been five fucking days!"

George Llewellyn took a breath and tried to calm down in response to the placating voice of his man in New Orleans, but there was no real point in trying to be civil. Instead, he tightened his grip on the telephone and continued his tirade.

"It better be in and she better be on it, or there'll be hell to pay.... No, leave it alone. I'll be down there myself tomorrow.... Damn right, I'll be there by noon.... No. We'll use Arnie's old captain for now. Let him run us up to Vicksburg - get to know him. I doubt if he's loyal to anyone but himself. You know the type.... No, God damn it! Stay away from there. The captain has orders to stay on the boat overnight and that'll have to be good enough. We don't want to draw any attention to it... "

* * *

"Afternoon, Cap'n! Welcome to N'Orleans!... Jody, catch that line! Give the Cap'n a hand there!... Good trip, Cap'n? Ole Nora gave us all a little extra work here, but no matter. Put the big ones upriver. Where'd you lay over?"

The weathered man glared at his interrogator from the fantail, then vaulted nimbly over the rail to the gas dock below.

"You sure are running your mouth a lot today, Watson. Something wrong, or did you just miss me?" the captain asked, without a hint of playfulness in his cool blue eyes.

"Just trying to make conversation, Rundy. Sorry," the fat man mumbled.

"Have your boy fuel her up and bring me some oil for that port engine."

"Jody, you heard the Cap'n. Fuel her up and check the port engine."

"I said 'bring me some oil!'" Pryor growled. "I didn't say check it. Nobody goes below, Watson. You got that? D'ya hear that, Boy? Nobody steps foot inside this boat."

"Yessir, Cap'n," Jody nodded, meeting the man's stare.

Watson jerked his head toward the office indicating the captain should follow him. When they were out of earshot of the mulatto boy, Watson turned to face Pryor and whispered, "Arnie lost the boat. You got a new owner."

"You're always boring me with old news, Watson. Tell me something I don't know."

"Arnie's plenty sore about it."

"Think I wouldn't know that?"

"Well, Arnie don't take shit like that sittin' down."

"Never has before."

"Damn it, Pryor, I'm trying to tell you something."

"So, tell me, Mouth, what's he gonna do about it?"

"Shit, Rundy, I don't know. Just cover your stern. These boys play for keeps."

"So do I, Watson. Don't lose any sleep over it."

"Say, that reminds me. Some guy called. Said he works for your new boss. He wants you to take the night off. Stay at the Royal Orleans on his tab. Sort of a 'welcome aboard,' he said."

"Hmmm ... "

"Yeah, the Governor's Suite is reserved in the name of Fred Perkins. Already paid. Got that? Fred Perkins."

Pryor glanced back at the boat.

"He doesn't want me to stay on board?"

"Call him yourself, if you don't believe me."

"I don't suppose he left a number?"

Watson laughed.

"Nope, but he did mention that your favorite kind of girl would be waiting in the suite."

"I like his style."

"Yeah. Sounds real classy. Anyway, you're not supposed to thank him or nothin' when he shows up in the morning because his wife will be along and she don't cotton to that kinda shenanigans."

"Why would he bring his wife down here?"

"You got me, Cap'n. Wait. Is that my phone ringing? Damn Gloria took off to the dentist. 'Scuse me a minute."

Watson huffed up to his small office and grabbed the telephone.

"Yacht club. Watson.... Damn it, Shimwell, are you crazy calling here?... It better be a pay phone. Why the hell aren't you at the store? You've just been on the job two months. Think, man, how it's gonna look. You're a fucking bean counter for the Llewellyn Department Stores. Those kinds of guys are always on the job.... No. Not here, you fool. You think I want 'em to blow up my place?... I told your girl it was all set for Friday at two-forty-five. Didn't you get the message?... Yeah, Llewellyn should be here by noon and he's always on time, but we added two hours in case of delay and then forty-five minutes for them to get outa here and upriver past the town.... It'll look like an engine caught fire and set off the explosions.... Nah. 'The Torch.' Same guy that did the warehouse. Always on time. Always does good work. Ex-military.... Can't. Shit, man, don't you think he'll check to see the stuff's there? It's his money that paid for it. We can't take it off without blowing the whole deal.... Heh, heh, yeah, that was funny, blowing the whole deal. So I'm a comedian. Now get your ass back to the store and stay there. We need to keep you inside. Don't call me back. I've got it handled.... Yeah, wife and kid too, but that's not our fault.... Hell, no! Everybody knows the rule. The captain goes down with the ship. I never did like the son of a bitch anyway. There's something weird about that guy.... Yeah, he'll be all right. Ole Arnie's tougher than they thought. He'll be keeping a low profile for a while, which is exactly what you better do. Now get back to the store...."

Watson hung up the phone and turned to the window. Jody was still pumping fuel into *La Muestra.* Apparently, the captain had gone below to check and oil the engines. Watson sighed and looked at his watch. Four-thirty. It would all be over at two-forty-five on Friday, less than twenty-four hours. He picked up the phone and called his night watchman.

"Schrader? Watson. Listen, I don't need you to come in tonight.... No. The wife and I had a little disagreement and I'll be sleeping on the couch in my office, so there's no use both of us being here. 'Course, I'm such a nice guy, I'll pay you for it anyway, but you keep this to yourself. I don't want my dirty laundry flapping in the breeze.... Heh, heh, you old reprobate. Go ahead. What you do on your night off is none of my business.... Now, why would I ever want to tell her anything? Your wife don't work here. You do.... Yeah, we guys got to stick together. These goddamn women are trying to run the world. Heh, heh...."

Watson's smile faded as he hung up the phone and looked down at the fuel dock. Damn nice boat. Damn nice.

Jody replaced the nozzle in the pump and looked up at the captain.

"Anything else, sir?"

"That'll do it, Boy."

Pryor turned the left ignition key, listened a moment, then turned the right. Twin spurts of water spewed across the river's surface, small jets forced into being by the boat's exhaust. Jody listened with admiration as the big Chris Craft settled into its deep muffled "bloo-bloo-bloo-bloo-bloo-bloo-bloo-bloo' and glided away from the gas dock to its reserved berth four slips down.

Fading afternoon sunlight glowed across the massive white stern with its arc of bold red lettering identifying *'La Muestra.'* Jody frowned. The "U" appeared to be a "Y." He squinted and read again from the increasing distance. *'La Myestra.'* He trotted down to her berth and waited to secure the lines. Then he stood still on the wooden walk, listening, while the captain went below to pack a bag and secure the boat for the night, finally locking the cabin door behind him and pushing the keys far down in his pocket.

"Anything else, sir?"

"That'll do it, Boy."

"Get in any fishing this trip, sir?"

"Too busy. Storm," Pryor added as he passed the young mulatto without a glance. He stopped halfway up the ramp and turned back.

"Boy."

"Yes, sir?"

Pryor reached into his pocket and pulled out a one-dollar bill as Jody approached.

"Here. Buy yourself some Halloween candy and a soda."

"Yes, sir. Thank you, sir."

Then the captain repeated his motion.

"Here. Buy some for your girlfriend, too."

"Yes, sir. Thank you, sir. Have a nice evening."

"Thanks, Boy. I plan on it."

Jody thrust his hands in his pockets and casually ambled off toward the supply shed, then cut back quickly to the main office when he saw the captain go inside. Out of sight under Watson's window, he could hear the two men talking.

"Go ahead and take my car. My night watchman just called in sick, so I'll be stuck here anyway."

"Okay. Where's the key?"

"Here. Now, remember, Royal Orleans' Governor's Suite, in the name of Fred Perkins."

"There you go boring me again, Watson. Ease up."

"Sorry."

"Just be sure no one gets near that boat, or it's your ass."

"Sure, sure, I understand."

"I hope you do."

"See you in the morning, Cap'n. Don't do anything I wouldn't do."

"Guys like you would do anything you could get away with, Watson. You're just too chicken-shit to try it."

The fat man laughed, then froze under the captain's stare.

"You don't need to call me chicken-shit, Rundy," Watson dared to mutter.

"You're right, Watson. I don't need to call you chicken-shit," the captain replied, tossing up the car keys and catching them in mid-air. "It's written all over your face."

As Pryor disappeared down the street in Mr. Watson's car, Jody gathered some cleaning supplies and headed back down to *La Muestra.* The agile boy climbed aboard without a sound and padded across the aft deck. He leaned over the rail to get a closer look at the lettering.

A thick red glob of something had hit the "U" and trickled down the stern several inches, changing the letter into a "Y." He stretched over to get a better look.

Blood. It could be blood. But the captain said he was too busy to fish. Hmmm.... Still, it looks like blood to me. Maybe even human blood.... Maybe I've been reading too many murder mysteries.

"Boy!"

Jody's heart skipped a beat.

"Yes, sir?" he straightened up with a jerk.

"What're you doin' on that boat, Boy?"

"Looks like a gull dropped a big purple one on the railing. It dripped down the stern. You know how the captain likes to keep her clean, sir."

"Yeah, but he don't want nobody on that boat, neither."

"So, I'll get down and let you scrape it off, if you'd rather."

The fat man heaved a sigh.

"Go ahead and get it yourself, since you're up there, but don't go bothering nothing else. Then you can take off early."

"Yes, sir. Thank you, sir."

Jody pulled a pack of chewing gum from his pocket, unwrapped one piece and folded it into his mouth. He held onto the foil wrapper very carefully as he reached down over the stern to scoop up the offending red globule.

Blood, Jody concluded, looking at the congealed residue on the gum wrapper. *Hmmm. Murder mysteries or not. This is definitely blood.*

Chapter 10
November 1, 1963
Morning

Christi smiled, walking down the hallway. Her blue, blue eyes sparkled up at Grover. He whispered something in her ear and she giggled. Grover turned toward his classroom alone, giving a wave to Kelly and Larry as they approached.

"I'm so glad y'all are here!" Christi stage-whispered.

"Why wouldn't we be?" Larry asked.

Flustered for a moment, Christi looked at Kelly and stammered, "Uh, because Kelly has a doctor's appointment in Jackson today. Don't you, Kelly?"

Christi was confused that Larry didn't seem to know the excuse. Surely he wasn't planning to leave school without a valid reason.

"Oh, sorry," Larry grinned. "I don't know what I was thinking. Of course, I knew she had a doctor's appointment in Jackson. By coincidence, I have one in N'Orleans. Dad and I are flying down. He's waiting for me, and chomping at the bit, I'm sure."

Carol Jean Tolbert passed by with a group of admirers.

"Good luck, Christi!"

"Same to you, Carol Jean!" Christi beamed.

"This is disgusting," Larry whispered to Christi with a grin. "You girls are so two-faced."

"The guys are just as two-faced," Christi laughed. "Wait until our class elections. The school population doubles."

"As far as I know, that's about par for all elections in Mississippi, and in Louisiana. Even dead people have the right to vote," Larry quipped.

"Dead white people, that is," Christi corrected him.

"Of course," Larry agreed. "Dead white people."

"Attention. Attention all students," the crackly voice of the vice-principal interrupted them. "The mimeograph machine should be fixed shortly and all the ballots should be ready in an hour or so. You will have until one o'clock to complete your voting in the Homecoming court run-off, so please be orderly. Thank you."

Christi's heart sank at the announcement. How could she ask Kelly and Larry to stay to vote for her?

"I'm staying," Kelly announced firmly, almost defiantly.

"That settles it," Larry nodded at Christi. "I'm staying."

Christi smiled in gratitude.

"I'll call my dad and tell him I'll be there as soon as I can. He'll just have to wait."

"Won't he be upset?" Kelly asked. "I thought that he was in a huge hurry to leave."

Larry shrugged, "It's no big deal. I'll go call him."

Larry left without another word, heading down the hall, leaving Kelly and Christi alone.

"He's awfully nice, Kelly. I really think you should take him more seriously."

"He's not Cameron. If you think he's so nice, you can have him, with my blessing."

"Now, Kelly, don't get testy. It's just that he's obviously crazy about you, and surely you realize by now that Cameron is only interested in Cameron."

"Shhh!" Kelly warned. "He's coming down the hall."

"Who?"

"Cameron."

"I don't see him."

"I don't either. I can just tell," Kelly whispered.

A moment later, Cameron rounded the corner.

"Good luck, Christi!" he smiled at her. Then he faced Kelly without a word.

Christi quickly excused herself to go to class.

"I hope you're all right," Cameron began.

"Why wouldn't I be?" Kelly asked.

"I heard you were going to the doctor in Jackson. Is it something serious?"

Kelly shook her head. "It's nothing. Really. Nothing."

Cameron nodded and tightened his jaw.

"Good. That's good. I..." he paused. "I..."

"What, Cameron? You what?"

"I hope you would tell me if you needed anything," he replied quietly.

"Of course," Kelly lied. "And you'd do the same?"

"Sure," he reciprocated her lie. "Sure, I would."

* * *

"God damn it, son! I told you we have to be there by noon! Fuck the run-off!"

"God damn it yourself, Dad! This is her best friend we're talking about. Aren't you the one always preaching about fucking loyalty to your friends? Kelly isn't just another piece of ass. I'm not even fucking her, for God's sake, but of course, I couldn't expect you to understand that. Shit, your brain's in the head of your dick."

"God damn it, boy, don't you talk to your father like that!"

"I'm fucking eighteen years old and I'll talk to you any goddamn way I want to. If you don't like it, you can get on the fucking plane and go without me. Kelly is one classy girl, and I'm going to treat her right. Maybe I'd be smart to keep her away from you and Mom anyway."

"God damn it! Don't remind me about your mother! I'm the one that'll have to tell her there's a fucking delay after I dragged her out of bed early. Shit, boy, you owe me for this!"

"Then you'll wait?"

"God damn right, I'll wait. She's probably worth it."

* * *

Christi and Grover were among the first to cast their ballots. Moments later, Carol Jean Tolbert was in the voting line with Larry Llewellyn right behind her. He had imagined for weeks that she wanted to "lose" the Homecoming Queen election so she would be "only" the Senior Maid, and thus would be escorted by the Senior Class President Cameron Coulter. Larry peeked over her shoulder and grinned at being right when he saw Carol Jean Tolbert boldly mark her vote for Christi Boudreaux. He would not have been so pleased to know that Kelly was about to cast her precious Homecoming Queen vote for the hated rival Carol Jean Tolbert.

* * *

"Would it be okay if I take off early today, Mr. Watson?" Jody French asked his boss. "I think it's going to be a quiet afternoon for a Friday."

Watson looked at his watch and at the clock on the wall before turning back to him. *Two-fifteen.* Watson frowned.

"You sick, Boy? You don't look so good. Got bags under your eyes. Been up all night?"

"Maybe I'm coming down with something," Jody lied, hoping his face wouldn't betray what he had seen and done the night before.

"You got everything done that needed doin'?"

"Yes, sir." *And more,* he thought, *not that you'd ever notice.*

The wall clock clicked another minute.

Two-sixteen, Watson noticed. *Twenty-nine minutes to go and the fucking Llewellyns haven't even called.*

"Is *La Muestra* out yet?" Watson asked casually, as if his eyes hadn't been back and forth from the entrance gate to the dock a thousand times in the last three hours. *Could PapaLew have heard something?*

"Hmmm? No, sir, I don't believe she is," Jody imitated his boss's nonchalant attitude.

"Well, maybe you oughta wait awhile. I don't know who all's coming and how much gear they might have. You better stay. Help them load up and shove off. They might be in a hurry," Watson advised.

Again, the old man looked at his watch, then at the wall clock. Click. *Two-seventeen.* The thin red second hand raced downward with the ominous sweep of a cockroach's feeler.

* * *

"Grover, no matter what happens today," Christi said seriously, "I want you to know how proud I am that you've been elected captain of the football team and that you want to be with me. I know that if it weren't for you, I wouldn't ever have a chance to be Homecoming Queen."

Grover gave her a squeeze right there in the hallway.

"Don't be silly, Christi. Everybody in Vicksburg loved you before they even heard about me. And they'll love you long after I'm gone."

"Where are you going?" she asked in a sudden panic.

"I'm not planning on going anywhere," Grover smiled. "It was just a figure of speech," he lied, worrying more than ever about the threat of the draft after graduation. If he couldn't get a scholarship to wreak havoc on a football field, he knew the Army would give him a scholarship to wreak havoc in Viet Nam. The thought depressed him, but he forced a grin for Christi. "I'm not going anywhere but to the Homecoming Game and the Homecoming Dance with my Homecoming Queen. Count on it!"

* * *

Rundy Pryor stared at his chronograph and felt a growing apprehension as the fractions of time rushed by. *Two-thirty-three-forty-seven.* Still no sign of his unknown passengers. He went below to down a quick gin and tonic.

Something could have gone wrong, he worried. *Maybe this is a set-up.*

He had re-checked the top layers of his cargo a dozen times. Everything seemed to be stowed as usual and nothing appeared to be missing, but maybe he should have looked deeper. He couldn't shake the feeling that someone had been on his boat.

Damn that Watson! He's got Arnie's old extra keys. The captain crossed the salon in three long strides and took the stairs in two more.

"G'd afternoon, Cap'n. Gonna jump ship?"

Pryor's eyes sought the voice on the ramp and found the young mulatto smiling up at him.

"Just going to pick up something from Watson before I go, Boy," he replied.

"Let me do it for you, sir. I sure enjoyed my candy last night. I hope you had a nice evening too. Now what can I get for you?"

"The keys. Watson has an extra set somewhere. I want them."

"Yes, sir. You just wait right there on the boat, sir, and I'll have them for you in a minute."

Jody immediately turned and started running up to the office. The captain checked his chronograph again.

Two-thirty-seven-twenty.

A yellow cab drove through the gates as Jody disappeared into the yacht club office. Pryor took a step forward, then decided to stay on board.

The captain watched a slim, balding man step from the cab's front passenger side and open the back door for an attractive fortyish woman with flaming red hair who greeted his gesture with a scowl.

A young man with a more subdued version of the same red hair opened the other back door and got out, followed by a tall, slim, blonde girl wearing navy blue slacks and a matching jacket. The cabby ran around to open the trunk and lift out the luggage.

As Jody emerged from the office, Watson huffed out to shake hands, and gesture toward *La Muestra*. The group looked over at the boat. Captain Rundy Pryor nodded a distant acknowledgment. Jody and the cabby picked up two bags each and trotted to the dock. The others moved more slowly, absorbing their surroundings. Watson walked a few paces ahead, leading them.

"Take those bags below and set them in the salon," Pryor ordered Jody and the cabby. "Did you get the extra set of keys, Boy?"

"Yes, sir," Jody smiled, setting down the bags, and fishing the keys from his pocket. "Here y'are," he grinned. He followed the cabby below, dropped the bags on the carpeted salon floor, and bounded back up the steps behind him.

"Here y'go, Boy," Pryor extended a dollar to Jody. "Thanks for picking up the keys."

"No problem," Jody answered politely. "If you need anything else, I'd better get it for you now. After all, I may not see you again."

"That's it," Pryor answered absently.

Jody grinned, and hopped off the boat behind the cabby.

Watson was ushering the group toward the ramp, gesturing widely with his arms and talking at a high pitch.

Wonder what he's so agitated about, Pryor frowned. *That fat man's gonna have a heart attack. Needs to learn to take it easy. Take your time.* He glanced at his chronograph. *Two-forty-one exactly.* He was anxious to get underway, but these unlikely people were taking their time about getting on board, gawking at the other boats like tourists.

Finally, the leader of the group looked at his watch.

"It's nearly two-forty-five," PapaLew announced. "I think we'd better get going."

Watson wiped his brow on his sleeve. "S'long, folks. Have a blast."

Though they were sixty feet away, Pryor could hear every word. At that last good-bye, he started the port engine, listened a moment, then turned the starboard ignition key. The engines settled into a comfortable idle at six hundred revolutions per minute, a deep rumbling bloo-bloo-bloo-bloo-bloo-bloo-bloo-bloo.

"Mr. Llewellyn?"

"Yes, Kelly, but please call me PapaLew. What is it?"

"Before we go, could I please run in the office real quickly and call the school to see if Christi won? Otherwise, I won't know until Sunday. I think I'd just die before then."

George Llewellyn's jaw tightened. *God damn it!* he wanted to shout, but his son's look stopped him cold.

"Sure, Kelly, go ahead," he smiled. "We'll wait right here outside the office. Charge it to the yacht club. Watson and I will settle up later."

Kelly ran inside.

Watson wiped his brow again and suggested, "Why don't y'all go get settled on the boat? I'll escort the young lady down in a minute when she's through with her call."

He looked at his watch. *Two-forty-three.*

Larry and his red-headed mother took a step toward the ramp, but George Llewellyn grabbed his son's arm. "Where are your manners, Son? We'll wait here, as we said."

Captain Rundy Pryor stood at the helm and reviewed the scene—the mulatto boy leaning against the storage shed, arms folded across his chest, expressionless; Watson, the frustrated shepherd, trying to get his flock to move; the red-headed boy and his parents, playing a three-way power struggle for all the world to see.

That's life, isn't it? Power struggles. Like Arnie and this new owner. Arnie's down now, but he'll come back. Suddenly, Pryor remembered Watson's words: *"Arnie don't take shit like that sittin' down.... Cover your stern.... These boys play for keeps."*

The apprehension he felt earlier returned. Someone had definitely been on board, though it didn't appear that the cargo had been disturbed.

"These boys play for keeps.... Arnie don't take shit like that sittin' down.... If you need anything else, I'd better get it for you now. After all, I may not see you again.... These boys play for keeps.... I may not see you again.... Cover your stern...."

Pryor blinked with comprehension, then fear. He vaulted down the stairs into the salon, cursing himself for not checking the engine room earlier. Rushing past the galley window, he saw the blonde girl come running out of the office, laughing, gesturing excitedly, hugging the red-headed boy. The mulatto pushed away from the wall and sauntered toward the group, while Watson stared at his watch, immobile. Involuntarily, Pryor looked at his own watch as he opened the engine room door. *Two forty-five.*

La Muestra's captain was blinded by a flash of light a millisecond before he heard and felt the full blast of the explosion that blew the port engine into a thousand steel missiles. In the next second, the starboard engine and fuel storage tanks blasted apart, hurtling steel and flaming raw fuel through gaping holes on both sides of the yacht. A third explosion in the forward cabin ripped open the bow, and destroyed all traces of the cargo that had been stashed there.

Fragments of wood and metal blew fifty feet in the air as the yacht tore apart from the inside.

On shore, the Llewellyn group ran for cover behind the office, then watched in awed silence as the remaining charred hull of *La Muestra* sank into the river amid burning patches of oil on the water's surface.

George Llewellyn responded instantly.

"Watson, give me the keys to your car. Pick it up later at the airport. We were never here. The boat is owned by a Cayman Island corporation. That's all you know. Got it?"

The fat man nodded and handed over the keys. George handed them to his son.

"Y'all get in the car," he directed quietly. Larry nodded.

PapaLew turned to the mulatto.

"Boy."

"Yes, sir?"

"We weren't here. Never here. You didn't see anybody here this afternoon," he whispered, folding a hundred-dollar bill into the brown hand. "You understand that, son?"

"Yes, sir."

"Good. Don't cross me. It isn't smart."

"Yes, sir. I believe that, sir."

* * *

"Kelly."

"Yes, sir?"

"I know we're all upset by what we just saw back there," George Llewellyn began in a soothing voice.

Kelly nodded and kept her eyes focused on the Mississippi River valley far below the King Air's window.

"But we're going to put that behind us now and forget about it," he suggested firmly.

"I don't understand what happened and why we left in such a hurry."

"It was obviously a terrible accident of some sort, but there are valid business reasons for me not to get involved in that. You're a smart girl. You understand, don't you?"

Kelly nodded a lie. "But what will we say to the people in Vicksburg when we get back early without the boat?"

"Nobody knows about the boat except your mother. You can tell her I didn't like the condition that boat was in and I'm going to get another one. I will, Kelly, and then we'll all take a nice trip on it. Trust me."

PapaLew was watching Kelly's face intently enough to notice the minute dilation and contraction of her pupils.

"Did you mention the boat to someone else?"

Kelly's chin quivered, but she looked straight at him.

"I did."

The same inscrutable poker face that had financed George Llewellyn's first years at Tulane and helped launch him in business continued to serve him well.

"Oh, that's all right, Kelly," he consoled her. "Don't you worry about it. Can you tell me whom you told?"

"Just my best friend, Christi Boudreaux."

PapaLew looked at his son with a question on his face.

"Clem's daughter?" he asked Larry. Larry nodded.

"Hmmm. Well, just tell her the same thing you tell your mother. I mean it, Kelly. It's important to my business that I not get involved in something like this. I'm counting on you to keep this our little secret."

She nodded and turned again to stare out the window.

The senior Llewellyn followed Kelly's gaze, peering down at the patchwork of farmlands and forests on either side of the river, their peaceful browns and greens unaffected by the turmoil all around the world. The tranquility below induced thoughts he would have sworn were lost to memory – images of faces, echoes of wisdom, lessons of a better life he had learned quietly on the family farm with his parents and grandparents - lessons well taught by their words and even more by their everyday example. For most of the flight, with unspeakable sadness, he questioned how and why he had left the best part of his heritage so irretrievably far behind.

Chapter 11
November 1, 1963
Early evening

"God damn it! You get hold of our man at the phone company. I want the long distance charges for all lines at the Crescent City Yachting Club and Marina for the month of October.... Yes, God damn it, and include today!... Tell him to be sure to get all lines. There may be one or two unlisted. Call me at home before midnight tonight.... I know it's Friday. God damn it! What do I pay you for? I want it tonight!..."

* * *

Helêne Lepeltier Boudreaux pulled her wool coat tightly around her slim body and stared into the black sky beyond the football stadium lights.

Comme moi, she mused in her mother tongue, and then corrected herself for the millionth time.

Like me.... Artificial light surrounded by infinite darkness.

Helêne saw Christi coming up the steps looking for her. She waved and smiled, forcing herself to sit up straighter on the backless wooden riser.

Two men in denim overalls seemed to be with Christi, though following a couple of paces behind. The younger of the two, who appeared to be about forty, was nearly as big as Grover Jones, and had his facial features.

Helêne shuddered involuntarily, but smiled and extended her hand when Christi introduced them. As Christi went back to join the other cheerleaders, and the two men settled themselves on the bench, Helêne uncharacteristically wished that Clem were there.

At awkward times like these, she resented the charade of his working late with that tramp secretary of his.

But who am I to call Vayda Jander a tramp? she asked herself, and smiled again for her daughter's sake.

Sandwiched between Lucky Jones and his friend Bubba Something-or-other, Helêne tried to develop an interest in the half-time show.

"Sure is easy to see where Christi gets her good looks, Miz Boudreaux."

"Thank you, Mr. Jones."

"You can call me 'Lucky.'"

"All right, Lucky. What's your real name?"

"Lucky's it. Yep, Lucky's it."

"Tell her the story, Lucky."

"Naw, Miz Boudreaux don't want to hear that old story."

"Sure she does. Don't you, ma'am?"

"Of course, if Mister, if Lucky would like to tell it."

"Go ahead, Lucky, tell her."

Helêne smiled encouragement.

"It ain't much really, but my mama always smoked Lucky Strike cigarettes. Well, right after I was born, my mama said, very first thing, 'Give me a Lucky,' and they handed me over to her instead of a pack of cigarettes. She thought that was so funny she decided to name me 'Lucky.'"

"What did your father think of that?"

"Aw, he don't care. A name's a name to him. Long as a kid comes when you call the name you given him, it don't much matter. Still, I wanted my boy to have a good solid name. Like 'Grover.' Has a nice ring to it, don'tcha think? 'Grover Jones.'"

"Very nice," nodded Helêne Lepeltier Boudreaux, whose precious daughter Christina Lepeltier Boudreaux wanted to be 'Mrs. Grover Jones.' "Yes, it's a very nice name," she lied.

"All this talking, I've worked up a thirst. Can I get you something, Miz Boudreaux?

"No, thanks, Lucky, I'm fine."

"Get me a RC Cola while you're down there," his friend ordered. "And a hot dog. Aw, make it two hot dogs. Lotsa mustard and onions."

Helêne shuddered.

"You cold, ma'am?"

"No, I'm fine. Just a little nippy out here."

Lucky Jones disappeared down the ramp.

"Finest time of year," Bubba nodded profoundly. "Gets a little cool in th'evenin.' Start a fire. Good sleeps. Real nice to take my grandsons camping."

"You have grandsons?" Helêne asked incredulously, then realized that she was also old enough to have grandchildren.

"Half dozen of 'em," Bubba announced proudly. "Two of 'em old enough to camp out."

"Have you known Mister, I mean, Lucky, long?"

"Years."

"Did you know his wife, Grover's mother?"

"Yes, ma'am. We all worked out'the plant, 'fore she went back to farmin' full time. Grover's mama was a good basketball player. When she hired on'the plant, they put'n her right on the team. What was her name? Marian Steele. Used to think it was Mary Ann, but it was Marian, I remember. Good lookin' woman. Good basketball player. Lucky, he'd go watch her play and he'd get crazy in the gym. I seen the coach and the refs come over try to quite him down. She couldn't hardly play for the noise he made. ... Lord, them was games!"

"I understand she's gone now."

"Dead," Bubba nodded.

"Was she ill a long time?"

"Never sick a day in her life, she always said. A tractor turned over on her. Cut both legs off. She bled to death before anybody knew about it."

Helêne shuddered again.

"I'm startin' to worry 'bout you, ma'am. You sure you're not too cold?"

Helêne shook her head as Lucky approached.

"Here y'go, Bubba. Didn't have no RC. Gotcha Coke."

"Wha'd I owe ya?"

"On me."

"Thanks. Here, Miz Boudreaux, why don't you eat one of them hot dogs? Warm you up."

"You cold, Miz Boudreaux?"

"No, Lucky, I'm fine. It's just a little chilly out here."

"Here. Take a nip o'this," Lucky offered. He pulled a half-pint of bourbon from his front pocket, poured a fourth of it into his Coke, and handed it to her.

"No, thank you, Lucky," she insisted. "Really, I'm fine. Plenty warm."

"Seein' that bottle reminds me the time we give that vodka to ole Jackie Duvall. 'Member that, Lucky?"

"Yep," he chuckled.

"Tell Miz Boudreaux that story."

"Aw, she wouldn't want to hear that old story."

"Sure she would. Wouldn't you, ma'am?"

"Of course, if Lucky would like to tell it."

"Go ahead, Lucky. Tell her."

Helêne smiled encouragement and mentally cursed at her husband for subjecting her to this misery alone.

Damn him! Damn that Vayda!

"It ain't much really," Lucky began, "but me and Bubba had some fun with it. We taken a quart of that Russian vodka and shaken some cayenne pepper in it. Yep, we shaken it up real good and let it set 'bout a week. It looked like liquid fire! Then ole Bubba here, he poured some of it in Jackie Duvall's coffee and, I tell you, if that boy hadn't a been a Cajun from Loosiana, he'd a died from it. Yep, me and Bubba had some good times outa that vodka."

* * *

"I appreciate your coming in on Saturday like this, Miss Hocking."

"No trouble, Mr. Llewellyn. Caramel Cat's new litter is doing fine, so no use me sitting at home. I'd just as soon make the money and..."

"Good. I'm expecting a call from N'Orleans. Otherwise, I don't want to be disturbed. That is why you're here, Miss Hocking. See that I'm not disturbed. Thank you."

Before his secretary closed the door, George Llewellyn was going back over the notes he had scribbled last night. Clearly, someone at the yacht club was calling someone at Llewellyn's store in Jackson. He tapped his fingers on the desk impatiently.

"'Scuse me, sir," Miss Hocking stage-whispered through the door with a timid knock.

"Yes?"

The door opened wide enough for a small head to enter.

"I wouldn't disturb you, Mr. Llewellyn, sir, but there's a young man on the phone who's quite insistent that you would want to talk to him. He's saying that he's Tawanya's brother."

"I don't know anyone named 'Tawanya,' Miss Hocking. He must have said 'Tom Warner.'"

"No, sir. I'm quite sure he said 'Tawanya.' I even had him spell it for me," Miss Hocking insisted with pride.

"Miss Hocking, if your hearing is that defective, I will have to replace you with someone more sensitive. I told you I never heard of anyone named 'Tawanya.' Is that perfectly clear?"

"Oh, yes, sir, Mr. Llewellyn. He must have said 'Tom Warner.'"

"God damn it! I thought so. Now get back on the phone and put him through."

"Yes, sir."

The door closed.

"...That's right. My name is Jody French. Tawanya is my older sister."

George Llewellyn felt the phone becoming moist in his hand.

"A long time ago, she gave me a sealed envelope to open if I ever got really worried about her. There was a code for a name and a local phone number. When I called, they said you had moved to Vicksburg and gave me this number. They said to ask for Mr. Llewellyn. Tawanya's been gone for three weeks without a word. She always calls, no matter where she is. Do you have any idea...?"

"Please deposit an additional ninety-five cents."

"Mr. Llewellyn, are you still there?"

"Yes, Jody, I'm here," the older man said quietly.

"Do you have any idea where she is?" Jody asked plaintively.

"I know for a fact that she was seen two weeks ago in Cartagena, Columbia."

"What would she be doing there?"

"That doesn't matter."

"Yes, sir. Was she alone?"

George Llewellyn decided to take a chance with this boy. Maybe together they could come up with something.

"She got on a boat called *La Muestra*."

There was silence on the New Orleans end of the line.

"Jody? Jody? Are you there?"

"Yes, sir."

"What's wrong?"

"*La Muestra* was blown up yesterday."

"How do you know that, Jody?"

"I saw it."

"You mean, in the paper?"

"No, sir. I mean, it was in the paper and I saw that too, but I saw the boat blow up."

"What do you mean? You were there? You live near the marina?" PapaLew recalled rows of shanties along the river.

"Yes, sir, I live near there, but I work there too."

PapaLew closed his eyes and tried to picture the young mulatto who had helped with the luggage. He had given him a hundred dollars and warned him against talking.

"You work at the marina?"

"Yes, sir."

"You were there yesterday when the boat blew up?"

"Yes, sir."

"Was anyone else there with you when it happened?"

"Yes, sir."

"Who?"

"Mr. Watson, the owner, sir. He's my boss."

"Anyone else?" PapaLew held his breath.

"No, sir."

"You're certain?"

"Positive, sir. It was only two-forty-five and none of the weekenders had arrived yet."

The boy sounded so honest that PapaLew had to convince himself that it had happened yesterday when he was there.

"Jody, what if I were to tell you that four people arrived at the marina in a cab about that time and that a man gave you a hundred dollars to keep quiet about it."

"I'd say you had received some bad information, sir."

Llewellyn smiled.

"And what if I said that Mr. Watson had given me this information?"

Without a moment's pause, Jody answered, "I'd say that Mr. Watson has his own reasons for saying what he says."

George Llewellyn almost laughed out loud.

"You're good, Jody. Really good. Now listen to me. I'm going to call you back in ten minutes at the pay phone where you are. Give me the number. We have a lot of things to talk about..."

* * *

"I'm sorry they changed their minds about the boat, Kelly, but I'm glad you insisted on waiting at school to vote for me," Christi confided over the phone. "That just shows what a good friend you really are."

"I'm not that great," Kelly insisted, glad that they were on the phone and Christi couldn't see her blushing from the shame of casting her valuable vote for the hated rival Carol Jean Tolbert.

"So, maybe you can go to the Halloween dance at the country club tonight. Did Larry ask you?"

"Yeah, he just called, but I think it's anti-climatic to have a Halloween party after Halloween."

"They had to. There was a big golf tournament and awards dinner last Saturday and they couldn't have it on the actual day because the B-team games are on Thursday nights and, of course, nobody would ever have anything on Friday night because of football. It'll be fun, anyway. Do you have a costume yet?"

"Larry said that his mother has a closet full of costumes from Mardi Gras, and he's sure I can find something that will fit. I'm going over to his house in a few minutes. What are you doing this afternoon?"

"Nothing. Grover's helping Miss Fennstemmacher. I've got a book report due."

"Do you think Cameron will be at the dance?"

"I'm certain of it," Christi reported. "Carol Jean made a big point of telling me she had invited him."

"Cameron would have invited me if his family belonged to the country club," Kelly said with feigned certainty. "Of course, if we still belonged, I could have invited him. Oh, well," she sighed, "at least I'll see him there."

"Kelly?"

"Hmmm?"

"You need to get over this Cameron Coulter nonsense. Larry Llewellyn is a great catch."

"Right," Kelly responded flatly.

"He is," Christi insisted. "Now, cheer up. Your trip may have been disappointing, but we'll have a real blast tonight."

Chapter 12
November 2, 1963
Afternoon

Christi took the last apple from the refrigerator and slowly walked outside. The sun was still warm, but the air had a crispness now and the grass didn't spring back after each footstep. She tried to settle down under her reading tree with *Wuthering Heights,* but a nameless agitation kept her from concentrating.

Maybe it's because I read this years ago when I wanted to and I don't want to read it again for a stupid book report. The words swam together on the page and suddenly Christi had the feeling that she had lived this moment before, or that she was foreseeing the future.

If I look up, I'll see the gardenia bushes against the side of the house and the sky will be a bright blue with a couple of puffy clouds to the southwest over the river. Then a dog will bark and I'll hear a screen door slam and I'll know I can predict the future.

Christi looked up and saw the gardenia bushes against the side of the house, thick and green as she had imagined. She let her eyes travel up past the windows and roof to the bright blue sky beyond. The constancy of its color was interrupted only by a couple of puffy clouds to the southwest over the river. A second later she heard a dog bark and she waited tensely for the slam of a screen door so that the spell would not be broken.

Prudence Washington took the last apple from the small refrigerator in the quarters' cramped kitchen and slowly walked outside. The sky was a bright blue with only a couple of puffy white clouds to the southwest over the river. The sun was still warm, but her heart was too heavy to feel it caress her dark skin.

She stood on the stoop for a moment, leaning against the open screen door, undecided on her course, and felt the quiet isolation of the white neighborhood where she had been born in the McCain's old quarters seventeen years ago. Moving to the Boudreaux quarters after Clayton McCain died had not made any real difference in her life. She was still a black girl in a white neighborhood and she would be expected to stay and serve until she died, as her mother would, as her grandmothers had done before her.

Down the street a dog barked and it sounded friendly. Prudence decided to seek its companionship. She took a bite of apple as she stepped down from the stoop onto the warm brick path. The screen door slammed behind her.

"Pru!"

She turned and saw Christi under the reading tree. Prudence took another bite from her apple and ambled across the yard. Her tall, thin body cast a long shadow as she walked. Christi motioned for her to sit down, and scooted over so that Prudence could lean back against the tree with her.

"What are you reading?"

"*Wuthering Heights*. For a book report."

"Didn't you read that a long time ago?"

"Yeah. How'd you know?"

"Mama watches what books you read and then brings them from your library when you finish with them. She used to do it at the McCain's too. Kelly reads a lot."

"No kidding," Christi laughed. "She's a maniac."

Prudence nodded, "But I like to read too, so it didn't bother me. Anyway, I figure if I read a book, you read it first. I hope you don't mind. Your father said it was okay for me to use your library."

"Of course, I don't mind. We're friends, aren't we?"

Prudence looked into Christi's sincere blue eyes. Then she scanned the expanse of the Boudreaux home from its magnificent towering trees to its massive porches to the many-windowed room upstairs that was Christi's own. She sighed and stared at the tiny out-building from which she had come, the old slave quarters that could have been set down inside Christi's bedroom and still leave space to walk around.

"You really do believe we're friends, don't you, Christi? You actually believe it."

"Well, what's a friend? Somebody you know and care about? Sure, I believe we're friends."

Prudence took another bite of the apple and stared at the sky.

"Oh," Christi sighed, "I know what's wrong with you today. Ray was here on leave and is gone again, isn't he? I'd almost forgotten. I'm sorry, Pru. I guess you miss him terribly. I know I would."

Christi leaned back against the tree and felt guilty for being so wrapped up in the Homecoming election that she hadn't remembered that Ray and Prudence were having their own homecoming. She thought about how she would feel if Grover had to go away.

"He's gonna get killed," Prudence announced matter-of-factly.

"Pru! Hush your mouth! Don't even say a thing like that!" Christi made the Sign of the Cross. "He'll be fine."

"No," Prudence shook her head. "He's gonna die over there. I know he is."

"You stop that kind of talk right now, Prudence Washington! You don't even know for sure that he's going over there. They don't send everybody to Viet Nam."

"Maybe not every <u>body</u>, but every <u>black</u> body. My people are just cannon fodder in this war."

"I know you're upset today, and so you're not thinking clearly," Christi consoled. "Even if, and I'm saying 'if,' every black body does get sent over there, they don't all get killed."

"Don't you read the paper, Christi? Everybody's getting killed over there. It's crazy!"

Christi closed her eyes and tried to remember what she had seen in the paper about Viet Nam. It seemed so far away. She didn't know anybody who was going. It wasn't like The War that was fought here in Vicksburg, where you could still, a hundred years after it was over, walk around and occasionally discover an old shell casing, or a button buried in the ground from a gray or a blue uniform. The War in Vicksburg felt real. Whatever was going on in Viet Nam was different.

Christi worried for a brief moment that Grover might go over there, but almost immediately remembered that he would have a draft deferment because he would have a football scholarship to go to college instead. She pictured the two of them strolling across the campus at Ole Miss, holding hands, kicking at newly-fallen leaves. One more year and they would be there together. They would have their whole lives together.

"It makes me mad, I tell you! Doesn't it make you mad?"

Christi glanced at her dark friend, embarrassed that she hadn't been listening, wondering what had made her angry all of a sudden. Taking a chance, the white girl nodded in agreement.

"Well, then, let's go."

"Go where?" Christi frowned.

"To Tolbert's, for an ice cream sundae."

"But Prudence, you know you can't go in there."

"That's what I just said. My people can wear a United States Army uniform and get their balls blown off in Viet Nam, but we can't get a sundae at Tolbert's. Doesn't that make you mad?"

So that was it. It was almost enough to make Christi mad too.

"Okay, Pru, let's give it a try," she nodded.

The two girls looked at each other and laughed.

"Why not?" Prudence shrugged. "The worst they'll do is shoot or hang me. Of course, it could be devastating for you. They might not invite you to be a debutante!"

Christi laughed again. "Got any money on you?"

"Enough," Prudence replied, "but we won't get that far."

"Don't be pessimistic. You're going to Tolbert's with me, Christina Lepeltier Boudreaux, of the illustrious Mississippi Boudreaux family. That's a name to be reckoned with."

Prudence drawled in a Southern belle imitation, "I reckon we'll find out soon enough."

The girls scrambled to their feet.

"Let's not take the car," Christi suggested. "It'll look more casual." She gently tossed *Wuthering Heights* onto the porch, and called through the front door to Nellie Mae that they were going to take a walk.

When the innocents arrived at Tolbert's, hungry for a sundae with extra whipped cream and nuts, Christi stepped in front of Prudence to open the big glass door. The popular

Homecoming Queen crossed the cool tile vestibule with her maid's daughter one pace behind.

Within seconds, the Saturday afternoon crowd was silent. Christi felt fifty pairs of eyes on her. She smiled at Old Lady Tolbert, Carol Jean's grandmother, who was nailed in place behind the cash register.

"We don't serve her kind in here."

"But, Miz Tolbert, she's with me," Christi tried to explain.

Old Man Tolbert came out from the back, startled by the sudden silence. He glared at Christi.

"What's that nigger doin' in here?" he asked harshly.

"We just came in for a sundae, Mister Tolbert," Christi answered respectfully.

"What's your name, Girl?"

"I'm Christi Boudreaux. Christina Lepeltier Boudreaux," she emphasized each word.

"Clem's daughter, I guess."

"Yes, sir."

"Does your daddy know you're in here with a nigger?"

Christi felt Prudence's hand on her shoulder.

"Come on, Christi, let's go," she whispered.

"No, sir, he doesn't. He's at the office."

Christi blushed from the confrontation, and from suddenly wondering what her father was doing in his office this late on a Saturday afternoon. The *July 25th incident* hit her again.

"You best get on home, young lady, 'fore I call him."

"But I want a sundae," Christi insisted respectfully.

"Fine. You just sit yourself down, order a sundae, and we'll forget all about this commotion."

"And my friend wants one too."

Kelly's neighbor, the giant Lefty Owens, with his three inseparable sidekicks, started easing out of the back booth, glaring at Prudence.

"Sit down there, boys," Old Man Tolbert growled. "This is my place. I'll handle it."

The four troublemakers sat, but on the edges of their seats, and never took their eyes off Prudence.

"Miss Boudreaux, you may sit down and order, and tell that nigger to leave, or you may leave with her, but right now, you are disturbing my business and in Warren County, Mississippi, that's still a criminal offense. If you wasn't Clem Boudreaux's daughter, I woulda already called the po-leece."

Christi's face burned, and her stomach grabbed her body. She turned to her accomplice.

"Come on, Prudence. I guess we'd better go."

The tall thin girl and the shorter plumper girl, one black, one white, left Tolbert's side by side and walked calmly down the block. When they were out of sight of the big glass windows, they collapsed together on a bus stop bench.

"Still mad?" Christi asked.

"Madder than ever!"

"You hide it well."

"My people have to."

"I know. I'm sorry."

After a long silence, Prudence said quietly, "I want to tell you that I'm sorry."

"For what?" Christi wondered aloud.

"For doubting that you were my friend."

* * *

"Watson. George Llewellyn here. Listen. That girl with us yesterday made a call to Vicksburg on your yacht club phone. Send a copy of your last four weeks' long distance logs to me with that one circled.... No, it's a matter of principle to me, Watson. I want you to understand that I always pay my debts. By the way, while you're at it, figure up what your marina is worth. You've decided to retire, Watson, and I'm going to take it off your hands.... Maybe you don't understand. Money is no object to me, Watson. It's just one way of keeping score.... My man will contact you...."

* * *

"This is George Llewellyn, Shimwell.... Drop the nicey-nice about the store. I won't have my employees making long distance calls during business hours, not even when they walk down the street to a pay phone. Do you understand what I'm telling you?... I want your resignation submitted in writing this afternoon, Shimwell. The picnic is over...."

* * *

Clem Boudreaux paced his living room floor, left hand rubbing his face, right hand grabbing the back of his neck, trying to calm down and collect his thoughts. Christi sat silently on the sofa, waiting. Finally, her father took a seat opposite her and spoke in his best sales voice.

"Old Man Tolbert called me at the office this afternoon, Christina."

She wondered what had been interrupted by that call.

"Wipe that look off your face, young lady. You could have gotten Prudence hurt. Maybe even yourself."

He paused and took a deep breath.

Christi stared at him and said nothing.

"You should have considered the consequences. Did you think about that at all?"

"Yes, I did, but I don't care about being a debutante."

"What? What are you talking about?"

"Nothing," she shrugged.

"Don't you realize what could have happened there?"

"All we were trying to do was order a sundae."

"There's a helluva lot more to it than that, young lady, and you have been raised to know better. Didn't you think for one minute about what just happened in Birmingham? The Klan blew up a downtown church, a Baptist church for God's sake, just to send a message to civil rights workers. Four girls about your age were killed in that church, Christi! Dozens injured – and it could've been more!"

"I know, Daddy, but that was Birmingham. Vicksburg is different!"

"Not so damn different, young lady. This is the South! Civil rights workers get shot. Their houses get bombed. Think I want you bringing that on us? We are the Boudreaux family, for God's sake! We are not civil rights workers!"

Christi thought about her daddy's brothers. At least two of them were in the Klan. They would all be furious when they heard about what she had done.

"But Daddy, I'm not a civil rights worker."

"Maybe not, but if you'd'a been a damn Yankee in there at Tolbert's today, instead of a Boudreaux born and bred in Mississippi, I doubt anyone would have been so tolerant. I doubt they'll ever be so tolerant again."

"I can't believe you're making such a big deal about this," Christi pouted.

For the first time in her life, Christi felt the intensity of her father's pent-up rage and fear. He rose abruptly from his chair, and paced back and forth across the rug in front of the fireplace. When he finally stopped and faced his daughter, the color had drained from his face.

"God damn it, girl!" he growled at his only child. "You could have been killed!"

Chapter 13
November 2, 1963
Evening

Jack-o-lanterns with hideous faces lined the country club drive, the flickering sentinels of doom casting their ominous warnings into the void of a starless night. Ghosts of a dozen cavalrymen hung suspended between outreaching fingers of ancient magnolia trees. A long, black Corvette glided into the drive with the sleekness of a fence-walking cat and came to rest under the columned portico where a cast-iron cauldron released its steamy vapors on the ghoulish Witch of Confederate Vicksburg who stirred and cackled and shrieked at arriving guests.

A black-faced scarecrow rushed to the Corvette's passenger side while Prince Charming, dressed in white satin brocade and a blonde pageboy wig, opened his own door. His Cinderella was magnificently attired in a long gown of matching white satin brocade, protected from the night chill by a flowing cape of white ermine and a pair of exquisitely-embroidered white gloves extending up past her elbows almost to the cap sleeves of her gown. Her thick blonde hair was piled high in a mountain of ringlet curls and upon her head rested a sparkling rhinestone tiara. Cinderella's true identity was hidden behind a white satin mask.

An ancient pick-up truck pulled in behind the Corvette, and a plaid-shirted Paul Bunyan, carrying his huge wood-cutting ax, stepped out. He was accompanied by an Indian princess in a gown of fringed chamois decorated with feathers and beads. Her dark braided hair was adorned with more feathers, and on her feet were beaded moccasins.

Cinderella and the Indian princess greeted each other with squeals of delight. Prince Charming and Paul Bunyan chuckled and rolled their eyes, feigning exasperation with the ordeal of assuming such disguises. They all entered the club together, pausing briefly in the vestibule for a newspaper photographer to take some pictures and get their names.

The party was already a success if judged by the noise level and the eerie atmosphere created by the elaborate Halloween decorations. The young newspaperwoman had all she needed for a full-page feature in Sunday's society section. A more seasoned reporter might have sensed a hard news story brewing beneath the artificial gaiety.

Three hours into the party, Christi and Kelly went to the girls' room together. A sudden silence greeted them. The other girls stopped their preening in front of the mirrors and walked out of the room. Christi and Kelly exchanged glances and wondered aloud what was happening.

"They're probably jealous of your costume, Kelly. It's incredible. I've never seen real ermine before."

"Me neither. You should see Mrs. Llewellyn's closets."

"I'll bet. How'd you like seeing Carol Jean and Cameron dressed up as Raggedy Ann and Andy?"

"Pretty disgusting," Kelly frowned. "I can't believe Cameron would wear that ridiculous red wig. I guess she made him do it. It's probably why they left early."

"I wondered if that was Carol Jean's way of making fun of Larry, with the red hair and all."

"I never thought of that," Kelly sighed. "Who would have imagined a costume party could have so much intrigue? But I'm not sure what's going on around here. Strange. Do you think everybody heard what you did at Tolbert's today?"

Christi shrugged, "If that's what's bothering them, it's a good thing the election was held yesterday."

"Do you suppose a Homecoming-Queen-elect can be impeached?" Kelly asked frivolously.

"Let's hope not," Christi grinned. "I imagine that Grover would probably start a civil war over it."

The two friends laughed and returned to Prince Charming and Paul Bunyan, who had just competed with each other in the apple-bob. They insisted that Christi and Kelly break the tie. The girls removed their respective feathers and tiara, handed the accessories to their dates, and leaned over the barrel of water with a dozen apples still floating on the surface.

"Nigger-lover!" was all Christi heard as she felt a huge hand on her neck, shoving her head under the water. Her nose burned as the cold liquid filled her nostrils. She tried to raise herself up, but the hand was on her neck so hard that it pushed her face down against the side of the barrel, bruising her cheek. For a moment, she thought she was going to drown, but mercifully, the hand released her and she jerked up, gasping for air.

Through the water dripping off her face, Christi could see Grover slugging Lefty Owens. Then one of Lefty's friends hit Grover from behind. Larry grabbed that guy and slugged him, and then another of Lefty's friends joined in. And another. All the football players who were there followed Grover into the fray.

Most of the girls, except Christi and Kelly, were screaming. Some of the guys immediately took their dates and left, but a lot of them stayed to fight. After a while, Christi couldn't tell for sure who was on which side.

Finally, someone pulled one of the beautiful porcelain lamps from its plug and threw it against the plate glass mirror above the fireplace. The glass exploded and everyone stopped for a couple of seconds. Before they could resume the brawl, a dozen Vicksburg policemen burst into the room.

"Police! Stop where you are! You are all under arrest."

Christi's heart caught in her throat. Her daddy would blame her for all of this. Maybe it was all her fault. She looked helplessly at Grover and was about to cry. The room was deathly quiet. Even Lefty Owens was still.

"Officer," she recognized Larry Llewellyn's distinctive in-control voice, "could you and I and the club manager talk for a moment?"

Everyone watched in silence as the three walked to the far end of the room and spoke for several minutes in low voices. Finally, they returned from their huddle, and the policeman announced, "Okay, the party's over. Everyone go home. Boys, you will show your driver's licenses to the officer at the door, sign out with your name and car tag number, then leave in three-minute intervals. You will take your dates directly home. No congregating, no parking, no cruising, no stopping at Tolbert's. Anyone on this list caught on the streets tonight more than a half-hour after checking out of here will be arrested. Is that clear?"

There was a general mumbling of assent. Christi sighed in relief and felt her swollen cheek. The club manager gave her an icepack and led her to his office to rest. Grover, Kelly and Larry went with her.

"What did you say to that policeman, Larry?" Christi asked when the four of them were alone.

Larry shrugged, "I told the manager he could put all the damages on the Llewellyn tab, so he didn't care about filing charges against anyone after that."

"Was it Lefty Owens who called me a 'nigger-lover?'" Christi wanted to know.

"Damn sonofabitch should'a been hauled in!" Grover exploded in response.

"Take it easy, Grover," Larry soothed. "It wouldn't do any good to have Lefty thrown in jail. His daddy would bail him right out, as usual, and we'd have a lot of bother having to be witnesses and all. There are better ways to deal with someone like Lefty Owens."

Christi smiled weakly at Larry and wondered why Kelly couldn't seem to appreciate him. She admired his confident aura, and trusted his good advice. Christi didn't have any idea what Larry meant when he said 'there are better ways to deal with someone like Lefty Owens,' but she was sure he would think of something appropriate.

Larry looked away from his stricken friends for a moment and clenched his fists at his side. Then with a firm, confident pat on Christi's shoulder, he reassured her again, "Don't worry about the police not doing anything to Lefty. I promise you, Christi, there are better ways to deal with someone like Lefty Owens."

Chapter 14
November 3, 1963

Prudence took an apple from the small refrigerator in the quarters' cramped kitchen and slowly walked outside. The sky was a bright blue with only a couple of puffy clouds to the southwest over the river. The sun was still warm, but her heart was too heavy to feel it caress her dark skin.

She stood on the stoop for a moment, leaning against the open screen door, undecided on her course, and for the thousandth time felt the quiet isolation of the white neighborhood where she had lived in slave's quarters for all of her seventeen years.

Down the street, a dog barked and it sounded friendly. She decided to seek its companionship. She took a bite of apple as she stepped down from the stoop onto the worn brick path. The screen door slammed behind her.

The tall thin Negro girl went in the direction of the dog's bark, but never caught up with it. Almost by accident, she found herself heading toward the river, to the spot where she and Ray had parked the night before he left.

Hard to believe that that was Friday night and now it's only Sunday afternoon. This Army experience is going to be an eternity. She looked up as a cloud momentarily darkened the sun and then passed on quickly. "You're right, Lord," she whispered aloud, "thank you for reminding me."

Prudence moped on alone, reflecting on her isolation. *I could invite a friend over sometime. Too proud, I suppose. Our place is no worse than anyone else's, but it's slave quarters. Neat, clean, efficient, remodeled slave quarters. And everybody probably thinks it's better than it is because of the Boudreaux name. Nice people, but so white.*

She looked around and felt the desolation of the river vantage point that had seemed cozy and romantic in the car with Ray.

A black station wagon turned down the dirt road and Prudence's first impulse was to hide.

I m*ust be getting paranoid after that incident at Tolbert's yesterday. Relax.*

As the car approached, she wished she had followed her first instinct.

"Well, well, well. Look who's down here by the river, boys. If it ain't the little Boudreaux nigger."

Prudence tried to ignore them, her eyes darting around quickly for an escape route. The hill behind her was almost straight up, and too slick with brown grass to climb. *Oh, God!* Her heart pounded out a plea. Another cloud passed in front of the sun.

Oh, God!

The car engine shut off. Lefty Owens was the first one out. Three others followed.

"We gonna have our picnic here, Lefty?"

"Looks good to me. Even got a little nigger gal to wait on us. Ain't that right, little nigger gal?"

God, I want to spit in his face. Lord, give me strength.

"I said, 'Ain't that right, little nigger gal?'"

"Yes, sir, that's right."

"Well, then, step on over to the car and fetch us some beer, nigger, and don't try to run off. That wouldn't be too friendly and I just might get upset."

"Yes, sir." Prudence walked quickly to the station wagon and looked in the back seat.

"Open the tailgate, nigger. Beer's in the cooler. Niggers are so dumb. Don't know where the beer is."

Prudence unlatched the tailgate, rolled down the window and lifted the cooler lid.

Oh, God! There must be nearly two cases in here. And they're already drunk.

She pulled out four cold cans from the ice, and a chill went through her.

Oh, God! Let them all pass out soon.

"You didn't get one for yourself, nigger."

"No, sir, I don't drink."

"Right. And you don't steal." They all laughed at her.

God, would it be so wrong to kill them? I could kill them all. If I had a knife, I'd kill them all.

She looked at her hands quivering in fear and rage.

"Bring me 'nother one, nigger."

"Me, too."

"Yes, sir."

God, how long can this go on?

She looked up and the sky was still a bright blue. As the afternoon wore on, pent-up terror and anger began taking their toll on the young girl's psyche. She wanted to run, to fight, to kill, to hide, to cry, to be white.

Where are you, God? Where are you?

"Beer, nigger!"

"Yes, sir." Prudence had lost count of her trips to the car, but she was exhausted from fear. Her mouth was dry. She took a piece of ice and sucked on it, trotting back to the group.

"There are only two beers left, sir."

"You been drinking our beer, nigger?"

"No, sir."

One of the group stood up and peed at her feet.

"I saw you take something out of that cooler and put it to your mouth. Was that some of my beer?"

"No, sir, that was a piece of ice. I was getting hot and just wanted a piece of ice. I didn't drink your beer."

"You're an uppity nigger, ain't you? Taking my ice without asking."

"Yes, sir. I'm sorry, sir."

"I'll bet you're gonna be sorry."

"Now, wait a minute," Lefty slurred. "Maybe this nigger gal ain't all bad."

"What?"

"Yeah, maybe this nigger gal ain't all bad. She's been getting that beer all afternoon without a word of complaint. Not as lazy as most niggers I've seen. I think she deserves a little reward."

"Shit, Lefty! You crazy? Reward a nigger?"

"Boys, boys, boys, when will you learn to trust ole Lefty?"

They all laughed.

"Didn't we have a good time last night? And you thought a costume party at the country club would be boring. Listen to Lefty, boys, and you'll go far."

"So what's her reward?"

"This is the same nigger that wanted an ice cream sundae at Tolbert's yesterday. Ain't that right, nigger?"

"Yes, sir."

"Well, boys, I think she's earned it. What's your favorite flavor of ice cream, nigger gal?"

"Vanilla, sir, but I don't think ... "

"That's right, nigger. You don't think. Ed, you take my car and get over to Tolbert's right now. Bring back a quart of their best vanilla ice cream. This nigger gal's gonna get her reward. You hurry back now. Don't let it melt."

The car and Ed disappeared, and Prudence felt the presence of the others more intensely.

"Go to school, nigger gal?"

"Yes, sir."

"Can you read?"

"Yes, sir."

"Write your whole name?"

"Yes, sir."

"Boys, what we got here is a exceptional nigger."

God, where are you? Where are you?

"This nigger is probably smart enough to know that if she mentions this nice picnic we've had to anybody back in town, we wouldn't take kindly to our reputations being smeared in the mud like we was some common honkies. Do you understand that, nigger?"

"Yes, sir. You don't want me to tell anyone about this."

"Wha'd I tell you, boys? This here is a exceptional nigger."

The bright blue sky was fading to a murky orchid. For the longest time, Prudence huddled quietly on the grass, pulling her knees tightly against her chest, her thin arms trembling from fright and fatigue. One of the group looked as if he might pass out any minute.

Prudence sprang to her feet and flew down the dirt road. Lefty's reflexes were quicker than she had calculated. He was only a few seconds behind her. Prudence ran and prayed.

Oh, God! Where are you?

Without looking back, she sensed that she was gaining distance from him, pulling ahead by at least thirty feet as she approached the creek bridge.

Oh, God! Let me make it over the bridge and around the bend.

She was halfway across the bridge when the black station wagon careened around the curve, heading right at her. Ed slammed on the brakes and jumped out of the car.

"If that's not a typical ungrateful nigger! Running off just when I went to all this trouble to get ice cream!"

Prudence collapsed against the hood of the car, knees trembling.

"Maybe she wanted watermelon instead, but I promised her a sundae," Lefty panted, "and, by damn, a promise is a promise, nigger or no nigger. Get in the car!"

Lefty grabbed her arm, shoved her in the back seat, and climbed in beside her. The smell of his beer breath almost made her nauseous.

Maybe I could throw up on him, Prudence hoped, but her stomach was too numb to cooperate. *Oh, God! Where are you?*

The car lurched forward over the bridge, up the dirt road toward the other two who had not bothered to chase after her. Lefty got out and pulled her with him.

"You sure are a skinny nigger. Don't your white folks feed you good?"

Oh, God! Don't let me spit in his face. He'd kill me.

"Well, no matter. We got some ice cream for you, just like I promised. What are you shaking for, nigger gal? You afraid of ice cream? It ain't poison. It's fresh from Tolbert's, just like you wanted. All us white folks like it. Now, take off your clothes, nigger gal. We wouldn't want to get your pretty dress all messed up with ice cream. I bet that dress belonged to Miss Christi Boudreaux before you got it, ain't that right? Or is that one of the bitch Kelly McCain's old dresses? I'll bet you've even got on some of those white girls' underwear. Let's have a look. I said, 'take off your clothes, nigger gal.'... Well, look here, boys. This is one skinny nigger. Bet she ain't even hardly got tits. Take off that bra and panties, nigger gal. Did you hear me? Boys, it looks like she's gonna need some help getting undressed here. Who wants to help her out of this fancy underwear so it don't get all messed up?... Well, well, now, this is one skinny nigger. Okay, nigger gal, we're going to treat you to our special chocolate sundae."

"But Lefty, I didn't bring no chocolate," Ed whined.

Lefty laughed, "We got all the chocolate we need right here."

Ed frowned, then laughed with him. The others joined in.

"Ain't that right, nigger gal? You're all the chocolate we need."

"How we gonna do this, Lefty?"

"Let's see here.... Shut up, you nekkid nigger! Your clothes is nice and safe, right over there, so you just shut up, lie still and relax. You're the one wanted a Tolbert's ice cream sundae. Ed, you grab hold this nigger gal's arms and hold 'em up over her head. You two each get hold one of her legs. Quit all that squirmin' around, nigger gal. We're going to a lot of trouble for you."

"Wha'cha gonna do now, Lefty?"

"Boys, boys, boys, don't you think I know how to make a chocolate sundae? Spread them legs."

Lefty pried the lid off the ice cream and grabbed a scoop of it in his hand.

"I said, 'spread them legs!'"

Ed and the others laughed hysterically as they realized what Lefty was about to do.

"Hold still, nigger gal. It ain't that cold.... Don't that feel good? Nice Tolbert's ice cream to cool down your hot nigger pussy.... How's this for a chocolate sundae, boys?"

Lefty laughed, scooping up another handful. "This here's what they call hand packed ice cream," Lefty explained. They all laughed hysterically.

"Let somebody else hold her arms awhile, Lefty. She's plumb wearing me out. Let me sit on one them legs and get a better look at what you're doin.'"

"Okay, swap out there. Now, what you bawlin' 'bout, nigger gal? Ain't that just like a nigger? Give'm what they ask for and they start cryin' for somethin' else."

"Maybe she wanted a cherry on her sundae, Lefty."

"Ed, sometimes you amaze me, boy. A cherry on top? Sure. Now, where we gonna get a cherry out here in the boonies? Shut up, nigger! That whimperin' is startin' to bother me. A cherry?"

"You don't s'pose this nigger got her own cherry?" Ed wondered out loud.

They all laughed again.

Lefty shook his head, "No nigger over eight years old got her cherry."

"I got me a hard dick here, Lefty. I could poke it in there and check it out."

"Don't you start screamin,' nigger. You made enough noise for one day. You want your tongue cut out? That's better. I'm kinda getting used to that sobbin.' Just keep it down or you'll never talk again. Don't you worry about ole Ed here, nigger. He ain't gonna hurt you none. He's just pullin' off his britches so's he don't get'em dirty and he's gonna poke around a little and see if he can find a cherry for you.... Wha'cha doin,' Ed?"

"Getting that freezing ice cream out. Think I wanna stick my dick in that?"

"Shit! You'd fuck a snake hole, Ed. Scared of a little ice cream? Besides, it's melting out already. That must be one hot pussy. Maybe I'll try it out when you're done. Go ahead. Hurry up now, Ed, I think I'll try it out.... Shit, you're lookin' good there, Ed. You found any cherry yet?"

"I'm... pokin'... 'round... in... here... pretty... good,... but... I... don't... feel... no... cherry... yet.... Aahhhhh," Ed finished.

Lefty nodded, "That's what I figured. No cherry. Well, get off there, Ed, and grab her arms again," he ordered, unzipping his pants.

"Let me try a little of that chocolate.... Yeah, just let me get in here and try a little of that chocolate....You like this, nigger gal?... You like... havin' ole... Lefty... in your... hot... nigger... pussy?... Bet you... always... wanted a... white boy,... didn't you,... nigger?... Don't... this... feel... good?... Yeah,... nigger... gal, ... don't... this...just... feel... good?..."

* * *

Prudence lay still, curled up like a kitten in the grass, long after the station wagon had disappeared down the dirt road.

She stared at a clump of weeds an inch from her eye and tried to hide behind it. The sound of a car approaching could not arouse her to move.

Maybe they've come back to kill me.... I don't care.

A black Corvette crawled up the incline, raising little dust in its wake. Prudence focused on it, letting the weeds blur in the foreground. The car looked vaguely familiar, but stirred an ominous feeling in her.

I don't care. I don't care.

She focused again on the grass and let the black car fade into the twilight.

"Pru!"

She looked in the direction of the familiar voice.

"Pru! Oh, my God, Larry! She's not moving!"

Christi jumped out of the car.

"Prudence! Prudence! Pru, are you all right?"

Prudence blinked her tear-swollen eyes and tried to focus.

It's Christi... Christi Boudreaux.

Pru tried to say her name, but no sound would come.

Christi? Is that you, Christi? You are so far away....

Prudence closed her eyes again.

"Larry, something's terribly wrong. Prudence, talk to me. We've been looking all over for you. Oh, God! I knew she was in trouble. I knew it. Larry, what are we gonna do? Prudence, tell me you're okay! Pru!"

Larry looked around at the scattered beer cans and cigarette butts littering the ground, then picked up an empty matchbook from the Vicksburg Country Club and turned it over in his hand. A quart container of Tolbert's Dairy Ice Cream dripped its remains into the dry grass next to the girl's discarded clothing. He handed the dress to Christi and she draped it over Prudence's still body. Larry knelt quietly a few feet away, not looking at her nakedness.

"Prudence," he said gently. "It's okay now. I'm Larry Llewellyn, Christi and Kelly's friend. We're going to take care of you. Nobody's going to hurt you anymore."

Christi searched his face and frowned, "What happened?"

Larry looked at her and shook his head.

Prudence opened her eyes again. She felt her dress draped over her. She saw Christi kneeling beside her, touching her shoulder gently. In the fading light, she saw a black Corvette on the road behind her friend.

"Christi…"

Christi breathed a sigh of relief at the sound of her name.

"Yes, Pru, I'm here. It's okay. I'm here."

"Christi…"

Prudence closed her eyes and when she opened them again, Christi was still kneeling beside her, touching her shoulder, stroking her back. The sky had darkened and the wind from the river blew colder. Prudence looked past the clump of weeds to the black Corvette. She couldn't shake the ominous feeling it gave her.

"Christi…"

"Yes, Pru, I'm here. Tell me what happened."

The frightened black girl looked at Larry and shook her head.

"It's all right, Pru," Larry said quietly. "I understand. You talk to Christi. She's your friend. You can tell Christi everything. I'll wait in the car. You take your time."

He rose and walked back to his car alone.

"Tell me, Pru. Tell me what happened," Christi urged.

"I can't."

"Why?"

"They'll kill me. You'll tell someone or call the police and they'll find me and kill me."

"Who?"

Prudence shook her head again.

"All right, Prudence, I swear to you that if you tell me, I won't call the police. I swear it, but you need to tell me. For your own sake, you need to tell me."

Prudence nodded and began to cry. As she dressed and sobbed out the story, her words seared the surface of Christi's soul. Christi's own anger and shame from the day and night before came rushing back to her, along with a thousand other hurts she had buried and never wanted to face. Feelings of devastation and rage fought for control of her.

"I swear to you, Prudence, I won't tell the police what happened here, but these are the same sick people who hurt me and I promise you this — they will pay for what they did to you."

"But you said you wouldn't call the police!"

"And I won't. I swear I won't."

Christi remembered the savage look on Larry's face after the fight at the country club last night. Savage, but under control. She remembered his words, she believed them with all her heart, and now she repeated them to Prudence, "Don't worry about the police not doing anything to Lefty. I promise you, Pru, there are better ways to deal with someone like Lefty Owens. There are better ways."

Chapter 15
November 15, 1963

Christi was having trouble making herself go to school. She would see Lefty Owens and his friends in the hall and she wanted to kill them. She had told Kelly what they did to Prudence, and, for the past ten days, Christi had wanted to tell Grover, too, but she was afraid that he might actually kill them. She was trying to relax and let Larry handle it. Kelly seemed to be absolutely certain that Larry would do something about it, but nothing had happened yet.

The bruise on Christi's cheek was finally fading enough that makeup would cover it. Still, she felt the pain of it, and the pain of being thrown out of Tolbert's. In her nightmares, she heard Lefty Owens hollering "Nigger lover!" She wondered how those civil rights workers kept on doing what they were doing. She decided that they must be more than a little bit crazy.

She tried to concentrate on her classes all day, but it was impossible. Her teachers decided that she must be excited and distracted about the Homecoming game that was only a few hours away.

* * *

"What are you moping about now? What more could a colored girl want?" Nellie Mae asked her only daughter.

"Here it is time for your Homecoming game, you got a new uniform on, and your team is going to the state championship. I don't know what's got into you. You haven't been the same since Ray was here."

"Mama, I'm tired of your acting like we have it so good, living out here in slave quarters, wearing hand-me-down clothes, and even a hand-me-down cheerleader's outfit from the white school, acting like I should be grateful for all this just because I'm black. Do you think it's right that we have to use their school colors so we can wear all their old uniforms? Just listen to you, Mama. 'What more could a colored girl want?' We're not colored. We're black, Mama."

"I don't like you calling us 'black.'"

"And I don't like being called 'colored' or 'Negro.' I'm black, and black is beautiful."

"Listen to you, now, picking up all that high-falutin' new talk that's just going to get you in trouble some day. The real trouble is that you don't want to be any of that. You want to be white!"

"If I were white, I'd have a white boyfriend and he wouldn't be going to Viet Nam to be killed."

"Quit talking like that, child. You're gonna bring it on, talking about it."

* * *

"Now, listen, Vayda darlin.' You know I'd love to be with you tonight, but my little girl's the Homecoming Queen and I can't miss it for anything."

"Okay, I understand. Just this one Friday, but when are you going to tell her?"

"Vayda darlin,' I promised I'm gonna do something about it when Christi graduates. Just be patient a little longer. Ole Clem will make it all worth your while."

* * *

"Mom, may I use your car tonight?"

"Well, sure, son, you know that I never go out after dark, especially when your daddy's out of town. What's wrong with your Corvette?"

"Nothing, but it's homecoming, you know. I just thought we might want to take some friends along later and we'd need more room, so the Cadillac will be better. I'll leave the Corvette in the garage, in case you need it."

Larry watched his mother pour herself another drink.

"You know I'd never drive that thing, son."

"Well, just in case, remember, I'm telling you that it will be in the garage all night and the keys are right here on the mantel."

"I'll remember," she nodded seriously, slurring her words slightly, "your Corvette will be in the garage all night and the keys are right here on the mantel."

* * *

"*Ah, ma chère!* You look beautiful in that dress!"

"Thanks, Mama. Are my bra straps going to show?"

"Let's pin them, just to be safe, so you won't have to worry."

"Good idea. Thanks."

"Now, remember, after Grover puts the crown on you, look over so your daddy can get a good picture."

"Yes, Mama, I will."

"And please don't expect us to entertain Grover's father after the game."

"I don't think his father will be there. They have a sick cow."

"My goodness, why don't they call the veterinarian?"

"They can't afford a vet, Mama."

"Oh, my dear, I'm so sorry."

"It doesn't matter."

"Yes, my child, it does matter. One of these days you may see that it matters very much."

* * *

"Yes, ladies and gentlemen, fans from Vicksburg and fans from Jackson, this is quite a game! A minute thirty-five to go and tied twenty-four, twenty-four. Only a few seconds left in Jackson's last time-out. No matter what the final score may be, this one will be talked about for years to come!

"All right now, play resumes and it's fourth and two on the Vicksburg twenty yard line. It looks like Jackson will go for it, but they better watch out! Here comes Grover Jones from the sideline! He is definitely limping, but he's back in the game!"

* * *

"Well, well, well, look at this, boys. Llewellyn's Corvette. Let's us follow a while and see what that little red-headed prick is doing out in our neck o' the woods. He ought to be at the Homecoming dance with Miss Kelly McCain."

"Maybe we should get his attention and invite him to have a drink with us, Lefty. Show there's no hard feelings."

All four in the black station wagon laughed.

"Sometimes you amaze me, Ed. Yeah, sometimes you just amaze me. Let's do that. Let's invite the little prick for a drink."

The station wagon speeded up as it followed the sleek sports car onto a dark narrow side road.

* * *

The scene in the gym was exactly as Christi had dreamed it would be — green and white crepe-paper streamers and balloons on the festive ceilings and walls; long folding tables set up around the room, each draped identically with rented white cloths and decorated with small centerpieces of green candles and white carnations. Sprigs of dark green ivy peeked from the centerpieces, trailed across the tablecloths and hung in garlands around the skirted stage where a six-piece band was playing the latest songs under a subdued spotlight.

Although everything looked right, it didn't feel right to Christi. This should be the greatest night of her life, but there was a pall over all of it. She was happy to be with Grover, but the rest of it was empty.

She watched Carol Jean, who was with Cameron, throwing herself all over him, but Cameron couldn't keep his eyes off Kelly. Larry, who was with Kelly, was being charming to everyone, but it was obvious that he might as well have been without a date for all the attention Kelly was giving him.

Finally, sometime after midnight, Larry excused himself from Kelly and walked around the table to the other unlikely couple. Kelly's heart beat faster as Larry leaned over to ask Carol Jean for the next dance, leaving Cameron and Kelly alone at their big table for the first time all evening.

Kelly smiled expectantly.

Cameron will have to ask me to dance now. And it's a slow one. He'll have to hold me now.

The lights dimmed as the bandleader announced in a whisper over the song's introduction that the very next dance would be the last one. Kelly held her breath, waiting for Cameron. He turned to her just as Larry took Carol Jean in his arms.

"Nice evening?" Cameron asked after a long look.

"Not yet," she replied with as much meaning as she dared.

Cameron leaned back in his chair and hummed the song's melody.

Oh, God! He's trying to drive me crazy. Cameron! Cameron! You can hum anytime! Dance with me! Hold me! Cameron!

"This is nice," he smiled. "I love this song."

He hummed again.

Cameron! Look at me! Hold me!

"Would you like to dance, Kelly?"

"I guess. If you want to."

"Oh, well, nevermind. The song's almost over and I'll bet you're tired. You've danced with every guy here."

Not with you, Cameron! I haven't danced with you, she screamed inside. *Why do you always do this to me?*

As the band repeated the final chorus, Cameron looked straight into Kelly's eyes and said, "I'm taking Carol Jean home at one. Could I stop by to see you after that?"

The song ended with a plaintive chord.

Kelly nodded, "Of course. I'll be home by one."

The lights dimmed their lowest for the last dance. Cameron rose as Carol Jean and Larry approached their table. He held out his hand to Carol Jean and led her to the dance floor. Larry sat beside Kelly, his arm draped over the back of her chair.

"Shall we?" he asked.

"Shall we what?"

"Go park by the river?"

"Lar-ry!"

"Well, then, how about a dance?"

"Okay."

He laughed as he led her onto the crowded floor.

"You're not being very romantic for the last dance," she pouted.

"Not much point in it, is there?" he asked, pulling her roughly toward him.

* * *

By the time Cameron arrived at one-thirty, Kelly had changed clothes three times and was waiting at the front door wearing slacks and a sweater. Cameron had traded his suit for a pair of jeans.

"Let's go for a drive," he whispered under the porch light.

Kelly nodded. "I'll leave a note on the refrigerator."

Cameron followed her down the dark hall to the dimly-lighted kitchen and watched as she wrote, *"Going for a ride with Cameron. 1:30. Love, Kelly."*

She stuck the paper on the refrigerator door with a Mickey Mouse magnet, then turned to Cameron in the semi-dark room. His eyes were on her as they had been at the dance and suddenly she felt too weak to stand.

Cameron reached for her hand and pulled her toward him as he leaned back against the kitchen sink. With his other arm, he encircled her and drew her body close. His lips found hers and touched lightly. She responded to his kiss and pressed her body harder against him.

All her hopes and fears and dreams of Cameron flooded into that kiss and, before their lips had parted, Kelly was wondering if it felt good to Cameron — if he would always want to kiss her like this — if he would always want her as much as she wanted him.

Without another word, he took her hand and led her out to the car. They drove in silence for a while, awkward at being together after the long evening of waiting. Kelly looked at Cameron's profile and dreamed.

He reached over to turn up the radio and began singing along with Elvis, *"There's no strings upon this heart of mine, It was always you from the start; Treat me right, Treat me good, Treat me like you really should, 'Cause I'm not made of wood and I don't have a Wooden Heart."*

Kelly closed her eyes, leaned back in the seat and hummed along, lost in the sound of Elvis and Cameron in stereo, daring to dream *"There's no strings upon this heart of mine..."*

Cameron drove aimlessly, listening to the music, painfully aware of Kelly sitting at the far side of the front seat, cool and aloof by the door, unaffected by the kiss he had tried to make perfect.

What do you want? Why are you here with me? Why won't you tell me what you're thinking? Kelly! Listen to the music! Listen! These words are for you!

He tried to be casual, reaching over to turn up the radio and singing along with Elvis, *"There's no strings upon this heart of mine, It was always you from the start; Treat me right, Treat me good, Treat me like you really should, 'Cause I'm not made of wood and I don't have a Wooden Heart."*

He looked over and saw Kelly close her eyes and lean back in the seat, humming along, probably bored with him.

Kelly, why can't you hear me? "There's no strings upon this heart of mine, It was always you from the start..."

Kelly opened her eyes and panicked.

"Cameron, are we going to Larry's house?"

Reflexively, Cameron put on the brakes and looked around, realizing that without thinking, he had been heading in the direction of the Llewellyn estate.

"I wasn't paying attention," he apologized, making a quick U-turn.

Now she's going to think I'm crazy. Why can't I ever do anything right with her?

Elvis sang alone, *"...And I don't have a Wooden Heart."*

Cameron drove south, parallel with the river, wondering what Kelly was thinking. In the dark silence, his heart skipped a beat when he saw flashing red lights on the road ahead. An ambulance without its sirens on approached at a leisurely pace, heading toward town. Seconds later, another one turned onto the main highway, following the first. Cameron slowed to a stop along the shoulder and peered down the intersecting asphalt road. In the distance, more lights flashed red and yellow.

"You want to see what's going on?" he asked.

"Sure," Kelly nodded.

Cameron turned onto the side road. Just over the first rise, where the blacktop curved downward and narrowed to a one-lane bridge, they came upon the accident scene. Red lights of a Warren County Sheriff's Department patrol car flashed in deathly silence. The yellow lights of Bennett's Water Street Garage illuminated a muddy, dripping, black station wagon hoisted up behind.

Kelly and Cameron got out of his car together.

"That looks like Nick Nichols," Kelly whispered. "Let's ask him what happened."

Cameron and Kelly approached the scene in respectful silence. The short, fireplug of a man was the youngest of the county's deputy sheriffs. He looked up from scribbling in his small spiral notebook, and grimly nodded in recognition.

"What happened?" Cameron asked.

"Drunk kids. Missed the curve, crashed through that low guard rail and into the water. All four of them drowned." Nichols shook his head and sighed.

"Who were they?" Kelly wanted to know for sure.

The uniformed broad chest and shoulders loomed large in front of Kelly as she looked squarely at his sober face and into his penetrating eyes.

"Your friend Lefty Owens apparently was driving," Nichols answered slowly, searching her face in the intermittent light from his patrol car and the wrecker.

Kelly returned his stare.

"Don't call Lefty Owens a friend of mine," Kelly declared boldly. "I'm just glad there wasn't some other car involved and that he didn't kill anybody else."

"He did. There were three others in the car."

"I'm sure I know who they were too. It's no great loss for Vicksburg," she added defiantly.

"Maybe not, but just keep quiet about this until I have a chance to get back in town and call on the families. By the way, does your mama know you're out this late, young lady?"

"I left a note on the refrigerator."

"Well, I suggest you take her home, Mister Coulter," he nodded at Cameron. "It's after two."

"Yes, sir, we were on our way home when we saw the ambulance," Cameron lied glibly.

Cameron and Kelly rode home in silence.

Nick Nichols finished his official report of the accident and filed away in his mind the unofficial 'open case' version which included the fact that Kelly McCain, known to have a vendetta against Lefty Owens and to be dating Larry Llewellyn, had arrived at the scene with Cameron Coulter, known to be dating Carol Jean Tolbert and to be a friend of Larry Llewellyn. He frowned.

What bothered the deputy was his nagging, as-yet-unfounded hunch that this had not been a random accident any more than the country club incident with Lefty Owens two weeks ago had been a random Halloween prank.

Nichols lit up a cigarette and leaned back against his patrol car, reflecting. He might be the youngest man on the force, but he was smart, and he had grown up in Vicksburg. He knew these people. Every instinct told him that something was not right.

Chapter 16
November 19, 1963

Everybody who was anybody in Vicksburg turned out for the funerals of Leftwich Ozias "Lefty" Owens and his friends. Deputy Sheriff Nick Nichols officially was there to pay his respects to the families. Unofficially, as always, he was observing everything and constantly adding to his vast knowledge of the inner workings of Warren County, Mississippi.

Cameron Coulter was there as president of the senior class, along with other representatives of the high school from which the four would have graduated in another six months. Kelly McCain was there because she knew Cameron would be. Larry Llewellyn had borrowed his mother's Cadillac to give Kelly and Christi a ride. He invited Prudence as well.

Prudence Washington, of course, had to stand outside the church, not daring to go in and try to sit among the white folks, and certainly not eligible to be placed with "the families' niggers" in the reserved pew immediately behind the next-of-kin. After the service, Larry asked the three girls if they wanted to go to the cemetery.

The thin black girl nodded, and murmured through clenched teeth, "I want to hear the dirt thud against those caskets. Then, maybe. I'll be satisfied." She sat in the back seat with Christi. The trio of girls rode in silence, each wondering if justice had been done divinely, coincidentally, or deliberately.

Larry drove his mother's car sedately, saying nothing, feeling the satisfaction and loneliness of competence.

* * *

"...for which let us give thanks as we gather together and bless this food to the nourishment of our bodies, from Thy bounty, through Christ, Our Lord. Amen."

That blessing is just like me, Christi thought as she made the Sign of the Cross during the silence following her father's Amen. *Part Boudreaux. Part Lepeltier. Part father. Part mother.*

Part old. Part new. What am I anyway?... Sixteen years old and what am I?... Well, whatever it is, it's better than being that turkey.

All eyes were on the perfectly browned bird in front of Clement Boudreaux. He stood to carve and the conversations resumed.

"Now, hurry up, Clement. You know those babies can't be good for long," Christi's mother interjected as her father poured his third glass of wine. "Everybody help yourselves to the vegetables and start passing things around."

Always the same admonitions. Every year more Boudreaux babies. Nellie Mae and Prudence would try to keep them all quiet during the Thanksgiving dinner. One o'clock. Nap time for most of them anyway. Christi was cousin to thirteen girls now, all but the eldest living in Vicksburg. Besides the teen-age Christi and her California cousin Maggie, the other girls were under six years old, all offspring of Clem Boudreaux's younger brothers, of whom Billy was the most vocal at dinner conversation, as usual.

"Well, I don't care. Somebody better stop them Commies before they take over the world. Once you let'em take over Viet Nam, there goes the rest of Southeast Asia. There won't be no end to it."

All nodded assent.

In the silence that followed, Christi asked, "How did it all start, Daddy?"

Clem Boudreaux took another sip of wine, looked at his innocent daughter, and sighed, "That's a hard question, Christi. It reminds me of a story John F. Kennedy used to tell about the outbreak of the First World War."

At the mention of Kennedy's name, a pall descended on the large family. It had been less than a week since the young president had been assassinated before their eyes and the wound was fresh in all of them. No one breathed as they waited for the eldest brother to go on with Kennedy's anecdote about how the war began. Clem poured himself another glass of wine and continued.

"Kennedy would tell how diplomatic negotiations dragged on through the long summer of 1914 and then terminated in hostilities. With war upon them, Prince Von Bulow approached his successor, the German Chancellor, and asked, 'How did it all begin?' And the German Chancellor answered solemnly, '*Ach*, if one could only say.'"

Silence.

"Sure is good dressing, Helêne."

"Thank you, John. Have some more giblet gravy on it."

"B'lieve I will."

"It's the same old thing it's always been. Commies trying to take over the world."

"Just like damn Yankees, trying to take over the whole country. Making promises they can't keep. Hard enough for a white man with good sense to scratch out a decent living and now they want to give hand-outs to niggers."

"But you know, this Viet Nam thing could turn out to be a blessing in disguise. Just keep shipping our niggers over there to get blown away. That'll cut down on the hand-outs we gotta give'm over here."

"For Christ's sake, I don't know what this country's coming to. Niggers are gonna be the ruin of it..."

* * *

"...Gracious Heavenly Father, we thank you again, as we leave to go our separate ways, for the opportunity to gather here together as a family on this Thanksgiving Day, in peace and love, to enjoy the fruits of Thy Harvest, this food for the nourishment of our bodies, from Thy bounty, through Christ, Our Lord. Amen."

"Amen."

Clem Boudreaux opened another bottle of wine. Chairs scruffed across the hardwood floor, china and crystal clinked to the kitchen, and televised football droned through the house, occasionally punctuated by lazy conversation and a few snores. Christi surreptitiously picked up the black hall phone.

"Kelly, can you come over?"

"Who's there? Did y'all eat yet?"

"Ate at one. Every Boudreaux in the county is here, but I don't care."

"What's wrong?"

"I don't know. Maybe nothing. Maybe it's just me."

"Okay. I'll be there in fifteen minutes."

Christi took the last apple from the refrigerator and slowly walked outside. The sun was still warm, but the air had a crispness now and the grass didn't spring back after each footstep. She tried to settle down under her reading tree with Pride and Prejudice while she waited for Kelly, but a nameless agitation kept her from concentrating.

Maybe it's because I read this years ago when I wanted to and I don't want to read it again for a stupid old book report. Being a senior is definitely not what it was cracked up to be.

The words swam together on the page and Christi had the feeling she had lived this moment before or that she was foreseeing the future.

If I look up, I'll see the gardenia bushes against the side of the house and the sky will be a right blue with a couple of puffy white clouds to the southwest over the river. Then a dog will bark and I'll hear a screen door slam and I'll know I can predict the future.

She looked up and saw the gardenia bushes against the side of the house, thick and green as she had imagined them. She let her eyes travel up past the windows and roof to the bright blue sky beyond. The constancy of its color was interrupted only by a couple of puffy white clouds to the southwest over the river. A second later she heard a dog bark and she waited tensely for the slam of a screen door so that the spell would not be broken...

"Christi!...Telephone!... It's Johnny Chambers!"

Christi was startled by the sound of her mother's voice calling from the front door at the same time Kelly turned into the driveway. Christi mumbled under her breath. *"Why does she care so much about Johnny Chambers and his money? I'll have plenty of my own money from Daddy."*

"Tell him I've gone for a ride with Kelly," Christi answered over her shoulder as she tossed her book on the porch and headed for the car, "and I'll see him at school sometime next week."

The determination and coolness in Christi's voice stopped her mother from protesting. She stood, immobilized with frustration, watching Christi get in the car and drive away, then, remembering Johnny on the phone, hurried back into the house. The screen door slammed behind her, but it was of no use to Christi. The spell had already been broken and she knew she could not predict the future.

* * *

"Well, Jody," the fat man huffed, "I guess this about finishes'r up."

"Yes, sir, Mr. Watson," the young mulatto grinned as he stacked the final box in Watson's station wagon, "That should do it. I was surprised you found a buyer so fast. I didn't even know the marina was for sale."

"Heh, heh," Watson chuckled, "lotsa folks may think I'm slow, but I do all right. Sold this place for more than it's worth. 'A fool and his money,' you know. Heh, heh. 'A fool and his money....'"

Watson absently followed the boy to the tool shed for a last look around, puffing from the extra weight of a huge Thanksgiving dinner. The late November sun sank unspectacularly over the Crescent City as they emerged from the small wooden building and ambled along the sea wall.

Relieved of the employer-employee relationship, the older man drifted idly into a monologue of reminiscing about the yacht club that Jody would soon be managing. Many of the unsavory details that Jody had heard earlier from PapaLew were carefully edited out of Watson's version.

Darkness sneaked up on them, and Watson seemed suddenly startled by it.

"Appreciate you coming down here on Thanksgiving to help me out, boy," he said gruffly, thrusting his hand toward Jody in a gesture of friendship. "Guess it's time to go now."

"Yes, sir," Jody nodded, looking intently at his own expensive new watch. "It's definitely time to go now."

With his right hand, Jody firmly gripped Watson's. With his left, he grabbed the old man's shoulder, whirled him around off balance, and shoved him from the sea wall into the cold turgid Mississippi River.

In the dim light, Jody saw the whites of Watson's eyes grow large, and watched his mouth open silently in horror like a fish when the hook sets. Watson flailed helplessly in the water for a few seconds, stiffened in pain, and sank out of sight. Jody peered intently into the black water and counted slowly to a hundred before turning toward the office to phone for help.

"This is Jody French at the Crescent City Yachting Club and Marina. I think my boss just had a heart attack..."

* * *

Dearest Ray,

I miss you so much, but to answer your question, not a single thing has happened in Vicksburg in the whole time you've been gone. Dull, dull, dull, as usual in this town. No news at all. I'm <u>fine</u> except for missing you! It seems you've been gone forever.

Speaking of forever, the whole Boudreaux clan was here for Thanksgiving dinner today and I had to keep all those babies quiet for two hours! <u>That</u> was forever! And, I helped cook, so I'm exhausted. Will write again in the morning.

See you in my dreams.... Love always... Pru

* * *

The weeks before Christmas vacation were hot, muggy, and interminably long. Christi and Kelly tried to befriend Prudence and cheer her up, but Prudence was becoming progressively more quiet and hard to reach. She spent most of her spare time writing in spiral notebooks that she hid between her mattress and box springs. She started learning to cook and made brownies to send to Ray for Christmas.

* * *

"*Mon Dieu! C'est magnifique!*"

"You really like it, Mom?"

"Christi, it's exquisite. And, Grover, what can I say? This is not simply a wonderful Christmas present for Christi, it is a testimony to your talent."

"That's nice of you to say, Miz Boudreaux."

"I'm not saying it to be nice, Grover. I grew up in Paris. Remember? I assure you that one cannot reside in Paris without learning something of art."

"She's right, boy," Clem added grudgingly. "The woman knows something about art, and, if she says it's good, then it's good, and that's final. Matter of fact, I like it myself. Reminds me of the flowers on Christi's wallpaper, but damned if they don't look alive in your painting."

"*Vraiment*. Alive. Such jubilant yellows bursting into a bouquet of life! Ah, Grover, now I understand," Helêne smiled. "Now, I understand."

Chapter 17
February 21, 1964

Margaret Rose Stevenson contemplated the initials on her pillowcase and, for the thousandth time, was amused at the irony of it. She would never be "MRS" Anybody. Her brown eyes wandered to the other pillowcase that was almost completely covered with a mass of dark curls. Gently, she smoothed them back.

"Time to get up, Sleepyhead. Your public is waiting."

"Oh, Maggie, can't you ever sleep late?" the soft voice purred.

Like a cat stretching after a long nap, Allessandra raised both arms up until her hands reached the mirror that served as a headboard for their king-sized bed. Pushing against it, she straightened her body and rolled over.

The white lace nightshirt that had been loosely wrapped around her fell open, fully revealing her flawless body. Allessandra smiled dreamily, her eyes still closed, and reached out with her right hand.

"Too late!" Maggie laughed on her way to the shower. She closed the bathroom door, then reappeared briefly.

"But, did I mention how exquisitely beautiful you are this morning? Like a *trachops cirrhosus* waiting for its prey."

"It's my business to be beautiful," Allessandra replied to the mirror.

She rolled over on her stomach, propped herself up on her elbows, and noted with satisfaction that she was indeed exquisite. Good for several more years. Maybe the eye job in a year or two. Not wanting to think about that, she turned again and relaxed on her back. Great legs, for sure. She lifted one up slowly in the air. Admired it. Let it down. Then the other. Exercise. Enough for today.

Allessandra rose languorously and padded barefoot to the front door, opening it cautiously to the full morning sun, retrieving the *Los Angeles Times* from its place on the mat, and lifting a handful of mail from the large brass mailbox that had recently replaced the small old black one.

"Your turn in the bathroom," Maggie called out. "Five minutes for me. Fifty-five for you."

Allessandra let the paper drop on the bed and continued leafing absently through yesterday's mail.

"What's a *trachops* whatever-you-said?" she asked languidly.

"A frog-eating bat," was the unexpected reply. "A truly fascinating creature," Maggie laughed.

"Speaking of fascinating creatures," Allessandra interrupted, "here's a letter from your twit cousin Christi in Vicksburg. It's marked *'Urgent!'*"

She continued in a faked Southern drawl, "Wondah what sort of melahdrahmah is unfolding along the Mississippi now. Could it be that precious Grover stubbed his toe on a cow patty, or perhaps the elusive Cameron has asked Kelly to return his Christmas card? Oh, Maggie, how evah will you solve this one?"

"Jealously does not become you, my dear," Maggie warned, taking the letter and walking toward the kitchen.

Heading for the bathroom, Allessandra shrugged grandly and glanced at the mirror for the effect. Somehow, it was unsatisfying.

Maggie poured a glass of orange juice and sat in a comfortable rattan chair under the indoor shade of a huge ficus tree. She sighed and opened the letter.

February 17, 1964

Dear Maggie,

The most awful thing has happened! Prudence's boyfriend has been killed in Viet Nam! He wasn't even there a week! Since he didn't have any relatives, he put Prudence's name down as next-of-kin and they just told her they're shipping the body back to Vicksburg for burial.

Pru's hysterical and Nellie Mae can't do anything with her. Their preacher is out back with them now, but Prudence didn't want to talk to him. She won't even talk to me or Kelly. She screamed at us that if Ray had been white, he never would have been sent over there to be shot at. The way she looked at us, you would have thought the whole war was our fault.

But, there's something even worse that nobody else knows but Kelly and me. Prudence (now swear you won't tell anybody this!) was raped a couple of days after Halloween. She thinks she's pregnant. What can we do? You're the only girl I know who's been around enough to have any sensible ideas. (I don't mean that in a bad way.) Mama would go into shock. You know how proper she is after growing up in Paris and all! I hate to think what Nellie Mae would do.

Please stop whatever you're doing and answer this letter or call me immediately. Thanks.

Love,
Christi

P.S. Cameron did not give Kelly a Valentine, which is exactly what I expected.

Maggie methodically tore the letter into shreds and mixed it into the garbage with yesterday's coffee grounds. With a glance toward the bedroom, she picked up the kitchen wall phone and dialed a local number.

"Hey, it's Maggie.... Didn't you tell me you knew a doctor in Memphis who does scrapes? Some guy who lived near you in Atlanta and got run out of town?... For God's sake, of course it's not me!... Somebody you don't know.... If you've got it, just give me the name and number. I've gotta get off the phone.... Okay, thanks.... Bye."

Maggie hung up the phone and busied herself making coffee and scrambling eggs until Allessandra appeared, towel-drying her luxurious hair.

"Well, what's the crisis in the Deep South this time?"

"Cameron didn't give Kelly a Valentine."

* * *

Prudence Washington lay absolutely still and tried to keep her breathing shallow and steady. She could hear her mother stirring in the next room.

Hurry. Hurry. Get out of here.

She felt the saliva forming in her mouth and knew it would soon be too full to swallow.

If only I could swallow a little. Just a little. Please, God!

Even as she prayed, she felt the flood of saliva and then the sickening bile rising to her throat. Her face prickled with heat at the same time her hands and feet turned cold and clammy. Damp perspiration coated her forehead.

Breathe! Lie still and breathe! I will not be sick! I will not be sick!

The bile was in her throat now, fighting to mix with the saliva. Slowly, Prudence turned her head to the side. Slowly, slowly, so as not to move any other part of her body, she opened her mouth and let some of the saliva trickle onto the towel she had placed on her pillow last night. The saliva poured out.

Breathe! Breathe! I will not be sick!

A trickle of perspiration dropped onto the towel as the foul-tasting bile nearly choked her.

Breathe! Breathe! Lie still and breathe! I will not be sick! Please, God, don't let me be sick!

The quarters' front door closed quietly, followed by the squeak and thud of the screen.

She's gone! Thank God, she's gone! Breathe! Breathe!

The knot in her stomach slowly began to rise, up, up, slowly, up, until it was caught in her throat and choking her. An involuntary chill and shudder passed through her entire body and the bile overpowered her. The taste of vomit was in her mouth, the smell of it everywhere. Prudence grabbed the towel, pressed it against her mouth, and ran gagging to the bathroom.

* * *

February 29, 1964

Dear Maggie,

You were right, as usual. Everyone did seem to calm down a bit after the funeral. Prudence looks really terrible, though, and is starting to lose weight. She's been throwing up all over the place, but everyone thinks it's because she's so upset over Ray.

Prudence grabbed me and Kelly after the funeral and made us swear that we hadn't said anything to Nellie Mae or anyone about "the problem." We swore we hadn't talked to anyone in Vicksburg, and we told her we had an idea to help her out, but wouldn't discuss it with her while she was acting so crazy. We're going to take your advice and leave her alone for a few days. Maybe she'll come around. I hope you're right!

Thanks for calling, and for everything!

Love,
Christi

P.S. Kelly won first prize in the George Washington Essay Contest at school. She wrote a series of letters between George and a fictitious friend of his in England during the Revolutionary War. The judges said it was creative and original, though stretching the contest guidelines. Kelly turned it in as a joke!

* * *

A skinny black hand, ungloved, protruded from a heavy coat sleeve, pointing straight out the old Chevy's window to indicate a left turn onto the muddy cemetery road. Five hundred feet behind, Nick Nichols slowed his patrol car carefully in the misting rain that turned these asphalt country roads into treachery.

He noted that the Chevy's right brake light was burned out. Old car. Young black girl driving. Probably no brakes, either. He sighed, snubbed out his cigarette in the overflowing ashtray, and turned into the mud rut made by the offending vehicle. No need for lights or siren. She would stop soon enough along the horseshoe-shaped drive.

He waited, a hundred feet back, while the girl got out of the car and plodded through the unkempt cemetery to a freshly mounded grave. Oblivious to his presence, she stood in a daze, unmoving, arms hanging limply at her sides. The rain became more insistent, but she did not flinch as it stung her face and soaked her uncovered mass of black hair.

Nichols glanced at his watch. He was officially off duty five minutes ago, but as usual, he had found something of interest to keep him later. He radioed his location and watched the unmoving black figure in the rain. For a second, he let his brain trick him into believing the girl had disappeared and left a statue in her place. Still, he waited. He tried to imagine what grief could hold a person immobile in the rain, but as always, he shifted back into his own reverie, which was a peaceful one.

Nick Nichols recognized himself as one of the truly blessed people on earth who had found a fulfilling career that made him look forward to getting up in the morning.

I may never be the Sheriff of Warren County, but one of these days, I'll get on the city force and I'll make Chief, the Deputy assured himself for the hundredth time in his short career. *And I'll be a damn good Chief. Who knows? After that? Maybe I'll even become the mayor of Vicksburg.*

Nichols smiled and unconsciously lit up another cigarette.

The last cigarette was cold in the ashtray before the young black girl moved, trudging slowly back to her car through thick, sucking mud. Nichols met her in the road, thankful that the rain had eased a little.

"'Scuse me, Miss," he interrupted her solitude, as politely as if she were a white girl.

She looked up, obviously surprised to hear a voice, but not startled.

"Yes, sir?" she answered calmly, looking directly at the man's face.

Nichols was momentarily taken aback by the directness of her gaze and her total lack of fear. Seldom did anyone, black or white, confront the deputy sheriff without a shadow of awe or fear or guilt. Then he remembered where he had seen this black girl.

"May I see your driver's license?"

"I don't have one, sir."

"Hmmm. Is this your car?"

"No, sir."

Still no awe or fear or guilt on her face.

This girl has been through hell, Nichols realized. *Nothing can hurt her now. Her own pain is her shield.*

"Whose car is it?"

"Mister Clement Boudreaux's, sir."

Nichols was not surprised to hear the name that had just been on his mind. He prided himself on being two steps ahead of the facts.

"Does he know you're driving it?"

"Yes, sir."

"Do you work for him?"

"No, sir, not exactly, but my mother does."

"And you don't have a driver's license?"

"No, sir."

"How old are you?"

"Seventeen, sir."

"And what's your name?"

"Prudence Washington, sir."

"And you live with the Boudreaux family?"

"Yes, sir. Out back, sir."

"Do you know Clem's office phone number?"

"Yes, sir."

Nichols scribbled the information in his notebook.

"Who taught you to drive?"

"Mister Boudreaux. Did I do something wrong?"

"Your car got my attention because the right brake light is burned out. Did you know that?"

"No, sir."

"And, of course, you've been driving without a license."

"Yes, sir," she maintained, with undeniable poise.

Nichols debated internally a moment. He could take the girl in, leave the car out here miles from town, and cause everybody a lot of aggravation, or…

"Am I in trouble, sir?"

Nichols looked past her to the fresh gravesite, and shook his head, "No. You've had enough trouble."

"Yes, sir," the girl sighed.

"Family member?"

"No, sir. Boyfriend, sir."

"Car wreck?"

"No, sir.… Viet Nam."

Nichols flinched, remembering his own recent tour. "I'm sorry," he nodded, and Prudence believed that he truly was.

Chapter 18
March 7, 1964

"Is there anything else I can get for you now, Miss Fennstemmacher?"

"No, Grover, thank you. You've been very kind. I'm surprised a young man like you could make such delicious chicken soup."

"I used to watch my momma," he paused, then went on with a catch in his voice. "She always said it was good for what ails you. Have some more before you go to sleep."

"I may do that, but I feel better already. To tell you the truth, I thought I was dying this afternoon. I've never felt so weak. It scares me to think what might have happened if you hadn't checked on me."

"Now, Miss Fennstemmacher, we know you're not going to die of the flu." In the brief silence that followed, they both, uncomfortably, remembered her father's funeral last fall, after his short bout of influenza.

"And, if I hadn't checked on you, one of your friends would have," Grover added hastily. Just as quickly, he realized that her phone seldom rang and no car ever pulled into the driveway except Grover's or those of his friends.

"Still," she smiled weakly, "it was you, and I'm grateful. Tell me what I can do to repay you."

"Nothing," he shook his head. "I don't need anything."

"I insist. Name it."

The image of Christi Boudreaux flashed through his mind.

"Okay," Grover grinned. "A place to come back to after I've gone off to college. Let me keep some things here."

"Consider it done. This will be your official Vicksburg home."

"Not a bad trade, I'd say," Grover laughed lightly. "A home in Vicksburg for a pot of chicken soup."

"'My kingdom for a horse,'" she replied. "Sounds fair to me."

"Fine. Now that the horse-trading's finished, you get some sleep. Call me if you need anything later. I think I'll run by Christi's for awhile," he said, pulling out a slip of paper and scribbling on it. "Here's the number where you can reach me."

"I have the number right here," the old lady tapped on her temple. "You gave it to me at Christmastime."

"Oh, yes, ma'am. Well, I'll be going now. Do you want me to turn out any of these lamps?" he asked, glancing around the dimly lit, ornate parlor, exquisitely furnished in pre-War antiques.

"No, no. You run along now. I'll be fine."

She watched him walk briskly to the truck, his huge shoulders hunched into the misting rain.

* * *

Christi and Kelly waited impatiently until the prominent couple left for the Warren County Chamber of Commerce dinner, and their maid Nellie Mae had gone with friends to a committee meeting at church. Then they dashed out the back door through the chilling rain to the quarters.

"Pru, it's us. Open up," Christi called, more brightly than she felt.

Prudence opened the door without hesitation, as if she had expected company. Christi and Kelly noted the Bennett's Water Street Garage wall calendar spread open on the tiny kitchen table.

"It's time to talk about this," Kelly stated boldly.

Prudence nodded her agreement, then sat impassively while the blonde girl told her the plan to drive to Memphis and take care of everything.

"Not that we generally approve of abortion," Christi added, shuddering at the word, and making the Sign of the Cross, "but in a case like this..."

The dark face across the table stared back blankly, then contorted in pain.

"But, what if this is Ray's baby?"

"Jesus God!" Kelly gasped. "Is that possible?"

Prudence nodded, looking down at her lap.

"The night before he left, we... I... well, we had talked about getting married... and... but... I... wanted to finish school first... and... I wasn't sure it was right... but... then,... he was going away and I wanted him so badly... and... we... in the car by the river... and... then... two days later, I was walking down there by myself... and... they... oh, God!... What can I do?"

Prudence broke into heavy sobs that wrenched a knot in Christi's stomach. Stunned and helpless at the agony of their friend, Christi and Kelly sat in numb silence, listening to the rain beat down heavily on the quarters' old tin roof.

None of the girls saw even a glimmer of a headlight when the old truck pulled into the Boudreaux's driveway and Grover ran up the front steps in eager anticipation, surprised at his own boldness in arriving unannounced. Seven times, he rang the bell and waited before dejectedly retracing his steps to the truck.

"If only I had married him," Prudence chided herself when the sobbing was over, "then it wouldn't be so bad."

"What if it isn't Ray's baby?"

"It is! It's got to be!" Prudence screamed at the younger girls. "It's all that's left of Ray. It's all I'll ever have!"

"But, what if it isn't?" Kelly insisted.

"It is," Prudence calmed down. "It simply is. And that's final."

"But," Christi began, raising her voice, "what if..."

The splattering rain stopped suddenly and the silence was startling.

Christi sighed and nodded in acquiescence, "Okay, Prudence. It is."

"If only I had married him," the pregnant girl repeated.

"Is that what you would have wanted?"

"Same as you would, if you loved somebody that much. I wish you could understand."

"I do understand, Pru," Kelly nodded, and Prudence sensed that she truly did.

"You know, Ray put me down on all his papers as his wife. He thought that if he believed it enough and acted like it was true, then, somehow, it would happen. He didn't have any other kin, so I guess he really needed to believe... that...

somehow it would happen.... Only, now it's too late... and..."

"Don't you start bawling again, Prudence!" Kelly interrupted. "It's not too late!"

"What are you talking about?" she asked with a frown.

"Well, of course, we can't bring Ray back and you may never have been his legal wife," Kelly paused, "but I've got a hunch that you can be his legal widow." Kelly grinned, nodded, and looked at Christi. "I'm going to give Larry a call."

The tall blonde girl stood up and hooked the wall calendar in place on its nail.

"Yeah, we may be approaching the Ides of March here in Mississippi," Kelly said, tapping her finger on the calendar, "but I've got a sneaky suspicion that it could still be early October somewhere in Louisiana..."

* * *

"Okay, okay, slow down, Racer. Therefore, they're dead. Watson and Shimwell were expendable. I'll miss The Torch, though. He always did good work. Wish I could have seen some of those 'accidental' explosions of his."

"Yeah, but Arnie, it scares me. How did PapaLew put those three together so fast? How'd he figure it out? And, if he does know, then he probably knows it was all your doing, and he'll be after us next."

"You scare too easy. Who said ole Llewellyn had anything to do with this? Maybe the fat guy Watson did have a heart attack. And that bean counter Shimwell? He could'a blown himself away. He never had no guts."

"Yeah, but The Torch? The Torch, Arnie? Hard for me to believe he got that careless," Racer insisted.

"The Torch was way overdue for an accident on the job, as many as he's done around the world," Arnie countered. "It could be just a coincidence. After all, we're talking New Orleans, Jackson, and Houston. Not all in the same town. Three dead guys in three different states don't prove nothing."

The phone rang in the next room, and Racer ran to answer it. When he returned, he was moving slowly, and the color had drained from his face.

"Another dead body?" Arnie asked sarcastically.

"Worse. Turns out that Watson, Shimwell, and The Torch all went out on the same day. All at the same time. The exact same time. That don't sound like no coincidence to me."

"Hmmm," Arnie agreed, shaking his head. "That ain't no coincidence. That's a message from my old friend Georgie."

* * *

March 27, 1964

Dear Maggie,

Things are looking up for Prudence. She's gone back to school, seems to be happy that she's having Ray's baby (I sure hope it is!), and she's gaining back some of the weight she lost. Still skinny, though.

Yesterday, she finally told Nellie Mae that she and Ray had gone over to Louisiana to get married when he was home on leave. Of course, Larry got it all taken care of officially, so she has a certificate and everything. He also gave her a little gold wedding band with 'For always - Ray' engraved inside.

That was thoughtful of Larry. He really isn't such a bad guy. It's too bad that Kelly is so hung up on Cameron that she can't see Larry's good traits. He's crazy about her.

And, speaking of "crazy about," Grover is definitely getting a football scholarship to Ole Miss! I can hardly wait to be there with him! Of course, Kelly thinks that she and Cameron will be going there together too. She can't seem to realize how much Carol Jean Tolbert has her claws into him. Any chance he'll ask Kelly to the Senior Prom? She's actually counting on it. I've got a feeling that's going to be another long night!

Love,
Christi

* * *

Hocking MacMillan Samuels stretched his long, lanky body, and pushed back luxuriously in his green naugahyde desk chair, surveying his new law office with approval. He had a nice view of the Ford County Courthouse, and a ten-second walk to the Tea Shoppe, that he considered the best gathering spot in Clanton, Mississippi.

Not bad for an old country boy raised on the banks of the Yalobusha River, he thought. *And not such an old country boy at that,* he added to himself, caressing the thick moustache from which he periodically removed all traces of gray.

Premature gray, he assured himself. *No harm in a little camouflage at the tender age of forty-six.*

"You have a visitor, Senator. A Mister George Llewellyn is here. Says I can call him PapaLew."

"Here?" he repeated into the intercom.

"Yes, sir."

"Well, don't keep him waiting. Bring him right in. No, I'll be right out," he corrected himself hastily, jumping to his feet and straightening his tie in one motion.

"George, ole buddy, come on in!"

"Big Sam, good to see you. Looking mighty spiffy these days. All that hair and none of it gray," he winked. "Now, who would believe we were ever classmates?" the balding visitor chuckled.

The disconcerting reference to gray hair put the state senator on the defensive. *Damn that George! He always says what I don't want to hear. Wonder what he's after.*

"Well, well, ole buddy, sit down and tell me what's going on in your life."

"I'd have to 'take the Fifth' on that one," PapaLew laughed. "I suspect you would too."

"Not me, ole buddy. I don't even talk to ole Arnie any more. Living clean. Three kids. Couple of hunting dogs. Nice wife."

"Hardly sounds like the famous 'Big Sam' of years past," George commented wryly, hoping he hadn't flinched at the mention of Arnie.

"Time changes a person, ole buddy. Look around. Don't I look respectable?"

"I'm sure you couldn't keep on getting re-elected if you weren't looking respectable, Big Sam," George winked. "Yeah, the fine folks of Mississippi put a lot of stock in respectability. Bet you're a deacon in the church by now."

Sam laughed uneasily. "If I didn't know better, ole buddy, I'd say you been checking up on me."

"Friends have got to look out for friends, Big Sam. You've always known that."

Facing the inevitable, the senator pulled on his mustache and sighed into his hand. "So, what can I do for you, ole buddy? I hear you're doing okay for yourself."

George nodded. "Can't complain, but I'm getting worried about this Viet Nam situation."

"Now, hold on right there, ole buddy. I'm just a state senator. I couldn't go to Washington and stop this thing if I wanted to."

"I'm not interested in the politics of the war. It's good for the economy and that can't hurt me. It might even open up some new Asian business connections."

"Well, then?"

"They keep escalating our troop involvement and I'm getting concerned that a student deferment isn't going to be enough to keep a boy out much longer."

"Is your boy draft age already?"

PapaLew nodded, "And I sure as hell don't want him drafted."

"Whoa, now, ole buddy. That's federal. You don't think I have that kind of power, do you?"

George Llewellyn leaned back in his chair, smiling, and stared at his old poker partner across the desk. The senator squirmed.

"Come on, ole buddy. I'm flattered, but surely you don't think I carry that big a stick."

The impertinent visitor laughed out loud.

"I might not have thought so, Big Sam, until I ran into this sweet little colored gal down in Jackson. Of course, I didn't look at any of the pictures she claims to have," he winked, "but this little ole colored gal swears to me you carry the biggest stick in the state legislature. And, she says you've got the imagination to use it right."

The senator leaned forward in his chair. "Now, ole buddy, you cain't believe everything you hear around the capitol. Besides, we're old friends, and I put a lot of stock in that friendship."

PapaLew rose from his chair slowly. "You're right. I'm gonna forget all about what I heard and I'm gonna rely on that friendship. I know you'll want to do a favor for an old friend," he smiled, laying a piece of paper on the desk and patting it. "It's none of my business how you do it. If it takes more money than you think I've got coming from that friendship, then give me a call. I'm counting on you."

"Wait a minute, ole buddy! You got <u>two</u> names written down here!"

The departing visitor shrugged. "And you've got that big stick, remember? Now, I'm counting on you,... ole buddy."

PART IV

LONG AFTER THE PROM

Chapter 19
July 24, 1968

Helêne Lepeltier Boudreaux stared at the ceiling. She reached toward Clem's side of their comfortable king-sized bed, and felt the loneliness overtake her once more.

He should have been here tonight, she thought. *He's the one who should have been talking to that awful man. Pourquoi moi? Why me? Damn that Vayda. Damn that Clem. How long can this go on?*

She tried to calculate how many years the affair had taken from her marriage.

This is, what? Nineteen-sixty-eight.

She felt funny and unsure after taking some sleeping pills earlier.

Yes, nineteen-sixty-eight. It is nineteen-sixty-eight and I am a grandmother now. My only daughter is going to have another child and I still have not seen the first one because my husband has disowned our child for marrying a hick farmer. Yet, Clem would have been proud to call Grover his son-in-law... if he had stayed at Ole Miss and become the football hero... if he hadn't been injured and left college without even trying any more... if he hadn't taken our precious Christi back to that terrible farm... where she doesn't have a phone... or a car... or any way to get out.... There is no way to get out....

Helêne dozed fitfully for a few minutes and woke with the loneliness pressing on her chest. She reached for the bottle of sleeping pills and took three more. She touched again the empty place on the far side of the bed.

How long? How long with no way to get out? This is nineteen-sixty-what? How long with no way out?

She stared at the ceiling and waited for the sleep that would not come.

I am a grandmother now. I should be happy. I have... what? I have... nothing. I had a daughter... and she is lost to me... as I was lost to my mother... and my daughter has a daughter... and she is lost to me.... I have nothing.... I have nothing.

She reached for the prescription medicine on the night table.

I have nothing.... Je n'ai pas de rien....

* * *

The hotel clerk looked up from his comic book when a tall, redheaded fellow approached the desk.

"I'd like to talk to Miss Dee LaSalla," he said politely.

"You can call her on the house phone," the clerk nodded toward the far wall, "if you have her room number. I can't give out room numbers."

"Please call her for me," the young man asked, placing a twenty-dollar bill on the counter without looking at it. "Tell her that Larry Llewellyn would like to see her for a few minutes, if it wouldn't be an imposition."

The clerk slid the money across the desk and into his pocket without taking his eyes off Larry, then picked up the phone and repeated Larry's message.

"Suite six hundred. You can go right up," the clerk grinned, hanging up the receiver.

Larry put another twenty on the counter.

"I wasn't here."

The clerk nodded, smiled, and picked up the twenty along with his comic book.

Hmmm, he chuckled to himself as Larry headed for the elevator, *ain't nobody here tonight.*

* * *

Clement Boudreaux huffed up the hotel's back stairway carrying flowers and champagne, and feeling very foolish.

Women can take to the damnedest notions about romance and anniversaries. Well, nine years is something, he mused on the second landing. *Who would have thought it? Nine years of screwing the same secretary. Now, that is something.*

He congratulated himself on the next landing, and paused to catch his breath.

Pretty slick to carry it off all this time without Helêne or anybody else noticing. And they say that everybody knows your business in a small town. Humph! Nobody knows any of Clem Boudreaux's business unless he has a mind to tell them.

He stopped on the fourth landing, put the champagne bottle on the floor, leaned against the wall, and massaged his calves.

Whew! Getting a little winded. There's that pain in the chest again, but the doctor said it was probably nothing. Just stress. Maybe a little out of shape, but not too bad for a grandfather.

Clem frowned and pursed his lips, thinking about the grandbaby he couldn't see because he'd popped off his mouth and disowned his only child.

Damn! If I just knew how to take it back. Well, it's the girl's own fault. She's too pig-headed to ask my forgiveness for marrying that lummox.

Clem resolutely began the next climb, heavier and slower, resting again on the fifth landing, where he remembered the champagne bottle sitting on the lower floor.

Damn!

He tromped back to retrieve it, then braced himself for two more flights.

* * *

Miss Dee LaSalla studied her generous body in the bathroom mirror and smiled her hoped-to-be-famous smile.

Still passing for early twenties, she convinced herself, leaning closer to the mirror and checking her brunette hair for signs of premature gray. She plucked out a few offenders from their roots. Then she straightened up and thrust out her ample bosom, straining the clasp on her pink chiffon robe.

The phone rang and she was amused to hear who was coming up to visit. She picked up the nearly empty ice bucket and hurried down the hall to refill it.

* * *

Clem Boudreaux cautiously opened the stairwell door, was momentarily relieved to see an empty hallway stretching out before him, and then was startled by the sight of a large pink-chiffoned rump protruding from the ice machine niche.

"Vayda?" he whispered, nervously fingering the champagne bottle.

The rump instantly materialized into the fully erect, voluptuous body of Miss Dee LaSalla.

"Oh, excuse me, Miss, I thought you were somebody else," the embarrassed man mumbled.

"Obviously," the woman replied, cocking her head slightly, and raising an eyebrow.

The two stared at each other a moment. The woman recovered first. A wry smile softened her features, and she chuckled lightly at his look of panic.

"Mississippi," she crooned in her low sexy voice. "If it isn't ole Mississippi, as I live and breathe. Where have you been so long, and what are you doing here?"

"I live here," he relied lamely, with a sigh of relief.

Dee laughed. It was a gentle, understanding laugh.

"And you thought that I'd come to get you where you live?" She shook her head, "No, Mississippi. I'm here to sing at some parties this weekend. You should know the boys don't send lounge singers to collect on gambling debts."

Clem shrugged his shoulders weakly and became acutely aware of the champagne and flowers he was carrying. Dee glanced knowingly at the label.

"Not a very good year," she frowned. "I'm sorry things aren't going so well. I always hate to lose a fan."

Down the hall, an elevator door opened. A young man stepped out and glanced at the two of them.

"Shit!" Clem exclaimed. "Oh, shit!"

"Don't worry about him, Mississippi. He's my guest for the evening. Hope to see you around."

Clem stood speechless as Dee approached the intruder.

"You must be Larry," she crooned, handing him the ice bucket and linking her arm around his. "Your daddy's told me a lot about you."

Larry was mesmerized by the lovely woman of indeterminate age. He glanced over his shoulder to see Christi's father disappear into a south-facing room, then was drawn back by the silky voice.

"Friend of yours?" she asked.

"Clem Boudreaux," Larry nodded. "He's the father of my wife's best friend."

"Wonder what he's doing here," she whispered.

"Banging his secretary."

"Why not at the office?"

"Oh," Larry chuckled, "every summer, late July, they meet here for their anniversary. He sneaks up the back stairs with flowers and champagne. A regular ritual, now, but from that red face, it looks like the old boy should have reserved a room on a lower floor."

"How do you know so much about it?" she asked.

Larry shrugged. "Everybody in Vicksburg knows. There's not many secrets in a town this small."

Dee pushed open the door she had left ajar, and took the ice bucket from Larry. He followed her into the room without speaking.

"Your daddy's a very, very special friend of mine," Dee confided, setting the ice bucket on a table. She walked around behind him toward the still-open entry. "He tells me that you'll be celebrating an anniversary this week," she continued, gently closing and bolting the door. "So, Larry," she turned back to him with a smile, "tell me just exactly what you'd like as your anniversary present."

Chapter 20
July 25, 1968

Christi knew there was something terribly wrong long before she heard the sheriff's patrol car clatter across the cattle guard and come to a dusty halt in the front yard. All morning she had had a sense of uneasiness that could not be attributed to her uncomfortable pregnancy, nor to last night's horrible fight with Grover. This was a foreboding far deeper than her usual worries about their precarious financial situation and bleak prospects on the farm.

She opened the squeaky door and led the baby out onto the porch. The stocky, uniformed figure of Nick Nichols emerged from his air-conditioned car into the sweltering heat and humidity. He nodded grimly, jaw set tightly, as he approached the house.

My God, Grover's been in a wreck, Christi shuddered.

She was afraid she was going to faint. Sensing her mother's distress, little Angelica began whimpering, but Christi barely noticed. The young mother leaned back against the paintless doorframe for support.

* * *

Jody French leaned back luxuriously in his comfortable desk chair, and took a moment to relax. The young mulatto surveyed his air-conditioned office with pride, enjoying the marine and brass motif. He especially lingered over his nicely framed eight-by-ten pictures with celebrities who had taken time from their busy schedules in New Orleans for a leisurely jaunt on the club's "courtesy cruiser."

The Crescent City Yachting Club and Marina had become a tonier place to berth a boat since Mr. Llewellyn, PapaLew, had bought it and turned over the management to Jody four years ago. Jody had been surprised at his own managerial abilities, and his flair for dealing with the wealthy clientele. He had thrived, and extended himself to the maximum under the free rein and seemingly limitless confidence that PapaLew handed him. Whenever Jody wanted to expand into a related field, the money and a green flag awaited him.

With the commissions Jody earned from yacht brokering, he had first bought the little house he shared with his younger brother, then started acquiring the surrounding rental property under an assumed name as the run-down shotgun dwellings became available. It did not offend his conscience at all to be a slumlord because he still lived in the slum himself and he did make occasional repairs if they were critical, which is more than he could say for the previous owners, most of whom shared the same last names, either "Inc." or "Ltd."

Jody shivered involuntarily, though, when he looked out the big picture window toward the new section of the marina where *La Muestra II* sparkled in the sunlight. The only disagreement he and PapaLew ever had was over the naming of that boat.

"My sister was killed on *La Muestra*!" Jody had shouted at his new boss. "I don't want to be reminded of it!"

"Yes, Jody," PapaLew had replied more gently than he usually spoke, "Tawanya was killed on *La Muestra* and I don't want either of us ever to forget that."

"But you didn't scrape her blood off the hull, like I did!" Jody had insisted. "How could I ever forget?"

And I might have been able to save her, George Llewellyn had silently rebuked himself, but Jody could not read his mind. All the distraught young man had heard was, "We remember what we want to remember, Jody. That's how we stay sane… or drive ourselves crazy."

Then the older man's patience ran out when Jody had asked, "So, what was Tawanya to you, that you even care to remember?"

PapaLew had shouted the last words yet spoken between them about the dead girl, "God damn it, son, if it mattered, I still wouldn't tell you!"

"Your brother's here, Jody."

The intercom startled the young man from his reverie, and he proudly pushed the button to reply, "Send him in."

"All set to go?" Jody asked as his brother's grinning face peeked around the door.

Naboth nodded.

Jody came around from behind his desk and gave his skinny brother a bear hug.

"Wish I could take you to the airport."

"It's okay," Naboth answered. For a moment, the thirteen-year-old mulatto seemed the elder of the two. "I'll see you at Christmas."

The brothers felt awkward, faced with separation for the first time in their lives. Jody, older by seven years, was the only father figure Naboth had ever known. With their mother dead of a drug overdose many years before, and Tawanya gone, the two boys had relied on each other more than they ever acknowledged.

"I still think you're a bit small to be going out for football up there," Jody advised for the hundredth time. "Oh, well, call me every week, collect, and let me know how they're treating you."

"Sure thing, bro," Naboth promised, looking at his watch. "Cab's waiting. I'm outa here." He stuck out his hand for their ritual handshake. Jody responded in kind, then hugged his brother, and hurriedly pushed him toward the door.

"I've gotta get back to work," Jody explained brusquely, to fight back any chance of tears. "Somebody's gotta pay the tab for that fancy prep school," he complained, gently shoving his brother out the door and closing it behind him.

Jody was sure he could have made it through the day without crying, if Naboth hadn't reappeared a moment later, just long enough to say, "I love you, Jody," before he ran for the cab.

* * *

"God damn it, woman, you are not going to start this day with a drink!" George Llewellyn shouted at his wife.

The sleepy redhead shrugged her shoulders and continued to pour the vodka into her orange juice.

"Did you hear me, God damn it?" he bellowed as he grabbed the bottle from her hand and hurled it through the kitchen window into the backyard.

The shattering of glass so near jolted the woman momentarily, then she smiled at her husband.

"Ahh, George, just like old times at home. You remind me so much of my daddy when you get mad."

Nothing that Cassiopeia could say would have inflamed him more than her reference to the old doctor they both hated for different reasons.

Cassi opened the cabinet door and casually reached for another fifth. This time, George grabbed her arm and jerked her around to face him as he sent the bottle hurtling after the first one.

"God damn it, woman! I am serious this time. Guests are coming in tonight. You will be sober when we greet them on the riverboat. You will be sober when we get off the riverboat. You will be sober tomorrow at the luncheon and golf tournament. And, most assuredly, my dear," he lowered his voice and twisted her arm, "you will be sober for our son's anniversary party on Saturday night. After that, you can drink your fucking ass into the grave with your precious father for all I care. I'm finished with you!"

With the last bitter words, he shoved her against the wall and stormed out of the room.

"Madras!" he shouted.

"Yes, suh," the big black woman appeared out of nowhere.

"Miss Cassiopeia is not to have anything to drink until we get home from the party on Saturday night. Do you understand me?" he glared viciously into her wide shining face.

"Oh, yes, suh."

He moved closer to her and lowered his voice.

"We've been through this before, Madras, and I realize that you've been taking care of Miss Cassi since she was a baby, but she is a sick woman… and she is smarter than you. Now, the last time, she tricked you. This time, you do not leave her for a minute. You go to the bathroom with her. You do not take your eyes off her. Do you understand?"

"Yes, suh. Oh, yes, suh."

"And, if by chance, sometime before Saturday night, Miss Cassiopeia Livingston Llewellyn gets hold of a drink," he said menacingly, grabbing the old black woman's big uniformed arm, "I am personally going to haul you all the way back to Louisiana to the Big Osprey Bayou and feed your worthless nigger ass to the goddamned alligators. Do you understand that?"

"Yes, suh. Oh, yes, suh. Ah unduhstayun!"

"Then get in there and watch her! Now!"

Chapter 21
July 25, 1968

Christi breathed a sigh of relief when the deputy asked to see Grover, and she silently thanked God that he hadn't been in an accident after all.

"Come on in and have some lemonade," she smiled at Nick Nichols, and opened the screen door for Angelica to toddle back inside.

"I'm afraid this isn't a social call," the young deputy demurred, removing his hat and wiping his brow as he strode across the porch.

"No matter," Christi replied lightly.

If Grover's not hurt, she thought, *what could be so bad? Probably one of the cows got out on the county road again.*

"The baby's thirsty anyway," she added.

The deputy followed her into the house and stood staring at the painting above the fireplace while Christi went to the kitchen and poured lemonade.

"I'm no connoisseur," he called into the next room, "but this looks like a right fair piece of art. I would've sworn those yellow roses were real."

"Grover painted that for me," Christi beamed, returning and handing the deputy his lemonade, "to commemorate a special occasion. My parents liked it so much that they had it matted and framed. My mother said it was as fine as many paintings in Paris."

"Hmmm," the deputy mused aloud, "just goes to show you can't always tell a book by its cover. I never would've figured Grover for an artist."

They all sipped their lemonades silently for a few minutes.

"Do you expect him back soon?" Nichols asked hopefully.

"Not until tonight. He and Paw left really early to drive to Jackson to pick up a hog. I don't know why it took the two of them, but they'll be all day about it, I expect. Is there something I can do for you?" Christi offered.

Nick Nichols drained his lemonade glass and looked around for a place to put it.

"Anywhere's fine."

"Look, Christi," the lawman said softly, putting the glass on the floor, "I didn't come here to see Grover. I was just hoping he'd be here to make this a little easier on you, but I'm afraid it can't wait until he gets back."

Christi's earlier discomfort returned and she leaned forward anxiously.

"Tell me straight out. What is it?"

"It's your father. He's..."

"Oh, my God! A car wreck! Is he alright?"

The deputy clenched his solid jaw and slowly shook his head. "I'm sorry, honey.... He's dead.... He was murdered."

Christi felt the blood drain from her face. Suddenly, the floor under her seemed to give way and she sank through a huge, gaping hole, falling helplessly down and down until she was floating in space with darkness all around her.

Then she blinked her eyes open and she was sitting on the sofa where she had been and there was no hole in the old linoleum floor and she wasn't falling anywhere and Nick Nichols was standing beside her with his strong hand on her shoulder, saying gently, "I'm sorry. I am so sorry."

Christi was too numb to think, but she heard a voice that sounded vaguely like her own asking, "When?... How?..."

"We won't know much until we get the coroner's report, but it appears to have happened early this morning. Bubba's hound came across them in the clearing behind Wayside Baptist Church and ran back to the house raising such a ruckus that Bubba followed after him to see about it. Otherwise, they might have been there undiscovered until Sunday."

"They?... You said 'they"... My mother too?" Christi gasped.

"No, thank God, not your mother. It appears to be your father's secretary, Vayda Jander, but there was no identification on her."

"'Appears to be?'" Christi frowned. "What do you mean, 'appears to be?'"

"Honey, it's pretty messy out there. It appears to be Miss Jander."

"It's Mrs. Jander," Christi corrected him, "the whore. I was always afraid she'd be the death of him, but I never expected anything like this."

"We don't know anything yet, Christi. Why don't you pack up the baby and ride into town with me? I've gotta go tell your mama now. I would've gone there first, but you were so close by, and without a phone and all...."

Nichols helped the pregnant young woman to her feet and picked up the baby, who sucked her thumb and stared at him silently.

"Leave Grover a note that you'll be at your mother's. I'm afraid he'll probably hear about this on the radio before he gets back."

"Probably not," Christi shook her head and muttered half to herself as she looked for some paper and began scribbling a note to her husband. "The truck radio's broken, just like everything else around here." She looked at the living room with distaste, deliberately left the lemonade glasses where they sat, and headed for the front door.

The trio drove to town in silence.

* * *

In suite six hundred of Vicksburg's finest hotel, Dee LaSalla smiled a wasted smile at the lanky redheaded young man who lay sleeping beside her.

Must be hereditary, she mused, thinking back on the past twelve hours. Every time she had stirred in the bed, he would be aroused and ready.

Gonna make his wife a good lover when he settles down a bit, she thought, and then chuckled lightly to herself, trying to picture the boy's daddy ever settling down.

The slight movement of her voluptuous body amplified across the bed and Larry half opened his eyes as he reached for her again.

* * *

Mississippi State Senator Hocking MacMillan Samuels was too excited about the impending trip to Vicksburg to make a pretense of going to the office this Thursday. He loaded the luggage, three sons and wife in the new station wagon he had bought her, and headed out of Clanton mid-morning.

He figured on checking into the Vicksburg Hotel early to get the full benefit of the daily room rate and to mingle with folks arriving from all over the state, even from out of state and Washington, D.C. Rumor had it that this would be the biggest party Mississippi might ever see, and Big Sam wasn't about to miss a minute of opportunity. His pulse quickened as he contemplated the numbers.

Most likely better than Memorial Day, the Fourth of July, and Labor Day picnics all rolled into one. And, quality people. These will be quality people.

Big Sam could hardly wait to introduce his three fine sons around. For a moment, he paused to remember the two names ole George had given him a couple of years earlier.

Can't say I blame him, using his money and influence where he can to keep his boy from getting blown up in Viet Nam, but what kind of connection could he have to that boy in New Orleans? Maybe I oughta check on that a little more.

Oh, well, I've done my part. Those boys are safe from the draft.

Best to forget about it now. Just hope it doesn't come back to bite me in the ass. That George has some nerve, expecting me to mess with the draft board.

But hell, I'd do the same thing for my boys, Big Sam thought self-righteously, and glanced at the three of them in his rear view mirror, sitting straight and erect, sensing their father's excitement about the upcoming events.

Big Sam could see only himself in each of his sons, and gave no credit, consciously or otherwise, to the contributions of his wife, as if the three healthy male specimens had sprung fully grown from the tool box in the back of his Chevrolet pick-up truck.

The senator was suddenly so overcome with pride and enthusiasm for life that, as he turned onto Highway 61 and headed south toward Vicksburg, he startled everyone in the car by calling out, "What a beautiful day! Let's all praise God in song!

'I wish I was in the land of cotton, Old times there are not forgotten, Look away, Look away, Look away, Dixie Land...'"

* * *

"Something's wrong," Christi's voice shook as the patrol car glided to a stop in front of the historic Boudreaux home.

The deputy's observant eyes took in the details — shades drawn, porch light on, newspaper on the sidewalk.

"You don't suppose that whoever..." Christi began tentatively, opening her own car door.

"Don't borrow trouble, honey," he tried to reassure her, but it didn't come from his heart. He picked up the baby and followed Christi up the walk, surreptitiously flipping up the leather strip that held his gun in place.

They waited what seemed an eternity to Christi for someone to answer the bell. After the fourth time, the deputy asked if she had a key.

"I might, if they didn't change the locks," Christi answered nervously, digging into her purse for her key ring. She found it, but couldn't get the key to go in.

"Here, let me try it," Nichols offered, noticing how nervous she was. He handed Angelica to her mother.

The door opened easily.

"Mama," Christi called, crossing the threshold. "Mama?"

Eerie silence was the only answer.

"Christi, I want you and the baby to sit here while I search the house," the deputy ordered gently.

Christi nodded numbly and followed his instructions. She looked dispassionately around the parlor. Every article was in the same place it had been throughout her childhood. Throughout her daddy's childhood too. And his father's before him. Nothing ever changed in the Boudreaux house.

Angelica sucked her thumb and observed the same room. Suddenly, Christi was overcome with anguish that her own daughter had never been in this house until today - had never met her grandparents, would never know her grandfather.

Christi clutched her daughter for comfort, when what she really wanted was for her own dear mother to hold her in a warm embrace and whisper that everything would be alright. The look on Nick Nichols' face when he returned told her that that would never happen.

"Don't tell me they got my mother too!"

"I'm sorry, Christi."

"I want to see her."

"She wasn't murdered. At least, not with a gun. There's an empty vial of prescription sleeping pills on the floor by the bed. You can go up there if you want to, but I wouldn't advise it, especially not in your condition. I'd say she's been dead eight or ten hours. Maybe more."

Christi started to get up, then sank back down into the old velvet sofa, the blood draining from her face.

"What do I do now?" she asked helplessly.

"Sit here while I make a couple of phone calls. Is there someone you'd like me to call to come be with you?"

Christi's mind wouldn't cooperate. She frowned.

Who are my friends? Where is everybody? How long have I been out on the farm without any company except Grover and Paw and the baby?

She stared at the young deputy blankly.

"You shouldn't be here alone. What about Kelly Llewellyn?" he offered. "Isn't she your best friend?"

Christi nodded assent, and Nichols quickly left the room to make the necessary phone calls in private. The young mother held her baby tightly and rocked silently from side to side on the Boudreaux family's vintage velvet sofa.

* * *

Across the Pacific Ocean, inland from the South China Sea, in the tiny village of Phú Nhuân, South Viet Nam, a young woman tossed fitfully, trying to get to sleep as the sound of exploding mortars violated the starry Asian sky. Nguyen Nhi Li closed her almond eyes and prayed fervently to the gods of her ancestors that nothing would spoil the sweet dawning of her long-awaited wedding day.

Chapter 22
July 26, 1968

"God damn it, boy!" George Llewellyn shouted at his visitor. "This is a fucking bad omen!" He slammed the newspaper down on his desk. "God damn it!..."

Jody French picked up the Friday morning issue of the *Vicksburg Daily Chronicle* and read the bold headline, "PROMINENT BUSINESSMAN SLAIN; SECRETARY SHOT; WIFE DEAD OF OVERDOSE."

"A fucking bad omen!..."

Jody watched the older man pacing the room, glanced through the article for more details, and realized that he had heard all the facts and more at the riverboat party last night. Apparently, there hadn't been this much excitement in Vicksburg since The Siege.

Everyone in town knew Clem and Helêne Boudreaux, that is, everyone who would have been invited to the Llewellyns' anniversary festivities, and all of them were uncomfortable with the unfortunate juxtaposition of two of the more gossip-spawning events in modern Vicksburg history.

Even those very close friends who might have been in real mourning over the deaths of Helêne and Clem (and what's-her-name, the secretary) could not force themselves to miss the gala party on the riverboat, convincing themselves that life is for the living and that Helêne and Clem, if surveyed, would have heartily endorsed participation in the celebration. So, the turn-out had been unaffected by the tragedy, except that most of the guests talked louder, drank more, and stayed later than they otherwise would have on another Thursday night when the threat of their own mortality didn't hang so heavily in the humid night air.

Jody's musing and George's pacing were interrupted by the secretary's announcement over the intercom, "Your daughter-in-law is here to see you, Mr. Llewellyn."

"God damn it!" the older man mumbled under his breath. "I was afraid of this."

"I'll wait outside," Jody nodded deferentially and opened the door for the beautiful blonde visitor. *What money can buy,* he pondered as he held the door for Kelly. "Good morning, Miz Llewellyn. If you'll excuse me, I was just leaving."

* * *

"I tell you what, Dep'ty, I'm gonna let you handle this entire investigation outa the sheriff's office," Vicksburg's police chief told Nichols by phone. "The murders happened in the county, at least the bodies were found there. We don't have any evidence of foul play in the wife's overdose, so no point in getting both the county and the city jurisdictions wrapped up in this mess. You handle it out of Warren County, and we'll cooperate if we get anything.... Sure....

"Oh, by the way," the police chief added, "I heard that Grover Jones got drunk at The Levee last Saturday night. Seems he spouted off that for two cents he'd blow away that rotten son-of-a-bitch Clem Boudreaux. The kid's known to carry a thirty-eight. You might want to check it out, Dep'ty."

* * *

Kelly McCain Llewellyn paused uncertainly in the office doorway, confused about her next move, as though she had planned her actions carefully and had now forgotten her lines. George Llewellyn stared across the room at her, as if seeing her for the first time.

My God, she is beautiful! he thought, and suddenly he was back in high school, dressed in his shabby farmer's-son clothing, gazing at the head cheerleader with an aching in his body and no way to close the gap between them. The silence grew uncomfortable for both of them. The girl recovered first.

"PapaLew," she began tentatively, "I... we..."

George Llewellyn took a step toward her and opened his arms in an awkward gesture. He had held innumerable women in his lifetime, but he had no experience with the proper hug for a grieving daughter-in-law. The girl ignored his gesture and sat in one of the large leather wing chairs facing the desk.

"We have to talk," she said with assurance, now remembering her prepared speech. He nodded and sat uneasily on the corner of his desk, looking down at her, needing the height advantage to maintain control.

"Alright, Kelly," he smiled lamely, "talk."

"PapaLew, I know you've gone to a lot of trouble and expense for this anniversary party, but I can't go through with it."

"Now, Kelly, I understand how you feel," he interrupted. "Clem Boudreaux was one of my best friends. Hell, we were in college together. Played poker. Got drunk. Chased whores. 'Scuse me, hon, I shouldn't have said that. I mean, God damn it, I know how you feel. Have you been talking with Christi about this? What did she say?"

"She said that I shouldn't let her family tragedy destroy the anniversary of the happiest day of my life."

"Well, there you have it, then."

"But, PapaLew," Kelly added pleadingly, "that isn't all there is to it. My wedding day was not the happiest day of my life. I didn't feel that way about it. I didn't love Larry enough to marry him. As much as he screws around, he probably didn't love me either. I don't really know how it all happened, but it wasn't fair to either of us."

"Fair? God damn it, girl, what's 'fair' got to do with any of this? You and Larry have a lot in common and you're good together. You've got two wonderful little daughters. You'll have more. This notion of love is just so much romantic nonsense. A bunch of Hollywood hype. Your mama even told me that she wasn't really in love with your daddy when she married him, but he cared about her and she knew he would take care of her. Now, that worked out fine for them, you gotta admit that. I think Larry offers you as much. Don't you agree?"

"Well, in a way, but…"

"Now, Kelly, it's natural to get upset when people close to you die. It colors your perception of everything else. This is a goddamn awful tragedy with your friends and I can see how you feel. Let me get our doctor to prescribe something to calm your nerves. You'll get through this like a trooper. I know you will. You're strong. Now, isn't that right?"

Kelly nodded, but realized that something had gone wrong. She frowned, but couldn't think of anything else to say.

George Llewellyn eased off the desk and walked toward her, ending the conversation. He placed an uncertain hand on her shoulder.

"We'll get you something for your nerves. And be sure to let me know if there's anything I can do for your friend Christi. We're all in this together now. Isn't that right, girl?"

The girl looked up at him with the softest, saddest, pale green eyes.

* * *

Christi woke up late and blinked in surprise to find herself in her lovely yellow bedroom in her big four-poster bed.

"Oh, God!" she whispered aloud. "I've had the worst nightmares."

Her mind flashed back to visions of a freshman year at Ole Miss, Grover's knee injury, moving out to the Jones' farm, being disowned by her father, giving birth to a daughter, the sheriff telling her that her father was dead, then her mother.

The door chimes that had awakened her rang again.

"Why isn't Mama answering the door?" she muttered half aloud. She threw back the light cover and reached for her robe.

As she sat up, the baby she was carrying gave a strong kick, bringing Christi's mind into sharp focus and present reality. She put both hands on her expanding abdomen and squinted her eyes tightly to keep from crying. Then she put on the robe and started down the stairs. Grover, holding Angelica, was opening the front door for Nick Nichols.

"Morning, Sheriff," Grover drawled amiably to the deputy who would never be sheriff. "Come on in. Coffee's on."

"I'm afraid this isn't a social call, Grover," the uniformed officer said gravely. "I need to ask you a few questions about your relationship with Clem Boudreaux and the whereabouts of your thirty-eight special. It might be more convenient if you come on down to the office with me."

Christi froze on the stairway, listening to the conversation.

At the sound of the deputy's suspicions, she ran down the stairs, screaming at Nichols, "What are you saying? Surely, you don't think Grover had anything to do with this!"

Angelica started crying and Grover automatically handed her to her mother.

Ignoring her outburst, Nichols calmly addressed Grover, "I can wait here until you get someone to come stay with Christi and the baby. They shouldn't be left alone."

"I'll call the next-door neighbor," Grover nodded. Then he turned to Christi. "Calm down, honey. I'm sure it's nothing I can't explain. The sheriff's just doing his job. It'll be okay," he finished, but he didn't sound convincing.

Christi glared at the man who had brought all this misery into her life.

"How can you do this, Sheriff?" she pleaded through clenched teeth. "You think Grover looks like a murderer?"

Christi turned and ran for her room, carrying her crying baby.

The deputy sheriff watched her disappear up the stairway.

"I didn't think he looked like an artist, either," he mumbled sadly to himself.

* * *

Friday, July 26, 1968

Dear Kelly,

It was more than kind of you to remember my little Ray's birthday in the midst of all that's going on there. He really loves the shiny red fire truck and feels so competent that he can work the pedals and make it go. Thank you for the perfect gift!

I'm sure that Ray would join me in saying we wish you could have stayed for a longer visit. It gets lonely here in Jackson, with everybody else still in Vicksburg.

Of course, I heard about Christi's folks yesterday. It was all over the news. I took a quick trip over there last night, just to offer my condolences in person. This morning, I've been trying to compose something to her, but I haven't found the right words yet. I feel so bad for Christi, and for you, too. I know you were practically a member of the family. Please accept my deepest sympathy, and let me know if you think of anything I can do for Christi, or you.

Fondly,
Prudence

* * *

Kelly was gracious, but subdued for the ladies luncheon at the club. She begged off the golf tournament, citing the heat and the need to go comfort Christi. A sense of depression plagued her into Saturday, enough to allow her to stare flagrantly at Cameron Coulter throughout the entire evening of her anniversary party.

More than one person at the elaborate gathering, in addition to her redheaded husband, observed her obvious lust for the recent college graduate who was home for only a few weeks. Kelly shamelessly followed him with her eyes all night. She directed most of her conversation to him. When they danced, she pressed her body scandalously close.

And, finally, as the evening drew to an end, with friends and couples leaving arm-in-arm, Kelly squeezed Cameron's elbow and whispered in his ear, "I want you!" She was looking over his shoulder as she said it, well aware that the only person observing this particular interchange and close enough to hear exactly what she said was the evening's genial and generous host, George Llewellyn.

* * *

"I'm sorry, Mr. Jones. There was nothing we could do for your grandmother. It was, in layman's terms, a massive heart attack."

"Miss Fennstemmacher isn't, wasn't, my grandmother. She was... my... friend." Grover stared at the stranger in the white lab coat, hoping for something.

"Well, then, I suggest you call her relatives and let them make the necessary arrangements."

"But Doctor, I don't even know her relatives. She didn't have any in Vicksburg. She might not have any at all."

"Perhaps her lawyer, then. If you will excuse me, Mr. Jones, I'm being paged."

"Yes, of course. Thank you. I'm sure you did all you could."

"There was nothing we could do. I'm sorry."

Grover walked in a daze through the glaring sterile corridor of the hospital and out the emergency entrance double doors to the dimly lighted lot where his old pick-up truck was parked. He got in the driver's seat, started the engine, and drove off into the black night, not knowing where to go or what to do.

* * *

Half a world away from Vicksburg, in the village of Đó Thanh, less than three kilometers from her home village of Phú Nhuân, the young bride Minh Nhi Li awoke early in the hut of her new husband's family. She smiled with the joy of beginning a life with the man she loved, and reached tentatively to touch his shoulder.

Minh Khoi Tien slowly opened his eyes and breathed a sigh of thanksgiving for the beautiful, untouched flower that had been entrusted to his care. The hope and the future of the Minh family gazed silently at each other in the dimness of dawn, then rose wordlessly from their mat to share the pleasant ritual of morning tea.

Chapter 23
July 30, 1968

Lucky Jones settled his large body uneasily into the ancient leather armchair across the desk from Nick Nichols. Lucky stared at the dust particles dancing in the early morning sunlight streaming into the small office. He tried to relax.

"Cigarette?" the deputy sheriff offered.

"Thanks," Lucky nodded, reaching across the old wooden desk to pull one from the pack. The two men lit their cigarettes and surveyed each other in silence.

Lucky spoke first.

"I guess you wouldn'ta hauled me in here if you'da b'lieved my boy's story, but I do appreciate you waitin' til after the funerals."

The deputy nodded in acknowledgement, pursed his lips, took another draw on his cigarette, and said nothing.

"Me and Grover done been over this a half dozen times. We got explanations for all yore questions."

The deputy nodded again, but didn't speak.

"Grover's plenty mad at me already 'bout that gun of his. Look, Sheriff, when he told you he left his thirty-eight in a wooden box on the front closet shelf, that was the Gawd's truth. I needed some money bad, so I tuk that gun to Jackson to hawk it. I didn't never tell him 'bout it."

"Got a pawn ticket on it?"

Lucky shifted again in his chair and looked around the small office, as if hoping to see a way out.

"Now, Sheriff, I didn't actually pawn the gun. I sold it outright."

"So, the pawn shop owner will have a record of it?"

Lucky nervously crushed out his cigarette in the overflowing ashtray.

"This here's the rub. I didn't never go into the pawnshop. I got there 'fore it opened, and was just settin' in the truck waitin' for them t'open up. Then, this here guy pulls up and gits outa his car headin' for the door, and I figure it's the owner, so I git outa my truck and go up and say 'mornin' to the guy. Well, turns out he don't own the shop or even work there, but's just a customer, like me, so, me and him stands around awhile shootin' the shit, and smokin' a coupla cigarettes, and turns out he's gotta mind to buy a twenty-five.

"Well, naturally, I start talkin' up a thirty-eight, that anybody knows is a better gun, and 'fore long, he's convinced he's gotta have a thirty-eight. Now, all this time, I ain't never told him that I'm there to hawk somethin' cause I got my pride, so, I says, 'I got a thirty-eight I'll just sell you, since I got a whole shitload of 'em at home.'

"Now, I know I shouldn'ta lied to him like that, Sheriff, but it just come outa my mouth, and next thing I know, I got Grover's thirty-eight out the truck and put that guy's money in my pocket."

"Did you get his name? Sign over the papers proper-like?"

Lucky writhed in agony and hung his head.

"I never had no papers on that gun. Anyway, it was Grover's gun, and he never had no papers on it neither. Now, Sheriff, you know for a fact that half the guns in Warren County ain't got no papers on 'em."

More like ninety-five percent, the young lawman considered to himself, but said nothing to Lefty.

"'Course, that's a crime, too, I guess. Me and Grover's guilty o'that, alright, but Sheriff, we ain't never killed nobody. We's just as sorry to hear 'bout Christi's folks as anybody. More than most. Why, me and them's got the same grandbaby."

"Did y'all see each other often?"

"Now, Sheriff, ever'body in Vicksburg knows that Clem Boudreaux disowned that girl when they left Ole Miss and she come back to the farm with Grover. Why would you even ask me that?"

"A neighbor saw your truck in front of the Boudreaux house late Wednesday night, about the time the coroner figured Miz Boudreaux took those sleeping pills. The neighbor said that a big man wearing bib overalls went up and rang the bell, then went inside when the door opened."

Lucky looked down at the bib overalls he was wearing, then back over at Nick Nichols. "They sure it was my truck?"

The deputy nodded. "Even jotted down the license number, since it was so late, just in case there was trouble."

Lucky turned pale and said nothing. Nichols continued.

"Grover didn't tell me you went to the Boudreaux house. He said you were asleep Wednesday night when he and Christi had an argument about money. The next morning, you and Grover were supposedly going in to Jackson for the day, but the truck broke down and you never got there. He said y'all fixed it yourselves. No one knows where either of you were at the time of the killings, or for most of the day.

"You must realize, of course, that with Christi's parents both dead, she'd stand to get that big house, the car dealerships, and whatever else there is. By your own admission, you were having financial difficulties, so, there was definite motive. Not to mention Grover popping off at The Levee last week that for two cents he'd kill Clem Boudreaux. Then, Clem gets shot with a thirty-eight, and you say you sold Grover's thirty-eight to some stranger in front of a pawnshop....

"Now, you tell me, Lucky, if you were sitting in a jury box and heard such a bullshit story, what would you think?"

Lucky squirmed again in his chair and stared at his hands for a full minute. When he finally spoke, his voice cracked.

"Let me have another cigarette, Sheriff.... I'll tell you the whole story."

Nick Nichols tossed the nearly empty pack across the desk, leaned back in his chair, and waited.

Chapter 24
July 31, 1968

Cassiopeia Llewellyn heard the poolside phone ring as a distant bell in the fog. When it stopped, she slowly turned her head toward the ghost of its sound, and opened one eye. The underwater pool lights reflected harshly against the midnight sky and, with a mild grimace of discomfort, she closed her eye to their glare.

Dimly, she became aware of a mosquito on her cheek, and made a feeble gesture to brush it away. The uncalculated movement knocked her glass of melted ice from the chaise lounge armrest onto the flagstone decking.

The explosion of shattering crystal somewhat roused the drunken woman from her stupor, and brought George to the balcony overlooking the pool. He cautiously opened one of the French doors, stepped outside in the shadow of the overhang, and saw his wife sprawled on the lounge below, not twenty feet away.

"God damn it, you drunken bitch! Are you trying to wake up the whole goddamn neighborhood?"

Through her fog, Cassiopeia thought she heard a familiar voice. Slowly she turned her head toward the sound, and struggled to gain consciousness.

"Do you hear me, you goddamn bitch?... Do you hear me?" he shouted louder.

"Daddy?" she mumbled in a childlike voice. "Daddy, is that you?"

George stepped toward the low railing and leaned over to hear her response.

"God damn it, bitch, speak up. What did you say?"

Cassiopeia moaned softly and tried to turn on her side.

"Daddy?" she whimpered softly. "Daddy, is that you?"

Suddenly, Cassi's body jerked rigid and she let out a dry, muffled scream.

"Blood! Oh, Daddy, there's blood everywhere!"

Her cry instantly shocked George back to that horrible night in New Orleans, when he had driven Elva Jean to the doctor's back-street clinic for a simple, though illegal, abortion. They had laughed and joked on the way over, deliberately not discussing any further the serious matter at hand. George remembered parking the car and running around gallantly to open Elva Jean's door. He remembered how pretty she was. Young and blonde and pretty. Really a pretty girl.

And then he had pushed the clinic buzzer and the door was opened by a breathtakingly beautiful red-head, who whispered, "I'm Cassiopeia Livingston. Come in. And don't say, 'Dr. Livingston, I presume' when you meet Daddy."

The redheaded young woman had smiled warmly and compassionately at Elva Jean.

"Here, honey, let me take your coat. Everything's going to be all right. This won't hardly take any time."

Then Cassiopeia had taken Elva Jean into the back room on the right, while George paced and fretted. Finally, an older man with fading red hair came in from a side door, reeking of alcohol, but walking fairly steadily.

George extended his hand. "Dr. Livingston?..."

The old man shot him a menacing glare and George remembered the warning.

"...I'm Hock Samuels," he lied. "We just can't afford to have a baby right now."

"No matter. Did you bring cash?"

George nodded and handed over a bulging envelope. The doctor's hands shook visibly as he counted the stack of twenty-dollar bills.

"Are you feeling all right?" George asked, in what he hoped was a casual tone.

He was answered with another of the menacing glares. The doctor counted the money twice, and then carried it into the back room on the left. George heard a safe being opened, then closed, then the sound of liquid being poured into a glass. From the other room, he could hear the muffled sobs of Elva Jean. George looked at his watch and resumed pacing. Finally, the doctor appeared with a glass of bourbon in his hand. It was George's turn to glare.

"Drinking on the job?" George asked sarcastically.

"Anesthesia," the doctor answered, holding up the nearly full glass and admiring its contents. "I never perform surgery without anesthesia." He gulped the drink, set the glass on a table, and disappeared into the room where Elva Jean was waiting.

George paced again. Finally, the girl reappeared.

"I hope you're not worried about Daddy," she smiled.

George stared at her before answering, "He looked drunk to me."

"No matter," she said. "He's never really sober, but I assure you that he's done this a thousand times."

"And you help?"

"I do what I have to do. He's my Daddy." She tilted her head wistfully. "Mama's dead. I'm all he has in the world."

"You'd be enough to make somebody's world. Do you have a boyfriend?"

"I don't even know any boys. Daddy made me drop out after my freshman year in high school. He told them I had some obscure disease and would have to be tutored at home. I don't really know anybody."

"And do you have some obscure disease?"

"No. He was just afraid I'd start dating and get pregnant. My mother died right after she delivered me. I think it did something to his mind. He's been doing this ever since."

"So, what do you do all day?"

"Work for Daddy. Madras, she's our maid, takes care of the house. I take care of Daddy. He never lets me be alone for more than a minute. I don't know why I'm telling you all this. I shouldn't be..."

"Cassi! Get in here!"

The girl jumped up without another word and hurried to help her father. In a few minutes, the old man returned. George looked for a sign of something.

"Want a drink, boy? She won't be ready to go for a while yet."

George shook his head. The doctor went back to his office and poured another drink. George watched him through the open door. He lost track of time.

"Blood! Oh, Daddy, there's blood everywhere!"

George rushed into the small room and saw Elva Jean pale and apparently unconscious. There was blood all over the sheets, and Cassi's hands were red from it. The doctor stumbled in.

"Get out of here!" he yelled with a slurred tongue.

George yelled back, "We've got to get her to a doctor!"

"I'm the doctor! Get out of here! Get out of my way!"

Cassi nodded and steered George back to the waiting room.

"She'll be all right, Hock. Sometimes this happens. Don't worry. She'll be all right."

George was torn, not knowing what to do. He looked at the blood all over Cassi and on his sleeve where she had touched his arm.

"Let's clean this up," he shuddered, " and I'll pour you a drink."

"I've never had a drink before," she replied.

"Try it, just this once. It'll be good for you. Here, I promise. A drink will be good for you."

The sound of Cassi's lounge chair scraping across the flagstone brought George back to the present. He watched in silence as his drunken wife struggled to her feet, clumsy in her heavy terrycloth robe. Cassi took an unsteady step toward the house, and then cried out in anguish as a shard of her broken drink glass sliced through the fleshiest part of her foot. She lurched sideways, squealing in pain.

George watched, immobile, as Cassi lost what was left of her balance and fell hard against the chrome pool ladder. The blow to her head cut short her scream, and Cassi's limp body slumped forward, spiraling silently into the pool.

George stared in fascination as his wife's blood billowed in smoky clouds, garish in the underwater lights. The heavy robe filled with water, dragging her unconscious body down. He wondered if she would drown, or die from loss of blood.

"Your wife died from loss of blood," Dr. Livingston had said matter-of-factly about Elva Jean, on that dark night in New Orleans. "Sometimes these things happen. There was nothing I could do."

Cassi had stared at her father in pain and disbelief.

"I am sorry about your wife, Mr. Samuels, but you'd better get her out of here." The doctor continued, "I have my reputation, you understand."

George had casually shrugged, "She's not my wife. Just a whore. She came here alone. You understand? It's your problem. But I will get her out of here," he had nodded toward Cassi. "Yes, sir. I will get her out of here."

George had taken Cassi by the arm and was leading her out the door when the older man lunged at him. George reeled around, knocked him unconscious with a single blow, and turned back to the frightened young woman.

"Let's go," George ordered gently, but firmly.

"Wait!" she whispered, and ran to the doctor's small office. George followed and watched with amazement as she deftly opened the combination safe and quickly filled a pillowcase with bundles of money. She paused briefly, then reached into the pillowcase and pulled out a small handful of bills. Counting out three hundred dollars, she put them back into the safe, closed the door, and spun the combination lock.

"We wouldn't want this to look like a burglary," she smiled wanly at her rescuer.

They walked to the car in silence. George drove aimlessly, stunned by the evening. When he finally parked, they talked all night, avoiding the one subject most on their troubled minds.

"So, she wasn't your wife?" Cassi ventured to ask, as dawn crept over the Crescent City.

George shook his head.

"Really a whore, then?"

George buried his face in his hands.

"No."

The young woman waited, staring out at the river.

"Maybe someday I'll tell you about her. Now, where would you like me to take you? Don't even think about going back to that crazy old man. You've got plenty of money. You can leave town. Start over somewhere."

"I won't go back to him," Cassi shook her head, "and I don't care about the money."

She dragged the heavy pillowcase from the front floorboard and put it on the seat between them.

"You take the money. I want to go with you. I want you to take care of me."

George was astonished at her naïveté and the direct simplicity of her request. He was even more astonished at his own reply.

"I'll take care of you," he had whispered. "I promise. I'll always take care of you."

George sighed a heavy sigh, staring down at her body in the pool.

"God damn it!" he muttered under his breath. He clenched his jaws, vaulted over the ledge, and dropped to the flagstone decking below.

The unmistakable sound of a forty-five shell clicking into its chamber stopped him cold. He looked toward its source and saw their huge black maid, crying, and aiming his own gun at him.

"Mistuh George, you done let my Miss Cassi die! I'm going to kill you like a dog!" she sobbed.

"Now, Madras, give me that gun," he answered calmly, taking a step toward her. "Someone could get killed."

"You don't care about Miss Cassi getting killed!" Madras screamed at him. "You knows Ah cain't swim, and you done let my baby die!"

Madras gulped back the next sob, and lowered her voice.

"There ain't nothin' left for me to do for my Miss Cassi but to pull this here trigger."

Before he could take another step toward her, George heard the gun fire. He flinched in anticipation of the pain. A split second later, he realized that he had not been hit.

As he opened his eyes, he saw the distraught, old, black woman slump into a heap on the flagstone, his gun still in her hand. In anguish, he turned from her and dove into the pool.

God damn it! How long has she been under?... God damn it!... How long?... God... damn it!... God,... help me!... God,... help us all!

Chapter 25
August 1, 1968

Deputy Sheriff Nick Nichols paused briefly at the nursing station before heading solemnly down the too-bright hallway to Room 509. He knocked softly, and paused only a moment before entering. George Llewellyn turned from his bedside vigil and rose to greet the deputy.

Nichols whispered, "Could we talk outside a minute?"

"No need to whisper," PapaLew replied in a normal tone. "She's still in a coma. Can't hear anything."

"I'm not so sure," Nichols continued in his whisper. "I've heard too many stories about people in comas waking up and remembering everything that had been going on around them. Would you mind?" He gestured toward the door.

George Llewellyn nodded, glanced a moment at his silent wife, and followed the deputy out of the darkened, flower-filled room into the sterile corridor.

"I'm real sorry about your wife's accident last night."

"Thanks. It was a real shock. The doctors don't know much yet."

"How long was she under?"

"I don't think it could have been more than a couple of minutes. I wish I knew for sure. It might give me more hope."

The deputy nodded.

"A couple of your neighbors reported hearing something like a gunshot several minutes before they heard the ambulance siren. Didn't add up to me. Gunshot. Apparent pool accident. Any connection?" the deputy asked.

"Madras, she's our maid, discovered Cassi in the deep end of the pool. I was upstairs asleep. Madras can't swim, but she reacted quickly enough to grab one of my guns from the cabana and fire a shot to wake me up. Otherwise, I'm afraid to think what might've happened."

The lawman nodded again. "Would it be all right with you if I drop by the house to ask Madras a few questions?"

"Sure, it would be fine, but she's not there. She was so upset that Larry drove her to New Orleans this morning to stay with her sister. There was nothing she could do for Cassi here. Besides, I was worried about Madras' heart. She's getting on in years. And, she is a big woman with diabetes. I told her she'd be more help to Miss Cassi if she'd go back home and rest up so she could take care of her when she gets out of the hospital. You know, she raised that girl from birth. It would kill her if Cassi didn't pull through."

"How about you?" the deputy asked politely.

"I've had a lot of pain in my life, Sheriff. This is the worst."

"And Larry?"

"Well, it's his mother. He wanted to be here with us, but I thought he'd be better off getting away for the day. Driving seems to clear his head."

The deputy pulled his small notebook and a pen out of his breast pocket. "Okay, then, just briefly, can you tell me how your wife fell into the pool?"

"The best we can figure it," George began, "is that Cassi had dropped her drink glass on the patio and then stepped on a piece of it as she was coming into the house. She must have lost her balance and fallen against one of the pool ladders. The doctors said she had a concussion and probably was unconscious before she hit the water. That might actually turn out to be her saving grace."

"And your maid Madras was...?"

"Madras was in her room, but she wasn't asleep. She heard the glass break and she went outside to see about it. She's incredible about cleaning things up right away. Thank God, she got there in time to see the water still rippling in the pool. Then she looked and saw Cassi at the bottom in the deep end. Cassi was wearing a heavy terrycloth robe. It must have taken her down like an anchor. Madras ran into the cabana, got one of my guns, and fired a shot to wake me up. The poor woman was so upset, she apparently fainted on the spot. When I got down there and saw Madras slumped on the ground, I was afraid she'd had a heart attack. Then I saw Cassi in the pool."

"Did the doctors check Madras over?"

PapaLew shook his head. "That stubborn old woman hasn't been back to a doctor since they told her she had sugar diabetes. Says she won't go around people that always have bad news. I couldn't do anything with her, and didn't want to make matters worse by arguing with her. I think she'll be okay after a few days at her sister's house."

"You have her sister's phone number, I suppose."

"Actually, her sister doesn't have a phone. I'm not even sure of the address. Madras was going to have to direct Larry to the house."

"Okay if I take a look at that gun?"

"Sure, Sheriff. We've got nothing to hide. I'll be home later this evening, if you want to stop by, pick it up and take a look around. Or, I'll drop it off at your office tomorrow. Whatever makes your job easier."

"That's generous of you. I'll give you a call and stop by on my way home. I'd like to take a look at the scene, just to clear it in my mind. I'm sorry about all this. I'll get my mama to pray for your wife. She's good about that sort of thing."

* * *

Grover sat in his truck until he was sweating more from the heat than from worry. That didn't take long in Mississippi on the first day of August in an old black truck without air conditioning. He took a deep breath, stepped down onto the radiating concrete street, fed the parking meter, and walked the twenty paces to the U.S. Army Recruiting Station without any trace of a limp.

Instant relief came from the office's air conditioning and from the fact that his information had been correct. The uniformed man behind the counter was a stranger to Vicksburg.

"You here to sign up? Do your duty to your country?" the older man asked without introduction.

"Yep," Grover replied in the same off-handed way, but quickly corrected himself. "Yes, Sir!"

"Fill out these forms," was the last thing Grover clearly remembered as he put his life in the toboggan that was the United States Army near the height of the Viet Nam conflict. Later, and often, he would wish that he had discussed it with Christi first.

* * *

Prudence Washington Purvis rang the doorbell as if this were any other home and realized that, in the years she had lived at the Boudreaux house, she had never walked through the front entrance unless she had just cleaned the porch. But it was too late to change course now, even if she wanted to, because Christi herself opened the door a moment later.

"I'm here to help," Prudence announced matter-of-factly.

Christi smiled at her and immediately burst into tears. "Oh, Prudence. That's so nice of you, but I don't have any money at all and I can't afford any help."

The baby in Christi's arms stared at the strange woman who had made her mother cry again, and then looked down at the dark little boy holding her hand.

Prudence smiled at the baby and then at Christi.

"I guess I could be insulted by that," Prudence replied gently, "but I know you're upset, so I won't take it personally. I didn't come here to be your maid. Once, about four years ago, you said we were friends. Remember? 'Someone you know and care about?' I came here because I thought we were friends."

"I'm so sorry!" Christi blurted out, sobbing harder. "I'm so sorry! Of course, we're friends! Thank you for coming!"

She sniffled, wiped her eyes, and invited Pru to come in out of the heat. "Have some lemonade," she insisted.

Prudence stepped across the threshold of the old Boudreaux family home and entered her own new era.

* * *

"...Listen, Chief, you said handle it out of our department and that's what I did. Hell, I'm not trying to sweep anything under the rug. Every damn piece of so-called evidence against Grover and his daddy is clearly circumstantial.... Hell, yes, we've taken circumstantial evidence to the Grand Jury before, but only when we knew the accused was guilty! I'm telling you, there's more to these murders than an angry kid like Grover.... Well, fine, you check it out all you like and you'll come to the same conclusion. I'm just not going to make their lives any worse after all they've been through. For God's sake, the girl lost both her parents, and I don't think she has any idea what kind of financial bind Clem was in when he died. She's gonna find out soon enough.... No, I don't think the wife knew either. She'd been seeing a half dozen doctors, taking enough pills for two or three people. She might have been a little more upset than usual, since it was Clem and Vayda's anniversary that night. Then Lucky showed up and seemed to get her more stirred up than ever. Said all she wanted was to hear about that grandbaby. She was heartsick over not being able to see her.... Sometimes when it looks like a coincidence, it might actually be a coincidence.... Hell, yes, I talked to the hotel clerk. He saw what he called suspicious-looking strangers at the hotel that night. Unfortunately, there were a lot of strangers in town for the Llewellyns' party, so it could be something or it could be nothing.... Damn right we're gonna keep it open. No Statute of Limitations on murder.... If you're wanting to move it to your department, you do the paper on it.... Fine with me. That's what I thought. We'll keep it all right here in the county...."

Nick Nichols smiled as he hung up the phone. He leaned back in his chair and pulled a pack of cigarettes out of his front pocket. There was little he would enjoy more than the prospect of solving his first really high-profile murder case.

* * *

Grover Jones waited a full twenty-four hours before telling his wife what he had done. He hadn't realized that each passing hour would make it more difficult. He certainly never suspected that his prepared speech would sound like a prepared speech. Christi didn't even let him finish it.

"Good Lord, Grover!" Christi shrieked. "What in the world were you thinking? How could you go out and join the Army and leave me like this?" She looked down at her huge mid section.

"I thought it was a good idea. We needed money and it's a job." Grover almost whined, "What could I do here?"

"Well, I don't know, but at least you'd be here. Don't you think that just being here matters?"

"Honest to God, Christi, I thought you'd be glad to see me go away for awhile. You can stay here in town now that, well, you know, anyway, now that you can live here in your old house and be around your friends instead of being stuck out on the farm."

"And how am I supposed to keep up this big house, and pay the utilities, and...?" Christ's voice trailed off.

"I'll send you my paycheck every month," Grover replied with an innocent smile. "The Army's gonna take care of all I need on base. And you'll have medical care for yourself and the babies. I checked on that. We can buy stuff cheap at the PX. Everything will be better than it was out on the farm. You won't have to put up with Paw. I know you don't really like being around him, but I gotta tell you that he is crazy about you, Christi. He just doesn't know how to show it. And he loves Angelica. I know he'd help you any way he could, if you'd let him."

Christi frenetically searched her mind for any solution that wouldn't include Paw. She sighed, hating to admit that Grover might have actually made a good decision.

"Well, maybe it won't be so bad," she speculated. "We do need the money. I've been through most of daddy's papers and I can't find life insurance policies or anything. Maybe he dropped them when, well, you know, when I left."

"No. He wouldn't have done that. He would have kept them for your mother. You'll find the policies. Maybe he had a safety deposit box."

Christi beamed. "I can't believe I didn't think of that! Of course, he had a safety deposit box!"

"Can I drive you to the bank?" Grover offered.

Christi shook her head. "No, it's so hot in that truck. I'll get Pru to take me. Her new little car has air conditioning."

"See," Grover smiled and nodded. "I knew you didn't need me. You've got friends, and they'll help you."

"Grover."

"What?"

"I do need you. You're my husband. I love you, and I do need you." As they embraced gently, Christi whispered in his ear, "I just don't need that old truck."

"Okay, honey, I'll see if I can trade it in on something better for you to drive while I'm gone. Maybe we can get a good deal at one of your daddy's used car lots."

"From what his lawyer told me, I don't know if he even owned them when he… died."

"I'll go see what I can find out from the guys who work there. Now, don't you worry, Christi. It'll be okay."

"You've been promising me that for a long time, Grover. I still love you and I still believe in you, but it's getting harder to believe that things are ever going to get any better for us."

"Of course, it's gonna get better. How could it get any worse? Why don't you go on upstairs and take a nap? I'll find you a car somehow. You've gotta have a car to drive."

As Grover backed his old truck out of the driveway, Christi tried to settle down for a nap. She looked around her beautiful bedroom and marveled at the irony of Clem Boudreaux's daughter being desperate for a car. Christi closed her eyes and realized that she was too tired to cry.

* * *

Cameron Coulter slowly climbed the steps to the front porch of the Boudreaux home, reacting as much to his feelings as to the heat. There had been a stagnant, discomforting air surrounding everyone in Vicksburg all summer. This time, leaving town would not be difficult.

A tall thin black girl opened the door before he rang the bell. Cameron was momentarily taken aback.

"Come on in, Cameron," the girl smiled. "Maybe you don't remember me. I'm Pru Purvis. My mother worked for the McCains."

"Of course, I remember you, Pru. We used to call you 'Prudence' though."

"Prudence, Pru, either one. I don't care." She smiled and shrugged. "Christi and the baby are taking a nap upstairs. Was she expecting you?"

"No. I should have called. I'm on my way out of town and I just wanted to say good-bye."

"Come on in and have some lemonade. She may wake up any minute and join us."

Prudence didn't give him a chance to decline. She quickly retreated to the kitchen and returned moments later with two icy glasses of Christi's locally famous homemade drink.

They sat facing each other in the old velvet-covered chairs in the parlor. Prudence broke the awkward silence.

"I heard you're going to Oxford on a Rhodes Scholarship. That's impressive. Congratulations."

"Thank you," Cameron replied automatically, feeling slightly disconcerted by something in the girl's attitude.

"Grover will be leaving soon, too."

"Grover? Where's he going? Back to school?"

"No. The Army. He's going to Dothan, Alabama, for a start. I hope he doesn't get shipped to Viet Nam after that," Pru finished emphatically.

"The chances are good that he will, " Cameron said.

"My husband was killed in Viet Nam. His first week."

"I remember hearing about that," Cameron replied gently. "It was during my senior year. I'm so sorry."

Prudence nodded.

They sipped their lemonades silently.

"Are you planning to enlist?" Pru asked bluntly.

"I haven't given it much thought," Cameron lied, knowing that right after graduation, he had been re-classified 1-A, and could be called for active duty at any moment.

"That's odd. It seems to be the main concern of every other guy who is anywhere near draft age.

"Well, actually, I meant that I hadn't given a lot of thought to the idea of enlisting," Cameron explained, realizing that his lie was obvious. "To be honest," he lowered his voice, "I'd be afraid to sign up, but I have to be careful what I do. I'd like to go into politics later on. A war record, or lack of it, can be an important political issue. I'm going to have to handle it carefully. In fact, I've been working on it from a couple of different angles."

He paused, frowned, and silently berated himself for being so candid with this black girl. He changed the topic.

"It's hard to imagine that Grover would leave Christi and the baby, especially now with another baby due, and her parents gone. Just enlist like that."

"Frankly, he was ready to go when he dropped out of Ole Miss and was reclassified for the draft. He just couldn't pass the physical with that knee injury," Prudence reminded him. "All this time, though, it has really bothered him to be '4-F.' When he thought he might be able to pass the physical, he went in again. He thought it would be best for the family, under the circumstances, but I have to agree with you. Not a good idea."

Prudence paused, as if considering her options, and then pressed ahead. "The bottom-line truth of the matter, though, is that Grover's a real patriot at heart. His father was in the Army. Actually, so was his grandfather and all those before him. Grover believes that it's his duty as a citizen to go. He doesn't think much of the cowards who try to shirk their responsibilities. Present company excepted, I am sure."

Prudence smiled. "More lemonade?"

Cameron could not believe that this impudent black girl would talk to him like that. Such a pleasant demeanor. Such a refined veneer. Such a brutal attack. He handed her his empty glass to get her out of the room for a few minutes.

"Are you moving back to Vicksburg?" Cameron asked as Prudence returned with the refilled glass.

"I don't think so. I just took some vacation time to lend a hand here. I'm well settled in Jackson now, going to school, and working part time for the Llewellyns."

"I didn't realize they had another home in Jackson," Cameron replied.

"They don't. And, I'm not a maid. I'm working at the store, while getting a degree in Business Administration, so I'm enjoying some hands-on training in retail. It's quite an education."

"That's very interesting."

"Is it?" Prudence asked, in that same disconcerting tone she had used earlier.

Cameron put his glass down on a silver coaster on the coffee table.

"Maybe I've offended you in some way," Cameron began, slowly rising to his feet. "I'm sorry. I'll be going now. Please tell Christi I stopped by to see her."

Prudence rose at the same time.

"No, please," she said quietly. "I'm the one who should be sorry. You came here to see Christi, to offer support at a bad time, and I was rude to you. I was very rude. I'm sorry."

Prudence knew that her bottom lip was trembling, and she felt her eyes becoming moist. She dropped her head, and blinked to stop the tears. She sniffled involuntarily.

"I really am sorry," she said, with her voice breaking. "I, I don't know what came over me."

Prudence was surprised, but not at all offended, when Cameron closed the gap between them and took her in his arms. For a brief moment, she stiffened, and then she relaxed into his embrace. It seemed so natural that he would try to comfort her. He held her for a long while without saying anything.

"It's okay, Prudence," he finally whispered. "It's okay. I know that you've been through so much. Christi and her parents were like family to you. You've been here all this time, being strong for Christi, but you're hurt too. It's okay for you to cry. You've been hurt too."

Prudence let the big, tall, white man hold her while she cried. She didn't know how long it was before she began to wonder what Christi would think if she should wake up now and walk into the room. Then she thought about Kelly McCain, and how she loved this man more than she would ever love her own husband. Prudence felt so comfortable in Cameron's arms that she allowed herself the time to wonder about all that and more. Finally, she straightened up and wiped her eyes with her hands.

"I'm sorry, again," she whispered. "I didn't mean to break down like that."

"It's perfectly alright," Cameron whispered in reply, only slightly releasing his hold on her. He leaned down and gently kissed her on the forehead. "It's perfectly alright."

Prudence looked up into Cameron's pale blue eyes. She had never felt such tenderness toward a white man. Cameron kissed her again on the forehead, and wiped her cheek with his finger.

"You can cry on my shoulder anytime," he promised softly. "We all need a shoulder from time to time."

"But you're leaving for England. Now's a fine time to offer a shoulder," Prudence chided gently.

"I'll be home as often as I can. I tell you what. You give me your address in Jackson, and I'll send you a postcard when I get to London. What do you want? Big Ben? The Tower of London? The Crown Jewels? You just tell me what you want, and I'll provide it."

"I predict you'll be a good politician one of these days," Prudence laughed. "You're already making promises you don't intend to keep."

"Try me," Cameron challenged. "Just try me. Give me your address, and you'll see me keep a promise. In fact, you might even see me in person the next time I'm in Jackson."

PART V

WORLDS APART

Chapter 26
August 2, 1968

Minh Nhi Li could scarcely believe her good fortune. "The Uncle" would arrive today, or maybe tomorrow. The visit itself would have been honor enough for their village, but The Uncle had invited the newlyweds to accompany him on his journey to Huế for the wedding of his niece, the daughter of his only surviving sister.

Even before she had married Minh Khoi Tien and moved to his village of Đó Thanh, Nhi Li had heard stories about The Uncle. His bravery, cunning and business acumen were legendary throughout the region. In fact, Minh Nhi Li had heard much more about The Uncle before she became a member of his family.

In her own village, people had felt free to whisper of the great Minh Quang Tung in her presence. Now, he was not only The Uncle, as the Americans had nicknamed him, but "her uncle." It would be unseemly of anyone to speak to her of a relative, especially one so renowned.

Though he had adapted to the presence of Americans, having served as well as used them, The Uncle had never demeaned himself by becoming like them. He did not brag about himself. He did not flaunt his new wealth. He did not abuse the people who worked for him. Minh Quang Tung was humble and highly respected — a credit to his ancestors.

Nhi Li tried to contain her excitement as she rose very early, cleaned their already clean bamboo hut, and wiped the best mat for the tenth time in two days, since it was likely that The Uncle might sleep with them. She went out into the field at the same time and in the same manner as she always did, so that no one could think she was drawing attention to herself on this auspicious occasion. Still, it was difficult to concentrate on the tasks at hand, routine as they were.

All day, and all the next day, Minh Nhi Li waited and tried to maintain a normal demeanor. It was late into the following black night before the Minh family and all the other villagers were startled awake by the sound of a loud diesel motor approaching. For a moment, they all felt the familiar sharp panic that it might be the *máy-bay-my*, the dreaded American airplanes, but this noise was different, not so shrill, rumbling across the ground as it grew closer. The Uncle and his famous truck had arrived in the hamlet of Đó Thanh under cover of darkness.

Twenty-four hours later, Minh Nhi Li climbed into the huge truck and took the middle seat between her husband and his uncle. It was dark, and the truck had been hidden under a huge cloth since arriving in Đó Thanh, so the young bride had little frame of reference for her position or for judging the truck's outward appearance. She had heard about trucks, but had seen only two or three of them in her lifetime.

She was startled by the noise coming from somewhere in front of her, almost under her feet, when The Uncle started the engine. The truck shuddered. For a moment, Minh Nhi Li was afraid it was going to explode like a bomb. Then, it settled into a rhythmic drumming that was loud, but not too threatening.

"Khoi Tien, help me remove the tarp. Nhi Li, you wait here and do not touch anything," the great man commanded quietly.

The men stepped out of the truck, leaving Minh Nhi Li huddled in the seat, her small frame made even smaller by hunching her shoulders over and crossing her thin arms for fear that she might accidentally touch something and cause a terrible tragedy. She began to wonder if she should be taking this trip.

The Uncle got back in the truck without Khoi Tien. Nhi Li was afraid to ask him anything. He moved the big stick on the floor in front of her. There was a grinding sound and the truck started to move slowly backwards, turning in a wide arc. Nhi Li closed her eyes and held her breath until the truck stopped. She opened her eyes and was relieved to see her husband standing several feet in front of them. The Uncle got out, again warning her not to touch anything. She would not have considered it.

Minh Quang Tung showed his nephew how to disengage the metal latch on the front grill of the truck. Then they pulled on some large pieces of metal which came out like a mat that had been folded back on itself. Nhi Li was curious and hoped that The Uncle would tell her about it. The thing was now protruding ten or twelve feet out in front of the truck, supported by wheels like a cart, but carrying nothing.

Then the men walked around to the back of the truck and climbed in. Nhi Li could feel the truck move with their every step. She was afraid it would start to roll away with her in it and she wondered what she would do. She decided that she would be able to jump out and she tried to see in the dim light how to open the door. There were two pieces of metal on the inside of the door itself. She decided that pulling or pushing on one, or both of them together, would be enough. She vowed to pay close attention to everything about this truck, so that she would not be harmed by it.

Finally, her husband and his uncle reappeared at the front of the truck and deposited something heavy on the platform between the wheels. She felt the truck move again from the weight, and caught her breath. She tentatively reached for one of the metal pieces that would lead to her escape. In that moment, Khoi Tien straightened up and headed for the door.

She decided to try to open it for him, but then she remembered The Uncle's warning not to touch anything. She wrapped her arms more tightly around herself, and waited.

The two men got back in the truck and Nhi Li felt much safer with one of them on each side of her. Minh Quang Tung moved the metal piece on the floor in front of her and Minh Nhi Li braced herself to move backward again. To her surprise, this time the truck moved forward. The Uncle reached out and touched something.

Lights came on, illuminating both the dirt road leading away from Đó Thanh and the huge metal thing sticking out in front of the truck. Nhi Li watched the thing roll and bounce with every rut, and she felt the truck itself bounce with every rut. Still, it was more comfortable than riding in a cart pulled by a water buffalo, and Nhi Li was again overwhelmed with gratitude at her good fortune.

"I see you staring at my sleeper wheels up front," Minh Quang Tung remarked after a while. "Do you know their purpose?"

"No, sir," Minh Nhi Li replied politely.

"Would you like to know?" he inquired.

"Yes, sir. I would like to learn as much as possible on this trip," Nhi Li ventured to confess.

"I was hoping that would be your attitude, Nhi Li. Khoi Tien, you have chosen well."

The Uncle shifted in his seat, and moved the floor lever again. The truck seemed to go faster. Nhi Li waited.

"The sleeper wheels," Quang Tung began, "are there as protection. Since you are family and you want to learn as much as possible on this trip, I will tell you the whole story."

Minh Nhi Li waited politely, as the truck bounced along the narrow dirt road. The Uncle seemed to be lost in his own thoughts. Finally, he spoke again.

"When I was a very young man, I married a girl from our village. She died giving birth to our son. The boy did not live. I decided that I had been cursed, and I left Đó Thanh so that I would not bring disgrace on the Minh family. In truth, my heart was broken and I was not thinking clearly, but that is the way of some rebellious youth. I moved to Saigon and did what I could to survive. I did not honor my parents.

"Many years later, I traveled by boat to visit the beautiful city of Hué. I have to tell you that it was very different then from the way we will find it when we arrive this week. You will see what remains after years of war. I was drawn to Hué, as so many of our people have always been. I wanted to be a part, if only for a while, of the intellectual and spiritual center of our country. I wanted to see the temples, the palaces, the tombs, the Citadel, the seat of the emperors.

"On a night when the moon was full, I spent a quiet evening in a sampan on Huong Giang, the River of Perfumes. I floated slowly and felt the quiet deep flow of the water, like the quiet deep flow of life among our people. I felt that I had an unfulfilled responsibility to keep that life flowing.

"The next day, I went to the Dien, one of the many ancient temples in the old walled part of the city. I stood and watched as ten men in ceremonial robes quietly lighted candles on ornate golden altars and invited the spirits of their ancestors to return. I listened to them read from a venerable tablet framed in red and gold. And all the while, silently, I prayed to the God who is above all gods that I could be forgiven for the disgrace I had brought on my family.

"I don't know how long I was there. The men in robes were lying prostrate on the temple floor. The fragrance of incense and flame tree flowers filled the room. The whole temple was lighted in an ethereal glow, and I felt something like the hand of God touch me.

"I walked out into a light misting rain, feeling cleansed. I roamed aimlessly across the Bridge of the Golden Waters, through a great courtyard, and past the Palace of Perfect Peace. I felt as if I were in a trance there in the Dai Noi, the Imperial City, as if I were one with my ancestors who had walked there. I could not leave. I could hear their voices in the winds whispering through the coconut palms, the frangipani, the banyan trees, and the soft-needled pines.

"Suddenly it was evening. I was startled to realize that I had lost the day. Yet, it was at that moment I found my life."

Minh Quang Tung stopped talking. Nhi Li's almond eyes glanced quickly away from his face to the road ahead. The truck continued to bounce slowly along, following its sleeper wheels. Nhi Li hoped that The Uncle had not forgotten the point of his story. She still wanted to know about the sleeper wheels, but would never be presumptuous enough to remind him. A moment later, he resumed his narrative.

"Two young women were wading side by side off a shallow bank of the River of Perfumes. They were identical in the twilight, wearing flowing, white linen robes. Each had adorned her long black hair with a lotus blossom. I thought I was having a vision.

"One of them felt me staring at her. She looked up and captured me with her eyes. I could not move. She smiled and touched the arm of the other. That one too looked up at me and smiled, and I saw that their faces were identical, but the smiles were not the same. The smile of the first one lit up the night. I knew I had been touched by the gods.

"Perhaps if I had been in Saigon, I would have let the moment pass. But that night in Hué, I believed that anything was possible. I approached them with courage and fear. They did not run away.

"I found out that they were, in fact, identical twins, and of the esteemed Nguyen family. Their father was a professor at the University of Hué. The next day, I presented myself to him and was fortunate to find that we had mutual acquaintances.

"Although I might have seemed too old to marry his daughter with the wonderful smile, Professor Nguyen was kind enough to honor me. It helped that the other twin was already engaged and was waiting for her sister so that they could marry in the same ceremony. Before I could fully appreciate my good fortune, the marriage was arranged.

"Nguyen Song Luong became my bride and moved with me to Saigon. It was the happiest time of my life. Everything I did prospered, and we had six children in the next seven years."

Once again, Minh Quang Tung fell silent. Then he asked, "Have you ever traveled on the Viet Nam Railway, Nhi Li?"

The young girl was not expecting a question. She hesitated. "No, sir. I have not traveled from my home village except to Đó Thanh. I have never seen a railway."

Minh Quang Tung nodded. "And you, Khoi Tien?"

The young man tried to sound humble as he talked briefly of a train trip to Nong Son two years ago, when he was allowed to help transport produce from their village to the larger market. The truck continued to bounce rhythmically along the dirt road. Minh Nhi Li had no idea how far they were from Đó Thanh. She watched the sleeper wheels in the lights and wondered what was hidden in the blackness on each side of the road.

"The Viet Nam Railway," Minh Quang Tung said, returning to his theme, "leaves Saigon in the far south of our country and travels eastward toward the sea, then turns north along the coast line. For about 700 miles, it roughly parallels the old Mandarin Road, the historic trade link with China. The Railway ends just south of the seventeenth parallel, where our country was divided by the Geneva agreements in 1954.

"The Railway was opened in the mid-1930's. It was repeatedly cut during World War II and during the eight-year French Indochina War after that. To this day, it continues to be sabotaged by our countrymen from the North. Even so, two million passengers board it each year, knowing the risks involved. It is the major artery of transportation for our country, and for many people there is no choice but to use it.

"I, too, thought I had no choice. It was well past the time for us to take our children to visit their grandparents in Hué. All eight of us boarded the Viet Nam Railway in Saigon. I rode in a front car with the armed guards, since I was capable of firing a rifle and helping in case of attack. I was certain that Song Luong and the children would be safe in the sleeping car far behind us. As the train approached a wooded ravine near Lang Co, guerillas waited in ambush. They let the armored car pass, then the two freight cars. They detonated a land mine directly under the first sleeping car.

"All those in the bottom bunks were killed instantly as the steel floor of the car rolled up like a carpet around them. The others were dashed against the ceiling and sides of the car, all injured and dazed. When they helped each other escape out the side doors, the guerillas opened fire on them.

"I watched Song Luong throw herself on top of our three youngest children to protect them. I saw their bodies jerk as they were hit. From the front car, the civil guards and I fired helplessly into the woods at targets we could not see. Minutes later, the guerillas ceased firing, and disappeared deep into the forest.

"In addition to dozens of soldiers, they had killed all five of the women and twenty-two children. I was the only one of my family who survived. But in truth," he added quietly, with a glance at Minh Nhi Li, "my life ended that day."

The Uncle returned his intent gaze to the road ahead and tightened his grip on the steering wheel. Minh Nhi Li responded to the long silence that followed by falling asleep.

She awoke with a jerk when the truck's right front wheel hit a particularly deep hole in the narrow dirt road. She was embarrassed to realize that she had been sleeping, and glanced furtively at The Uncle to gauge his reaction. He seemed oblivious to her presence beside him as he continued to drive along without a saying a word.

Glancing the other way, Nhi Li noticed that her husband was asleep too, leaning against the door with his head back and his mouth slightly open. He had been unaffected by the bounce that had awakened Nhi Li. Perhaps she need not be embarrassed by falling asleep. Perhaps it was to be expected that passengers would fall asleep in a truck. Gratefully, Nhi Li closed her eyes again.

It was the light of dawn that awakened her the next time, along with a growing awareness of the muted voices of her husband and his uncle Quang Tung. Nhi Li was embarrassed again, realizing that they were speaking softly in deference to her. She felt inadequate, not knowing the etiquette of riding in a magnificent vehicle like The Uncle's truck. She took a deep breath, stirred slightly, and opened her eyes.

The Uncle greeted her warmly.

"Good morning, my niece. I trust you rested as well as possible under these circumstances."

Nhi Li's heart flooded with gratitude. "Oh, yes, sir. I had a most pleasant rest. I hope I wasn't rude to fall asleep."

"To the contrary," Quang Tung replied. "It is considered a high compliment to trust a driver enough to fall asleep."

Nhi Li dared to look at The Uncle's face as she smiled. Then she turned to her husband, knowing that he too had slept, and asked, "Minh Khoi Tien, did you also honor your uncle by trusting his driving?"

"I slept well," Khoi Tien replied, "but I wish I could have honored my uncle more by performing this task for him."

"I will teach you to drive today, if you like," Quang Tung offered, and Nhi Li's pulse quickened as she thought of her husband in command of this huge, powerful vehicle. She tried not to let her heart swell with pride.

Chapter 27
August 4, 1968

In retrospect, Minh Nhi Li was sorry she had been so curious about the sleeper wheels. If she hadn't asked, it would never have occurred to her that the dirt roads they were traversing under cover of darkness could be booby-trapped with land mines. She took little comfort in The Uncle's assurances that the weight of the sleeper wheels was designed to detonate any explosives buried in the road and to divert serious damage from the body of the truck.

She didn't understand his technical talk about some parts of the truck being armored with an extra coat of steel. And, she certainly was not pleased to realize that they were heading in a northeasterly direction toward some of the most dangerous places in their war-torn, long-divided country.

Khoi Tien, on the other hand, seemed not only to have absorbed everything The Uncle had told them, but he was also excited and animated by all of it. Already he was driving the magnificent vehicle fearlessly, as if he had been doing it all his life. Li stared intently at her husband, knowing that he was too focused on his task to notice her boldness.

Tien was consumed with manipulating the steering wheel in the dark cab of the truck while The Uncle slept peacefully on her other side, leaning against the door. Without taking his eyes from the road ahead, Tien was constantly pushing one or both of the pedals with his feet, and frequently moving the stick on the floor as well, totally in command.

Nhi Li was fascinated with Tien's newly developed talent and she finally had the motivation and the time to wonder about the man she had married not so many days ago. She even had some time to wonder about herself.

She happily recalled meeting Tien in the spring of the previous year, and was glad that their villages had adopted the thrilling country ritual of *Quan Ho* that was so popular with their northern relatives in the province of Ha Bac.

Li had looked forward to participating in *Quan Ho* since she was a little girl, but as the time approached, she had become fearful that she wouldn't be able to respond quickly enough to entice a suitor. Her mother and her grandmother had both coached her as they all worked side by side in the fields and at home. One of them would make up a verse and sing it *a cappella* while the other would whisper suggestive responses for her to sing.

Although the words she sang had to be lyrical and witty, she also learned to use double entendres and puns to convey thinly disguised sexual meanings. When the festive day of *Quan Ho* finally arrived, Li was somewhat confident that she could make a good impression.

Minh Khoi Tien had stood out in the group of young men from the village of Đó Thanh who came to court the girls of Phú Nhuân with bawdy singing and earthy bravado. He was the first boy to sing and Nguyen Nhi Li was the first girl to respond. She would never forget his simple but pointed refrain:

"Let me ask the orange flower: is there a path leading to the garden where you grow?"

With her mother and grandmother cheering from the sidelines, Li had not so coyly responded in her lovely clear soprano voice:

"The fragrant path to the orange blossoms is lined with bamboo hedges so a bee can easily find his way."

To her delight and surprise, Nguyen Nhi Li had a marriage proposal from Minh Khoi Tien that very day. There was no reason to decline nor demur, so the engagement period began immediately with the blessings and enthusiastic support of both families and villages.

Nhi Li was still grateful in her heart that her village had adopted the *Quan Ho* ritual instead of the rice cooking competition that unmarried young women faced in the northern parts of the country. During festivals in Lang Son, Cao Bang and neighboring provinces, the competing women would each be placed in a small circle less than her height in diameter, and handed the baby of a stranger to hold while she cooked a pot of rice.

The contestants had to start by chewing a stick of sugar cane to yield dry fiber to make a fire under the pot of rice, that was suspended from a pole and attached by a sash to the woman's back. She would have to keep the pot steady in order to cook the rice properly, so all her movements had to be small and graceful.

To make the contest more interesting, the judges would place a frog in the same circle with each woman and she had to keep the frog inside the circle during the entire time allotted to her. As if that were not enough, the crowd of spectators would set off fireworks, bang on drums or anything handy, and tell jokes to distract the girls. The baby she was holding, of course, would be terrified by all the noise and would have to be comforted.

The winner was the girl who made the best-tasting rice in the shortest time, while keeping the frog in the circle, and having the happiest baby. Minh Nhi Li once again thanked the gods of her ancestors that she had not needed to win Minh Khoi Tien's proposal by impressing him with her domestic skills.

There was no question in her mind that she and Tien had been physically attracted to each other, but they had not had the opportunity to spend time alone before their wedding day. Thinking about the simple ceremony that had bound them together for life, Li realized that she and her husband were still virtual strangers to each other.

She had thought that he was a young man much like any other young man of their province, and that she was a young woman much like her friends. She would never have suspected that Tien could learn to drive a truck. This newly acquired skill gave him added stature in her eyes and she wondered how it might affect them when they returned to Đó Thanh.

Would Tien be content to stay in their small village, tending crops and making an occasional trip to the market? Or, would he feel so comfortable in the grand city of Hué that he would want to live there? Would he want to go to school at one of its famous and grand universities?

Or, would her husband become like The Uncle and travel the country alone? Would he risk his life on dark dirt roads to transport supplies and contraband to and from the

Americans? Would it be unseemly to ask him about these things? She knew immediately that it would.

The omnipresent danger from the war around them had added an intensity to each day since the beginning of their life together, and these new thoughts and fears only compounded Nhi Li's natural tendency toward worry and seriousness. As she stared at the sleeper wheels bouncing along in the lights of the great truck that her husband was driving, Li considered her limited education and skills, knowing that most any girl in the village could work faster and harder than she.

Then she thought about the lack of surviving males in Tien's line of the Minh family and was suddenly burdened — almost overcome — with her as-yet-unspoken responsibility to become pregnant and bear a son. Minh Nhi Li's face flushed in the darkness as she realized how inadequate she would be to the tasks before her. She was small and weak, and her husband could drive a truck.

Chapter 28
August 5, 1968

Jody French was feeling guilty, but it had taken him quite a while to figure out exactly what the feeling was. For all his life, he had been able to rationalize or justify his actions so that he had never before been assaulted by guilt. Now it hit him. And it hit hard.

La Muestra II was heading southeasterly from Punta Gorda, Nicaragua, by way of Colón, Panama, to the Columbian port of Cartagena, after an uneventful run from New Orleans. The illicit cargo of small arms and munitions for their friends in Nicaragua had been unloaded swiftly and efficiently, in contradiction to the natives' reputation for laziness.

The captain had assured Jody that the homeward-bound cargo of marijuana and cocaine would be waiting as usual in Cartagena. Everything was functioning like a Swiss watch. Even the weather was perfect.

A cabin steward who helped on the boat when there were guests aboard silently delivered a perfectly mixed Margarita to the table at Jody's side. Salt on the rim. A juicy slice of lime. A small plate of sliced fruit, softened Brie cheese, and assorted gourmet crackers.

The same attendant had helped the captain oversee the unloading in Punta Gorda. They had not allowed Jody to lift a finger to do anything since the boat left New Orleans. PapaLew had insisted that Jody should take a vacation, which happened to be his first vacation ever, and everyone wanted it to be perfect for him. No one wanted to cross PapaLew.

But, Jody French was lounging on the stern of *La Muestra II* feeling guilty. He had never considered the possibility that doing absolutely nothing for a couple of weeks would make him feel so bad. He didn't like the feeling at all.

It's easy enough to make money, Jody mused as he took a sip of the Margarita, *but I'm not sure I'll ever get the hang of sitting around enjoying it. The guilt caused by inactivity is a terrible thing.*

He took a deep breath as the yacht cut effortlessly through the rolling Caribbean Sea. Jody wished upon a passing white cloud that he were back at work in New Orleans.

* * *

Margaret Rose Stevenson carefully resealed her passport into its waterproof pouch and stashed it in the hidden pack under her cotton shirt. She took a deep breath of the warm air that was being circulated by lazy ceiling fans and looked around the open, tropical-style airport lobby, scanning the crowd for her previously arranged translator *cum* guide. He had been described to her only as "Juan with one arm."

Maggie hoped she could count on him because her Los Angeles Spanish consisted mostly of instructions for her maid, and she had not studied anew for her trip to the world's smallest Spanish-speaking country, that was peculiarly located in Africa.

Worse, Maggie knew absolutely nothing about the Fang tribe's language, nor of the Bayele pygmies' native tongue; nor did she know which she would encounter in the jungle.

"Señorita Maggie?" came a masculine voice from beside a large stucco column.

Maggie nodded at the short, dark man with one good arm and one elbow-length stump. The very tall woman raised her index finger in the wait-a-second gesture, and mumbled *"Momento"* as she compulsively checked her camera bag one more time.

Although Bata was the capitol city of Río Muni, Maggie knew that any film or equipment that might have been pilfered by the custom's agent or damaged on her journey would be difficult to replace in the small province on the equatorial west coast of Africa, and impossible once she was up river in the jungle. The quick review of her camera bag assured Maggie that a side-trip north to Cameroon for supplies would not be required.

"Bueno," Maggie announced with a smile and a nod, resealing her bag. *"Vamanos, Juan."*

Maggie walked out into the intense sunshine, staying close beside Juan in the bustling throng, insisting on carrying her own bags as she always did. She deposited her small suitcase and generous camera bag with tripod in the back of his ancient open Jeep.

Minutes later they were darting in and out of the city traffic and soon speeding past great green fields on the outskirts of town, with Juan jabbering in Spanish at a pace that Maggie could not clearly follow. She closed her eyes and wished there were a door to lean against so she could take a short nap. Sleep on the loud, lumbering, poorly air-conditioned prop plane had not been satisfactory.

Maggie surmised from Juan's monologue that he was very impressed with the acres and acres of coffee and cocoa plantations, and he thought that she should be impressed too. She had known before her arrival that they were the pride of Río Muni, and provided most of its income. Her own interest, however, was farther inland. She nodded politely when he glanced at her for a response, but wished he would pay more attention to the highway, though the traffic was light.

The road soon became more narrow and curving. Maggie estimated that they had traveled over twenty miles of winding jungle track when Juan stopped at a small, unmarked clearing on the side of the road.

"Oye!" he commanded unnecessarily. Maggie was already listening to the booming cascades of the Mbía River as it tumbled noisily over the rocks somewhere in the jungle ahead.

Juan was referring to something else, though. Moments later a very dark-skinned Pygmy appeared from the shadows of the forest and smiled a greeting. Juan called him *"Amigo"* and that was good enough for Maggie. She could use a friend with two good arms out here in the jungle.

Juan began telling Maggie about Amigo and his tribe of hunters who lived in this part of Río Muni and southern Cameroon. He seemed genuinely excited about this week's photo assignment, and proud of the arrangements he had made, but Maggie soon became frustrated trying to understand his very fast Spanish.

"Please speak to me in English," Maggie asked her hired translator.

"I do not speak the well English much too so very good," Juan replied somewhat sheepishly, with a heavy accent. He immediately continued his story in Spanish, faster now, not caring that neither Maggie nor the Pygmy seemed to understand most of what he was saying.

It didn't take Maggie long to realize that Juan the translator didn't speak the Bayele Pygmy language "much too so very good" either.

Frustrated, during a pause in Juan's monologue, Maggie turned directly to the Pygmy who was hardly half her height.

"Niamoa?" Maggie asked earnestly, pointing into the jungle. She was hoping that he would recognize the term that the neighboring Fang people of Río Muni used to describe the world's largest frog. They called it "mother's son" because its seven or eight pound size and long limbs made them think of a small child.

Maggie had traveled half way around the world to capture on film one of the gigantic yard-long frogs that had until recent decades been considered either a myth or an extinct species. She was certain that they existed because a female of the species had been caught several years earlier in West Africa by a curator from the Barcelona Zoo, but photos of the amphibians in their natural habitat were scarce, and therefore valuable.

One known photograph had sparked Maggie's interest and that of her magazine's editors nearly a year earlier. Now that she was so close to the gorge where the giant frogs reportedly thrived, but having to rely on a one-language translator, she was concerned that all her plans might have been for nothing.

"Niamoa?" Maggie repeated hopefully.

"Niamoa!" her new Amigo nodded brightly, gesturing toward the sound of cascading water.

Maggie waved him ahead, grabbed her camera bag, and unhesitatingly followed the Pygmy into the thick, dark jungle. One-armed Juan left the keys in the Jeep and cautiously made his way behind them on the barely-defined trail that turned and twisted downward through the moisture-laden shadows.

* * *

Kelly left her husband napping in the second-floor master suite of the Llewellyns' small palace on the west side of the Bosporus, and descended the marble stairway alone, carrying only a towel and her sunglasses.

This anniversary vacation in Istanbul was promising to be no more of an auspicious occasion than their honeymoon had been. Although they had delayed the trip for a week because of her mother-in-law's pool accident and hospitalization, PapaLew had insisted that she and Larry leave Vicksburg as soon as Cassi came out of her coma. PapaLew planned to send his alcoholic wife somewhere for further treatment and he argued convincingly that there was no need for them to stay in Mississippi on her account.

Kelly had a funny suspicion that PapaLew wanted Larry to get out of town for some reason, though she couldn't imagine why, and, as she had been well trained, she didn't ask. *At least it can't be "business" this time. Certainly not in Istanbul!* she thought.

As Kelly walked through the salon, one of the young French maids approached and asked if she needed anything. Without even pausing to look at her or to speak, Kelly just shook her head *no*.

I suppose she thinks I'm an arrogant American, Kelly decided, as she settled herself into a chaise lounge on the marble loggia, but she was too heartsick to care.

She put on her sunglasses and leaned back in the shade, observing the broad panorama before her. Gentle waves lapped against the seawall fifty feet away. Beyond that, countless ships of all shapes, sizes, nationalities, and registers plied the historic strait that linked the Black Sea by way of the Marmara Denizi and Aegean Seas to the Mediterranean.

Kelly recalled studying the history of Constantinople, now called Istanbul, and for the first time began to understand its strategic importance in the world. She hadn't checked the guidebook, and didn't know for sure, but she guessed that were it not for so many vessels moving through these turbulent waters, she could swim across the strait right from their dock. Whoever controlled this small area could have indeed controlled much of the ancient world.

In many ways, it reminded her of Vicksburg, with its strategic location on a bluff overlooking the Mississippi River. Her vantage point from the palace was almost directly on the water, but she transported herself back home where she had so often sat on the bluff watching the barges pass. It made her even more homesick for her babies.

She wondered who else had sat on this loggia, taking a vacation but thinking about children far away. The palace was only about three hundred years old and not at all grand, but it had housed a family, or a succession of families, in its two dozen rooms swept with sea breezes and filled with exotic furnishings and art. Kelly had thought it odd that a villa so relatively modest would be called a palace. She was told that it had that title because it was built for relatives of a royal family.

Probably the poor white trash branch of that royal family, Kelly cynically surmised. *How appropriate.*

Once again, she found herself resenting the fact that PapaLew and Larry always left out the most interesting details. Had another young mother sat on this loggia missing her children? Had she pretended that everything was fine because she didn't know what else to do?

Disturbed by her thoughts, Kelly rose and walked to the far southwest side of the loggia where worn marble steps descended to the garden. She strolled aimlessly for a while and then began picking up small stones that caught her attention. With both her hands full, she headed to the seawall and carefully placed the stones in a little pile. Then she sat on the wall, with her feet dangling toward the water, and one by one, threw the stones as far as she could into the channel.

She saw Larry's shadow a moment before she heard his voice.

"Bored?" he asked sarcastically.

"Throwing rocks into water has never bored me," Kelly answered sweetly. "Otherwise, I wouldn't do it."

"Would you like to go sightseeing?" he offered.

"Not today."

"Shopping then?"

"I don't need anything."

"You could buy some souvenirs," he suggested.

"I'll do that before we leave. All I want is a doll or two for the girls' collection."

"I was thinking you might want to buy a nice Russian samovar for your mother."

"She has a teapot she likes. She'd just have to polish a brass samovar."

"Maybe a nice rug for her entry?"

"Maybe. Maybe tomorrow."

"I made plans for us to have dinner at the Galata Tower tonight. They have the best bacon-wrapped beef filets in the world, after Coy's in Hot Springs, of course. I know you can't resist that," he smiled.

"You got me on that one. A nice, juicy filet sounds good."

"And, by the way, we'll be having company at dinner."

"Company? Whom do we know in Istanbul?"

"He's sort of a friend of PapaLew," Larry began.

Kelly's heart sank at the words "sort of a friend of PapaLew." That could only mean "Business."

"What's the story?" Kelly asked.

"The guy is the equivalent of one of our Senators in the United States. He controls the committee that controls the gambling industry in Turkey. We've decided to turn the palace into a very exclusive gambling casino and bring junkets here from home."

"You're kidding, right?" Kelly asked incredulously. "Gambling in this little palace?"

"I'm certainly not kidding. We've already had an architect look at it, and the plans are underway. All we have to do now is complete the... necessary process."

"Which includes what?" Kelly wanted to know.

"In a word... bribes."

Kelly frowned. "Surely you're kidding about that!"

Larry shook his head. "Bribery is not a dirty word over here. It's the accepted way of doing business. In this case, we bribe the Senator, and he greases the wheels to get his government's approval of our gambling rights."

"You mean, a gambling license, don't you?" Kelly corrected. "Not gambling rights."

"Actually, no. What's at stake here is the exclusive right to control gambling for the whole country. You see, the Turkish laws, that are written in French by the way, reflect their Islamic prohibition against gambling, so no citizen of the country is allowed to promote or personally participate in gambling in any form. They certainly would not be eligible to have gambling rights. But a couple of interesting loopholes make the right to run gambling establishments an exclusive one for the entire country and, fortunately for us, only available to foreigners.

"And here we are," he paused, "foreigners."

Kelly was astounded at the notion.

"So," Larry continued, "the greedy, hypocritical, Islamic Senator will put it all in place legally. We'll bring planeloads of gamblers from the States on free junkets. The international tourist business will help the Senator's status, and everyone wins. It's no big deal, really. Just a good opportunity."

"And we do this over dinner?"

"As I said, bribery is the accepted way of making these things happen here. The other part is making sure that it's all done among friends. Therefore, we'll have dinner with the man. You will be your usual charming self. We'll entertain him at the Paris Revue afterward, and I'll transfer the money from our Swiss bank account to his tomorrow. Then..."

"I didn't know we had a Swiss bank account," Kelly interjected.

"Everyone has a Swiss bank account, Kelly."

"Oh," she replied sarcastically, "how did I ever miss that?"

Chapter 29
August 7, 1968

"Wait a second, guys," Cameron said to the trio of new friends who seemed ready to leave the table. "I want to send a few postcards before we head back."

His companions simultaneously glanced at their watches, nodded their approval, and signaled the waitress to bring more coffee.

Cameron sauntered out to one of the huge kiosks in front of Victoria Station and twirled a tall rack that was brimming with the famous, colorful sights of London. Being so far from home made it easier for him to push the nightmare of his recent draft reclassification to the back of his mind once more.

Thankful that he would be sending the handful of identical cards from London instead of Viet Nam, he flirted with the clerk while paying, and re-joined the other Oxford students.

Cameron tossed the cards on the table, pulled a pen and small address book from his pocket, and started writing.

"Hey, they're all the same, old man," Edward chided, pawing through the stack. "The Crown Jewels?"

"Just what every woman wants," Cameron smiled. "Or, thinks she wants," he added with a wink and an attempt at mystery in his voice.

"Thinking about the Jewel of Jackson… Cheers — Cameron," he scrawled on each of the dozen cards.

He addressed the last one to Prudence.

* * *

"The seventh hour of the evening of the seventh day of the seventh lunar month is a propitious time for a wedding," The Uncle began solemnly over their mid-day meal. "My niece and her husband will be favored on this day of the first autumn rains."

The Uncle smiled and nodded at his prophecy. Then he focused his attention on the newest member of the family.

"Minh Nhi Li," he addressed her formally and with the honor of her full new family name, "do you recall the story of the Weaver and the Shepherd?"

Nhi Li was not sure if she should admit knowing it, and thus risk ruining The Uncle's opportunity to recount the popular myth, or feign ignorance and let him think she knew so little about her country's holidays.

"I do know the story, Uncle, and I would love to hear you tell it," Nhi Li answered truthfully and with tact.

The Uncle smiled at her wise answer.

"And so I will tell it," The Uncle replied, looking for further approval from his sister. The widowed mother of the bride nodded, honored to have her illustrious brother filling the role of host in her home.

"Many, many years ago there was a shepherd who loved a beautiful weaver girl. They spent so much time together, enjoying each other's company, that they became careless about everything else. They neglected their very important work of shepherding the sheep and weaving the cloth that people needed."

The Uncle paused, looking around at the small remnant of family that was his. All were paying close attention, smiling at him, and nodding in recognition of the story.

He continued, "Because they were so derelict in their duties, the Lord of Heaven felt compelled to take action. He separated them by placing them on opposite sides of the galaxy. The Queen of Heaven, who was as romantic as all women are, felt compassion for the loving couple and begged the Lord of Heaven to have mercy on them. She pleaded for him to grant some kind of concession to honor their love for each other."

The young bride-to-be blushed at the thought of such love. The Uncle pretended not to notice.

"The Lord of Heaven, who could usually be swayed by his own love for the Queen, honored her petition on behalf of the young lovers. He arranged that on one day of each subsequent year, a flock of magpies would form a temporary bridge across the Milky Way. The shepherd and the weaver girl would be allowed to cross over the bridge to meet each other and to spend that one day together. When they parted at the end of the day, showers of tears would fall from heaven, and all the people on the earth would see the first autumn rain."

The family sat in respectful silence for a few moments after The Uncle finished his story.

Nhi Li was pleased that her husband gave the first compliment.

"That is always a beautiful story, Uncle, but even more so with your skillful telling of it, especially on this auspicious day of my cousin's wedding. You have honored us all by sharing your gift of speech with us, and I thank you."

Nhi Li beamed at his words and looked down to avoid appearing proud. Once again, she was thankful to be a part of this wonderful Minh family. Silently, she prayed that she would soon conceive a son to carry the Minh name for her husband, and for The Uncle. She knew she was their only hope, though no one would ever speak such unseemly words to her.

In her heart, Nhi Li truly believed that the simple wedding ceremony they would all attend in a few hours was destined to be blessed with the falling of the first autumn rain. The overcast sky gave her hope that at least a gentle mist would grace the union of her new cousins. She prayed that it would be so. And even more fervently, Nhi Li prayed that her union with Khoi Tien would be especially blessed on this night.

* * *

I'm so sorry I couldn't get here for the funeral," Maggie apologized to her younger cousin as they greeted each other with a hug on the front porch of the ancestral Boudreaux home.

"That's okay," Christi responded quickly. "I'm just glad you're here now."

After a very long embrace, they walked into the cool, high-ceilinged entry.

"Let's get you settled in the guest bedroom," Christi offered, "and then we'll talk. Or, would you like to take a bath first? Maybe a nap?"

"A bath would be great!"

Christi led the way up the stairs, slowly and empty-handed. Maggie followed, carrying two bags.

"I slept on the airplanes and anywhere else I could for the past three days," Maggie said to Christi's back, "but I haven't had a shower since I fell into the Mbía River."

"The what?" Christi asked, pausing halfway up the stairs.

"The Mbía River," Maggie pronounced carefully, pausing behind Christi. "It flows through Río Muni, on the west coast of Africa. I managed to get some great photos of the largest frogs in the world. At least I'm hoping they're great photos," she added. "I had enough trouble getting them. I'll tell you all about it later. Anyway, I haven't had a shower since then, so I hope I don't smell too bad!"

"Not at all," Christi replied, "though I have seen your hair look better."

"But not often!" Maggie laughed. "Thank goodness, I'm always on the viewer side of the camera lens! The world might be shocked to see what a mess hides behind the photo credits of one Margaret Rose Stephenson."

Maggie followed Christi into one of the front guest rooms and dropped her suitcase unceremoniously on the Oriental carpet that covered most of the room's hardwood floor. She leaned over and gently placed her camera bag on the green velvet Victorian side chair closest to the door.

"I had forgotten what a beautiful home this is!" Maggie exclaimed as she straightened back up and looked around the room. "I'd love to do a photo shoot here someday."

"Anytime you like," Christi offered. "It's been here, looking just like this, for a hundred fifty years. I don't think it's going to look any different a hundred years from now, but you're welcome to shoot anything you like. Most of the pictures we have, of course, are in black and white, so it would be nice to have some professional shots done in color. Who knows? I may have to use them for advertising rooms to rent."

"I hope you're kidding," Maggie said softly.

Christi shrugged her shoulders. "Who knows? Anyway, I guess this will be my permanent home again... now that..."

Christi's voice trailed to a whisper and she started to cry.

Maggie wrapped her arms around her younger cousin, paying no attention to the protruding abdomen between them, and let her cry for several minutes. Only after the tears subsided did Maggie pluck a tissue from its box.

"Thanks," Christi said, wiping her eyes. "Most people are quicker with a tissue than you were."

"Most people are uncomfortable around tears," Maggie explained, "so they hand you a tissue as a subtle signal to stop crying. I learned in therapy to withhold the sop towel until the crying begins to subside on its own. Most people can't cry for more than ten minutes at a time anyway, even if they try. Ten minutes is little enough to give to a friend."

Christi blinked and looked at her cousin in a new light. Maggie was still the six-feet-tall, angular tomboy with short-cropped hair whom Christi had always known, but there was an indefinable something different about her.

"Therapy?" Christi asked. "You were in therapy?"

"Yeah. Everyone in California's in therapy. You have to have a letter from a shrink to get a driver's license."

Christi's blue blue eyes widened. "Really?"

"Oh, I'm kidding," Maggie chuckled. "Any nut can get a driver's license — exactly the same as in Mississippi."

"Well, if you don't want to talk about the therapy," Christi's voice trailed off.

"No. That's not it. I wasn't trying to change the subject. I'm glad to talk about it. A couple of years ago, I admitted to myself that I was an alcoholic. I went to Alcoholics Anonymous and when I was doing my personal inventory, I realized that I had a lot of deep issues to deal with, so I got professional psychological help too. Taking the first step was the hardest part."

Maggie paused, and then shook her head.

"That's not entirely true," she resumed. "There are lots of hard parts and each one seems the hardest at the time. It's worth it, though. It's all worth it."

"Something has changed about you, that's for sure," Christi said. "There is a different look on your face. Even though you're tired and all, you look, I don't know, you look somehow…" Christi searched her mind for the right word.

"Peaceful?" Maggie asked, taking a seat on the bed.

Christi nodded and plopped onto the nearest chair.

"Yeah, peaceful. You look peaceful, and not so stressed as before."

"It's called serenity in the AA program," Maggie explained. "The first time I experienced a momentary glimpse of it, I had to call my sponsor to describe the feeling and ask if she knew what it was!"

Maggie sighed and continued. "It's amazing now to realize that I had lived my entire life to that point without a moment of true peace or serenity."

"I always thought that you had a tough time, with your parents getting divorced and all," Christi empathized. "No wonder you started drinking!"

"I can't blame it on my parents," Maggie injected quickly. "I had to take a long, hard look at my history, not blame anyone for it, deal with it, and let it go."

Christi thought briefly of the many issues that were unresolved in her own life, then asked her older, and now noticeably wiser, cousin, "How did you do it? How did you let it go?"

Maggie sighed again. "That's a bigger question than you realize, Little Cousin, and there are Twelve Steps to get there. The main thing is that you give it all to God, called our Higher Power in AA. The program is a process of learning how to do it, and keep doing it. Our slogan is 'One Day at a Time.'"

"Wow!" Christi sighed, "that's more than I bargained for!"

"Me too," Maggie smiled. "How about that bath break?"

"Sure!" Christi responded enthusiastically. "Everything you need should be in here," she said, opening the door. "Now, don't sing too loudly in the tub. I wouldn't want you to wake up Angelica with the infamous family screeching."

"She might as well get used to it," Maggie countered. "She probably inherited the same vocal cords as the rest of us."

"It worked for cheerleading," Christi reminded her, "but not for chorus!"

"Play your best game with the cards God dealt you. That's what I always say."

"I'm trying to do that," Christi responded quietly. "I'm trying to do just that."

Maggie nodded sympathetically, "You'll do fine, Christi. Just fine," she assured her, picking up her toiletry bag and heading for the bathroom. "I'm sure it will be hard for awhile, but you'll survive this. Remember that what doesn't kill us, makes us stronger."

PART VI

1969 – NEW BEGINNINGS

Chapter 30
January 20, 1969

The inaugural address of the United States of America's new President Richard Milhous Nixon was heard, or could have been heard, around the world. Every listener, however, had a conscious or not-so-conscious agenda that influenced what words would be retained.

* * *

Northwest of London at Oxford University, Rhodes Scholar Cameron Coulter from Vicksburg, Mississippi, with his very well known political ambitions, told himself that he was listening as an enlightened, well-traveled citizen of the world.

He knew that he would eventually be standing on that same precipitous podium, but of course he would arrive as a Democrat, not a Republican. Though his current leanings were far to the left of his Dixie compatriots, he was much less ideological than he was simply ambitious. His politics could change. His ambitions were set in rock-hard southern clay.

Cameron heard Nixon say: *"I ask you to share with me today the majesty of this moment. In the orderly transfer of power, we celebrate the unity that keeps us free."* Cameron liked the word "power" and his whole life was focused on attaining it.

Nixon continued: *"Forces now are converging that make possible, for the first time, the hope that many of man's deepest aspirations can at last be realized."* Cameron knew that his Rhodes Scholarship was a ticket to his deepest aspirations.

"The greatest honor history can bestow is the title of peacemaker." A younger Cameron had frantically tried to be the peacemaker in his chaotic, dysfunctional home, but he had failed miserably, despite the heroic stories he had conjured in his own mind about facing his violent, alcoholic stepfather.

"This is our summons to greatness." Amen to that.

* * *

In her nearly empty apartment in Los Angeles, California, Margaret Rose Stephenson found the last hidden-from-herself bottle of Scotch, and poured a double shot into one of the four remaining juice glasses. For a moment, she looked around, and then headed to the guest bedroom where she turned on the small surviving television set, and settled alone on the carpeted floor, leaning back against the barren wall. There was nothing to watch on any channel except the inauguration.

Maggie recalled that Nixon had graduated second in his high school class, second in college, and second in law school. He even came in second when he ran for governor of her great state of California. She remembered hearing somewhere that "second is the number one loser."

She raised her glass to the television set in a toast to the "number one loser," but before she could touch the glass to her lips, she heard Nixon say:

"Because our strengths are so great, we can afford to appraise our weaknesses with candor and to approach them with hope."

Maggie frowned and immediately got up from the floor. She carried her glass to the kitchen and poured its contents down the drain, and did the same with the entire bottle of 12-year-old Scotch. She dropped the empty fifth bottle into the trashcan on her way out the back door. It was a short six-block walk to her former home away from home, and if she hurried, she could get there before the next meeting started.

"Hi. I'm Maggie, and I'm an alcoholic. I've missed seeing you guys for the past coupla months. I've been off on a shoot in the Australian outback and New Guinea. I'm hoping that the article with my photos will appear in National Geographic later this year. But, I'm struggling today, and I really wanted a drink. Some of you have heard me speak about my friend, my roommate, Alessandra. She's moved on, which I should have anticipated. After all, she's a gorgeous young woman and she was determined to make it in films. I won't say any more about her because what we say here has to stay here, and I know you'll be tempted to talk about her if you read the tabloids. Besides, it's not about her problems, it's about mine.

"I know this day is just a bump in a very long road, and I'll survive it, but I really did want to drown all my pain in a bottle. Just knowing that you guys are here supporting each other, somehow supports me no matter where I am. Thank you for helping me to take it one day at a time."

* * *

"We see the hope of tomorrow in the youth of today. I know America's youth. I believe in them. We can be proud that they are better educated, more committed, more passionately driven by conscience than any generation in our history."

When he heard Nixon's words, Jody French thought of his younger brother Naboth, safely away from New Orleans, working diligently to make a better life for himself by excelling in his prep school and beyond. He thought about his sister Tawanya as well, though her hope of tomorrow never came. Jody didn't think about himself in Nixon's context, because he didn't consider himself to be a youth, though the calendar would call him that. Jody felt old. He felt worn.

"We have found ourselves rich in goods, but ragged in spirit; reaching with magnificent precision for the moon, but falling into raucous discord on earth."

Jody pulled the well-worn file from the back of his desk's top drawer. It was all there in the report. The blood he had scraped from the back of *LaMuestra* five years earlier was a certain match to his own and to Naboth's, even accounting for the fact that they all had different fathers. PapaLew had insisted that Jody file a missing person's report on his older sister, but was even more insistent that Jody not disclose the information about the blood on the stern of that luckless boat. Jody had been amply rewarded for his silence, his cooperation and his loyalty, while his sister had become nothing more than one of millions of persons missing around the world.

"To a crisis of the spirit, we need an answer of the spirit. To find that answer, we need only look within ourselves."

Jody rarely looked within himself, and when he did, he didn't like what he saw.

"When we listen to 'the better angels of our nature,' we find that they celebrate the simple things, the basic things - such as goodness, decency, love, kindness."

Remembering his cold-blooded murder of Watson, Jody wondered if he would ever be able to celebrate "goodness, decency, love, kindness." His mother would not be proud, though PapaLew always assured him that what he had done was the right thing to do, under the circumstances.

It was like war. Watson had played a critical role in the attempted murder of PapaLew and his innocent family, not to mention the actual murder of the captain who went down with the ship. Watson clearly had been the bad guy, but he would never be tried and convicted because PapaLew wouldn't get involved.

Jody had bravely done the right thing. It always sounded so simple and right when PapaLew said it, but listening to Nixon's words about "goodness, decency, love, kindness," was filling Jody's head with disturbing thoughts.

* * *

Deputy Sheriff Nick Nichols was enjoying his own view of this inaugural time. Along with Nixon, one of the other Warren County deputies had run successfully for the office he had coveted for years. Though Nichols was still only a deputy while his older compatriot was the new sheriff, Nick took heart from knowing advancement was possible. Anything was possible. He could be mayor someday. A local legend.

Though he didn't realize it, Nick Nichols already was a local legend. He knew or knew something about every person – male or female, black or white – in Vicksburg and in the rest of the surrounding county. He had a formidable network of friends and informants who daily added fodder to his files.

"To match the magnitude of our tasks, we need the energies of our people - enlisted not only in grand enterprises, but more importantly in those small, splendid efforts that make headlines in the neighborhood newspaper instead of the national journal."

* * *

Larry Llewellyn was sprawled on the huge leather sofa in the den, watching the Nixon inauguration with his wife Kelly. It was something they could do together without arguing, since neither one of them had supported McGovern for president.

"We cannot learn from one another until we stop shouting at one another - until we speak quietly enough so that our words can be heard as well as our voices."

"Did you hear that?" Larry asked sarcastically.

"What?"

"'We cannot learn from one another until we stop shouting at one another - until we speak quietly enough so that our words can be heard as well as our voices.'" Larry repeated Nixon's words verbatim.

"Of course, I heard it," Kelly answered. "I was wondering if you did. After all, you're the one who shouts around here. When you are around here."

Larry turned back to the television, knowing that this conversation would be no more successful than most of theirs.

"Sorry," Kelly said quietly. "There's no point in arguing with you."

In her mind, Kelly replayed the words her mother had frequently spoken to her, "You made your bed, and now you have to lie in it. Fortunately for you, it's a comfortable bed in a big comfortable house." Kelly signed in a kind of gratitude for her physical surroundings.

Nixon ruined the moment with his next sentences: *"I do not offer a life of uninspiring ease.... I ask you to join in a high adventure - one as rich as humanity itself, and as exciting as the times we live in. The essence of freedom is that each of us shares in the shaping of his own destiny."*

Kelly realized that she was living a life of *uninspiring ease,* at least materially. There was certainly no *high adventure,* and there was nothing exciting in her life except the rare times she shared with Cameron. The *entire essence of freedom* was missing, and she was taking no role in the shaping of her own destiny. What in the world could she do that was inspiring, exciting, and fulfilling?

"The way to fulfillment is in the use of our talents; we achieve nobility in the spirit that inspires that use."

Larry was relieved that Kelly had backed off about his not being around the house all that much. He figured that she knew he was running around on her, but he also figured that she didn't care. After all, she was still seeing Cameron every time she had a chance, so how could she complain about his affairs? They didn't mean anything. He decided the balance was acceptable. Maybe someday, they could even discuss it.

"After a period of confrontation, we are entering an era of negotiation."

* * *

Prudence Washington had allowed the McGovern rhetoric in Cameron's letters to persuade her that the Democrat would be a better president. She watched the inauguration intently, hoping that Nixon would somehow speak to her concerns.

"We have given freedom new reach, and we have begun to make its promise real for black as well as for white."

The young black woman leaned forward in her chair as Nixon addressed her directly.

"No people has ever been so close to the achievement of a just and abundant society, or so possessed of the will to achieve it."

Prudence nodded, knowing that she had the will to achieve, and that she was well on her way. She wished her mother would be more open to change, but Nellie Mae was of the old school, and she would be left behind.

"Those who have been left out, we will try to bring in. Those left behind, we will help to catch up.... No man can be fully free while his neighbor is not. To go forward at all is to go forward together. This means black and white together, as one nation, not two."

"Thank God that the Llewellyns are not so racist as most of the folks in Mississippi are," Prudence murmured under her breath. "Not many businesses in Jackson or Vicksburg would have given a black girl all the opportunities they've given me. Of course, it's because of Kelly, but I'll make them all proud."

* * *

After her initial anger at Grover for joining the Army, Christi had become comfortable with the idea. After he finished basic training, she even became proud of him for it. Nevertheless, her overriding concern now was for his safety. He would, no doubt, be going to Viet Nam, unless the awful war came to an end quickly. Christi wanted to hear Nixon's promises for peace. He did not disappoint her.

"For the first time, because the people of the world want peace, and the leaders of the world are afraid of war, the times are on the side of peace."

Christi could have cheered, but didn't want to wake the babies from their naps.

"The greatest honor history can bestow is the title of peacemaker. This honor now beckons America - the chance to help lead the world at last out of the valley of turmoil, and onto that high ground of peace that man has dreamed of since the dawn of civilization. If we succeed, generations to come will say of us now living that we mastered our moment, that we helped make the world safe for mankind."

"Amen!" Christi spoke aloud.

"Standing in this same place a third of a century ago, Franklin Delano Roosevelt addressed a Nation ravaged by depression and gripped in fear. He could say in surveying the Nation's troubles: 'They concern, thank God, only material things.'"

For a moment, Christi contemplated the financial bind she was experiencing in Vicksburg with Grover gone, but her natural optimism surfaced soon enough. Despite her dwindling bank account, she would look forward with hope.

"As we reach toward our hopes, our task is to build on what has gone before – not turning away from the old, but turning toward the new."

* * *

The village of Đó Thanh had no televisions, but the young Minh Nhi Li would have been thrilled to hear talk of peace from the new American president. Perhaps, with peace in her land, her husband would be able to return home safely. Though she hoped for the best, she knew that most of the young men and boys who were seized in their villages were never seen again after being carried away to fight in the war alongside their "brothers" from the north of Viet Nam.

She refused to believe that that would happen to Minh Khoi Tien. After all, he was smart and resourceful, and he had learned much from The Uncle in the time they had shared. Surely, even now, he was making a plan to escape and return to her, and to the son who was growing inside her.

"Each moment in history is a fleeting time, precious and unique. But some stand out as moments of beginning..."

* * *

"With those who are willing to join, let us cooperate to reduce the burden of arms, to strengthen the structure of peace, to lift up the poor and the hungry. But to all those who would be tempted by weakness, let us leave no doubt that we will be as strong as we need to be for as long as we need to be."

Pfc. Grover Jones nodded his agreement, and offered a salute toward his new Commander-in-Chief's unseen voice from the radio. He personalized it with a vow whispered under his breath:

"I'll be as strong as I need to be for as long as I need to be."

Chapter 31
January 25, 1969

Deputy Nick Nichols leaned back in his chair, lit another cigarette, and thought about his most troubling open file. This quiet Saturday marked exactly six months since the murder of Clem Boudreaux and his secretary Vayda Jander. It was unusual that Nichols had not heard one word of information about who was behind the crime. Thus, the deputy had concluded that the killer was an outsider. The method of execution and dumping of the bodies also led him to conclude that it was a professional hit, probably by at least two men.

Nichols knew, from too many sources to count, that Clem Boudreaux had been in financial straits at the time of his death. The rule had always been simple - follow the money - but so far, in this case, the money trail had been obscure.

As for Vayda Jander, she had just been in the wrong place at the wrong time. From what Nichols had learned, that had been the story of Vayda's life.

"You have a visitor," came the familiar voice over the intercom.

Nichols sat up straighter in his chair, and was somewhat surprised to see the enormous figure of Tiny Hamlin filling the doorway. The sheriff stood and smiled at one of the nicest guys in all of Mississippi.

"Good to see you, Tiny. Come on in and take a load off. What gives me the honor?"

"I come to confess to a crime, Sheriff."

"Tiny Hamlin, you've never done anything wrong in your whole life," the lawman replied.

Tiny looked down at his big hands.

"I did one thing, Sheriff, and it won't let go of me."

"Okay," Nichols said, "you have the right to remain silent."

"I know that, but I just cain't. It's abotherin' me somethin' fierce, and been abotherin' me somethin' fierce for five years."

Tiny hung his head and stared at this hands, the hands of a man who had been fixing engines and transmissions for most of his life, as his daddy had done before him. Nichols waited.

"Sheriff, you 'member when them four boys ran off the road and got drowned in their car back in sixty-three?"

"You mean Lefty Owens and his friends?"

Tiny nodded.

"Sure, I remember," the deputy answered quickly, and his mind replayed the scene of a muddy, dripping, black station wagon being hauled out of the water by a wrecker from Bennett's Water Street Garage. "Yeah, I remember. And, you were driving the wrecker that night, weren't you, Tiny?"

The big man nodded.

"So, you committed a crime that night?" Nichols asked.

Again, the big man nodded.

"Okay, Tiny. You're here. Tell me about it."

"Ain't you gonna get your notebook out first, Sheriff?"

"I don't always write things down, Tiny. Just tell me."

"You know that was a nice station wagon, Sheriff. And it had a new set of tires on it."

"Okay."

Tiny looked around the office and over his shoulder before continuing. He leaned forward and whispered.

"Sheriff, 'fore anybody knew it, I tuk them four new tires and swapped 'em for the old ones offa my truck. Course I muddied 'em up first, so's no one would notice."

The deputy sheriff grinned.

"That was smart, Tiny. No one did notice. Not even me."

"You didn't notice?" Tiny asked in disbelief.

Nick Nichols laughed his big laugh. "No, I didn't. Why?"

"Ever time I seen you since, you looked at me funny."

"That thought," said the deputy with another laugh, "was coming from your own guilty conscience."

Tiny's jaw dropped, and he said nothing in response.

"Don't worry about it, Tiny. It was more than five years ago, and the Statute's already run. You're off the hook."

"But the Lord knows I done it."

"Then you confess it to the Lord, Tiny, and tell him you're sorry. That's that," the deputy counseled, rising from his chair. "Jesus hung on the cross so you wouldn't have to."

Tiny didn't move for a moment, and then he repeated his look around the office and over his shoulder.

"There's more, Sheriff."

Nichols sat back down in his chair, smiling at the penitent.

"There's this, too," Tiny whispered, gently placing a clean blue shop rag on the desk. He carefully unrolled it to expose a brassy projectile, nearly three inches long.

"Whew," Nichols whistled. "Where'd you get that, Tiny?"

"It was stuck up in the firewall of them kids' car. I just tuk it fer a souvenir, Sheriff. Later, I got to thinkin' about it, and I'm purty sure that this here bullet musta went right through the front tire and come out clear the other side. They was two holes in that tire I had to fix afore I could put it on my truck."

Nick Nichols couldn't decide if he wanted to slug Tiny or hug him, so he just took the time to light another cigarette. He held up the pack toward Tiny, knowing the big guy didn't smoke. Tiny shook his head.

"Who else knows about this, Tiny?"

"Nobody, Sheriff."

"You sure?"

"Yes, sir. Nobody saw me when I tuk it, nobody saw me when I hided it, and nobody saw me brang it here today."

"Okay, Tiny. I'm not gonna file charges against you for obstruction and accessory after the fact, if you swear not to talk about this, unless I ask you to testify. You understand?"

"I don't know about no construction and accessories, Sheriff, but I give you my word that I won't say nuthin' about nuthin' to nobody, lest you ast me yoresef."

After Tiny left, the deputy thought intently about the night Lefty and friends died in that car. Kelly McCain and Cameron Coulter had arrived at the scene, without Larry Llewellyn.

Nichols picked up the shell, still in the shop rag, and decided it was from an old M14. A sniper with that gun could have hit the tire from 500 yards, or even farther with a scope. He knew a few hunters in Mississippi who could manage that shot, but there would be no trace of a sniper in the woods after all this time.

Nichols had kept his temper in check, but he was more than a little aggravated at Tiny for not turning this over to him sooner. Still, the lawman was pleased to know that his nagging hunch that night had been right.

The car wreck that killed those four boys was no more an accident than the brawl started by Lefty Owens at the country club two weeks earlier had been a random Halloween prank. PapaLew had fixed that ruckus for Lefty, and had paid for all the damages at the country club. Why?

What was going on between Lefty and the Llewellyns? Nichols realized that everybody in the county had some sort of beef with Lefty Owens, but a professional hit? Who would have ordered and paid for that? Who could have?

With this new information from Tiny, and the bullet that could have been red-hot evidence five years earlier, Nichols now counted six apparent contract killings in his county since the Llewellyn family had moved to Vicksburg.

Nichols hadn't heard a word about a connection between the Llewellyns and Lefty Owens, other than Kelly's well-known dislike of the bully and his three friends. PapaLew and Clem Boudreaux had been connected as old friends, hadn't they? Everyone knew that, but now the deputy was wondering if Vayda had actually been an innocent bystander. Or, were they all in together on something bigger than he knew?

It could have been a coincidence that six civilians were all dead at the hands of strangers in Warren County, Mississippi, but coincidences always troubled the deputy — especially coincidences in his county, on his watch. Nick Nichols sighed, stretched back in his old wooden chair, and lit another cigarette.

Chapter 32
March 3, 1969

Despite the cold, Christi felt her face flush with prickles of heat. Her breathing was quick and shallow. Her mouth was dry, but her eyes were wet with tears. Her hands shook as she tried to re-read the official-looking document. She had never seen anything like it, but it had arrived by way of certified mail, and she had signed for it, so she could only assume it was true. As she stood on the porch, letter in hand, watching the mail truck disappear around the distant corner, Christi had a sick feeling in the pit of her stomach.

Christi thought of her young daughters, innocently taking their afternoon naps in the ancestral home of the grandparents they had never seen. What would become of them? Christi had no education past high school, no special skills, no plan to implement, and no idea of what to do next. She walked back into the house, surveying its grandeur as if she had never seen it before.

The old black phone in the hallway jangled its harsh alert. Christi's first instinct was to ignore it, but she didn't want it to wake up the girls. It was Prudence Washington on the line.

"Christi, are you okay? I just had the worst feeling about you," came the concerned voice from Jackson.

"Thanks for calling, Pru. No, I'm not okay. I just got an official notice."

"Oh, my God! Grover?"

"No," Christi whispered. "No, thank God, it's not Grover."

Prudence breathed an audible sigh of relief.

"Then, how bad could it be?"

"It's a foreclosure notice, Pru. They're going to take the house."

"Not the Boudreaux house!" Prudence exclaimed. "How?"

"Before my daddy…, oh, Pru, I can't talk about it now."

"Go lie down," Pru advised. "I'll call you later."

Christi placed the receiver on the phone cradle without even saying good-bye.

* * *

Pru's next call was to George Llewellyn's office.

"PapaLew, thank you for taking my call. I just found out that they're going to foreclose on the Boudreaux home."

"God damn it! What the hell is going on? Who's going to foreclose?"

"Christi was so upset that she couldn't even talk to me," Prudence explained. "I don't know anything other than what I just told you. I called because you're the only person I know who could help her."

"You did the right thing, honey. I'll take it from here," he assured her. "Don't you worry. I'll take it from here."

George Llewellyn hung up the phone and called his lawyer. Then he got in his car and drove immediately to the Boudreaux home. When Christi finally answered the bell, she was startled to see PapaLew on the porch.

"What's wrong?" she asked as she opened the door.

"God damn it! You tell me what's wrong. Prudence just called to say you got a foreclosure notice today."

Christi nodded, and began crying again. "I didn't know Pru was going to call you," Christi said simply, "but I'm glad she did. I couldn't think of anything to do. Please come in."

* * *

Dear Christi,

I started to write a letter to you on the plane, but it sounded so bad that I tore it up and started over. That seems dumb now, but that's what I did. I hope you'll understand, but I'm sure you never would do anything like that because you always say what you feel.

Anyway, I was feeling sad and missing you and feeling sorry for myself for being on my first plane ride alone. Well, not really alone, with all the other Army guys crammed up against me, all going to the same place. I looked around on that plane and figured that not all of us would be making it back from Viet Nam in one piece, but I'm sure that I will. Maybe we all think we will, and maybe we all will, but maybe we won't.

Grover snatched up the offensive piece of paper, crumbled it in his huge paw, and threw it on the floor in disgust.

Dear Christi,

Flying turned out to be not so bad, but it seemed to take three days to get here. We flew forever over the Pacific Ocean and then over the South China Sea, but I couldn't tell the difference.

Then we flew over dark green land for a while and then we landed so fast that I thought we might be crashing, but there was a big ole airport right in the middle of nowhere. It's hot in nowhere, but the guys who have been around a while say to enjoy it. The rainy season starts in May.

I always liked the rain. Maybe it's the farmer in me. I played some of my best games in the rain too. Remember that Jackson game when I hurt my knee the first time? Sure you do. Anyway, I might not of caught that interception in the last seconds of the game if it hadn't of been raining that night. The Jackson guy might of been able to hang onto it with his little hands and he would of had the winning touchdown instead of me.

I sure looked funny in the game film, limping and running down the field. I can close my eyes and hear the crowd going nuts. You were so pretty that night. You still are. Give the babies a kiss for me. Tell them that daddy loves his little girls, and his big one too.

Love,
Grover

* * *

Cameron Coulter hunched his shoulders against the dank English chill, and walked carefully down the dimly lit cobbled alley. The girl had given him good directions, and he had little trouble finding the turquoise blue arched doorway that distinguished her tiny quarters from the others. Perhaps he should have carried a book or two, since he had invited himself to her place to study, but he was in no mood to study on such a deliciously gloomy evening.

She answered his knock quickly, though he was a good hour later than they had arranged.

"I expected you immediately after dinner," she chided, with no hint of humor in her voice. He ignored her tone, and focused on her delightful British accent, though, of course, he was the foreigner with the accent.

Cameron studied her face and her clothing. No makeup. No fancy dress. Nothing different from the plain wool leggings and oversized sweater that the English country girl had been wearing when they had met on campus a few weeks earlier. Either she never did anything to fix herself, or she didn't consider his visit worthy of special attention.

"I got tied up," he lied, without bothering to apologize.

"Where are your books?" she questioned.

"I wasn't in the mood to study," he responded truthfully, closing the door behind him.

The room was small and over-furnished, in that way of Dickens' settings, with too many books and not enough lamps. He headed to the small heater in the corner that made a spot of warmth in an otherwise chilly space, and stretched his hands over it. The movement of his long slender fingers cast strange shadows on the wall.

The girl did not ask him to sit down, nor did she offer a cup of tea.

"I must study tonight," she said simply. "I thought it might be nice to have some company while I studied, but I can't have you just sitting here watching me. Perhaps you can come at another time, when you are in the mood to study."

Cameron could not believe he was being rebuffed by this very plain girl. She actually had her hand on the doorknob. He pulled the wool cap from his head and shrugged off his jacket in one move, then quickly covered the few steps back to the door and wrapped both his arms around the girl.

"What are you doing?" she asked incredulously, trying to push him away.

Cameron began kissing her cheek, her forehead, her neck, whatever he could reach as she twisted her head violently.

"Stop!" she cried.

"Didn't you know why I was coming here?" he asked.

"I thought we were going to study. I have a fiancé coming home from the navy. I have no romantic interest in you. Stop this right now." Pleading, she looked directly into his eyes.

Cameron used that moment to catch her upper lip in his teeth. He clamped down, but not enough to break the skin.

"Stop!" she cried again, and then whimpered "Stop!" as if she could think of no other word to say.

Still biting her lip, Cameron half-carried, half-dragged her to the lumpy sofa that served as her bed. She felt her leggings being ripped off, but his full weight was on top of her, and her lip was being bitten unmercifully. She could not move, other than to flail her arms uselessly. She tried to scratch him on the back, but his sweater was too thick.

"Stop!" she whispered hopelessly as she felt him force his way between her legs. She closed her eyes and tried to tell herself that she was having a nightmare while he bit her lip and thrust himself into her voraciously. Her whole body was throbbing in pain, and when she thought she couldn't stand another moment, she mindlessly started counting to herself "one-thousand-one, one-thousand-two, one-thousand-three, one-thousand-four, one-thousand-five, one-thousand-six, one-thousand-seven," and it was when she reached "one-thousand-twenty-seven" that he shuddered to a finish.

When it was over, Cameron got up and straightened himself, while the girl lay on the sofa, crying hopelessly. He casually picked up his jacket from the floor where he had dropped it, and put it back on as he walked across the room. He put on his wool cap, opened the door to the dark night, glanced both ways down the alley, and, seeing no one, he headed out without a word, leaving the stricken girl alone.

Chapter 33
April 29, 1969

The Uncle arrived in Đó Thanh unannounced, under cover of darkness, as was his custom. Minh Nhi Li heard his truck, as did the other villagers, but she alone rose to greet him. She had hoped, prayed, and dreamed that he would have found her beloved husband by now, and would return with him in triumph. She tried to conceal her disappointment that The Uncle had arrived alone.

"There is no word of my dear nephew," The Uncle announced immediately, with compassion in his voice. "I fear that your husband will not return, though I continue to pray."

Minh Nhi Li nodded stoically and invited The Uncle inside.

"You will be pleased to see your nephew's son," Nhi Li whispered with a trace of pride in her voice. The Uncle nodded, and peered at the sleeping baby on the mat.

"A son?" The Uncle asked. "A son?" he repeated.

Nhi Li smiled. "A son."

"What have you named him?" The Uncle wanted to know.

"He has been called 'The Minh Son' since his birth one month ago," the young mother answered simply. "I was waiting for… for… his father… to return, or…"

The Uncle laid his hand gently upon the sleeping child.

"He will be called Minh Quang Khoi, for he will be my son and his father's," The Uncle announced solemnly.

Minh Nhi Li nodded and smiled. "This is a high honor, Minh Quang Tung, and I will do everything I can to make you proud of this son."

"I am already too proud," the old man answered. "Come, let us sit and talk. I have many things to tell you."

For the next two hours, Nhi Li heard stories that she would not have believed from any other source. Many of the facts and numbers were too astronomical for her to comprehend - a million tons of American supplies a month coming into her country, air traffic so heavy that her country's airports were now the busiest in the world, sophisticated technology, napalm bombs that roasted their victims alive, and smuggling networks for everything a man could want.

"I am not proud of everything I have done since the Americans began to arrive in our country, and I will make no excuses. I am responsible for many of the 'irregularities' that have occurred with American supplies. On paper, they have sent enough concrete to pave all of Viet Nam, but though the payment arrives, the concrete does not.

"Perhaps I have contributed to the soaring inflation that has made our piaster worth so little while the GI's are paid in what is called 'scrip' and many of us make a percentage on the exchange, putting our profits into gold. War is a dreadful business, Minh Nhi Li, and I am a business man."

Minh Nhi Li nodded politely, wondering why The Uncle was telling her all these incomprehensible things in the middle of the night. Just as strangely, The Uncle had not hidden his truck, as he customarily did.

"I must go now," The Uncle announced, rising to his feet. He enjoyed a lingering look at his namesake, the only hope for the Minh family name to continue. Then The Uncle removed a small packet from his many-pocketed shirt, and held it in front of Minh Nhi Li.

"This," he explained slowly, "contains everything that you and your son will need. Soon, or maybe not too soon, our country will collapse. I advise you to leave Đó Thanh as soon as you are able, but do not go to live in the cities. Too many refugees already, and no safety for a young woman and child, even, or especially, with gold I could transfer to you. I would take you from here myself, but my life is in danger now, and I would only put you in harm's way. Do you understand?"

Minh Nhi Li nodded, but her eyes betrayed her confusion.

The Uncle sighed. "I have troubled your mind with too many things tonight, and I regret the need to do that, but you are the future of the Minh family. I trust you will choose a wise and safe path for yourself and for Minh Quang Khoi."

As if responding to the sound of his new name, the infant awakened from his sleep. The Uncle wordlessly went to the baby and lifted him from the mat. The old man and the baby stared at each other in silence, and Nhi Li saw tears forming in the eyes of The Uncle. He gently handed the child to her, and left the hut in silence. His truck rumbled into the darkness.

* * *

Through the plate glass window of his office twenty feet above the warehouse floor, Arnold Robert Neely absently watched trucks backing up to the loading docks. Sometimes, and this was one of those times, Arnie actually missed driving the big rigs himself. With that thought, his phantom left leg reflexively tried to engage a clutch, but the clutch wasn't there and neither was his left leg. For the millionth time, Arnie cursed his fate, and the former friend he blamed for his injury.

If he had been a more introspective man, Arnie might have wondered why he would be cursing George Llewellyn at the exact moment that George rapped on his open office door. It took Arnie less than a moment to recognize the hated face that he had not seen in decades.

"How did you get in here?" Arnie growled at the intruder.

"God damn it! Same way you got into my sister's pants – lying, manipulative, southern charm," George answered with a smile. "Nice receptionist you got out there. Big tits."

"You'll surely excuse me if I don't get up?" Arnie asked sarcastically.

"You probably can't get anything up these days. I won't take it goddamn personally,." the unwelcome guest retorted.

George Llewellyn dragged a heavy chair from its place against the wall, and moved it uncomfortably close to Arnie. Neither man spoke for a full minute.

"You have a nerve showing up at my place. I oughta have you shot for trespassing."

"God damn right, you oughta have me shot, or you oughta have a boat blown up under me. You sure as shit don't have the balls to do it yourself. Gonna call the same guys you sent after Clem?"

"What happened between me and Clem is between me and Clem. If that's why you're here, it's none of your business, and we got nothing to talk about."

"God damn it! I'm making it my business!"

Arnie sighed in resignation. "Okay. Why?"

"It's a long story, but it has to do with family. Clem's daughter is my daughter-in-law's best friend. I gotta do something."

"Clem shoulda thought about his daughter before he dug into me so deep. A man's gotta pay his debts," Arnie averred self-righteously, as if he were quoting scripture, "and a man's gotta collect what's owed him. One way or the other. Dead or alive. Clem might've forced me to do it the hard way, but it's just business."

"God damn it! I understand business, but Clem was our friend. Isn't that worth something?" George asked.

"If he's such a good friend, why didn't he ask you for the money? You were right there in Vicksburg with him."

"Probably his pride. Probably figured everybody in town would hear about it." George shook his head, thinking that everybody in town knew about it now.

"Listen, Arnie. I want the Boudreaux homestead," George announced simply. "I'll pay fair value for it."

"It's not for sale," Arnie answered quickly.

"God damn it! Everything's for sale – it's just a matter of the price."

"Not this," Arnie insisted. "I want that house."

"God damn it! You are not going to move to Vicksburg! I swear, if you put your one lousy foot in Mississippi, I am personally going to haul you all the way back to Louisiana to the Big Osprey Bayou and feed your worthless honkie ass to the goddamned alligators. Do you understand that?"

Arnie laughed out loud.

"I can't believe you're still using that old threat. The Big Osprey Bayou dried up years ago," Arnie informed him. "It's a shopping center now. Progress, old buddy. Progress. Don't worry. I have no intention of moving to Vicksburg, or anywhere else. I've got a nice setup here in N'Orleans."

"God damn it! If you're not moving to Vicksburg, why do you want that house?"

"Progress, old buddy. Progress. Going to bulldoze her down. It's a perfect spot for a convenience store and gas station, with plenty of room for a car wash."

"God damn it! Are you outa your fucking mind? That's a fucking historical treasure. It could be a museum!"

"Ha! When did you get so god damned cultured that you care about a museum?"

George Llewellyn stared at his former college friend and poker partner. He knew Arnie well enough to know this wasn't a bluff. A fucking car wash? The usually stoic PapaLew felt his lower lip quiver. He coughed into his hand, hoping that Arnie had not seen any sign of weakness.

"God damn it! I don't care about any museum. I just told the kid I'd try to help. If your mind's made up, then that's it."

"It's not like you to give up so easy," Arnie commented.

George shrugged. "Maybe I'm getting mellow in my old age. By the way, speaking of old age, I ran into Big Sam a while back. He's doing pretty good for himself."

"Yeah. That's what I heard. State senator now. Too good to talk to me," Arnie complained.

"He doesn't have much to say to me either. Turned into a god damned deacon in the church. All righteous now."

Arnie nodded. "It happens. Gotta think of his reputation."

"God damn it! That reminds me. Speaking of reputations, those guys you hired to do ole Clem did a bang up job. Not a trace of evidence anywhere. Who'd ya use? The Twins? Are they still around?"

Arnie simply nodded once.

"Are you saying that's who you used, or that they're still around?"

"Both," Arnie answered.

George laughed out loud.

"What's so funny?" Arnie wanted to know.

"You said 'both' and we're talking about The Twins. It just struck me as funny. Where can I find them?"

Arnie stared at George and didn't say a word.

"God damn it! I'm not going to have them take you out. I just like to be able to get in touch with the right people at the right time. You know. Insurance."

Arnie scribbled a number on a pad of paper that had a fancy crest and "Arnold Robert Neely" engraved at the top.

"You can always find them through their mama. Here's her number."

"What'll they charge?"

"Hell, they give me a volume discount," Arnie bragged. "You're on your own, but you can use my name."

George rose slowly from the chair, folding the piece of paper and sticking it in his front pocket.

"Thanks," he said, patting the pocket.

"Don't mention it," Arnie responded. "And don't ever show your face around here again. Next time I might not be feeling so neighborly."

"God damn it! Speaking of neighborly, why do you really want Clem's old family homestead?"

"You remember when we were all at Tulane?"

"God damn right, I remember. You, me, Clem, Big Sam. Hustling those rich kids at poker. Easy pickings."

"Yeah," Arnie agreed. "And remember that weekend we all drove up to Vicksburg and stayed at Clem's house?"

George nodded.

"You know what happened there?"

"We all got drunk," George volunteered.

Arnie gave a look of disgust, and said nothing.

"Clem's old man butt-fucked you?" George tried again.

"Shit, no. Worse. I heard that old man and his prissy wife talking about us. They was worried about poor little Clemmie boy because they thought I was a bad influence on him. They called me 'poor white trash.' Said if Clem kept hanging out and gambling with the likes of me, he'd go down the toilet with me. Said I was lucky to even see the inside of a house like theirs."

"God damn it! So what?"

"I decided right then and there that someday I would own that fucking Boudreaux house and bring it to the ground."

"Hmmm," George nodded slowly on his way out the door. "I guess they were right about you after all."

Chapter 34
April 30, 1969

It had never occurred to Grover Jones that writing to Christi would be the hardest part of being in Viet Nam. If she knew everything that was going on there, she would be too worried to think straight. He was having trouble thinking straight too, but only because he was trying to assimilate too much new information and become a part of an Army culture that was almost as foreign to him as the Viet Cong, whoever they were — wherever they were.

Guys in his unit smoked pot that was sometimes soaked in opium. They used heroin and drugs he had never heard of. Every time they went out on patrol, Grover felt like he was getting in the car with a drunk driver. Once, he was almost certain that their patrol leader was shot in the back by one of their own guys. When he whispered his concern to another soldier, he heard that guys got "fragged" all the time. It was a new word that he was sorry to know. He quickly figured out that it was best to keep his mouth shut.

Grover also decided to avoid the poker games. First, of course, he was a lousy poker player, even when it was Penny Ante with Christi just for fun. These guys were too serious for Grover, but a lot of them lost their entire "scrip" paycheck every chance they got. Worse, Grover suspected that Sarge was getting the guys drunker than they should have been and then cheating them when they could have beat him fairly. He knew it was best to keep his mouth shut about that too.

Once, at the showers, Grover noticed that Sarge took off a padded belt-like thing from around his waist and put it on the floor between his feet, not even worrying about the water getting on it. Grover was curious, but not curious enough to ask about it. It was bad enough to get shot at by unseen guns in the jungle. It was another thing entirely to risk getting "fragged" for asking a stupid question. Grover kept his curiosity under control, but sometimes exercising that control took a lot of energy. He had never been so tired in all his life.

* * *

April 30, 1969

Dear Christi,

It was great to get a letter from you. I'm glad that things are going so well at home. I told you that you would be fine with me gone, but I hope that you're missing me as much as I'm missing you.

I got a letter from my dad too. He says things are fine out on the farm, best crops in years, but he misses you and the girls. I won't ask you to go out there, but I hope you will invite him over to see the kids. He said he had some mail for me. Maybe you can see about that too, but it's probably nothing important.

Things aren't so bad here, considering there's a war on. It's still hot, but the rain is due any day. A change will be nice, I hope.

I'm going to cut this letter short tonight. We're going out on another patrol early in the morning. I probably shouldn't mention that, because I don't want you to worry, but going out on patrol is what we do, and I don't want to lie to you about it.

I love you more than I have the words to say. I only hope that you just know it in your heart. I miss you and the girls.

All my love,
Grover

* * *

May Day! May Day! May Day!

Grover woke up thinking that the First of May was called May Day all over the world, but he had no idea why. And, why was that same term used as a distress signal? He was starting to realize that there were too many things he didn't know. He wondered if Christi knew about May Day, and figured she probably did. If she didn't, surely Kelly McCain would know. That girl knew all the English words.

It would never have occurred to Grover that Mayday as a distress signal came from the French phrase "venez m'aider" that means "come to help me." Dropping the "venez" or "come" part leaves "m'aider" that is pronounced "mayday" all over the world.

Grover also didn't realize that many of the words in common usage in Viet Nam came from the French because the French had occupied Viet Nam for years, with soldiers as well as missionaries. The French influence was most obvious in the large cities, but there were traces of it in the most remote villages. The missionaries had been zealous.

Grover was uncomfortable with the words "May Day" ringing in his ears as he headed out on patrol. Thankfully, he had never been asked to "take point" on these sorties. He knew all too well that the point man was the most likely to step on a land mine. He had seen it happen, and it was the worst sight of his life, but he never mentioned it to Christi.

Somehow, stepping on a land mine seemed worse than getting shot and killed, even if the end result was the same. Grover tried to shake the thought out of his head as they entered into heavy cover where the huge trees had such thick canopies that it seemed like night time in the middle of the day. May Day.

It was still hot. There was no sign of the promised rainy season, but Grover was soaking wet from perspiration. He could smell the guy in front of him. He supposed that the guy behind him could smell him too. There were other smells in the jungle that Grover had not come to recognize, but he was assaulted with all of them in the age-old fear response that heightened the senses of hearing, sight, and smell.

Grover listened to strange birds in the distance and the tromping of leather boots and the shifting of heavy packs and guns. Finally, after what seemed like hours of silent and blessedly uneventful trekking through the darkness, he heard the screaming sound of a jet engine ahead. He heard explosions, followed by screams of human beings. Screams in Viet Nam sounded just like screams in Vicksburg. Grover wondered if screams sounded the same in every language. Could it be the thing that all people had in common?

Moments later the point man stepped on the one land mine guarding the eastern jungle path into the village of Đó Thanh.

Grover heard a click, and then silence as the entire troop stopped without a signal. The point man had heard the click too. He knew that as soon as he took his weight off the mine, it would detonate. The man behind him very gently touched his shoulder. The next one made the Sign of the Cross. Then all of them stepped back away from him, staying on the path.

Another plane, or the same one, screamed overhead. There were more explosions, and more screams from the village. All Grover could hear was the reverberating sound of that click. Then he heard the point man say, "Tell Vicki I love her," right before he dove off the landmine. He was one of the lucky ones. He died instantly.

For no reason that Grover could understand, everyone broke rank. They ran into the village, shooting everything that moved – old men, women, children, water buffalo, dogs, chickens – and then someone set a hut on fire and then another hut and another. Grover stood watching, as if he were only a distant observer and not a part of the assault. May Day. May Day. May Day.

Suddenly, Grover was sure that he heard someone crying "May Day! May Day! May Day!" Pointing his rifle in the direction of the sound, Grover looked down and noticed that his feet were moving toward a hut that was starting to smolder. He opened the door with the barrel of his gun just as something that looked like a football hurtled across the room toward him. Instinct honed by years of defensive play caused him to reach out with his left hand to catch the ball.

Fourth and two on the twenty yard line. Jackson is going for it. The crowd is wild. "Gro-ver! Gro-ver! Gro-ver!"

Grover started to tuck the ball under his arm and run when he realized that in his hand was a baby, wrapped tightly in a cloth. He blinked. He heard a click. He saw two little brown eyes staring at him out of the football in his hand.

"May Day! May Day! May Day!"

"Soldier!"

Grover snapped to attention. The football baby was still in his left hand. He saw Sarge on the other side of the hut, with his hand on the throat of a very small woman. Sarge must have thrown the football at him, or thrown it toward the side of the hut, out of bounds, intentional grounding.

"Let her go, Sarge!" Grover heard his voice command. "Let her go!"

Sarge scowled at Grover and started to draw his side arm. In two steps, Grover was standing over him, beating him with his M-14. Sarge collapsed in a bloody heap on top of the very small woman. Grover kicked him off her and felt the padded belt-like thing around the non-com's waist. Still holding the football baby in his left hand, Grover dropped his gun and removed Sarge's belt. He shoved it and the handgun under his shirt. Then he grabbed the dead man's rifle, along with his own. With his right hand, he slung the rifles over his shoulder and dragged the woman from the hut as the smolder grew into a fire. The football baby was still in his left hand.

When Grover emerged from the hut, there was no sign of his unit, or of life. He walked in a trance toward the center of the village that was engulfed in flames. He turned to the woman, but she was running back to the hut. He could not believe that she would leave the football baby to go back to a burning hut. She must have gone crazy. He saw her crawl into the hut, like Alice Through The Looking Glass. He could not believe that he was going to follow her. He must have gone crazy too. Then he realized that he was dreaming.

"Touchdown! Jones has made the touchdown! Vicksburg wins it! Yes, folks, Grover Jones is the hero tonight!"

Now the woman was running toward him from the hut, waving a small packet in one hand, and clutching a white football in the other. Everyone must have a football in this dream, Grover thought, but he could not awaken himself.

The woman handed the small packet to him, exchanging it for his football baby. She was crying and kissing the baby, and the stadium crowd was going wild, "Gro-ver! Gro-ver! Gro-ver!" and the dying village of Đó Thanh was burning all around them.

Chapter 35
May 2, 1969

The last thing Prudence expected on her day off was a call from Nick Nichols. The deputy wanted to see her the next time she was in Vicksburg. Nothing official. Nothing to worry about. Just stop by for a chat. It was the sort of summons that would strike fear in the heart of anyone guilty of a crime, but Prudence's conscience was clear, and she was planning to spend the weekend in Vicksburg anyway, visiting Christi. Would the sheriff be in his office on Saturday? Yep.

Prudence arrived mid-morning and was waved into the deputy's small office without ceremony. He rose to greet her.

"Thanks for coming so quickly," he said cordially.

Prudence nodded and smiled. "No problem."

"How are things going for you in Jackson?" he asked.

"Great. You must know that PapaLew gave me a nice job in the Jackson store and I'm enjoying the work. I'm going to Jackson State University part-time, and I'll eventually finish with a degree in Business Administration. Little Ray loves his school and his day care. Things couldn't be much better."

"I'm glad to hear that," the deputy said sincerely. "I know you had quite a hard time for a while."

Prudence nodded.

"I want to discuss something with you that's extremely sensitive and important. I think I can trust you to maintain confidentiality. Am I right?"

Prudence frowned and looked inquisitively at the lawman.

"I can't imagine why you would want to confide in me," she responded honestly.

"It's about PapaLew," Nichols replied.

Prudence crossed her arms and leaned back in her chair, frowning. "PapaLew has been more than kind and generous to me. I wouldn't feel right talking behind his back."

"That's understandable," the deputy said, nodding. "Still, this is really important, and I think that you can help."

"I don't think so, Sheriff. I don't know anything about the Llewellyns' businesses, other than the store in Jackson, though I've heard the same rumors that you must have heard."

"Pru, I need someone inside, and you're the perfect person. You've been involved with the family for such a long time that no one would suspect you of anything."

"Sheriff, you can't ask me to trade on that friendship to be a spy for you."

Nick Nichols was almost taken aback by the young woman's bold response. He remembered the way she had looked at him the first time they met, after standing forever in the rain beside Ray's grave. Her pain had been her shield back then. Now she had some maturity to go with it. The deputy was impressed. He would have to be more insistent.

"I was hoping you would be cooperative," Nichols said simply. "I didn't want to twist your arm."

"I don't think you have a way to twist my arm," Prudence said firmly, rising from her chair. "I'm sorry I can't help you."

"Not so fast," he said, raising a hand in the air.

Prudence sat again. The deputy walked around behind her to close the door. When he went back to his chair, he took his time, lit a cigarette, and offered her one, which she declined.

He let out a deep sigh, with a cloud of cigarette smoke.

"I didn't want to do it this way," the deputy began.

Prudence felt the slightest twinge of fear.

"Do you remember the day we met? At the cemetery? A little over five years ago, right?"

She nodded.

"I remember it too, and I remember very well what you told me that day. You said that Ray was your boyfriend."

Prudence tightened her lips, but said nothing.

"Not long after that day, but definitely <u>after</u> that day, Ray was your husband."

"Perhaps I misspoke at the cemetery."

"I don't think so. In fact, I know you didn't. You were not married to Ray when he was killed in Viet Nam. I am really sorry for your loss, but he was definitely not your husband."

Prudence gave an innocent little shrug of her shoulders.

"I have papers."

"I know about the papers. You're not the first person to get a marriage date adjusted, for whatever reason."

"Is that a crime?"

"As a matter of fact, it is, but not one that I'm interested in prosecuting. The more serious crime came later. You falsified documents to get government assistance. You knew that if you were just Ray's girlfriend, you would not be entitled to widow's benefits from the VA, and you wouldn't be receiving those Social Security checks. Therefore, every dime that you have received by virtue of being his 'widow' has been fraudulently obtained. That, missy, is a federal offense."

Prudence sighed, dropped her head, and stared at her hands that were trembling in her lap.

"So, you're going to arrest me?" Prudence finally asked.

"If I get you thrown into prison, you won't be any use to me at all. I'm hoping that you will reconsider my request for help so we can work on this together, and I'll forget I ever happened to find out about that bogus marriage license in Louisiana. That's not in my jurisdiction anyway.... Well?"

"I don't like it one bit," Prudence spat the words at him.

"I don't either," said the deputy, with a touch of sadness, "but I also don't like unsolved murder cases in my county."

Prudence's eyes widened. "Murder cases? Surely you don't think that PapaLew has murdered someone here?"

"That's what I aim to find out. Are you going to help me?"

"I don't really know how I could help you, but I don't see that I have any reasonable alternative, except to cooperate."

"You got that right," Nichols said with authority.

"Fine," Prudence responded sarcastically. "What do I have to do?"

* * *

Jody French had enjoyed the entire morning meeting with PapaLew. As usual, all his plans for summer activities at the marina had been approved with enthusiasm.

"God damn it, Boy! You're doing a great job at the yacht club. I wish I had more for you in New Orleans."

"PapaLew, I've been thinking about some commercial development along the riverfront. I don't mean just wharves for loading and unloading freight, but nice restaurants, shops, and high dollar tourist attractions. I haven't run numbers on it yet, but my instinct tells me it would work."

PapaLew beamed at his protégé, and nodded.

"You're on to something there, Jody. I bet it would work, too, from a popularity standpoint. My biggest concern, and the reason I wouldn't want to pour a lot of money into it, is simply the goddamned geography of the whole area.

"You've got Lake Pontchartrain north of the city. What? Thirty-five miles wide. You've got the Mississippi River flowing into the delta. You've got the whole fucking Gulf of Mexico up her butt. And you've got pretty little N'Orleans just sitting there waiting to get swept away because her God damned levees can't stop all that water in a really big storm.

"It's been four years since Hurricane Betsy, so we're due for another big one this season. Just about the time we'd get something built, we'd have a hurricane wipe it out. No, we're lucky the marina is still standing. Jody, you're just too young to realize this from personal experience. Go back and check the weather history. N'Orleans has never gone more'n twelve years without a hurricane. We can't afford those odds."

Jody was visibly disappointed. It was the first denial he had experienced from his mentor, and it didn't feel good at all. Maybe he should have spent more time on numbers before broaching the subject with PapaLew.

PapaLew got up from the big chair behind his desk and walked around to Jody. He patted him on the shoulder and said, "I'm glad you're always thinking of new projects, Jody, and I wish I could go along with this one, but I don't trust Mother Nature with that much money. Come on. Let me buy your lunch. It's not the end of the world."

"I don't suppose we're going to the Vicksburg Country Club for lunch, are we?" Jody asked disingenuously.

PapaLew laughed out loud. "You'll be the first to know when a black kid can get a meal at the VCC without being kitchen help. I was thinking about Sambo's for barbecue."

"That sounds great, though I wasn't hungry until you mentioned Sambo's."

As PapaLew and Jody left the office, Prudence was walking up to the door.

"Hi, PapaLew," she greeted him casually. "I was just in town to visit Christi and I thought I'd stop by to see you. I'm sorry. I should have called, seeing you have company."

"Jody and I were heading out to Sambo's for lunch. Would you like to join us?"

Prudence looked at the handsome young man with PapaLew, and thought she would like nothing better than to join them for lunch. She had not been attracted to another man since she met Ray, and she was surprised at herself for being instantly interested in whoever this was.

"Pru, this is Jody French. He runs our marina in New Orleans. Jody, this is Prudence Purvis, an old friend of the family who's our right hand in the Jackson store. It's funny that you two haven't met before now."

PapaLew noticed that Pru was suddenly silent, and that Jody didn't say anything either. The two were simply staring at each other. PapaLew stifled a laugh. This could be cute.

* * *

Grover had never been very good at geography, and his map reading skills were limited at best, but he had never been so motivated to figure out where he was and where he was going. For nearly twenty-four hours, he and the woman and the baby had hidden in the jungle, far enough from the village not to be sighted, but close enough to hear if someone returned looking for him. There had not even been the sound of a jet or a helicopter, nor had Grover spoken to the woman. Nothing but the strange birds, and now the sound of thunder.

It was time to move. Grover opened Sarge's pack and found maps, but they were the strangest maps he had ever seen. All the big words were in an unknown language, which he assumed was Vietnamese. He showed one of the maps to the woman. She studied it carefully, and then nodded. She put her finger on the printed words Đó Thanh, and then pointed back to her village.

Grover laughed out loud, and the woman looked at him as though he had lost his mind, which he probably had. The last time he had looked at a map was when he was lost in Dothan,

Alabama. Now he was lost in Đó Thanh, South Viet Nam. He wished there were someone to laugh with him. The woman just stared, and cradled her baby closely, as if he were in danger of going crazy too.

Grover realized it was time to try to communicate with her. Clearly, she could not go back to a burned-out village alone.

He put both his hands on his chest and said, "Billy Jack Rucker" without thinking beyond what he had seen on the passport in Sarge's pack. He knew enough to know that the passport had to be illegal, but Sarge must have bought it for a way out, if he ever needed it.

"Billy Jack Rucker," Grover repeated his new name.

"Ban-Li Giác Rach-Khê," she said, pointing at him. "Ban-Li Giác Rach-Khê."

"Hmmm. You can just call me 'Jack,'" Grover said. He put his hands across his chest again. "Jack," he repeated simply.

"Giác," she mimicked clearly. "Giác."

Then the woman smiled, nodded, and tapped her chest. "Minh Nhi Li," she said clearly. "Minh Nhi Li."

Grover laughed again. "Minnie Lee?... Minnie Lee?... What's a girl like you doing with a good southern name like Minnie Lee?"

Minh Nhi Li smiled again. They were communicating.

"Minh Quang Khoi," she said, lifting the baby toward him. "Minh Quang Khoi."

Grover had no idea what she was saying. He smiled and patted the baby gently. "Yes, you have a handsome son. Let's just call him 'Sonny,'" Grover suggested. "Sonny Lee."

Minh Nhi Li remembered the name of The Uncle's young wife, and smiled her assent at using a family name.

"Song Nhi Li," she agreed, nodding. "Song Nhi Li."

Chapter 36
July 19, 1969

Kelly was refreshed and well tanned after two weeks on the spectacular blue waters of the Aegean Sea. Exotic names of islands that she had first noticed in her high school Latin classes were now intimately familiar, and the mythological gods and goddesses of the ancient Greeks had become comfortable travel companions. Even Larry was agreeable.

From the bow of the *Aegean Lover*, Kelly watched the port of Pireaus come into focus at a leisurely speed of five knots. She faced the harbor with mixed emotions. Undoubtedly, this had been the best two weeks of her marriage to Larry, and she didn't want it to end, but maybe Athens could provide a fresh start. After all, Athens was the cradle of Western Civilization. Perhaps it would birth something new for them.

* * *

Christi finished packing her clothes and the assorted paraphernalia of two little girls. Deputy Sheriff Nichols had warned her that she could not take any of the *Boudreaux family furniture, household items, or heirlooms.* There had been *a photo inventory.* She would be *financially responsible* for anything that was missing. His words, from the *official papers* he had delivered, rang in her ears. Clearly, she must leave with only her clothes and the personal property she had brought from the farm, which was practically nothing.

Looking around her bedroom, Christi could not cry. She did not have enough emotional strength to summon the tears.

An unusual noise out front shook her from her reverie. A large diesel truck, pulling a flatbed trailer, was stopping on the street directly in front of her house, its engine idling.

Leaving the girls napping, Christi went outside to inquire.

It was obvious. A large metal ramp was lowered from the back of the trailer, and a bulldozer fired its engine, shooting a cloud of black smoke into the air. Slowly, with its blade raised, the giant yellow machine made its way down the ramp, and unceremoniously drove over the curb and into the Boudreaux front yard.

"What are you doing?" Christi hollered at the driver.

"We're just unloading today when there's not any traffic," the operator answered over the roar of the dozer engine. Then he cut it off and said, "We'll be back on Monday morning to start taking down the house."

"But they haven't sold the furniture, or anything, yet."

The man shrugged his shoulders, and started toward the truck. "All I know, Ma'am, is that we're supposed to drop off the dozer today and come back on Monday morning to start the demolition. No one said anything about furniture. I guess you have time to move it out," he said politely, as he climbed into the cab, "but that's not my business."

He closed the door, released the brake, and drove away.

Christi was still standing on the curb when Nick Nichols drove up in the Warren County Sheriff's Department car. He parked, but left the engine running, and got out to talk to her.

"I seem to be a part of the worst days of your life," he said.

Christi nodded, but didn't say anything.

"I wish there were something I could do," he offered.

"Everything is still in the house," she said. "The man told me he'd be back Monday for the demolition. Surely, they're not going to bulldoze it with all those antiques inside."

"I'm afraid that's what they have in mind," the deputy replied. "It sounds crazy to me, but you're not allowed to take anything out, and I don't suppose that anyone has made arrangements to get in the house."

"I haven't heard a word," Christi said with a frown. "I really don't understand what's happening here."

"Excuse me, Christi. There's a radio call for me."

Nichols walked around to the driver's side, leaned in to take the call, then stood upright, and turned to Christi.

"I have to get back to the office," he explained. "Please leave everything as it is. I don't want you to get in trouble."

* * *

Grover Jones, now called "Giác" by the small Vietnamese woman, had learned a lot about survival in the past couple of months. After nearly a week in a makeshift shelter within shouting distance of the burned-out village of Đó Thanh, the unlikely trio had begun their dangerous southward trek.

At first, Jack wondered how he would deal with the burden of a woman and an infant, but soon realized that, although he had spent plenty of time hunting and camping, Minnie Lee was more adept than he was at dealing with the elements in a jungle in Viet Nam. As predicted, the rain had hit with full force, and the monsoon was upon them. Still, remarkably, the woman was able to start a fire using only bamboo and a knife.

Minnie Lee had grabbed a package of rice from her burning hut, and they had found more rice when they ventured back to the village the next day. They ate a dead chicken on the day after the conflagration, but after that, Jack had no stomach for road kill.

Minnie Lee knew how to make small traps for lizards and birds, and she could cook rice in an upright hollow shoot of bamboo stuck in the fire. She knew which vines in the dense foliage contained clear liquid to drink, and she showed him how to protect his mouth from the often sharp or sticky ends of the strange plants. She knew which plants to eat, and which ones to avoid. She nursed the baby, and Sonny Lee was thriving. He seemed twice as big as the day he was a football.

Jack and Minh Nhi Li had no real conversations. She would say, "Giác," or tap on his sleeve, and then point and gesture. He called her "Minnie" and she responded. That was enough. She did talk to the baby, but none of it made any sense to Jack.

Nothing made any sense to him except to survive. He thought he had kept track of the days since May Day, but he wasn't certain. All he knew for sure was that he had never been so hot and so wet and so miserable in his entire life, and he wondered how in the world he would ever get back to Christi and his daughters.

The trio had arrived at a fairly wide stream, and with all the rain, it appeared to be moving at a good clip. The map that he had found in Sarge's pack made more sense to Jack the more he used it. He had never seen topographic maps that showed so much detail. It seemed that every little puddle of water was identified, and in the monsoon season, there was plenty of it. Jack figured out that a stream of water was a *song*.

He studied the map carefully and decided that they had arrived at Song Vu Gia, a large stream that twisted and turned, and ran into Song Thu Bon, which ran northeasterly before it became Song Ky Lam. After some widening and narrowing and widening again, it became Song Dien Binh for a very short way south, and then there was Song Cau Lau that appeared to grow quite wide as it approached Song Hoi. After the stream called Song Hoi was divided by several deltas, it became Song Cua Dia and, almost unbelievably, it finally dumped into the South China Sea.

The words "South China Sea" were written large and in English. To Jack's tortured mind, getting to the South China Sea was almost like getting back home. He had no idea who or what he might encounter along the way, so he took his time building a large raft that he hoped would make a safe journey.

Grover remembered being jealous of Tom Sawyer and his friend Huck Finn, rafting on the Mississippi River in his childhood books. Now, from his vantage point on the bank of what he hoped was the Song Vu Gia, water travel no longer seemed so adventurous and fun. Minnie Lee was very clever and resourceful, but she was no Huckleberry Finn, and she wasn't physically all that strong, so the heavy work fell to Jack, while the woman quietly pointed out the best vines and stalks of bamboo for him to cut. Worse, through all the days of Jack's raft design and building, the rain never stopped.

* * *

Beginning at dawn on that Saturday, people streamed from their mountain villages toward Athens. A mass evacuation poured down the steep and winding roads like lava to the sea.

Margaret Rose Stevenson checked her passport, camera, film, and notes in preparation for leaving Delphi, though she was suddenly reluctant to go. From her balcony at the Hotel

Acropole, she had lingered over coffee, enjoying a magnificent view of the Corinthian Gulf and the olive groves of Itea.

The quiet, family-run hostelry with several dozen decent rooms was near the center of town, and not far from the Oracle. For a few precious moments, Maggie actually thought about staying. She could settle. She could live here. Seldom, if ever, in her travels had she entertained such an idea.

Maggie had all the photos she needed for an article about Delphi and its famous Oracle. She could tell about the Greeks and visitors who still believe that the spirit of the ancient god Apollo continues to reside in Delphi, just as he did thousands of years ago. Whether or not there was ever anything at all to the Oracle, tourists and visiting dignitaries still flocked to the stone temple to get answers to their deep questions, personal problems, and even affairs of state.

For Maggie, though, and for the mountain visitors and dwellers, it was time to leave Apollo in his temple, and travel to Athens. The only way to see the USA Apollo 11's projected landing on the moon the next day was to be somewhere with a strong television signal. That somewhere was Athens, and it was 180 kilometers away. A hundred miles was a real journey on the mountain roads, especially in heavy traffic. Maggie reluctantly loaded her rented Fiat, checked out of the Acropole, and joined the caravan headed toward the coast.

* * *

Nick Nichols recognized PapaLew's unmistakable stretch Mercedes parked in front of his office. Of course, it stood out everywhere in Vicksburg, as did the Llewellyn boy's black Corvette, but the deputy didn't begrudge them their luxuries, nor did he look down on the hardscrabble poor of Warren County. He just took people as they were. People.

Still, he had some concerns about the Llewellyns' "business" dealings, and he was more than a little curious about why he had been called to his office by George Llewellyn on a Saturday afternoon.

"Sorry to interrupt your weekend, Sheriff," PapaLew said.

Nichols shook his head. "No problem. Come on in."

They settled quickly in the small office, Nichols behind his desk. He pulled a pack of cigarettes from his front pocket and offered one to George. PapaLew waved it off.

"I'll get right to the point," PapaLew began. "I talked to my lawyer about this first."

The deputy was intensely interested now, but didn't show it. He just nodded, silently encouraging his visitor.

"It's my understanding that if a person commits a murder, he can't collect on the life insurance of the person he killed," PapaLew stated flatly.

Nichols' mind raced back to the night that Cassi Llewellyn had had her pool "accident." She had gone into a coma that night, but she had recovered. The deputy knew that George had sent her to an alcohol treatment center. He had also heard that she occasionally fell off the wagon. Surely, she was not lying dead in a puddle of blood now. Nichols just nodded.

"By analogy, then, God damn it, it would seem to me that a person who committed a murder should not be able to benefit from it in any way," George Llewellyn continued, warming a bit, "especially not from the estate of the person he killed."

Nichols simply nodded again. PapaLew reached into his own front pocket, and pulled out a small black object, hardly larger than a pack of cigarettes.

"This new-fangled gadget," PapaLew explained, "is not yet available on the market, but we're testing them to put in our stores. God damn it! It's a pretty good little recorder," he said, placing it on the desk between them.

The deputy leaned forward in his chair, looking closer.

"I don't suppose you're here trying to sell me this thing," Nichols quipped.

"Nah. Just listen, and then I'll answer any questions you have. The first one would be, 'Who is that other voice on the tape?' It's an old friend who isn't so friendly any more. The second would be, 'Has anyone tampered with this tape?" and the answer is no. The third question is, 'Would this hold up in court?' That, I don't know, but I'm trusting you can help."

"I'm listening," Nichols said. PapaLew pushed a lever, and the male voices were clear as if they were in the same room.

"How did you get in here?" … "God damn it! Same way you got into my sister's pants – lying, manipulative, southern charm. Nice receptionist you got out there. Big tits." …

"You'll excuse me if I don't get up?"… "You probably can't get anything up these days. I won't take it god damn personally."… "You have a nerve showing up at my place. I oughta have you shot for trespassing."… "God damn right, you oughta have me shot, or you oughta have a boat blown up under me. You sure as shit don't have the balls to do it yourself. Gonna call the same guys you sent after Clem?"

At the sound of the name "Clem," the deputy slowly pulled out his notepad from his cigarette pocket, and started jotting down key phrases.

"…a man's gotta collect what's owed him. Dead or alive. Clem might've forced me to do it the hard way, but it's just business."… "I want the Boudreaux homestead."… "It's not for sale."… "Going to bulldoze her down."… "…those guys you hired to do ole Clem did a bang up job. Not a trace of evidence anywhere. Who'd ya use? The Twins? Are they still around?" Silence, and then: "Are you saying that's who you used, or that they're still around?"… "Both."… "Where can I find them?"… "You can always find them through their mama. Here's her number."… "What'll they charge?"… "Hell, they give me a volume discount."

"Whew!" Nichols whistled. "That's some conversation!"

"God damn right it is," PapaLew agreed.

"And the mama's phone number?" the deputy inquired.

PapaLew pulled a folded piece of paper from his pocket. "The handwriting is Arnie's."

The deputy took the paper from George and noted the fancy crest. The name "Arnold Robert Neely" was engraved at the top. A phone number was scribbled at an angle.

"That's a N'Orleans phone number, Sheriff. That old lady is easy to find. Meanwhile, do you think we can find a judge to give us a restraining order to save Clem's house?"

"Hmmm… a tricky legal issue," the deputy demurred, "but, hell, this is Warren County. We take care of our own."

"God damn right, we do! Let's get going."

* * *

Jody was only slightly disappointed that PapaLew wasn't in his office, though they had an appointment that afternoon. His secretary had no information about when he would return. Jody smiled, and asked to make a long distance call.

As luck would have it, Jody caught Prudence as she was walking out the door, heading to Vicksburg. They arranged to meet at Christi's house later that evening. Jody decided to spend the afternoon, hot as it was, sightseeing in Vicksburg's historic district.

* * *

Larry took Kelly's hand and led her out onto the rooftop terrace. There was a gentle breeze far above the streets of Athens, and a breathtaking view of the Acropolis, where the ancient marble temples glistened in the night.

"Champagne," Larry said to the waiter. "Something very sweet for the lovely lady who doesn't usually drink, and something very dry for me." He didn't need to add that it was a very special night, as he pulled out a chair for Kelly.

Rather than protest, Kelly smiled, and graciously used the one word she had learned for the trip to Greece. *"Efharisto."*

Over the past two weeks, she had found that saying, "Thank you" was a very effective way of communicating with the Greek crew on the yacht. Later, she would learn that in shops, she could point and say, *"Efharisto"* and lovely gifts would magically be wrapped for shipping to Mississippi. Of course, that would only work when Larry was standing beside her with plenty of American dollars, but he always was, and so Kelly was charmed by the romantic atmosphere of Athens.

"Efharisto," she said to the waiter when he appeared with her champagne. He smiled, nodded, and said something she didn't understand. *"Efharisto,"* she repeated.

"To my beautiful wife, the mother of my gorgeous daughters," Larry toasted, lifting his glass toward her.

"Efharisto," Kelly acknowledged, lifting her own glass. The champagne was sweet, just the way Kelly liked it, and over the next hour, she enjoyed much more than she had planned.

* * *

The Athens Hilton was at capacity, with the usual summer festival visitors from around the world, and the huge influx of Greeks in town to see the Americans' moon landing the next day. The event was special to Greeks not just because of its historical significance, but because the ship carrying the three astronauts was named for their ancient god Apollo.

Maggie had booked a room at her favorite small hotel near the port of Piraeus, but along with everyone else, she was drawn to the magic of Athens at night. After a quick drink on the Hilton's terrace overlooking the Acropolis, she headed downstairs to the club, where the young and not-so-young beautiful people were dancing.

The room was crowded, the music was loud, and the lights sparkling off the large mirrored ball hanging from the ceiling gave an air of excitement that was intoxicating. A tall blond fellow with a Swedish accent asked Maggie to dance, and she did. Then another, and an Italian, and more, until she knew it was time to go if she expected to return safely to the port. She left alone, through the huge double doors, as several young couples were entering. Maggie held the door open for them.

"Efharisto," said a lovely blond woman with a slightly slurred speech and a definite American accent.

"Parakalo," Maggie answered reflexively.

* * *

From their comfortable cushioned settee on the backyard terrace, Prudence and Jody noticed the light go out in Christi's bedroom upstairs. Suddenly, Jody seemed much closer to her, and Prudence felt slightly afraid.

"Was that a hint from Christi?" the young man asked, looking toward the darkened window. "It is getting late."

His question made Prudence relax a bit, knowing that he was willing to leave if that would be best for her. When Pru didn't answer, Jody started to get up. She touched his hand.

"No. It's okay. You may stay awhile, if you want."

When Jody sat down again, it seemed he was even closer. He put his arm along the back of the settee, behind Prudence, but not touching her. He sensed her fear, and wondered.

"Talk to me," he whispered gently. "Have I scared you?"

Prudence was taken aback by his direct question. She hadn't thought about it herself, but she knew she was afraid.

After a long silence, she answered, "It's not you. It's about something that happened a long time ago."

It wasn't at all hard for Jody to guess what might have happened to this beautiful young woman. Who and when and where and why didn't matter. It only mattered that she had been hurt, and he never wanted to hurt her. He stretched both arms up behind his head, got up from the settee, and said, "Let's take a little walk."

Pru rose from the cushion, eager to keep Jody's company, but grateful for a chance to have a little distance from him. Side by side, but not touching, they crossed the stone terrace and stepped onto the lawn that was too dry, even for July.

"Someone forgot to water the lawn," Jody suggested.

"Someone can't afford to pay the water bill," Pru corrected.

They walked silently to the far edge of the property, where Jody unlatched and pushed open the wrought iron gate.

"We'd better just walk around the grounds," Pru said.

"Is there a bogeyman in the neighborhood?" Jody asked.

"No. There are only white men in the neighborhood," she answered simply, "and they all have guns."

"We're not doing anything wrong," he insisted.

"Sure we are," Prudence countered. "We're being black. At least, I am. You might be able to pass, in the dark. Either way, it's not safe for us, except on the Boudreaux property."

"You know that because you wandered off the property, and someone hurt you. Is that right?"

"It's not what you think," Prudence answered, but Jody was quite sure that it was.

"I'm planning to be around a long time," Jody said gently, reaching for her hand, and looking into her eyes. "When you're ready to tell me, I'll be listening with all my heart."

Before she could get scared again, Jody released her hand, and pulled the wrought iron gate closed.

* * *

After a short walk from the Metro station, Maggie arrived back on Kapodistriou Street in Pireaus, the site of one of her favorite little hotels in the world. She never told anyone its name, cherishing the knowledge of a secret place she could count on for a room, no matter the season. Like the Hilton, it was also at capacity on this night, but located on a side street with the cracked and bumpy sidewalks typical of the ferry port area, it always promised local flavor and no Americans.

Maggie enjoyed an early, enormous breakfast of homemade honey-soaked *loukorides,* followed by eggs with cheese and ham, and an especially strong cup of coffee. As she sipped the last drop, the owner's wife appeared with *spanakopita* warm from the oven. Maggie looked at her watch, and sighed.

"Another cup of coffee with some *spanakopita, parakalo.*"

* * *

Kelly woke up at first light. Seeing the radiant glow on the marble of the Acropolis, she remembered reading about rosy-fingered dawn in her high school Latin book. She was glad that Larry had left the drapes open the night before, or she would have missed the unforgettable view that recreated the ancient poet's thoughts.

Moments later, Larry woke up and reached for her hand.

"You look rosy this morning," he said sweetly. "How do you feel after all that champagne last night?"

Kelly hadn't been thinking about herself at all. She took stock, thankful to not have the headache that had followed her two previous indulgences in champagne. How did she feel? Startled by her own thought, she said, "I feel pregnant."

* * *

The Monday July 21, 1969 edition of the *Vicksburg Daily Chronicle* sprawled across the kitchen counter, its headline proclaiming "TWO MEN WALK ON THE MOON." Christi stared at the huge, color photos, and was grateful to see that the entire front page was dedicated to the story of "one small step for man, one giant leap for mankind."

There was some modicum of relief in seeing that the moon landing had relegated Christi's own sad story to page three.

"HISTORIC BOUDREAUX HOME GOES DOWN TODAY"

A four-column-wide color photograph showed last night's rally protesting the demolition. There must have been two hundred people with lighted candles, standing vigil before the priceless treasure. Smaller photos showed the mayor and the head of the historical society giving impassioned speeches on Sunday afternoon. An old black and white photo showed three past governors of Mississippi standing together on the front porch. A downtown map showed the home's location.

Too many of Vicksburg's old homes had already been lost to strip malls and parking lots, but none had been so grand and so much a part of the town's heritage as the Boudreaux home. For well over a hundred years, the family had opened the house and its expansive grounds for weddings, debutante parties, and political gatherings, not to mention its well-known role during "The Siege" of Vicksburg in 1863.

Christi was sickened and humiliated to be the Boudreaux giving up the home that had survived the Union Army. Any thoughts of sneaking out quietly with her private shame had been ruined, however, by her foolish determination to spend the last night with her daughters in their ancestral home. This morning's paper had brought another onslaught of protesters.

Peeking through an upstairs window, Christi saw neighbors and strangers beginning to encircle the bulldozer. About thirty of them joined hands around the offending machine. Then a larger group formed a circle around them. A third group was forming an outer concentric circle when the bulldozer operator and his crew drove up in a large truck. The crowd began to jeer as the men approached the house, intent on doing their jobs.

Christi was afraid there could be violence. It was time to go. She walked her daughters to the entry hall, where their meager personal belongings were waiting. When she opened the door, the jeers from the crowd turned to whispers, and then to applause. Christi tried to hold her head up high, but it was not easy, carrying the baby and holding Angelica's hand. She heard the click of photographers' cameras, but she could not see them through her tears. She could not have been more humiliated if she were being stoned, naked in a public square.

Someone carrying a coffee cup turned and hurled it at the bulldozer. Seconds later, people started throwing whatever they had handy. A couple of them picked up some stones from the front garden. A neighbor who was building a new patio ran across the street and started pulling bricks from a pallet. After he threw them at the bulldozer and went back for more, several dozen men joined him. Some of the bricks shattered against the side of the dozer. The front windshield and side windows cracked, splintered, and finally exploded.

The dozer operator and his men had taken refuge in their truck right after the coffee cup was thrown. They were Vicksburg folks, too, and they knew when to get out of the way. They called their office on the truck radio, and their dispatcher called the Vicksburg Police. Minutes later, two squad cars came squealing around the corner, with lights flashing and sirens blaring. Christi's humiliation was complete when two more squad cars arrived from the other direction. The crowd got quiet again, but no one slunk away.

Christi numbly sat down on the top step, with her young daughters beside her, looking at the spectacle that her life had become ~ a bulldozer stalled in the yard ~ hundreds of people futilely trying to help her ~ eight uniformed police officers in charge of mob control ~ photographers having a field day, frantically snapping photos they hoped would qualify for Associated Press national distribution the next day ~ a young reporter from a local radio station, thrusting his microphone at people for sound bites that he could use on the noon news.

"Mommy, I have to poo-poo," Angelica said loudly enough for everyone to hear. Christi broke into hysterical laughter, and decided that she had officially lost her mind.

Just as Christi and the girls went back into the house, Deputy Sheriff Nick Nichols drove up the street quietly, no siren and no flashing lights. He pulled up beside the demolition crew's work truck and got out of his car. One of the senior policemen at the scene walked briskly over to him.

"We've got it covered here, Dep'ty," the officer advised.

Nichols nodded deferentially, mindful of the jealousy factor that sometimes intruded on jurisdictional issues. This was a hot news item, and inside the city limits — clearly a case for the Vicksburg Police Department. The county sheriff's deputy pulled a folded piece of paper from his front pocket and showed it to the city policeman, who looked at it briefly, then nodded and handed it back. County business, for sure.

The deputy sheriff held the paper up to the closed window of the crew's driver-side door. The driver opened the door and got out, glancing nervously over his shoulder at the crowd that was now quiet and still.

"It's a restraining order," the deputy explained, loudly enough for the listening crowd to hear, "issued this morning by a county judge, who has jurisdiction over property matters in Warren County. It's official. You can trust me on that. All you have to do now is get that bulldozer off the property."

The dozer operator grinned. "I sure don't mind doing that, Sheriff, if everyone will let me get to it."

Without another sound, the crowd started easing away from the bulldozer. The city police headed back to their cars. From inside the house, Christi heard the unmistakable sound of the bulldozer firing up its engine. She hurriedly washed her hands and Angelica's, and panicked at the thought of the dozer crashing into her house while she was still in it.

What had happened to all the protesters? She knew they couldn't really stop the demolition, but why had they given up so quickly? Stepping onto the front porch, she could see why. Nick Nichols, as usual, had arrived to ruin her life.

The deputy sheriff took the steps two at a time, rushing toward the young mother whose girls were watching silently from inside the screen door.

"NO!" Christi screamed at him. "NO! Get away from me! Haven't you done enough?" She beat him on the chest with both fists, and he let her beat on him until she was exhausted. Then he encircled her with his strong arms and held her close.

"It's okay, honey," he whispered in her ear. "We have a restraining order. No one can take your house. Not today. Not for a long time. And, maybe, just maybe, not ever."

* * *

Classified 1-A for the draft, Cameron had orders to report for active duty that day. He decided simply not to show up, but joined the crowd celebrating with Christi. A month later, he joined the Reserves, swearing an enlistment oath. A month after that, he failed to report to his duty station. His Reserve status was revoked, making him 1-A and AWOL, while his friend Grover Jones was officially declared Missing In Action.

PART VII

1975 – MORE NEW BEGINNINGS

Chapter 37
October 16, 1975

"If you like cowboys, you should'a been here for the rodeo in July," Jack said amiably to the tall American woman with the fancy camera. "What'd you say your name was?"

"Maggie. Maggie Stevenson. And you?"

"Billy Jack Rucker," he answered. Then, looking around the corral, he added, "but all my friends call me Jack."

"Wait a minute," Maggie said, resting her camera on a fence rail and taking a closer look at him. "I know that name. I met a Billy Jack Rucker in the States."

Grover panicked for the first time in years. His face heated. Who the hell was Billy Jack Rucker anyway? It was a question he always tried to avoid, since first seeing it on the passport in Sarge's belt pack, but here it was again. What could he say?

Before Jack could formulate a reasonable response, Maggie had already decided that he was one of the many runners she had met in the past couple of years. Sad. From Calgary to Cartagena, from Zambia to Zevengergen, they were all the same — Vietnam vets who, for one reason or another, were trying to make a new life somewhere. Anywhere. She figured that she would never get any real background information on him, and it didn't matter for her story. She recovered first.

"Oh, yeah, I remember," Maggie said sincerely. "He races boats, in California, or Nevada, or somewhere out west. I covered an event for a racing magazine. Are you related?"

"I don't think so," Grover answered truthfully, and then changed the subject. "What brings you to Mareeba?"

"Other than the climate?" she laughed. "I'm here to do a story about the cattle business in Australia, and I'm going to focus on the area around Mareeba because the growth has been so phenomenal over the past quarter century. By the way, how long have you been here?" Maggie asked.

"About five years," Jack answered truthfully. "I bounced around a little, but this seemed like a good place to settle. So, you write about boat racing and cattle?"

"I write about anything that will pay the rent, but I admit to a travel bug that keeps me moving as much as possible. I'm a free-lancer," she added, handing him her card. "May I ask you a couple of questions about the cattle here?"

"Sure. I'm no expert, but I run a few head. Mainly, I haul cattle to Indonesia and bring back plywood."

"I didn't realize there was a wood shortage in Australia," Maggie commented.

"No shortage of wood here. It's just that when I started hauling cattle for some of the ranchers, I was looking to find a return load, so's I wouldn't be running empty. I used to haul logs and veneers that I sold to our mills, but they started using some local pines a coupla years ago. About that same time, the Indonesians started making their own fine grade interior plywood, and the Australians started making coarse exterior plywood. I just got lucky in the changeover."

"That sounds like more than luck to me," Maggie said, opening an opportunity for Jack to talk more about himself.

"Well, that's probably more than you ever wanted to know about plywood from Indonesia," Jack concluded. "What can I tell you about Australian cattle that you don't already know?"

"I know that the first Europeans arrived in Australia about 200 years ago with six head of cattle, that there are about 30 million head now, and that world cattle prices have been falling over the past year. That's about it," Maggie said.

"That's a good start," Jack replied. "If you'd like to see a big operation up close, you're welcome to tag along with me."

"I thought you said you just ran a few head."

"Right, but my neighbors have a big place, and they have a guest house that's open for anyone who wants to visit. We don't get all that much company up here, especially since all the tourists have to go to Sydney now to see that new-fangled opera house they opened a coupla years back."

Maggie nodded, and hoped she wouldn't have to say that she had done a story on its history and construction.

"I'd certainly appreciate the hospitality," Maggie answered. "I always get better stories when I can get to know the locals."

"Just one thing," Jack cautioned. "I don't want to be in any pictures."

"No problem," Maggie agreed. Her theory about this Billy Jack Rucker being a runner had just been confirmed.

* * *

Remarkably, Christi still went to the mailbox every day hoping and expecting to hear something from Grover. No matter how many times people told her that the soldiers listed as "Missing In Action" were probably dead, Christi refused to believe that about Grover. She was sure she would "know" if he had died. So far, the "MIA" label was better than "Killed."

The long-awaited letter did not arrive, but there was one from Cameron Coulter. She opened it eagerly, leaving the bills for later, and was disappointed to see that it was a slightly personalized form letter. "Dear Friend" had been crossed out, and Cameron had written in "*Christi.*" Cameron was going to run for Attorney General of Mississippi, and he was soliciting the help of his dearest and closest friends.

Christi wondered what made him think she would have any extra money to contribute to the campaign, and then she asked herself if she would have supported him even if she had a big stash of money in a Swiss bank account. She had not seen Cameron since the night of their tenth high school reunion over a year ago. Neither in that interim, nor in the distant past, had he done anything to demonstrate integrity. He was probably still AWOL from the Army, after reneging on his reserve enlistment about the time Grover went missing.

She had not read anything about that in the newspapers. As far as she knew, no one had tried to arrest him before he fled to London to avoid being prosecuted for desertion, and no one had said anything about it since he brazenly returned.

She did wonder why he had left Oxford after completing only two years of a three-year program, but she knew that with Cameron, the truth would be very difficult to uncover. She wasn't interested enough to try. She dropped the letter in the kitchen trashcan, and didn't give it another thought.

* * *

The sound of Larry's car pulling into the driveway roused Kelly from her reverie. She ran through the darkened house to the bedroom, slid into bed, and pulled up the covers. Larry walked in moments later and flipped on the overhead light.

"You awake?" he asked loudly.

"Sure," Kelly answered sarcastically. "I was just going to get up and turn off the light."

"Don't you want to know where I've been?" Larry asked petulantly, with a slight slur to his voice.

"Of course, I want to know where you've been. I just don't think that asking you would shed any light on the situation."

He walked over to the bed and sat down. "You really don't trust me, do you?"

"I trust you completely, my dear. I trust you will always be true to your nature."

"Don't be mad at me," he pouted like a little boy. "I brought you a present."

"I would have been happier to have you here for our anniversary dinner and to spend some time with your children," she replied, extending her hand for the gift.

"I told you something came up."

"I'm sure I know what came up," Kelly replied absently, focusing on unwrapping the small Neiman-Marcus box. Inside was a lovely crystal bird.

"It's a songbird," Larry explained. "Like you."

"Thanks, Larry. That was very thoughtful."

Kelly placed the gift on her bedside table and turned back to Larry, who was walking toward the bathroom, undressing on the way. He took a very quick shower, returned naked, and turned out the light. Once in the bed, he reached up under Kelly's gown with one hand and pulled her toward him with the other. He kissed her and rolled on top of her.

"Happy two-month anniversary," he whispered.

"Thanks. You too," Kelly responded, hating herself for being aroused by his touch. She hated herself for remarrying him after she had finally gotten away from all the Llewellyn business. She hated herself for uprooting her children and moving to Dallas, thinking that law school was going to make her life better. She hated herself for believing that Larry could ever change, so she just closed her eyes and thought about Cameron, while her roving husband did what he did best.

At breakfast three hours later, Larry was cheerful and the girls were back to normal, which was loud. Kelly was glad it was finally Friday, though that was the hardest day of the week, ending with her Oil and Gas class at four o'clock in the afternoon.

"Who wants to go with me to Galveston?" Larry asked unexpectedly as they were all finishing their pancakes. "One last weekend at the beach before it gets too cold?"

"Me! Me! Me!" the girls chorused at once.

"Great!" He laughed and clapped his hands.

"Larry, you know I have a paper due next Monday," Kelly demurred.

"Right," he nodded. "So, you can come with us and write on the beach, or stay here and have some peace and quiet."

It seemed to Kelly that Larry's gifts and plans always had some hidden agenda, but she was too tired to think about it.

"Can you girls have a good time without me?" Kelly smiled and nodded, prodding for an affirmative answer. "I know you can," she added in an aside to Larry.

"Yes, Mommy, we can," Laurie obliged. Being nine years old, and the oldest, she usually took the lead in answering.

"And we'll be good and not drink Cokes even when Daddy says it's okay," the innocent five-year-old Leesa added. The baby could always be counted on to divulge Larry's secrets.

"What about you, Lily?" Kelly asked their middle child solicitously. "Would you have a good time?"

"Lily's scared of the water and she's scared of the sharks," Leesa volunteered, her eyes getting big. "She's even scared of walking on the beach and stepping on something squishy!"

"I'm not scared," seven-year-old Lily protested, sticking two fingers of her left hand into her mouth, and twirling her hair with her right index finger. "I'm not scared of anything!"

"It doesn't matter if you're scared, Lily. We all get scared," her mother assured her. "Just don't let it stop you. Daddy will be there to hold your hand, so you can be scared and brave at the same time. Okay?"

Lily nodded uncertainly, and twirled her hair faster.

"Kelly, will you pack their things so I can pick them up at school and get out of town before the rush-hour traffic?"

Kelly looked at her watch, sighing at the added pressure.

"Sure," she agreed, realizing that a few extra minutes now would yield forty-eight hours of solitude. "Excuse me," she said, pushing back her chair and carrying her utensils to the dishwasher. "Y'all clean up the kitchen while I pack for you."

Kelly took the stairs two at a time, packed the three tiny suitcases, rushed back downstairs with them, brushed her teeth, grabbed her book bag and ushered the girls to the car.

"Larry," she called, as he headed for the bathroom, "the suitcases are in the hallway by the phone stand. Have a good time! Bye!" Her husband seemed oblivious to her, so Kelly followed him into the bathroom.

"I said…," she began.

"I heard you," he cut her off. "By the way, I forgot to show you this yesterday." He reached into his jacket that was still hanging from the hook behind the bathroom door, and handed her an envelope folded in quarters.

The car's horn blasted the quiet neighborhood and Kelly groaned, "I've told them a thousand times not to honk."

Larry nodded and looked at his watch. "You'll be late if you don't go now."

"I know. Well, y'all have a good time at the beach."

Kelly smiled and gave him a quick kiss on the lips, while absently tucking the folded envelope into the side compartment of her big leather purse. She didn't notice it again until halfway through her Oil and Gas class when her pen ran out of ink and she reached into the purse for her spare, always-hidden-from-the-children pen.

Extricating and unfolding the envelope, she saw that it was addressed to "Mr. and Mrs. Lawrence Llewellyn." The return address in Oxford, Mississippi was Cameron's. Kelly's heart skipped a beat as she opened the letter and began to read.

It was a personalized form letter, letting them know that Cameron was going to run for Attorney General of Mississippi and soliciting the help of his dearest and closest friends. Kelly sighed. She had not seen Cameron since the night of their tenth high school reunion over a year ago.

Larry had actually sent Cameron an invitation to their disastrous second wedding, which Kelly thought was absurd, but didn't know how to avoid it. Cameron had not formally responded to the wedding invitation, but the day after the event, he had called Kelly's sister Mandy to ask about it. The day after that, Cameron proposed to Mallory Cheatham and married her in front of a justice of the peace a few weeks later.

Now, married and appearing to be more mature, Cameron was running for office again. Kelly felt a certainty that he would be the next Attorney General of Mississippi. She pondered the hand-written postscript at the bottom of the letter. *Larry - give Kelly my love - tell her to call me next time she's in Mississippi - hugs and kisses to the children - Cameron*

* * *

George Llewellyn casually flipped through the day's mail and was not at all surprised to see Cameron Coulter's return address. The envelope contained a slightly personalized form letter. "Dear Friend" had been crossed out, and Cameron had written in "*PapaLew*." Cameron was going to run for Attorney General of Mississippi, and he was soliciting the help of his dearest and closest friends.

"God damn it!" George said aloud as he pulled out his checkbook. He had already funded the two candidates who announced early, and he knew he would write another check when his ole buddy Hocking MacMillan Samuels finally got around to announcing.

He buzzed his secretary and gave her the freshly written check, along with Cameron's letter. Then he quickly went through the other papers that required his personal decisions. The only troublesome document remaining on his desk was the *subpoena duces tecum* that had arrived the previous day.

"God damn it!" he said again, as he thought about the legal summons. The last thing in the world he wanted to do was testify at Arnie's trial for the murders of Clem and Vayda.

Although "The Twins" had already been tried, convicted, and sentenced for pulling the triggers, Arnie's lawyers had managed to wrangle over seven years of relative freedom for the guy behind the hit. George derived some pleasure from knowing that the impending trial had forced Arnie to clean up his act, and to deed the Boudreaux property back to Christi.

Chapter 38
November 20, 1975

Minh Nhi Li awoke shortly after dawn, and listened for the house sounds. As usual, all she could hear was Giác in his bedroom next to hers. Every morning, he got up at dawn and started painting. Though he had done a nice job fixing the old house and painting the other rooms in colors she had chosen, Jack kept adding yellow roses to the walls in his own room.

In studying English by reading captions under magazine pictures, Nhi Li had seen enough fancy rooms to know that Giác's room was highly unusual for a man. It was definitely feminine, yet he had never invited her into it. He also had never gone into her bedroom again after he finished painting it the pale green color she had picked.

Sometimes she wondered if something was wrong with Giác, that he didn't want a woman. Or, perhaps he just didn't want a Vietnamese woman. More likely, he just didn't want her, but he had saved her life, and her son's, and he was kind.

Not a day went by without Nhi Li missing her husband and wondering what had happened to him. Their son Minh Quang Khoi was six years old now, and it was time to tell him about his father, but she didn't know what to say. Giác called the boy Sonny Lee, and Sonny seemed to understand Giác quite well. Perhaps Giác could explain these things to him.

Nhi Li dressed quickly and went to the kitchen to prepare breakfast. Giác had invited an American woman to the house this morning, and Nhi Li wanted to make a good impression so she would not embarrass Giác or herself.

She was pleased with the new tea that Giác had brought back from his last trip to Indonesia, and was grateful that he thoughtfully always brought something nice for her and for Quang Khoi. She was hoping that the American woman would enjoy the tea as much as she did.

* * *

Maggie rose early, dressed quickly, and gathered her camera and equipment. She left the guesthouse before dawn, leaving a note for the housekeeper that she would be back that night. Though she had not planned this much time for the cattle article, the magazine had extended her deadline to accommodate some other stories, and she was happy to stay.

Her hosts were gracious, though usually absent. They had flown to Hawaii a few days earlier, and invited her to stay in their guesthouse as long as she wanted. They would be gone until after Christmas, or perhaps until the first of the year.

Maggie never lacked something to occupy her time. She soon discovered that the land area of Mareeba Shire was a fascinating conglomeration of geographies. It had pristine rainforests and vast coastal ranges. Its fertile plains provided sugar cane, coffee, macadamia nuts, cashews, bananas, pineapples, and mangoes, as well as many more exotic crops.

Going west across the Mareeba Shire area of Queensland, Maggie had explored a small part of the famous Australian outback, where the vast sunburnt savannah plains stretched beyond the imagination. Its sunsets were spectacular. The air was clean and arid, the humidity was always low, and there were at least 300 sunny days a year in Mareeba Shire. She would get three complete articles from this trip to Australia, and she was quite pleased. One would go to National Geographic, her favorite magazine, and her favorite buyer.

Now Maggie was anxious to meet Jack's family, though he had not spoken much about them. Maggie knew that the woman would be quiet, shy, and deferential to her husband. Mostly, she was curious about the boy. The mixed races were endlessly fascinating to her, and usually made good subjects for photographs. She hoped that Jack would let her take some shots of the boy and his mother, though his face was off limits.

* * *

Mallory Cheatham busied herself counting contributions to her new husband, the candidate. The hicks in Mississippi were coming through in spades. Though she had not found one of them to her liking, their money was good, and she felt confident that Cameron would be the next Attorney General of Mississippi. At least, then, they could move to the capital.

* * *

"It's one week until Thanksgiving," Jody announced over the phone to Prudence.

"I know that, Jody, and I'm getting ready as fast as I can. I'm looking forward to seeing you and Naboth at Christi's."

"Pru, one other thing. What does Ray want for Christmas? If it's something big, I'll get it now and bring it up in the car, since I'll probably be flying up at Christmas."

"Here, ask him yourself," she said, handing off the phone.

"What do you want for Christmas, buddy?" Jody asked.

"I want a daddy," Ray said. "I want you to be my daddy."

"Ray!" Prudence grabbed the phone from her young son. "I'm sorry, Jody. I don't know what got into him."

"I'm not sorry, Pru. Let's not disappoint the boy. You know I love you both. Make it happen. I'll bring the ring."

* * *

As soon as she saw the very tall American woman smile and bow toward her through the screen door, Nhi Li knew that she would not be embarrassed.

"Good morning," Nhi Li pronounced in her best English.

"Chaøo. Toâi teân Maggie Stevenson."

Minh Nhi Li and her son smiled to hear their native tongue.

"Welcome to our humble home," said the very small boy.

"Caùm ôn nhieàu," Maggie continued, thanking him.

Jack watched silently as his new American friend charmed her way into his home with just a few Vietnamese words.

"Minnie has fixed quite a breakfast for us," Jack offered. "Did you bring your appetite?"

"Daï coù," Maggie affirmed. Then, setting down her camera bag, she asked, *"Phoøng veä sinh ôû ñaâu?"*

"Beân tay maët," the woman nodded, indicating a hallway on the right.

When Maggie returned from washing her hands in the small bathroom, Jack pulled out a chair for her. Noticing that the table was set with traditional English knives, forks, and spoons, Maggie turned to Minh Nhi Li and asked, *"Toâi phieàn anh laøm caùi naøy duøm toâi? Cho toâi xin moät ñoâi ñuõa."*

"Daï coù." Nhi Li clasped her hands together, smiled, and bowed deeply. She simply looked at the boy, and he quickly ran to the kitchen. When he returned with the chopsticks, Maggie bowed her head and thanked him, *"Caùm ôn nhieàu."*

"Daï khoâng coù gì," the boy answered properly.

"Anh aên thöû baùnh cuoán chaû luïa ñi. Ngon laém," Nhi Li gestured toward the crepes. Maggie helped herself, and put one on the boy's plate.

"Caùm ôn nhieàu," he thanked her.

"Daï khoâng coù gì," she responded, and then asked, *"Ni hoïc chöa?"* wondering if he were old enough for school yet.

He demurred shyly, *"Daï khoâng."*

"Maggie, I didn't know you spoke Vietnamese," Jack said.

"Toâi noùi ñöôïc tieáng Vieät moät chuùt thoâi," she replied.

"You may think that you just speak a little bit, but it's too much for me. How about we switch to English?"

Maggie smiled with relief. She had already used most of her Vietnamese vocabulary. By the time they had shared the delicious breakfast and innumerable cups of tea, along with lively conversation in English, Maggie was feeling like part of the family. She had decided, however, that Jack was not the biological father of the Vietnamese boy. No similarity at all.

"Maggie, I'm taking a boatload of cattle to East Timor in the morning," the huge man announced. "Would you like to go with us?"

Maggie looked at the woman, who smiled and bowed.

"What's this? A family vacation? With cows?"

"No," Jack laughed. "Minnie and the boy always stay here. I thought you might like to take some photos when we load and unload, maybe talk to the crew, the buyers, whatever you like. We'll be back in a couple of weeks. How's that sound?"

"Sounds great to me!" Maggie exclaimed. "I'll be back first thing in the morning, with a fresh load of film. And, speaking of photos, I know you don't want me to take pictures of you, Jack, but I would love to get some candid shots of your beautiful wife and son."

Jack and Minh Nhi Li exchanged a look, but said nothing.

"I'm sorry," Maggie apologized after the longest silence of the morning. "I didn't mean to offend any of you."

"No offense," the woman said sweetly. "My son and I will be happy to have our faces on your camera. And I will be happy to send food for your boat journey with the cattle."

* * *

It had been many years since the Boudreaux parlor served as a wedding chapel, and never on such short notice, but Christi managed to have it all decorated and filled with flowers, thanks to PapaLew's generous offer to "take care of everything" for his favorite young couple. On the Saturday after Thanksgiving, the small group gathered.

Christi served as Maid of Honor, while her daughters Angelica and Alexandra - Angel and Alex - were flower girls. Naboth, handsome in his West Point uniform, served his older brother as Best Man. Nellie Mae was dressed in fine purple silk as the mother of the bride. Ray Purvis, Jr., now eleven-and-a-half years old, the instigator of this marriage, was going to give away the bride. He thought of it more as gaining a daddy, than giving away a mother, so he was excited.

Larry, Kelly, and their three daughters had arrived from Dallas. A couple of Pru's friends from Jackson had driven over for the ceremony, but Jody's only guests were PapaLew and his wife Cassi, who rarely appeared in public. She was quiet, but did not throw a wet blanket on the festivities. Pru's old pastor, who had baptized her, performed the ceremony. As always, snippets from his message stayed with Prudence.

"Being married is like having a Swiss bank account that someone opened for you.... You can't enjoy the benefits of it, if you don't know those benefits exist.... The key to open the account and to enjoy the benefits is to be completely honest.... Keep no secrets..."

Jody was listening carefully too, and after the long evening of celebrating with their guests, and the long-awaited union of Jody and his precious bride, he whispered in her ear.

"Are you awake?" he asked.

"Mmm-hmmm," she murmured.

"You remember what the preacher said about not keeping secrets?"

"Mmm-hmmm."

"Do you think he's right about that? Is it important to tell everything?"

"Mmm-hmmm."

"May I tell you something really serious, even if it's bad?"

"Mmm-hmmm."

"Will you still love me, no matter what?"

"Mmm-hmmm."

"I killed a man."

"Mmm-WHAT?!?" Prudence sat straight up in bed.

"I killed a man," Jody repeated clearly.

"But you weren't in the Army. Was it an accident?"

"No. It was deliberate."

Pru sighed and said, "Tell me everything about it."

When Jody finished telling the story about the marina and Watson, and how Watson had been complicit in blowing up PapaLew's boat, and how PapaLew had told him to do it, then Prudence said, "I have something I have to tell you too."

Jody listened compassionately as she related the story of her pregnancy, the rape by Lefty and his friends, how Larry had arranged for a record of a bogus marriage in Louisiana, and how she had wondered throughout her pregnancy whether her son would be Ray's, or the son of a rapist. It was almost dawn before she finished talking and crying and being comforted by her new husband.

"There's one more thing," she added, "and I really hate to tell you this."

"Go ahead. I'm listening."

"The sheriff here, who seems to find out everything about everybody, found out about the fraudulent marriage. He said that I had committed a federal offense by taking Army support and Social Security money as a widow. He made me agree to be a spy against PapaLew because he thinks PapaLew is guilty of murder. And, I don't think he even knew about your Mr. Watson. Until tonight, I had no reason to believe his suspicions about PapaLew."

Chapter 39
December 1, 1975

Monday morning was busier than usual in the Warren County Sheriff's office. Prudence wanted to use that as an excuse to leave, but Nick Nichols spotted her among the waiting visitors, and invited her in before she lost her courage.

"You probably thought I forgot about my promise to you about PapaLew," she began tentatively. "I mean, it's been..."

"Nope. I'd didn't think that for a minute. I figured you just didn't have anything to report yet. I trust you," he said, "and there's no rush — no Statute of Limitations on murder."

"I don't know if what I have will be helpful or not."

"You can let me decide about that. Thank you for coming."

Prudence sighed. "May I ask you a question about another case first?"

The deputy sheriff nodded. "Sure. Go ahead." He leaned back, pulled a pack of cigarettes from his pocket, and lit one. "You still don't smoke, right?"

Prudence found his knowledge about her disconcerting, but she went on with her question.

"Have you heard about that girl who got raped in Clanton over the weekend?"

The deputy nodded.

"She was a white girl, right?"

"They're not officially giving out that information yet, but you probably have good sources."

"Okay, if they find out that this white girl was raped by a black boy, what would happen to him?"

"He would get a fair trial with a public defender before he was convicted and given the death penalty," the deputy sheriff replied with assurance.

"What if it's a black girl, raped by a white boy?"

"You know this is Mississippi, and that's a whole different story. He might get a sexual assault charge, or maybe just a battery charge, depending on his family, his lawyer, and how good a football player he is. Probably get probation. So, was the rapist a black kid? What do you know about that case?" the deputy asked, pulling his notebook from his pocket.

"Nothing. I was just curious." Prudence sighed again, and asked, "Did you hear that I got married over Thanksgiving?"

"I did. I wish you and Jody all the best. I've heard nothing but good reports about that guy, and about his brother at West Point. You must be very happy."

"I was," Pru lowered her voice to a whisper, "until he told me that he murdered a man under orders from PapaLew."

"Whew! That's some heavy pillow talk," the deputy said. "Does Jody know you're here telling me about it?"

"Yes, sir," Prudence answered directly. "He said that I had to do what I had promised to do." Tears were forming, but she continued, "So, I have to tell you what he told me."

"You realize that you won't be asked to testify against your husband? Or, against PapaLew, since your testimony would be hearsay?" He put his notebook back in his cigarette pocket.

"Aren't you going to take notes?" Pru wanted to know.

"I'll just listen to what you have to say," he explained, and then sat quietly as Pru told everything she knew about the boat being blown up at the marina, and Watson who was part of the plan to kill PapaLew, and how Jody pushed him off the seawall, letting him drown or die of a heart attack in the river.

"That's quite an interesting story," the deputy said, "I hope you don't think it's right to take the law in your own hands."

"I don't think it's right," Prudence said, "but I do think that sometimes it's the only thing to do. Think about that girl up in Clanton who was raped. Wouldn't it make sense that a black girl raped by a white boy in Mississippi would want justice, but not be able to get it through the courts?"

Nichols shrugged, giving a grudging nod. "Still, not right."

"Maybe not, but I know how she would feel," Pru sniffed, feeling tears forming in her eyes again. "It happened to me."

The deputy sheriff leaned forward. "What? You were raped? When? Do you know who did it?"

"Yes, I was raped. November 3, 1963. On a bluff down by the river. Lefty Owens and three of his friends did it."

"And you never reported it," the deputy stated, not asking.

"Of course not," Prudence spat the words. "What would have been the point? They wouldn't have been convicted, and they might've followed through on their threat to cut my tongue out if I told." Pru started crying again in earnest.

The deputy opened a drawer, pulled out a box of tissues, and handed it to the distraught young woman.

"I'm sorry that happened to you, Prudence, and I wish I could have done something about it. I don't like that sort of thing happening in Warren County."

"I'll tell you this for a fact, Sheriff," Pru said, wiping her eyes and nose, "I would have killed them if I could."

The deputy nodded. "That's an understandable reaction, but what did you do? Did you tell anyone?"

"Larry Llewellyn and Christi Boudreaux came looking for me, and found me there on the bluff. I told them, but I made them swear not to breathe a word of it, and not to tell the police. Larry said there were better ways of dealing with people like Lefty than to call the police. I thought he might actually try to retaliate in some way, but then those animals were killed in a car accident. I was happy, and relieved."

The deputy stood. "I hate to rush you out of here, Pru, but I have a waiting room full of people this morning, and I've got to go testify at a hearing right after lunch, if I get lunch. Maybe you could bring me a sandwich and a pickle later?"

"What about Jody?" she asked.

"I guess you oughta fix him a sandwich too."

* * *

Tiny Hamlin was the deputy's next visitor of the morning.

"Sheriff, I got this here *sub penis*, and I figured I'd better talk to you about it. What's gonna happen to me?"

"It's not about you, Tiny. There's a murder trial going on, against the guy who ordered the hit on Clem Boudreaux."

"And his secretary?"

"We think she was just in the wrong place at the wrong time, but it was a definite hit job on Clem."

"So, why do they wanna ast me stuff, Sheriff? I don't know nuthin' bout no hit on Clem Boudreaux."

"Okay, Tiny, you watch cop shows on television and at the movies, right?"

"Yes, sir."

"And you know that sometimes people who did bad things try to cut a deal with the law so they don't have to serve so much time in jail? Right?"

"Yes, sir."

"There were two bad guys who killed Clem and his secretary. They already went to jail for pulling the triggers. They're serving life without parole. Know what that means?"

"Yes, sir. They cain't never get out. No way."

"Right, but they want to have a chance to get out on parole, someday, so they are trying to cut a deal. These two convicted bad guys have agreed to testify that Arnie, who is on trial this week, is the bad guy who hired them."

"But what's that got to do with me?" Tiny questioned.

"The second thing is that these same two bad guys are trying to tell a story that a guy named Llewellyn from Vicksburg hired them to kill Lefty Owens."

"They talkin' bout PapaLew?" Tiny asked. "PapaLew ain't been nuthin' but nice to me. He give me gift certifications to his store ever time I wax his car."

"PapaLew's a good man, Tiny, but these guys who are telling the story are bad men, and they need to stay in prison."

"What do I need to do?"

"Well, Tiny, when you get on the stand in a courtroom, you always need to tell the truth. You just don't have to tell every little thing you might know. They're going to ask you about pulling Lefty's car outa the water. I'll bet you remember that, but I'll bet you don't remember anything else about that car."

"But Sheriff, what about them tires?"

"What about them tires, Tiny? I examined that car the day after the wreck, and the tires looked fine to me," said Nichols. "I'd sure hate to look stupid on the stand if there had been something wrong with those tires and I missed it. Ever seen bloodier wrecks than that one, Tiny?"

"Sure, Sheriff. I seen 'em all. I seen blood and guts and hair stuck to broken glass. I seen body parts. I seen 'em all."

"Then, when you get on the stand, Tiny, you might want to be thinking about all those bloody wrecks you've seen. You might want to tell as much as you can remember about bloody wrecks in Warren County. I'll bet you've seen more wrecks than any person in this part of the country. Of course, that might make it hard for to you to remember every little detail about every wreck. It's okay to say 'I don't remember' when you're on the stand. It won't make you look bad."

"But what about them tires, Sheriff?"

"Did I ask you to say anything about those tires? Did I, Tiny? No. I told you that I looked at those tires the next day, and they looked fine to me. That's all anyone needs to know. Now, I've gotta go see some other people. Let me just walk you out the back door, so we can talk on the way to my car."

* * *

The sandwich was good, the pickle was crisp, and there was a big bag of chips, along with a Coke. The deputy was glad to have a decent lunch under his belt for the hearing.

Tiny took the stand first, and swore to tell the truth. Nearly everyone in Vicksburg knew Tiny, and they knew he always told the truth. The judge and special prosecutor, however, didn't know anything about him. It didn't take them long to conclude he was a stupid country oaf, not worth their time.

"Yes, sir, I pulled that wrecked car outa the water, but I seen bloodier wrecks than that. I seen blood and guts and hair stuck to broken glass. I seen body parts. I seen 'em all."

"Mr. Hamlin, we're just examining the pertinent details surrounding this particular event. Please confine your verbal responses to relevant issues addressed by counsel."

"Huh?"

"Was there anything unusual about the tires on that car?"

"They was right for the car. Not too big, not too small. But I seen bloodier wrecks than that, and all kinds of tires."

"No further questions for this witness."

Then Deputy Sheriff Nick Nichols swore his oath and stated that he had examined the tires early in the morning after the wreck. He had found no bullet holes in any of them. After that, the court declined to hear further accusations from The Twins against "some Llewellyn guy in Vicksburg." They testified against Arnie anyway, and he got a life sentence.

Chapter 40
December 5, 1975

"Christi, the house looks great!" Cameron exclaimed as he greeted her with a hug. "Thank you for doing this for me."

For some reason, Christi felt herself stiffening with the hug.

"No problem. The flowers are left over from Pru's wedding last weekend," she said. "PapaLew bought them. I just pulled out the dead ones, and fixed the rest to make fewer, but fresher-looking arrangements. I think they look fine."

Uninvited, Cameron started walking around the house and through the kitchen where he picked up some finger food.

"What's with this ramp up to the back door?" he hollered.

Christi went to join him, not wanting to raise her voice.

"Right after the first of the year, I'm going to have a few older ladies move into the house with me. They're not sick or anything, but they don't want to live alone. All of them are moving from large, lovely homes, and they'll be comfortable living here. It will be nice because I need the money."

"How many will you have, and who's going to help you with all the extra work?" Cameron wanted to know.

"There will be four ladies, two of them in each of the two downstairs parlors. They've been together in the same Bridge club and sorority since college, so I know they are compatible. Nellie Mae and a younger woman she knows will live here and help me. Nellie Mae will cook, and the other will clean. I might even have an easier time than ever. Plus, the income."

Cameron nodded. The doorbell rang, announcing the first guests, and Christi ran to answer it. The fund-raising event turned out to be a huge success, and Christi was pleased to be a proper hostess in her ancestral home. It had been years since anyone had entertained there. Christi's delight was diminished only by the fact that she was not truly supportive of Cameron's run for Attorney General. *He has neither the experience nor the integrity to hold such an office. Yet, what integrity do I have, pretending to support him?* She sighed, and further derided herself for not liking the smelly witch of a woman he had hauled down south and married. As usual, fortunately, the irritable and irritating woman was absent.

When the last guest was gone and Nellie Mae had retired to the quarters out back, Cameron took off his sport coat, poured another glass of wine, and offered it to Christi.

"No, thanks," she said, "but you go ahead."

Cameron lifted the glass toward her, nodded, smiled, and said, "Thank you for a wonderfully successful evening. You should be my campaign manager." He swallowed the entire glassful of white wine in one gulp.

"I'll be busy running this place," Christi said, shaking her head. "I think that will be enough work for me."

"Right," Cameron agreed, "and I hope it goes well for you. If you run into problems, let me know. When I'm Attorney General, I'll be in charge of overseeing nursing homes, even little ones like this. I'll be in a great position to help you."

"Thanks," Christi said, barely stifling a yawn, "but it's getting late." Heading toward the front door, she suggested, "Why don't you take the rest of that bottle of wine with you?"

Cameron could not believe he was being dismissed after such an exciting evening. Christi actually had her hand on the doorknob. He quickly covered the few steps to the door and wrapped both his arms around her with more than a hug.

"What are you doing?" Christi asked incredulously, feeling suddenly trapped, and trying to push him away.

Cameron began kissing her cheek, her forehead, her neck, whatever he could reach as she twisted her head violently.

"Stop!" she cried.

"Why did you invite me here?" he asked.

"I agreed to host a fund-raiser for your campaign. I have a husband. I have no romantic interest in you. Stop it."

"Sorry to remind you that Grover has been missing for over five years," Cameron said cruelly, not releasing his grip on her. "I'll bet you haven't been laid since he left."

"Stop it right now! What in the world has gotten into you, Cameron? You can't be that drunk. Please leave me alone, and go home. Take the wine with you."

Pleading, Christi looked directly into his eyes.

Cameron used that moment to catch her upper lip in his teeth. He clamped down, but not enough to break the skin.

"Stop!" she cried again, and then whimpered "Stop!" as if she could think of no other word to say.

Still biting her lip, Cameron half-carried, half-dragged her to the Victorian sofa in the front parlor. She felt her pantyhose being ripped off, but his full weight was on top of her, and her lip was being bitten unmercifully. She could not move, other than to flail her arms uselessly. She tried to scratch him on the back, but his sweater was too thick.

"Stop!" she whispered desperately as she felt him force his way between her legs. She closed her eyes and tried to tell herself that she was having a nightmare while he bit her lip and thrust himself into her voraciously. Her whole body was throbbing in pain, and when she thought she couldn't stand another moment, she mindlessly started thinking about Pru 's rape by Lefty Owens. By the time Cameron shuddered to a finish, Christi was thinking of ways to kill him.

Cameron got up and straightened himself, while Christi lay on the sofa, crying hopelessly. He casually picked up his sport coat from the chair where he had dropped it, and put it on as he walked across the room. He opened the door to the dark December night, then turned back to her and said, "You'd better put some ice on that."

Stepping onto the front porch, Cameron glanced both ways down the quiet street, and, seeing no one, walked out without another word, leaving the stricken young woman alone.

Moments later, Nellie Mae hurried into the house through the back door. She heard Christi sobbing in the front parlor, and rushed to her. "What happened to my baby girl?" Nellie Mae cried out, seeing Christ's cut and bleeding lip. "I knew it. I knew something was wrong."

"I, I, I fell down," Christi lied.

"Don't be telling this old woman a lie like that. You tell me right now who hurt you," Nellie Mae insisted.

"Cuh, Cuh, Cameron raped me," Christi blurted out, and broke into sobs. "He raped me, right here in my own house!"

Nellie Mae gently put her arms around Christi and held her close. "Shh. Shh, Baby. It's okay now. No one has to know."

Christi wondered about that strange reaction, and almost immediately realized that Nellie Mae had the wisdom of age.

Chapter 41
December 6, 1975

"That's the little town of Tatuala," Jack informed Maggie with a left-handed gesture over the port bow. She considered taking some photos, but the sun was too intense for a meaningful shot at such a distance. She could barely make out some ramshackle buildings at water's edge, typical of a thousand harbors in underdeveloped countries.

As the small port faded from view, Jack turned the boat to a westerly course. "We're going into the Selat Wetar now. It's a strait between the island of Wetar on the north, and Timor. "

Maggie nodded. "Thanks. You're a good tour guide."

"No problem. It's nice to have company for a change, especially someone who is interested in everything. So, what do you know about where we're heading?"

"I know that for the past year and a half, the Portuguese government has been in the process of decolonizing most of its overseas territories, and that includes East Timor."

Jack looked at her with obvious surprise on his face.

Maggie laughed. "Just my luck. Last April, I was in Lisbon during the military *coup d'état* that started the recent turmoil."

"Okay, you're ahead of me," Jack admitted. "I knew there was some trouble in Dili last summer, but I didn't pay much attention to the politics. Nobody bothered me or my boat."

Jack sensed Maggie's disappointment with his response, so he asked, "What's the connection between Lisbon and Dili?"

"Portugal controlled East Timor for over 300 years. So, the Timorese speak Portuguese and are Catholics, though I've heard that they practice an interesting blend of papal ritual and ancient animistic rites. It's one of the poorest countries on earth, per capita. I'd like to do a story there someday."

"Sounds like you've already done the research," Jack said.

Maggie shrugged. "I read a lot," she admitted.

"Okay, then tell me what happened last summer."

"In August, there was a *coup* in the capital city of Dili."

"Where we're heading at a pretty good clip," Jack inserted.

"Right. Now, in a nutshell, you can think of the Timorese war like the U.S. Civil War, except in this case it's between the East and the West instead of the North and the South."

"Who are the bad guys in Timor?" Jack asked.

Maggie laughed. "In other words, who are the Yankees? Well, the West wants a union of the whole island, and the East wants independence for East Timor. The West started the civil war this past August. The East pushed them back into Indonesian West Timor in late September."

"Sounds good so far," Jack applauded. "Then what?"

"The Indonesian government got involved, making raids into East Timor, trying to take over. It got pretty bloody."

"Is it over now?" Jack asked, realizing that he had been foolishly oblivious. "I mean, are we heading for trouble?"

"Sorry to worry you," Maggie said. "I assumed you knew."

Jack was thoughtfully quiet for a few minutes as his cattle boat cruised peacefully through the warm waters. Maggie closed her eyes and inhaled deeply, enjoying the smells of the sea and the salt air. She could be on the Mediterranean, the Caribbean, or any of a dozen seas she had recorded on film.

"Is there anything else I need to know?" Jack finally asked.

"Just one thing," Maggie said seriously. "Yesterday, when I went to the bank in Mareeba, the manager showed me a copy of a month-old Telex. Back in October, in fact it was the day you and I met, five journalists were murdered in Balibo."

"Where's that?" Jack asked anxiously.

"I don't know," Maggie confessed. "It's not on my map, but it has to be between Dili and the East-West boundary in the middle of the island. Those guys were filming the regular Indonesian Army invading East Timor, and the Indonesian government killed them rather than admit its involvement."

"Maybe you'd better leave your camera on the boat," Jack quipped, though there was serious concern in his voice. "But you're American. Were they American journalists?"

"No. They were from Australia, Britain, and New Zealand, but that's no comfort. In a war zone, people shoot Americans all the time. No one asks to see a passport before firing."

"Maybe it's all over," Jack hoped aloud.

"That's possible, of course," Maggie agreed, "but the bank manager had a more recent Telex saying that just last week, on the 28th of November, the East declared its independence."

Jack searched his little-used and almost forgotten classroom memories for something about a Declaration of Independence. Of course. July 4, 1776. He brightened. That had turned out well for the cause of independence.

"When in the Course of human events," he began in a near whisper, "it becomes necessary for one people to dissolve the political bands which have connected them with another," he paused for thought, resuming in a more forceful voice, "and to assume among the powers of the earth, the separate and equal station to which the Laws of Nature and of Nature's God entitle them..."

He stopped and looked at Maggie for help. She concluded, "...a decent respect to the opinions of mankind requires that they should declare the causes which impel them to the separation."

"Do you think it was like that for East Timor?" Jack asked, after a few moments of silence.

"I hope it was like that for them," Maggie said simply. "but I hope it won't be the start of a full-scale war, like our ten years with England. Some of these primitive third-world people think nothing of slaughtering whole villages."

Maggie's mind raced back to the ravages she had seen and photographed in previous years – terror and vicious genocide in far-flung locales – from Cambodia to Cyprus to Africa. Jack thought only of the tiny Viet Nam village of Đó Thanh.

Maggie was the first one off the boat after they docked in Dili. Despite Jack's concerns, she took her camera equipment and photographed not only the cattle being unloaded, but also the port area and other ships. Jack tried to keep one eye on her while supervising his deck hands and the local cattle handlers who did all the dirty work. He had spent enough time doing it himself when he started this cattle shipping venture.

After refueling and tying up, Jack told the deck hands to stay on board for the night, in case there was trouble. He didn't really expect any, but the conversation with Maggie had worried him more than he wanted to admit.

Jack took Maggie to dinner at a typically run-down, open-air restaurant within eyesight of his boat. She took photos as if they were at a fancy resort. The fish was as good as anywhere on earth, and they indulged in a second course of it. Maggie declined to drink, telling Jack that she had struggled with an alcohol problem for years. He seemed sympathetic.

"I think my father-in-law might have had that problem too," Jack confided in her, surprised at himself for his candor.

"Minh Nhi Li's father was an alcoholic?" Maggie asked.

For too long a moment, Jack didn't respond. He heaved a big sigh. "Minnie is not my wife," he said reluctantly, "and Sonny is not my son. They were, uh, they were, uh, refugees, and I, uh, well, I, uh, it's a long story."

"We have all night," Maggie said, "and you know how much I like hearing stories about people, places, and events. Off the record, of course. I won't tell anyone about this."

Jack began cautiously, hearing the words aloud for the first time. He omitted everything about the village of Đó Thanh, the weeks of trekking through the jungles, the dangers of being spotted skirting the rice fields, and the fear of rafting down swollen streams with a woman and baby on board.

Instead, Jack started the story on the banks of the South China Sea, where he found Minnie, with her son, trying to get passage on a boat to Singapore. He was going there too.

Maggie was wise enough not to interrupt his story with the questions that were swirling in her trained observer's mind.

"I was very surprised that she had a passport," Jack said, "but I found out later that passports, even American ones, were easy enough to get. All you needed was money, and Minnie had some, from her family, I guess. It was kinda funny at first because we just pointed and grunted. Anyway, we got on the same boat going to Singapore. One day we were standing on the deck when it started to drizzle. Minnie held out her hand and said, '*crachin*.' Know what that is?"

He was not very surprised when Maggie nodded, and said in fluent French, *"Le crachin est une précipitation persistante, particulièrement fréquent près des rivages océaniques."*

"Right, I think," Jack agreed. "So '*crachin*' means 'drizzle' in French and in Vietnamese. Minnie picked up some French from her father who learned it from the old missionaries."

"And you?" Maggie asked, hoping for some background.

Again, Jack's pause was too long for Maggie's satisfaction.

"I took French in high school," he answered. "So, that's how we talked 'til she learned English, watching television."

"Speaking of television," Maggie said, "I'll bet the networks are showing those reruns of Pearl Harbor tonight."

"Hmm. That's right," Jack agreed. "Tomorrow's the 7th."

"Can you even imagine what it must have been like to be rousted out of bed on a quiet Sunday morning by the sound of airplanes dropping bombs? In Hawaii, no less? Paradise."

"It's almost like paradise here, too," Jack suggested. "Would you like to take a walk along the beach?"

"Is it safe?" Maggie asked.

"I sure hope so. I need to work off some of that dinner."

Jack and Maggie walked until very late, and talked about everything except what Maggie really wanted to know. What was Jack's true story? She decided that accepting his offer to share a room might open up more conversation.

"I don't mind sharing a room," Maggie said sleepily. "but you do know that I'm not interested in men. Right?"

Jack nodded. "I just need a good night's sleep before we start back. I hate to admit it, but talking about Vietnam and the Civil War and Pearl Harbor gave me the heebie-jeebies. I'm about halfway expecting some gook to shoot off an M-14. I could use a fast-talking American girl as back-up."

They both laughed, and headed to a harbor-side inn where Jack had stayed before. It was fairly dirty and the bed was lumpy, but they were too tired to care. Sleep came fast.

Jack woke up with the long-familiar nightmare of a plane screaming overhead and the sound of bombs exploding. He tried to ignore the distinctive tat-tat-tat-tat of M-14's and the piercing screams of women and children. Maggie shook him.

"Sorry," he mumbled, "I shoulda said I have nightmares."

"Wake up, Jack!" Maggie whispered urgently. "It's not a nightmare!" Both of them heard a jet scream overhead.

"Oh my God!" Jack exclaimed. "What's going on?"

"I don't know," Maggie fired back at him, "but let's get outa here." She rolled off the bed, still fully dressed from the day before, and grabbed her camera. They clambered down the rickety wooden steps to the alley, where a tank rumbled toward them, fifty feet away. Maggie snapped pictures of it.

"Are you crazy?" Jack yelled at her, trying to be heard over the sounds of bombs exploding from more planes overhead.

Maggie got pictures of the jets, including two with falling bombs clearly visible in her cross sights. Jack grabbed her arm, causing her to miss the shot of a tank mortar exploding.

"Damn it! I could've gotten that!" she hollered at him.

"You coulda gotten it down your throat!" Jack yelled back. "Come on!" he insisted, pulling her down the alley as more tanks rolled through the streets. "We've gotta get to the boat!"

Jack led the way while Maggie took pictures. "Better get a shot of my ass too!" he yelled. "I'm about to kiss it good-bye!"

* * *

The following spring, Maggie wrote a compelling personal account of the December 7, 1975 attack on East Timor, and her dramatic escape past gunboats in the harbor. In her article, she stated that U.S. President Ford and Secretary of State Kissinger had met face-to-face with Indonesian General Suharto in Jakarta the previous day. She boldly suggested that America had supplied Indonesia with the arms and ammunition used in the full-scale air, land, and sea invasion of the small, struggling country. She accompanied the text with the only photographs known to have survived the attack.

To her article, Maggie appended a copy of United Nations Security Council Resolution 389, adopted 22 April 1976:

"Reaffirming the inalienable right of the people of East Timor to self-determination and independence in accordance with the principles of the charter of the United Nations…

"Calling upon the Government of Indonesia to withdraw without further delay all its forces from the Territory…"

Maggie was disappointed that the United States abstained from voting on that Resolution, and equally disappointed to have her article rejected by every newspaper and magazine group in the country. Later, she was denied a visa to return to Timor, and was unable to cover the story of 250,000 freedom seekers being slaughtered in their homes and on the streets.

Chapter 42
January 3, 1981

"What am I going to do now, Kelly?"

"You're not going to make love to me in the back seat with a trooper driving us down the highway at seventy-five miles an hour. That's for sure!" she answered firmly.

Cameron chuckled, "I didn't mean now, at this moment. I meant now, in my life. What am I going to do in a couple of weeks, when I'm not the governor any more?"

"What do you want to do?"

"I've been offered the chairmanship of the national party."

"Is that what you want to do?"

"Everyone thinks it would be a good political move."

"Is it what you want to do?"

"Even my mother thinks it would be a good move, and she doesn't often agree with the other women around me."

Kelly noticed he still avoided saying Mallory's name.

"Is that what you want to do?" Kelly repeated, shifting around to get more comfortable in his arms.

"There are a lot of political advantages, but it does have a potential downside."

"Is it what you want to do?"

"It would keep me in the public eye and allow me to travel around the country... a long-term benefit in making contacts."

"Is that what you want to do?"

"So, I guess maybe that's what I should do. Everybody seems to think so. What do you think, Kelly?"

"It doesn't matter what I think. What matters is what you want to do. What do <u>you</u> want to do?"

"Haven't you been listening to me?" he asked, annoyed.

"I've been listening to you more than you've been listening to you — rattling on about other people's notions for your life. I'm more interested in what you want for yourself."

"I don't know what I want, Kelly. That's why I'm asking you. You know me better than anyone else. Help me."

Kelly closed her eyes and sighed. A thousand thoughts went through her mind before she spoke again.

"I care about you. I want you to have what you want."

"No one but you ever asks me what I want. And when you ask, I never know how I'm supposed to answer."

"Cameron, it's simple. Close your eyes and pretend you're about to wake up on the first day of your own special life. You can have absolutely anything you want. Money is no object. You can have anything you want," she repeated with meaning. "Anything."

Cameron sighed and relaxed against her.

"Good," she whispered. "Now, picture the room you will be in. Anywhere you want. Anywhere. Picture what clothes will be hanging in your closet. Your morning will be totally free to do whatever you want. What clothes do you want to put on? Tell me. Just tell me what you want to wear today."

"Jeans and a flannel shirt," he answered quietly.

"And what is the first thing you want to do?"

"Have breakfast with…" he paused.

Kelly's heart skipped a beat, waiting for him to finally say Mallory's name aloud. Or maybe hers. She held her breath.

"Carrie," he finished, sighing with relief, as if he had just let out an awful secret.

Kelly pictured his little, blond, two-year-old daughter and began to breathe again.

"Good," she encouraged. "You would have breakfast with Carrie, and then?"

"Take her for a walk, go to the park, show her off at the grocery store. What? I don't know what. This is crazy. I just want to spend time with her."

"It isn't crazy, Cameron. It's beautiful. I hate to think what my life would have been if my daddy hadn't spent time like that with me." Kelly swallowed hard and continued, "Now, tell me. Could you spend time with Carrie like that if you were the chairman of the National Democratic Party?'

"Of course not."

"Then it's simple. You don't want to be party chairman."

Cameron sighed again. "You make it sound so simple."

"Things are simple, Cameron. Mostly, we try to complicate them. If you want to stay home and be with Carrie, do it."

"But I'd have to get a job, too."

"Any law firm in Jackson would love to have you."

"You don't understand. I don't know how to practice law."

"So what? Go to the best firm. Tell them you'll work for them if they give you a guaranteed salary, a great office and the best legal secretary they have."

"Then she'd find out I didn't know how to practice law."

"Right. But she won't tell, if you let her practice for you. Nobody gets to be a top-notch legal secretary in Jackson unless she has the brains to be a lawyer. Use her. She'll love being your invaluable assistant. Everybody wins."

"You're still making it sound so simple, Kelly."

"It is."

"How will I get from there back into elected office?"

"Is that all you ever think about? What about your life? You need to take the time to grow up and figure out who you are and what you really want. Can you live forever with your personal life in shambles? Can you keep seeing me like this, year after year, and not have it affect everything else? I can't do this. This is too hard on me. I really care about you, and it doesn't matter to me if you're the governor, or the president, or a high school teacher. As far as I can tell, little Carrie is the only other person in your life who loves you unconditionally and isn't looking for you to provide some status by what you do. Wake up, Cameron! You better not jeopardize your relationship with Carrie."

"I won't," he whispered, pulling Kelly closer. "God help me, I won't."

* * *

"Are you fucking crazy? You fucking stupid asshole!"

Mallory slammed her book down on the kitchen table. "What do you mean, you want to stay home with Carrie? What kind of a chicken shit job is that? You think you're going to go from being governor to being a fucking nanny? I didn't have that fucking kid to ruin our career! Remember the deal? Nothing about fucking staying home and baking shit cookies! Not for either one of us. You got that, asshole?"

She picked the book up again, and threw it across the room for emphasis. "You fucking cock sucker!" The book skidded along the white tile countertop, crashing into a stack of bowls.

The sound of shattering glass brought a state trooper running into the kitchen from his post on the back porch. He took one look around, shrugged, and left quickly, though he wished that once, just once, he could pistol whip that bitch across the face. It might actually be worth the jail time.

* * *

Kelly glanced through the *Dallas Morning News* as she was sipping a second cup of tea. She was troubled enough by the article about Cameron to put down the newspaper and pick up some stationery. She sat at the desk in her sunny office, having some very dark thoughts. Finally, she wrote.

Saturday, June 6, 1987
Early in the morning

Dear Cameron,

I've read in the papers that you are trying to make a decision about running for President, yet I sensed when we visited last month that you're already in the race....

Kelly thought about the night they recently spent together at the D/FW Airport hotel. Cameron had tearfully confessed that he was a sex addict — that he could not help himself – that he had had sex with hundreds of women. He knew he was out of control, and he vowed to get outside help, but there was no way he had managed to do that in less than two weeks. Running for President now was the height of arrogance, or insanity. She picked up her pen and continued.

I woke up this morning with a feeling of 'déjà vu' and recalled the time after you lost the governorship when you were considering whether or not to head the national party. Your mind seemed to be made up to do it because your intellect thought it was the best thing to do at the time, but you admitted that in your gut, you wanted to stay home with Carrie, and, thank God, that's what you did.

Now you've developed yourself well ~ intellectually, socially, politically ~ yet you know there are other parts of you that are less strong and mature. I've always believed that God wants you to be a great leader someday. I'd hate to see you settle for being a great politician....

Kelly considered whether that paragraph was too blunt, or not blunt enough. As usual, she couldn't spell things out in plain English, for fear that the letter might fall into someone else's hands. It wouldn't be prudent to use the words *"out of control sex addict."* She realized that she was simply repeating some of what she had said in detail when they were together. It would be clear enough for Cameron, and innocuous enough for anyone else. She continued with a new paragraph.

Get quiet. Look inside yourself. Feel. Forget about the polls, the political 'facts,' the supporters who have their own reasons for wanting you to run. Do what you did when Carrie was a baby: Listen to your gut. Trust it. Are you ready to be a great leader? Is your own house in order?...

This would not be a good letter for Mallory to see. The simple phrase *'house in order'* would launch her on a blue-streak tirade. Still, the chances were slim that she would ever see this letter, or any of the others that Kelly and Cameron had exchanged over the past decades. It was safe to persist.

I was just now looking in the Bible to find that quotation from St. Paul about "all things working to the good..." (Remember I used to tell you that "everything will work out for the best?" I do believe that!) Anyway, some of us Catholics never learned how to handle a Bible read well, and I couldn't find that passage, but I was praying for guidance for you and my eyes fell upon 1 Corinthians 14:8 ~ "For if the trumpet give an uncertain sound, who shall prepare himself to the battle?"

Whatever you decide, I support you. Just remember that I care about you as a human being, not a human doing.

Love,
Kelly

It was exactly a week later when Kelly received his reply on the lovely cream-colored stationery with its gold seal.

STATE OF MISSISSIPPI
CAMERON COULTER
GOVERNOR

Under the gold embossed print, Cameron had written "6/12" without including the year. The entire letter was in Cameron's hand, and he had taken time to write legibly.

Dear Kelly —

Thanks for your letter — It's good advice and you sound good in it —

I am in a quandary and exhausted. We're about to take a few days off so that I can quietly "feel" what I should do —

Best,
Cam

Thanks for coming by the office too — Let me know when you're here again — Your letter was on target — You know me —

* * *

Kelly sighed. Surely, Cameron would not expose himself to the world yet. *Expose himself?* she thought. Surely, not yet.

* * *

Another week passed before Kelly realized that Cameron had made the wrong decision, despite his assurance to her that he would take the time to "feel" what he should do. He had called a press conference for the following Tuesday. All the television networks and newspaper groups were sending teams of reporters, photographers and support personnel to Jackson, Mississippi for the big circus event.

Kelly knew she had to do something to save Cameron from his blatantly foolish choice. One letter had not been enough.

She finished packing for her vacation in the Bahamas, and tried to put Cameron out of her mind while she took care of necessary details before leaving the house for two weeks. It was in times like this she was glad she had made checklists on the computer. She would never forget things by being rushed at the last minute, but she did get plenty of teasing about it from her family and friends. Compulsive, they said.

For the rest of the afternoon, Kelly considered what she should say to Cameron that would be safe to write in a letter, but strong enough to make the point. She was truly afraid that, not only would he be exposed for his decades-long relationship with her, but she would catch some flak too – and Mallory would launch attacks on women he had messed around with over the years. It could get very ugly. Suddenly, Kelly was glad she just happened to be leaving the country.

The next morning, Kelly was still contemplating what to write when her airport shuttle arrived. She stuck an extra piece of stationery and an envelope in her purse, and headed out the door, thinking that some words of wisdom would surely come to her on the way. Finally, when she was in front of the American Airlines terminal at D/FW Airport, she did it.

Kelly addressed the envelope to Cameron Coulter, Office of the Governor, State Capitol, Jackson, MS 39201. She took a lingering look at her personalized letterhead - "Kelly McCain" printed in block text. Without writing a word, she folded the paper in thirds, put it in the already-stamped envelope, sealed it, and dropped it into the D/FW mailbox, with a prayer.

* * *

Kelly was watching the evening news with some friends outside Nassau when she heard Cameron's name as a teaser.

"Thank God, he's going to pull out of the race," Kelly said.

"No way," one of the news junkies opined. "He has a big press conference scheduled for tomorrow to announce."

Kelly just smiled. "We'll see."

She knew exactly what must have happened. Cameron received her letter that morning. He read between the lines, which was tricky since there were no lines to read, and he finally decided to stop the insanity. She was relieved when the newscaster announced that Cameron had announced to the press that at his press conference the next morning he would announce that he wasn't going to run for president.

It was a bizarre occurrence, and an unorthodox way to make such a non-announcement. Speculation ran rampant on the networks about the unexpected turn of events. Kelly knew that Cameron would catch hell for it at home, but she felt so good about his decision that she treated herself to an extra helping of dessert that evening. Life was good.

Life was not so good in the Governor's Mansion that night.

"Are you fucking crazy? You fucking stupid asshole!"

Mallory slammed her briefcase down on the kitchen table. "What do you mean, backing out at the last minute? What kind of a chicken shit maneuver is that? You think this is all about you, cocksucker? I haven't put up with your fucking shit all these years to go down the toilet now! Remember the deal? The fucking deal? Now I'll be sixty fucking years old before it's my turn to run! You stupid cock sucking asshole!"

She picked the briefcase up again, and threw it across the room for emphasis, yelling, "You fucking stupid cock sucking asshole!" The case skidded along the white tile countertop, crashing into a couple of monogrammed crystal tumblers.

The sound of shattering glass brought a state trooper running into the kitchen from his post on the back porch, unsnapping the leather strap on his gun holster. He took one look around the room, shrugged, and left quickly, snapping the gun strap back in place.

"Trailer trash," he muttered under his breath. "What was he thinking when he married that piece of trailer trash?"

Chapter 43
October 17, 1989

Maggie was pleased with the past three days of shooting and interviewing in and around San Francisco. It was nice to be so close to home, though she was rarely in Los Angeles anymore. It was even nicer to be working on a story that had maintained her interest for such a long time.

Her 1976 article "Following the Refugees" had flowed directly from her visit with Minh Nhi Li in Australia. It had been well received, and the photos had generated praise. At the same time, though, she had been disappointed that her East Timor article never made it to print. The government's position was still a denial of the invasion. Maggie got mad every time she thought about it, but she shifted to the present.

"Vietnamese Babies Now American Teenagers" was going to be one of her best features ever. She had a good feeling about it, and the photos were extraordinary, even if she did say so herself. She had spent the day in San Lorenzo, where a talented young Vietnamese actor was trying his hand at writing and directing a documentary. He had allowed Maggie free access to the set and to his Vietnamese subjects, in exchange for one still shot he could use in promoting his film.

On the way back to San Francisco, Maggie stopped to buy more film. She wanted to have plenty on hand for the Battle of the Bay. The Oakland Athletics and the San Francisco Giants were warming up for the third game of the World Series, and Maggie had treated herself with the purchase of a great seat. On the way to the game, for a moment, she felt self-pity about traveling alone, but the moment didn't last.

* * *

Minh Khoi Tien and his friend Nguyen Cuong Boi were driving home from a day of filming in San Lorenzo, where one of their young acquaintances was doing a documentary on Vietnamese refugees. Khoi and Cuong had one of the more interesting stories, being abducted by North Vietnamese and forced to serve in their army before finally escaping and returning to their home village of Đó Thanh. When they had arrived, they found almost nothing of what had been their homes, and nothing at all of what had been their families.

The two had men vowed to stay together and to keep looking for anyone who might have escaped, but Minh Khoi Tien had found himself unable to look at the newspaper and magazine articles. Cuong Boi, the artist and writer, gathered and filed the stories, while Khoi Tien, the house painter, searched every pair of almond eyes he met on the streets. He still had hope.

A few artists lived in West Oakland in 1989, but the area where Khoi Tien and Cuong Boi lived was best known for its crime, poverty, and pollution. It was a rough area, where auto body shops, metal companies, and tattoo parlors competed for space with once-lovely but now-dilapidated Victorian homes.

West Oakland had been all they could afford when they managed to get to the bay area a decade earlier. They never decided to stay. They simply never decided to move.

On the way home from San Lorenzo, Cuong Boi was driving the old Pontiac while Khoi Tien was entertaining him with often-told stories about The Uncle from days long past. Khoi stopped in mid-sentence when the earth shook beneath them, and Cuong swerved the car to the right side of the road. They were northbound on the freeway, under the Cypress Street Viaduct, nearly home, when the upper deck bearing the southbound traffic suddenly collapsed.

In slow motion, Khoi heard and saw the massive columns of concrete buckle and explode. He heard metal screaming and glass shattering as cars in front and behind them were crushed flat under tons of concrete. He could hardly believe his good fortune that Cuong's quick reflex had moved him out of danger. He sighed in relief and turned to thank his friend.

The horrors of Vietnam had not prepared him for what he saw in the front seat beside him, and he could not escape until rescuers cut him free. There were at least forty people dead under the viaduct, and Cuong had died faster than some.

Devastated by the loss of his only homeland connection, it would take five years for Khoi Tien to force himself to search through the files his friend had gathered, and to take his unique art to a San Francisco gallery to share with the world.

* * *

"Comeback Cam" was his new nickname, and he liked it. At least, he liked what it represented — a narrow escape from political oblivion after lounge singer Sindy Towers, with her blond hair and black roots, had peddled a story about their long-term extra-marital affair. Mallory, as usual, stuck with the deal, and after sufficient rounds of yelling "You fucking stupid cock sucking asshole!" at him, she had devised a plan.

They would appear on national television, if they could get Kelly to do it with them. Cam would admit to an affair with her, since a tabloid reporter had already uncovered the story. The candidate could defend that one affair as an outgrowth of his childhood crush, and Mallory would forgive both of them.

Then Mallory could condemn Sindy as a "fucking liar" — though Mallory would omit the word "fucking" in public. Her problem was that Kelly refused to participate in their charade. She and Cam decided to perform, and lie, together.

* * *

Kelly checked her calendar, February 27, 1992, and noted the appointment time – 2 p.m. She arrived early and skimmed through a couple of magazines while the others straggled into the office, but the session, as usual, started promptly. Kelly looked around the small, cheerful room at the six faces that had become so familiar to her over the past several years.

"I'm embarrassed to be back here," she confided when it was her turn to speak. Her female therapist and the other five members of the mixed group nodded their understanding as she added, "I should have known it would happen sooner or later."

"Don't beat yourself up, Kelly. We'll listen to anything but that," Lucy reminded her. The small raven-haired therapist smiled warmly. "We're glad you had the strength to admit you need more help."

Kelly forced a smile. "Thanks. I know. I appreciate your letting me come back," she paused, trying to find the right words. "I thought I was over the sex addiction mess when I limited myself to Cameron and quit getting involved with other guys. I was wrong about that," she paused again. "The whole affair with Cameron was as sick as the rest of it. He's married and that's that. It was psychologically unhealthy and, worst of all, morally wrong. I've rationalized and deluded myself long enough. I've asked God to forgive me and I know that He has. I'd just like a little help to put it all behind me."

"When was the last time you were with Cameron?" Lucy asked for the group.

"A few weeks ago. We were in San Antonio. I thought everything was fine. Then he didn't call me and I don't think he'll ever call again. I'm angry that he's the one who made that decision. I should have done it myself."

Kelly was comforted by the quiet nods in the small circle and she sighed with some relief.

"Why isn't he going to call you again, Kelly? What happened?" Lucy asked.

Kelly felt trapped. Suddenly, the small circle felt stifling. Her face flushed. She tried to form some words, but nothing came out of her mouth.

"It's a long story," she finally managed to say, "but under the circumstances, I don't think he'll call."

"You're being evasive, Kelly," Lucy admonished quietly. "Tell the long story."

Kelly nodded slowly, braced herself against the back of her chair and took a deep breath before she began tentatively, "You remember I said a long time ago that Cameron is a prominent person and he's married?" All nodded.

"Well, he's running for political office now and it looks like the story about us is going to get publicized."

"You said his wife already knew about you, Kelly, so, what difference would an affair make to anyone else?" Lucy questioned. "It's not like he's running for President of the..." The therapist's soothing voice dropped to a barely inaudible whisper, "Oh, my God!"

Kelly stared at the floor, averting the looks of the others as they finally realized who Cameron was. She tried to think of some plausible justification for withholding this information from the group for years.

"Alright, Kelly," Lucy stated gently, but firmly, "I could tell you how I feel. We could all tell you how we feel, that you didn't trust us with this information, but I want you to tell us, right now, straight out, in therapy terms, why you withheld this from us."

Kelly felt her face and neck getting hotter. She could hardly breathe in the small room. Her mind raced through a dozen possible answers, all of them bullshit.

Finally, she whispered, "I was protecting him."

Lucy nodded as the others glared.

Sixty-five-year-old Herb, who rarely said anything without prodding, suddenly blurted out, "That sorry son-of-a-bitch never deserved a woman like you!"

Instantly, the glares were all directed at Herb, and Kelly felt incredible relief in the momentary respite. Herb's words rang in her ears, over and over, until Kelly felt herself believing them. Then she felt a deep, overpowering hurt forming in the pit of her stomach, making its way up through her chest to her throat, lodging there until she almost choked on it. Finally a sound came from her mouth that was part moan, part cry, part scream, and she began to sob uncontrollably.

No one moved or tried to stop the flood of tears by offering a tissue. Kelly was left to wipe her eyes with her sleeves until they were saturated, and still the tears flowed. Finally, Kelly, exhausted, felt Lucy put her arms around her and then, one by one, the others went to her and embraced her and whispered words of comfort. Kelly had never felt so grateful.

"Now, go home and write it," Lucy insisted. "All of it. Don't hold anything back. Don't protect Cameron any more."

"But," Kelly began.

Lucy shook her head, "No 'buts,'" she admonished. "You don't have to publish it. We all keep journals, Kelly. We don't have to publish them. Just write what's in your heart so your heart won't have to break from trying to hold it all."

Chapter 44
January 20, 1993

It was after midnight, and the church was getting stuffier by the minute. The music had been beautiful and moving, but it seemed like hours ago, and Christi felt herself nodding off while the various speakers droned on and on. Now, former President Jimmy Carter was telling stories and Cameron was enjoying all of them. Christi knew that Cameron could easily stay up all night. She never could. She stifled a yawn.

Carter paused his story about a Habitat for Humanity home to ask Cam, "What was that nice lady's name?" and Christi wasn't surprised that Cam answered immediately — he remembered everyone's name. She wondered if he had raped that woman, or had one of his infamous flings with her. Word on the street in Mississippi said he was colorblind.

She chided herself for such thoughts in church, and said another prayer for Grover's safe return. She still refused to believe that he was dead, and she worked diligently with the POW/MIA groups around the country. Christi would not leave D.C. without a promise from the new President, her old high school friend, the rapist who owed her something for her silence. On his third day in office, Cameron swore he would not normalize relations with Vietnam until every prisoner was returned and every record searched for the Missing In Action.

As president, Cameron wanted to put the Vietnam War behind him. It was bad enough that his draft dodging had been partially exposed during the campaign. Thankfully, Jimmy Carter had pardoned him back in 1977 before anyone tried to prosecute him. Cameron could easily rationalize every crime he had ever committed. He gave Christi a parting hug, and reached for her breast. She just wanted to slap him.

* * *

Grover Jones saw his own hands trembling on the steering wheel as he turned into the Boudreaux driveway. He glanced at Minnie in the front seat. Her face was inscrutable, as usual, but Sonny gave Grover an encouraging pat on the back

The front door was closed to the winter weather, and Grover took a deep breath before ringing the bell. His mind raced back to that September day in 1963 when he and Christi had made love for the first time. He wondered if her bedroom still had the yellow rose wallpaper. He wondered how Christi would look after all this time. He wondered how he would look to her. He wondered if he should have called her, or sent a letter, instead of just showing up at her door. Mostly, he wondered if she would forgive him for the past 25 years.

Grover's heart nearly stopped beating as the door opened. After all this time, there stood Christi herself, looking exactly as she did when he left. Her brunette hair had not a touch of gray, though it was a bit longer now. She was still pregnant and beautiful. *Still pregnant?* Grover blinked in disbelief.

"Daddy! Oh, Daddy! Daddy, you're home!... Alex, come down here right now! Daddy's home! Daddy's home!"

Angelica had recognized him before he knew his own daughter. Seconds later, an almost-identical pregnant woman came rushing down the stairs. Both girls threw their arms around Grover, hugging him and crying, "Daddy! Daddy!"

After a few glorious minutes, Grover managed to stop his own flow of tears to ask, "Where's your mother?"

"She's gone," Alex said, and Grover broke into tears again.

"Oh, God, what have I done?" he cried.

"No, Daddy, not 'gone' like forever gone, but gone for a week to Washington for Cameron's inauguration." They all laughed together for the first time. "She'll be home tonight!"

"Come sit in the parlor and have a cup of tea," Angelica suggested. "We have so many questions."

The word 'tea' reminded Grover of Minnie and Sonny.

"Before I sit down, let me tell you that I brought some people with me. It's not what you might think and I'll tell you the whole story in time. I hope you'll welcome them."

The happy girls nodded together, "Of course, we will."

Grover walked back to the door, and motioned for the little Minh family to join him inside. They all sat in the parlor in front of a roaring fire, talking and laughing and crying and trying to cover a quarter century of news in an afternoon.

Alex, named for Alexandra Fennstemmacher, wanted to hear all about the early days with their mother in Vicksburg. Angel wanted to know about Vietnam, but Grover skipped most of his own Army story, and just said he was counting on Cameron for a pardon, as Jimmy Carter had pardoned Cam.

Grover was amazed to hear the girls tell their love stories. Twin brothers who were attending West Point had visited Vicksburg during the "Sons of the Siege" reunion. They were the great-great-great-great-grandsons of Jacques Boudreaux who had built the family home in 1848. When the cadets toured the house, which was opened to the public that day, they met their distant cousins Angel and Alex. The tale was a syrupy southern romance, and the girls giggled in telling it.

Finally, Grover said, "I need to call my dad." His daughters looked at each other sheepishly before Angel said, "We used to visit him all the time,... especially after he moved into the nursing home,... but he died two years ago."

Grover dropped his head, and covered his face with his big hands. He sobbed uncontrollably, from sadness and guilt. When he finally recovered, Angel told him that there was a box of things from Paw in their mother's bedroom upstairs.

"Mom has always been expecting you to come home. She has shown us your picture and talked about you and prayed for you every night of our lives. We knew you'd come home."

Grover was waiting at the front door when Christi arrived that evening. A quarter century of pain and separation melted away in one moment. Even the rose wallpaper was the same.

* * *

There were many adjustments over the next few months. Grover learned that Miss Fennstemmacher had left her home to him, stipulating only that the downstairs be open for public tours one day a week. A fund established by her father would take care of the upkeep for a hundred years. Grover recalled her long-ago promise to him — a Vicksburg home in exchange for that pot of chicken soup he had made when she was sick.

Grover and Christi decided to start fresh in "his" house and let their daughters take over the Boudreaux homestead. They were blessed with four grandchildren at once, when the girls each delivered twin boys. Grover became a fine "PaPa" for them while the Boudreaux husbands were half a world away.

Minh Nhi Li and Sonny moved in to help Angel and Alex with the house and the newborns until Sonny could find a job and his own place to live. Nellie Mae was still staying in the quarters, but she was slowing down and could use some help.

Christi's cousin Maggie came to visit that spring, on her way to Atlanta. There was another round of surprises as she recognized 'Jack' and Minh Nhi Li from two decades past.

"Small world," Maggie said. "Last night, I called Australia trying to find you, Jack. I got a letter from a guy in California who was going through some old magazines. He came across my article with Minh Nhi Li's photos, and he swears she was his wife." She showed Nhi Li a photo of Minh Khoi Tien.

"This is your honorable father," Minh Nhi Li said simply, handing the photo to her son. At age 24, they were identical. Maggie arranged for their reunion, and for the right to publish their story. Sonny wanted to turn it into a movie, and Maggie found the funding for it in a packet Nhi Li shared with her.

"You're rich, Nhi Li," Maggie said. "This is the record of a trust account at Standard Chartered, one of the oldest banks in Singapore. In 1966, a Minh Quang Tung deposited nearly a million dollars for your family. That bank invests well. There's no telling what this is worth now."

* * *

Christi waited until after his pardon came through to tell Grover about *the incident* with Cameron. Grover wanted to kill his wife's rapist with his bare hands, so Christi insisted that they avoid their high school reunion the next summer.

Cameron's phone call after the reunion made Christi realize that avoiding painful issues wouldn't make them go away. It was never too late to deal with reality. Maybe she could even stand up to Cameron someday. Christi took a deep breath, and a small step. She would make that appointment with the eye doctor tomorrow. It was finally time to see everything clearly. Maybe she would even write it all in a journal.